Beautiful House

Raye Cain

****

This book is NOT a story of Black trauma. While the story deals with difficult situations and has painful moments, as does all of my writing in the pursuit of being realistic and speaking the truth about the world, my intention was to tell a well-rounded, thoughtful tale with a satisfying ending. I've done my best as an honest chronicler to represent these women accurately, passionately, and meaningfully.

Thank you for reading. Enjoy!

Chapter 1

North Carolina, 1960

Berry was especially thorough when she cleaned homes, so she could tell when one of the women she worked for was giving her a hard time about the results. She was standing in the spacious main bathroom of the house she'd just cleaned, examining the large mirror that adorned the top of the cream vanity.

"How about," said Mrs. Perscher, tilting her carefully coiffed blonde head—"How about you just take some white vinegar and try it one more time, but wipe it real light?"

The two of them, one dark and one pale, were as visible as they could be reflected in that mirror. But Berry had cleaned too quickly for Mrs. Perscher's satisfaction. She hadn't struggled enough. She should be more sweaty, more crumpled. But Berry always took her unruffled time.

"Alright, ma'am," Berry said crisply.

"Yeah, yep," said Mrs. Perscher. "That'll be good." She looked around, her gray eyes searching. "And how about run around the bottom of the tub just one more time, too."

Berry nodded in pretend meekness. Inside, she seethed. She despised Mrs. Perscher.

"Right," said Mrs. Perscher. "Right. So you just do that, and then we can get you on outta here for the evening."

She smiled her usual fake smile and clasped her hands. Berry grabbed the white vinegar out of her cleaning bucket. She rolled her eyes when Mrs. Perscher walked out. Slavery, picking up behind this lazy woman. Why couldn't people clean their own houses?

A couple minutes later, facing each other in the hallway, Mrs. Perscher detained Berry again. She wasn't done yet. "Sweep the porch before you go."

As always when their eyes met, they went stiff.

It didn't take Berry long to sweep the wide porch and straighten the rust-colored pots of miniature decorations. She popped back in, almost colliding with Mrs. Perscher in the foyer.

Mrs. Perscher said it was good without even checking and smiled. Her teeth were tiny, her nose was long, and whenever she smiled, she looked quite like a witch from a fairy tale. Mrs. Perscher was slim, in her early forties, and her hair was always set firmly and shining blonde. She had put on gray gloves and a matching-colored hat and was holding her purse, which meant she was headed out.

They made their way around each other. Berry replaced the cleaning things in the cleaning closet. The smell in the house was always so strong. Citrus. Powder. And in the closet, bleach. She peeled off her gloves. She always washed them in water with half a cap full of the bleach, to avoid cross-contamination.

Berry washed her hands at the pump. They didn't like the maids using the sink. She went back into the house and grabbed her things. She wanted to be away before Justine came. The cook was a stubborn looking woman, and for some reason she thought Berry wanted her job. Berry did not want her job, she didn't even want this damn job.

As she headed down the walk, she saw the dark red car pull to the curb and let out Justine. Berry kept walking, looking the other way.

***

It wasn't like Berry wanted to clean homes, but there were few other job options in the small town of Springville, North Carolina. The paper mill was for men, she refused to go to the fields, and what she intended to do was get out of this little town and go up North to college. At nineteen, she already felt she was wasting her life. She'd never have nice things, a nice house—happiness—as long as she stayed in this desolate, limiting place.

She'd figure it out. As soon as she could convince her mother Lilah to move away with her. Berry's mother was too attached to her own mother, Grandma Maple. Lilah was afraid of moving. Or of doing anything, really.

Berry didn't see herself staying much longer as a maid for Mrs. Perscher, regardless. The county commissioner's wife was witchy on her best days. Berry was young, slim, and a threat. Mr. Perscher had winked at her a few times, often watched her with a heavy stare, and once had held the front door open for her, but blocked her so she was forced to duck under his arm.

Handling nice things but not having them was pure pain. Berry's own house, as she approached it, was a stark contrast to Mrs. Perscher's. Just enough space for Berry, her grandmother, her mother, and her sister. It was bare-looking, and rigorous tidying up could only take it so far. As usual, Berry was disheartened by the sight of the short concrete steps, the leaning porch, the general feeling of lopsidedness and the reminder of plain rooms. Berry wanted fancy, like the houses she cleaned.

The whole neighborhood landscape consisted of similar small, square homes, usually preceded by one or two steps leading to a modest front door accompanied by a rocking chair. The neighbors had gardens, junk, cars, and dirt drives but no garages. Fields of different crops at differing seasons surrounded everything. Berry reached her house and rounded the back.

She knelt on the ground by the back door, turning the boards she'd collected this way and that. For the past month, she'd been attempting to build what she called a hangout spot. She wanted a spot to crawl into and nap in peace and silence. All she needed was a board on the ground, some walls, and a covering.

She'd gotten two pieces put together so far. Would it stay, though? It was stupid crooked. Something was missing. She really didn't know the first thing about carpentry. And she'd had to beat the nails to death just to get them to go in. All of it was so much harder than what she thought it'd be when she first envisioned it. She sat back on her heels with her chin in her hand, thinking. What did she need to do?

She looked up at the sound of rumbling. Her sister Lucille and her boyfriend Zachary were coming up in his old green pickup. Zachary drove recklessly, skidding to a stop. He jumped out, stretched, and loped over toward Berry, and, as usual, Lucille trailed right behind him. She followed him everywhere, an obedient puppy who happened to be a slim, brown-skinned, 5'6 girl with doe eyes for her tall, well-built man.

"Berry baby, what you doing now?" Zachary said, grinning and tilting his cap.

He walked like he was rich. He had nothing.

"Still at it," said Berry.

She moved out of the crouch, feeling the burn in her legs. Lucille clutched a little black pocketbook under her arm. "That look rough," she said. She was smacking her gum. "But cool."

"Ima make it work," said Berry.

They laughed at her and left her to it, Zachary touching Lucille on the waist as they rounded the corner.

The idea of a house consumed Berry. She knew every nook and cranny of Mrs. Perscher's house, Mrs. Hayward's house, Mrs. Lauden's house. And it wasn't just the external build of a nice home or size of the rooms or the fresh bright paint or the expensive plush furniture. It was the details too: the decorative bed covers, the artistic lamps, the gold-plated edges. That was what got to her.

Nothing to do but compare when she came back to her own home. And be frustrated. The nails didn't hold the wood steady, and she couldn't figure out what to do. She kicked it, then sat back down and stared at it. She wanted something nice, too. Something pretty to lie down in, look around at, and call hers. Hers. She couldn't get stuck here. She had to find a way to make that happen. She had to make it work.

Chapter 2

Aunt Millie was arriving from New York on Saturday, and since Zachary had a truck, he'd pick her up from the train station. Aunt Millie was coming to stay with Grandma Maple. It was short notice, but that was because Aunt Millie had suddenly left her husband. He was beating her, so she had to leave. That was all Grandma Maple said about it.

Berry rode with Zachary to the town's train station. He parked on the edge of the large parking lot and waited, while Berry sat with her head laid against the window.

"Dang," said Zachary, glancing at her. "You look tired as hell."

"You gonna be tired too when Aunt Millie come out," said Berry.

"Is she that bad?" asked Zachary, laughing.

Aunt Millie talked too much. She was Lilah's sister, and just like Lilah, she had too much going on. As for why in the hell she would move back to the South—the ex-husband situation must be dire. Grandma Maple didn't like to tell people's secrets, though, so Berry would have to try to gauge the situation herself.

Berry and Zach waited a while, straining to see the people leaving the large, dark concrete building. Was that Aunt Millie? Nope. No. Still not her. Then, finally, there she was, a familiar shape even though Berry hadn't seen her aunt in years.

Aunt Millie made her way across the lot, clutching a wide-brimmed hat atop her head. She was slightly chunky and had a slight limp. She had someone with her, which made Berry lean forward to look. A few paces behind, a girl in a tiny blue-striped shirt and flared blue pants was lugging Aunt Millie's suitcase and clutching a small bag in her other hand.

"Come on here now," said Aunt Millie to the girl. The girl was clearly struggling with the luggage, but she wasn't complaining. Aunt Millie probably couldn't help either. It looked like something was wrong with her knee.

"Get out," Zachary told Berry. "Let your auntie get in the front seat."

"Lord, Lord, baby, look at you, look at you!" Aunt Millie said to Berry as she got out.

She grabbed Berry and very near suffocated her in a hug. Berry endured it in complete familial submission. Aunt Millie was saying all sorts of stuff, rocking her back and forth. When she finally let her go, she turned to the girl and fixed her hat and said to Zachary, "You gonna put the stuff up there or ride with it?"

"They can hold it down," said Zachary, turning in the driver's seat to look out at them. "Truck bed be fine." He must have remembered his manners then. He jumped out of the truck and came around the side, passing Berry, who was wiping away the kiss Aunt Millie left on her cheek with her sleeve.

"Lemme help ya," Zachary said to the girl. They had the gate down. Aunt Millie got in the truck and shut the passenger door.

The girl hopped on the back as Zachary pushed the second piece of luggage onto the bed. She was slim like Berry, and her movements were quick and sharp like a cat's.

Berry and the girl got a good look at each other. The girl had smooth dark skin, almond eyes, and a sniffy expression. Her straightened hair hung past her shoulders and her edges were as kinky as Berry's. She must be around nineteen too, Berry's age. No coat on, but it was the first day since winter they could get away with it.

"So you from New York?" Berry said to her as the truck rumbled off.

The girl, sitting with her knees up and pressed together, shaded her eyes against the sun behind Berry and nodded.

"You kin to my aunt?" said Berry. "We might be cousins."

"Nah."

"Everybody cousins in the South," said Berry.

"I'm not kin to Mrs. Varner, though."

"OK."

She rude as hell, Berry thought, and looked away, squinting at the passing scenery of fields and houses. The truck had picked up some speed, and the wind ruffled their clothing. She could feel the girl looking at her. Berry decided she hated that chick.

***

Bernadette Smith was a down-to-earth country girl. She said what she meant, she threw with a straight aim, and if she liked somebody, she spoke to them. If she didn't like them, she'd have a whole lot of thoughts about them that she kept to herself. Apparently, that girl with Aunt Millie didn't want to be befriended.

It didn't make sense, Berry thought, as the road raced by. She didn't look at the girl sitting right in front of her. This girl would be staying at her house. They could've been friends—why not? Because Berry would have loved that, someone she could share every secret and laugh with.

The girls she'd gone to high school with always got on her nerves, though. Always falling out over something stupid. She said, he said. I don't like her, she's stuck up. So if this girl was like that, then shoot. Why bother?

There were more important things than other girls and friends, anyway, Berry thought as the truck stopped in the yard and she got to her feet. Berry had to stay focused. This was the same town where her father had been murdered by the Klan, where her mother wasted her life, where everybody knew her as Maple McKinley's granddaughter. She needed to leave. She had to leave.

She knew the image people had of her. Berry Smith. Dark skin girl, walking down the lane in her white Chucks, her little black handbag swinging from her shoulder, pretty smile, clever dark eyes, kept to herself but nice if you talked to her. Took after her grandmother—they were the smart, capable ones from that family. Everyone in town knew them. Maple McKinley had cooked for the mayor and his wife for years. But the granddaughter was young, and there was something different about her. What would she make of herself?

There was nothing here, nothing to look forward to. She'd talk to Lilah again as soon as the company got settled in and they had a moment together to discuss it. Go North, go to college, and find a good job so she could get a nice place to stay for her and Lilah. They'd have a nice house, they'd finally be happy.

So crazy that Aunt Millie and the girl came to Springville, North Carolina, of all the locations on the map, Berry thought, to a place she longed to escape. That ex-husband situation must really be something dire.

Chapter 3

Little Miss Rude—as Berry had dubbed her—was actually named Josephine. Josephine Walker. Aunt Millie called her Jo. She treated the girl as if she were some kind of apprentice, but Josephine seemed to regard being by her side as a duty. Aunt Millie left her hat in the pickup that same evening she arrived, and Josephine ran out in the dark and fetched it for her.

Grandma Maple stood over the stove while everyone else sat around the table. Zachary held his terrier puppy, which had wandered into the house. When Josephine took her spot beside him, Berry noticed that she kept glancing sideways at the dog with a funny look. She don't like dogs, Berry thought. She felt the same way. They all smelled funky and their fur felt gross. Josephine was seated directly across from Berry, where it was hard not to look at her.

Lilah lit a cigarette. Berry gave her mother a hard look. Lilah—just cooking up her lungs.

"Lilah," said Aunt Millie. "Put that thing out, girl. I come back from the city where all the heathens at and I still got more manners than you."

"I can't help it," said Lilah. She puffed.

"Lord have mercy," said Aunt Millie.

"She can't help it," said Grandma Maple. "Don't y'all start arguing, ain't been here for a day and already acting like girls again. And Zach, get that dog out. He stinks."

Zach went to the door with the dog. Grandma Maple took the pot and set the whole thing on a plate on the table. Jo stared hungrily. Berry kept glancing at her, she couldn't help it. The girl was right in front of her. Jo looked at her then and Berry looked away to the food, but when she looked back, Jo was still looking at her, unsmiling dark eyes observing.

***

The women divided household tasks equally, and no one ever complained about her share of the work. Berry always did the dishes. After the meal, Berry started on them as usual. Lucille went to help Josephine unpack, while Lilah went outside to smoke some more. Grandma Maple still sat at the table with Aunt Millie. They spoke in undertones, but the kitchen was small, so it was easy to hear them.

"Just stay here," said Grandma Maple. "As long as you need to. No, don't you worry. Long as I got a room, you welcome."

There was a chair shuffle, something like a sigh. Berry dried a plate and pretended not to be listening. She put the plate on the open shelf. They didn't have cabinets all around like there needed to be. Open shelves were such a sore eye. When Berry finally learned how to build, she was going to finish the kitchen with real cabinets.

Aunt Millie's boisterous affection was all gone. When Berry stole a glance at her face, her aunt looked soft and weary, sitting with her chin in her hands. She was only about forty, a little ahead of Lilah. Aunt Millie acted a lot older than that. It struck Berry with shock. Aunt Millie wasn't old, she was tired. Berry felt sad as she turned back to the stack of pots. She didn't want to be like that.

"I just wish he wasn't such a dog, Ma," murmured Aunt Millie.

"Then you shouldn't have been with a man," said Grandma Maple.

***

Poor Aunt Millie, having to return to her mother. A woman could always come home to other women once the men were done dragging them through the mud and abusing them. Over and over, and over again, Berry had seen it.

Berry didn't want to be like that, she thought as she lay in bed later that night. She'd never be like that with that boy she was sneaking around with, Charlie Johnson. Charlie was the Avery farm tenant's son. He had nice long legs and they'd been messing around since last spring. She wouldn't be like that with him, even if she married him. She'd never let him step on her, dry her up, wear her out, make her old.

She was always going to be happy, no matter what. Even if she had to go to the ends of the earth to find her happiness, then she would. She deserved that.

Restless, she sat up. Lilah kept coughing and going back to sleep, lightly snoring later. This house, this freaking house. It was really getting on Berry's damn nerves. Why, all of a sudden, when she was nineteen, was she so frustrated and angry with everything?

She slipped out of bed and padded across the bare floor to the door. It was impossible to see in the dark. But she was used to it. She made her way down the short hallway and into the kitchen. Just as she went to pull the string for the light, she heard a rustle. She paused, frowning, and then pulled the light anyway.

Little Miss Rude—Josephine, leaned against the counter, holding a glass of water to her lips. She wore a pink floral nightshirt and green pajamas. She stopped mid-sip.

"Oh," said Berry. "Lookie here."

The silence was punctuated by the sound of Berry's heartbeat. She could hear it and she was sure that Josephine could, too. The other girl drank her water as casually as you please and set the glass on the counter. She looked at Berry with a smirk.

"Your grandma said, I can make myself at home."

"Oh, I see you did that."

The glass was straight, with no marks, and the single cup that Berry always polished the most—until it was transparent and looked like she could put her finger right through it. It was Berry's favorite glass, and it irritated her tremendously to see someone else drinking from it.

Nobody at the house knew, of course, that it was Berry's favorite glass. Or that she even had one. It was not normal for a person older than six years of age to have a favorite drinking cup.

Josephine studied her nails. Berry sat at the kitchen table and put her hand under her chin. All the sleep—not that there was any in her—had vanished.

"Just gonna sit there and watch me?" said Josephine. She shook her head. Then she took the glass, filled it with more water, and gave it to Berry.

Berry didn't think about what she was doing. She drank the water straight down while Josephine's dark eyes bored into her.

"I don't have no problem with you, honestly," Berry said. "Okay? So stop acting weird."

The last words were expressed with irritation, but she was relieved just to say something sharp, and her body was at ease as she stood and put down the glass. Josephine said nothing in reply. Berry left the kitchen without looking back.

In bed again, she lay on her back, trying to make out the marks on the dark ceiling. She realized suddenly that she'd done something not like her, because she was fastidious. She'd accepted a drink of water, right behind the mouth of someone else, without rinsing the glass.

Chapter 4

"There's nothing to do around here," Josephine said. She'd been looking for a job. She was standing on the porch with Lucille and Berry, who were going through a cardboard box of preserves the neighbors dropped off. Neighbors always gave and vice versa. "Nothing," continued Jo. "That dumb man at the mill told me off."

"Berry cleans," said Lucille, who babysat and did other odd jobs. "You could try that."

"Not a real job," Berry huffed. "I'm saving money. I'm gonna move."

"Well, you should," said Josephine. "You all don't have shit."

"Hey," said Lucille, straightening from the box and glaring at Josephine. "Watch your mouth. You here on Southern hospitality."

"What y'all fussing 'bout?" Grandma Maple stepped out. "Always fussing and doing."

"We not fussing," said Lucille. "Josephine think she from Paradise and we living in Hell."

Grandma Maple snorted and then her mouth quirked. "We are living in hell."

"I didn't say that," said Josephine. "I just said it wasn't shit down here."

Grandma Maple turned on her. "Huh?"

Jo suddenly looked uncertain, shifting from one foot to the other.

"Did I hear what I thought I heard?" said Grandma Maple. "I know you didn't just cuss at me. What you cursing for?"

Josephine looked even more unsure. "It's a bad habit. I'm sorry, Mrs. McKinley."

"You too young for habits. You ought to be 'shamed of yourself, having filthy stuff like that come out of your mouth. You a young lady, Josephine."

Jo dropped her head. Berry and Lucille exchanged glances, Lucille stifling a snicker. They must do it differently in New York, because Berry could not imagine cursing in front of her grandmother. She couldn't even say the word "lie" to Grandma Maple. Or "hate". Or "mad". Or any such thing that implied real human emotion or behavior.

"You need to wash your mouth, girl," Grandma Maple told Josephine. "Don't let me hear you talking like that ever again."

Josephine mumbled another apology and went into the house.

***

"You really clean for people?" Josephine asked the next day, standing on the lower step, hands tucked into a thin jacket, as Berry leaned against the porch post. Without being asked, Josephine had started to help with all the chores, such as clearing sticks out of the yard earlier that day and laying them in a heap. She talked a lot of trash, but already her being here was helpful.

"Yes," said Berry. "Mainly for Mrs. Perscher's. I hate it."

"Who's that?"

Berry told her that it was the county commissioner's wife.

"Town hotshots, oh okay. They make you wear some sort of uniform?"

"You don't have maids in New York? Yankee town?"

"Yankee town is not a real place."

"You don't wear a uniform," said Berry, ignoring her. "It's just, I'm not going to somebody's house looking tacky. I don't go out looking tacky."

"Yeah," said Josephine. "Me neither." She came higher on the steps and stopped on the top one. "And I did work in New York," she said. With a funny tone, she added, "Yankee town."

They gave each other sarcastic smiles. "It was at a restaurant," said Josephine. "Dishwashing, two shifts. And I was taking night classes."

"Night classes? Really?" That hit Berry like a ton of bricks. She stared at the face before her, eyes focused on hers. Josephine had an entire life before, and of course she was upset, having to move South and to nothing when that wasn't her choice.

"What were you studying?" Berry asked.

"Nursing." Josephine pulled a face. "I didn't like it, though. You need a strong stomach to do it. I would act like I did, then I'd go home and couldn't eat my hamburger sandwich."

"Ew." Berry was conjuring up images of sick people.

"Yeah...Couldn't finish my lunch one time. That hamburger started looking like diarrhea."

They broke out in laughter.

***

After that conversation, Berry and Jo were no longer weird around each other. They weren't friendly, but they were hesitantly interested, calm, and neutral. Jo took the trash out to be burned. She did the dishes whenever Berry didn't. She hung the clothes on the line. She packed food that Grandma Maple cooked. Berry told her thanks, and she meant it.

Berry, being the youngest of the women, was used to listening to her mother, grandmother, and sister do their thing. They complained about men, life, their bodies, men. Berry worked, she bought herself lollipop treats, she messed around in the yard, and she fantasized about having the bigger and better things that she saw in magazines. She had no one to relate to...

Then Jo came along. Finally, someone in the house who was on her level, someone she felt all at once a sense of rivalry and curiosity towards. This other girl also had been studying in college! Something Berry wanted to do so badly. And she was actually funny. Berry didn't hate her anymore. Berry was generally irritated by most things and most people, but admittedly, not by Jo Walker.

***

Always irritated. Among the innumerable thoughts she kept to herself, Berry's main emotion was a belabored resentment. Resentment because she didn't own nice things, resentment because her world was limited, resentment because her mother's absentmindedness frustrated her.

Lilah would sit on the front steps, blowing out smoke. She didn't go to the club, she didn't even drink, and as far as Berry knew, she never stayed with a man too long, either. She just smoked those darned cigarettes. A mother was supposed to be active, fussy, interfering. That was the comfort of having one. Lilah didn't care. Berry could probably jump off a cliff and Lilah would just keep on smoking, looking in one direction.

If Lilah wasn't so checked out, Berry's sister Lucille wouldn't be such a bird. Lucille flitted here and there, a movement of confusion and igno-rance. Her world was Zachary. Berry had asked her multiple times to come to New York with her. Lucille always said, "I can't leave my man, Berry." As if he was the most precious treasure she'd ever found. As if a two-legged Negro was a reason to put her life on hold. Her love for him was nauseating.

The final time she and Berry made plans to go out together, Zachary drove up thirty minutes before, and guess who Lucille ran outside to and ended up leaving with.

Berry had a lot of thoughts. She had to keep them all to herself, it hardened her resentment.

It wasn't her mother's and sister's fault, though. Nor could it be blamed on the house.

The real truth was that Berry had a chip on her shoulder. Her father, Raymond Smith, had fought in the war. When he got back home, Raymond loved his whiskey and his women. Where did folks find the hours in the day? Lilah left Raymond when Berry was five and Lucille was six. The three of them came traipsing back from Texas to North Carolina. Raymond followed, begging his wife to come back to him. They were together for about a month before Lilah left him again and came back to Grandma Maple.

A week later, they found Raymond in a ditch with his neck broken, right eye gouged out, his hands tied behind his back, and his privates stuffed in his mouth. The women sobbed and begged. The police scratched their heads and said they didn't know. The adults didn't spare her the details, so Berry understood it all. This was the world they lived in.

Raymond had a closed casket funeral. He'd gotten drunk and taken the wrong road home. Grandma Maple had no choice but to drop the case, Lilah discovered smoking, Lucille accepted it. Berry grew up thinking, year after year, that her father was a fool to be drinking in the first place when he had a wife and two daughters who needed him in this hostile world.

Why couldn't he have had the sense to stay alive to be there for them? What kind of man was so weak that he could be butchered like an animal, disgraced like that, while his women watched helplessly?

Chapter 5

The five women sat at the round kitchen table: Berry, Grandma Maple, Lilah, Lucille, and Jo. Aunt Millie was in bed. During a lull in the conversation, Jo casually announced that she'd gotten a job cleaning the sheriff's office and running errands. They broke into gasps and murmurs. "Yeah," said Jo, shrugging. "They had the hiring sign in the window. But I'm surprised, too. Why everybody looking at me like that?"

Grandma Maple shook her head. "I hope you up on why you got the job."

"Well, I'm doing something nobody wants to do. For pennies."

"That's exactly why they hired you. That and because you got a nice build. You know that don't you? Don't let them use you, don't never let them white men put they filthy hands on you."

Lilah and Lucille nodded. Berry watched with an eyebrow raised.

"You know how they like to do," Lilah added, shaking her head.

Lucille smacked her gum. "You from the city, you might be a little confused."

"I'm not confused about anything," Jo retorted. She glared at Lucille.

"City ain't no different from here," said Grandma Maple then.

"Be careful," said Berry evenly, and, as dusk was falling, she half-rose from her seat to pull the light switch overhead. The conversation progressed to a different topic.

The sheriff's department though. Of all the places in town Jo could've found a job, she had to step into the den of vipers. She was bound to get herself molested or in some kind of trouble. Didn't she know none of the other women wanted the position because they didn't want to be messing around there?

Also, Deputy Frazier. The heavy-set, flushed one who wore wire-framed glasses. Berry was ninety-nine percent sure that he was in the group of men who killed Raymond Smith fourteen years ago that night. It just made sense every time Berry looked at him. His pale blue eyes. That black baton. Other details. Many details.

"Be careful," she told Jo again as they stood at the sink later. "Just be careful."

Jo didn't retort this time. "I will."

Berry hated the idea of Jo getting hurt. By a white man or a black man. Different ways of hurt, and any man could hurt. Was it worth the trouble of sleeping with one, for anything at all?

***

Berry said this often to herself, and usually when she was leaving the house where Charlie Johnson lived, but always her resolve would weaken. And eventually she would return. It wasn't so much that she liked Charlie as a person, as it was the simple fact that his dick felt so good.

This place: pure pleasure—and frustration. Simultaneously, or alternating. Charlie's bed in his house, while his parents and his brothers were out. And she was here now, under him. And boy did he know how to use his dick. He wasn't afraid to pound her. The hard sharp feel of his slim hips felt divine. She wanted it hard, he gave it good.

"Shit," he said. He was enjoying her too, clearly.

He had a good-looking face, but she didn't like looking at him. She just liked the way he felt. She kept her eyes closed, her hand on his chest. His heart was beating fast. Hers was, too.

Her hand fell away as he went faster. She was almost there, he was hitting that spot in her that was just right, just right, right there—she was almost there—

"Keep going," she whispered, melting back into the mattress, knees shaking. "Keep going."

She focused. His hips, the feeling, the rhythm.

Then he tensed, breathing hard, and—stopped.

She lost it all, just like that. It was all over in one moment. He was out of her. Her eyes flew open to the sight of him finishing himself, shuddering—

She looked away. She hated his face when he was coming. He wasn't hot when he was. No idea why, it just didn't appeal to her. In fact, it pissed her off.

He flopped down beside her, wiping with a random t-shirt that was already on the bed. She ignored his gaze and pretended to be patting down her hair, which she would soon have to put the hot comb on again. It wasn't about the hair though, not at all. She was pissed at him. She was so, so close to a place she had been trying her damn hardest to reach forever. And she'd never gotten there, in all this time with him. Doing him for a year now, and the times when he had made her finish: not once. Because he always stopped too soon.

"Berry," he muttered, as she leaned over the side of the bed and reached for her underclothes on the floor. But he wasn't really trying for a conversation either.

Ugh. He just couldn't go long enough. Why couldn't he go long enough?

A few moments passed while they lay in their respective places and drifted to their own thoughts. She was bored, and he was already lightly snoring.

***

Berry had everybody fooled. Every time they asked her if she was talking to any of the neighborhood boys, she said the same thing: If I like him, I'll talk to him. But I don't like nobody. Grandma Maple just told her not to let anybody get her caught out there. Berry wasn't stupid. She always made Charlie pull out and do it somewhere else.

Not the best situation, but that was what it was. Her body needed touch. She just couldn't give it up.

And one day, hopefully, she'd climax. She kept returning in hope of that.

As she approached the lane of her own house, she set her expression to steel.

Jo and Aunt Millie stood together at the kitchen table when she walked in. Their backs were turned. Aunt Millie was speaking in a low voice to Jo. Berry would've greeted them, but remembering where she'd just come from and what she'd just done, she crept past them instead. As she did, she stole a second glance at Jo, and wondered very randomly what kinds of men she liked to be under, and if she'd found anybody in this town to be with.

***

The next day, that Saturday, Berry sat on the back steps of the house again, rubbing her temples. Where was she before Aunt Millie and a girl named Jo moved in and threw off her thinking?

The scrap boards lay there in the dirt. She nudged them with the toe of her Converse.

It occurred to her, as she stared at the neighboring house with its faded gray shutters and slipshod underpinning, what the tiny house needed. A foundation. Something to hold it all together. And she thought, How the hell didn't I think of that before? I can't just slam some pieces together and expect them to stick without something solid holding it together.

An actual tear of joy came to her eye at her profound genius and the ability to teach herself. She took the board and lugged it out into the space. She put scattered bricks down. There was always junk lying around. Junk nobody was using.

She could make something of this. She was excited again.

She was sawing hard enough to break her arm when someone laughed. She stopped, turned slowly, and glared over her shoulder. Jo grinned down at her, fingers at her mouth. Berry had thought it was Lucille, coming to tease her like she always did. But it was Jo, looking sneaky and curious and wearing the outfit from the first day Berry met her.

Heat rushed into Berry's face.

"What you doing?" Jo asked, not mockingly. "Building something?"

"Er, yes," said Berry.

"Ooh, cool. I like it." Jo hopped over the board where she now faced Berry. Berry dropped the handsaw and sat back on her heels and looked at her. She was preparing to defend herself for looking crazy, but Jo was still assessing the boards and the tools.

"You for real know how to use this stuff?"

The question was flattering, the way it was posed. "Not really," Berry said easily, fingers tapping and smoothing the board. "But I try my hand. Zach works with a carpenter. He gave me some things."

Their gazes met. There was some agreement of understanding, of admiration, respect. Jo said, without breaking her gaze, her voice softer, "What you doing it for?"

"It'll sound silly," said Berry, laughing a little, hesitant.

Jo shrugged. Her face was encouraging, her eyes wide.

"It's like an on-the-ground tree house," Berry said then, her own voice soft, too. "That's what I'm trying to make. I just want somewhere where nobody can bother me."

"Neat," Jo said, sincerely. Berry smiled tentatively. And in that moment, for the first time in her life, she felt that someone truly saw her.

Chapter 6

"God!" screamed Reverend Jackson that Sunday morning, "is a healer! He's a healer!" He pushed Aunt Millie and she fell backward. Grandma Maple swiftly caught her and straightened her. Aunt Millie pressed her face into her hands, her shoulders shaking.

Reverend Jackson was an older, skinny man, built like a reed—and he was always pushing his members as they stood before him at the mourner's bench in Beautiful Jerusalem Baptist Church. The mourner's bench was a low, blue upholstered structure where people would kneel not just to pray—but to mourn. Howl, weep. Tarry. The church had a mourner's bench because Reverend Jackson was in the Holiness movement before he switched denominations, and boy did the Holiness folks love to pray and cry and scream before the Lord.

Berry mostly watched dispassionately. But that morning, she felt sorry for Aunt Millie.

Also like the church he had left, Reverend Jackson believed in faith healing. It could all work if they just had faith. Every Sunday he said it. And Aunt Millie believed him, because although she rarely went elsewhere, she always came to church to stand in Reverend Jackson's prayer line, in her best black pumps and dress, hands folded before her before she inevitably pressed them to her face, weeping.

The music played and people cried.

And Aunt Millie came home in the same condition as she was before.

Aunt Millie was taking the long rest she needed. Maybe she'd need a few weeks? The women discussed her in low tones during their kitchen chat time in the late evening. "Be easy on her till she gets herself together," said Grandma Maple, who was doing crossword puzzles.

"We know," Lucille said. "I'm just saying nobody should be in bed during the day. I can't wash my sheets if she's sleeping."

"You act like you both don't take a bath every single day and every single night."

"Oun care," said Lucille, popping her gum. "I like my clean sheets."

"Cille, have some sympathy." Lilah pulled her cigarette away from her face and blew out smoke. "You wearing the fabric out anyway, washing the sheets every day. She probably don't sleep much at night. I think she having nightmares."

"Heck yeah," said Grandma Maple. "Heck yeah she having nightmares. That man beat the living daylights outta her, 'course she having nightmares. That's why her spleen like that."

"I do hope her spleen get alright," Lucille conceded, pulling her gum in and sighing.

Grandma Maple glanced at Berry, who was coming to sit at the table with them. "You wanna switch rooms with her, Berry?"

"Nope," said Berry, glancing at her annoyed sister. "I like staying with Mama. 'Cille got it."

"Y'all act like you don't understand." Grandma Maple sighed.

"I do understand it," said Berry, voice rising. "I do."

***

If only they knew the things she understood! Deputy Frazier was getting out of his blue and white patrol car, and Berry was walking past that little red and white brick store she never went into, because she wasn't going to spend one brown cent there when she had to go through the back door. Broad daylight.

Deputy Frazier. Nobody would believe her if she said it, but she'd seen it in a dream. Six nights straight, in 1954, Berry was fourteen years old and she dreamed of him. There was a circle, torches and men. Even as a dream it was terrifying as hell. Even to wake up from. A man's harrowing wail. The man was her father. And someone was whacking him as he balled up in the dirt, and the fist that held the baton was white and meaty, and the wrist connected to it had a flaky pale splotch. More hard black shoes surrounding the man, kicking out. But that wrist.

Standing in line at the post office a few days later, she saw that wrist exactly as the image had pierced her dream. Deputy Frazier was talking to a town hotshot and another cop near the counter, and his short sleeves revealed meaty arms. And Berry's gaze traveled down and snagged on that blob on his wrist. That image had been made for her, as if it was meant to be revealed. That's him.

Maple McKinley's granddaughter. She could've sworn his body language changed every time he passed her. He was leaning against the pickup window of the store. She crossed to the other side of the street and passed by, only glancing back once, feeling him staring through his tinted sunglasses at her.

She quickened her steps. This time, seeing Deputy Frazier left her with a bad feeling. Usually, Berry could swallow the emotion and go on. But now she kept thinking about him, and he came to her even while she was lying in bed next to Charlie at his house.

They had the heater up even though it was warming quickly with spring. Berry was in a white bra and panties. Charlie was shirtless in long brown pants. He was talking, she wasn't listening. He was always talking about himself. Always after he finished before she never did.

"You know, Berry?" he said then, to whatever he was talking about.

"Yeah," she said, without even looking at Charlie. Deputy Frazier. She had a hunch about him. But there was something missing about all this. Something completely unrelated to the deputy. This thing niggled at her. This thing. Was she forgetting something important? Was she anxious? Confused? Hell yeah, she was, but why?

What the hell was it? Something was bugging her. A thought she needed to have, that wasn't coming to her mind. She sat up and reached for the rest of her clothes.

***

Berry stood on the steps of her own house when she returned home, still trying to remember what it was that she was forgetting, thinking that maybe she'd never thought of it at all. What was it? What was worrying her? The distinct smell of collards wafted outside. Her grandma must be making dinner.

There was no creeping past Grandma Maple. "You wanna help?" she said when Berry came inside. She was at the stove, stirring something in a large gray pot. She'd made sure Berry knew how to cook, started teaching Berry when she was six.

Berry ran through her mind for an excuse. She couldn't find one.

"Where you been anyway?" Grandma Maple fanned away heat. "Where you been this long?"

"I stopped by the store," said Berry.

Grandma Maple didn't even look back at her, but Berry could tell just by the set of her shoulders that she didn't believe her.

"Come on help me cook," she said.

Everything Maple McKinley did, she did hard, and she did well. She worked hard—she'd trekked to the fields for years, cooking after that, raising four girls, worked right through carrying them, her husband dying young—everything. She was a lean, well-built woman with a perfectly upright posture, and she dressed up whenever she left the house. Grandma Maple said a woman should never look sloppy. She cooked the best food, she sewed every piece of clothing that split, and her daughters could always come to her for advice. And they eventually always said, whether or not they butted heads with her, that she was right.

"I know so," she'd say. "And when you live sixty years on this earth, then you'll be right about some stuff too."

She'd been eyeing Berry hard lately, trying to figure her out, sizing her up. She was giving Berry that look now, as they stood across from each other and kneaded dough together on the wood tabletop. Berry made a show of pummeling the dough. She watched her dark hands go underneath and over and squeeze the pale paste. Grandma Maple could look right into her eyes sometimes and guess things, and if Berry looked at her too long, Grandma Maple might guess just where she'd come from.

If Grandma Maple got too curious, she just might have a dream about Berry. Berry wasn't the only one who had odd dreams come out of nowhere. Maybe most women did. The women in her family got their little hunches about random and sometimes serious things too, though none to the degree that Berry did.

Berry just reminded herself, over and over, that what she was doing was really none of Grandma Maple's business. Not really, not truly.

"Think it's good," Berry said, and pulled a ball of dough away from the original lump to pat onto the pan. Grandma Maple didn't say anything. Why should Berry tell her everything? They kept secrets from her.

Chapter 7

Jo sat on the back step, watching Berry as she hacked at that little house. Berry couldn't get the sides to stand up. Just one side so far, and she couldn't get the board to act right. For one, the nail wouldn't go through in some places. This wood was tougher than nails.

"Want me to help you paint it when it's finished?" Jo said. She smiled when Berry emphatically said yes. But it had to be built first.

"So," said Berry after a while. Still trying to nail to no avail. Those darn sides. She got one nail in. She sat back on the grass. "You miss anybody from the city?"

The reply was quick. "If you asking if I had a boyfriend, no."

Berry grinned. She wasn't asking that, but it was funny that Jo thought she was. She cut her eyes at Jo again. Surprising that a cute girl like Jo didn't have a man.

"Hey, what?" said Jo, noticing the look and looking amused. Then she said, "Oh, you mean, who's my people?"

"Yeah," said Berry, banishing her smile. "I was just wondering. No big deal."

"I can tell you. I don't claim them. My people. They're buzzards."

Berry raised her brows in surprise at the frank harshness. She was expecting a generic answer. "You call your family buzzards?"

"I mean," said Jo emptily. "They don't mean a thing to me. They're not good for me."

"Dang." Berry immediately felt sorry for her.

Jo shrugged. But something flickered across her face that wasn't bravado, for the first time that Berry had seen. It made her look even younger than nineteen and so vulnerable. "I'm just telling the truth. I don't really have a family."

"I shouldn't have asked you that. I'm sorry. Sorry about all of it."

"I don't care. I do not care. Berry, can I ask then? Did your parents separate?"

And see, that was one thing that Berry was just dying inside to rant about. She also felt bad for making Jo sad, so she was happy to change that subject to herself. And she'd never had anyone to talk to about herself. Before she knew it, she'd told Jo all about the murder, Deputy Frazier, and her dream. Jo sat there with her mouth open at the end, her eyes fixed on Berry as she took it all in.

Talking to Jo was a deep breath of relief, thought Berry after she spilled it all. Berry felt she could tell her anything, even about her stupid dreams that made her sound insane. It was so easy it shocked her.

Then Jo opened up to her. Her own father died in the war in 1945. "Maybe God will be our Father." (Berry laughed at that.) Jo's mother, Elaine, was an unstable individual even before that particular event, but she just got worse. Her next three marriages were each one worse than the last.

"Boy, my mama could pick a man," said Jo, rolling her eyes. "She really could pick."

"That's crazy."

"Oh no, it gets worse," said Jo. "It gets worse."

Somewhere between the second and third marriage separation, Elaine's drinking habit intensified. They lost their apartment. They crowded in with cousins. The cousins were drunks, creeps, and everything else in between. Jo's mother wound up in a mental institution, but fortunately, one of the neighbors was a hardworking, serious woman who went to church.

That particular neighbor knew Aunt Millie. That's how Jo came to know her. Jo ditched the fucked up cousins and moved in with her. But surprise—this was not a safe place either, because the estranged husband, Clyde, was abusive as hell. By the end, Jo and Aunt Millie had all they could take.

"She's never going back to him," said Jo squarely. "And I told her not to."

Berry listened intently. She realized that Jo was telling her secrets.

Lighthearted topics. The next morning, hanging out on the porch, Berry sat in a chair and Jo stood behind her. Jo had nimble fingers, she could make a clean, sleek braid, even on straightened hair. Chatting about nothing. Girls being girls. Later, Berry came back from the store with six lollipops and gave four of them to Jo, whose eyes lit up with surprise as she smiled.

***

Their most interesting conversation happened at the clothesline two days after that. Berry folded the clothes as Jo took them down and passed them to her. Berry asked her again about nursing. She'd thought about doing that herself. It was either that, or teaching. Those were the only professional paths for Black girls.

"Nursing just wasn't for me," Jo explained. "But if you feel it fits you, hooray." She dropped more pins into the bag. "When I go back North, I don't know what I'll do. But it won't be nursing, I know that."

"Maybe we could be teachers," said Berry.

"Ooh, maybe!"

"Doctors and lawyers," said Berry, and they both laughed.

"We'd be so cool!" They laughed again.

"Jo though, really. I know. Okay, hey. Wanna know another secret?"

They stopped. Jo nodded vigorously. Berry said, "But only if you tell another one, too."

"Hey!" Jo whipped a towel at her. "I'm all out!"

"No you're not!" Giggling. They were holding each other's hands now, the white shirt and white towel between them crumpled in the dirt.

Laughing. "Okay, okay. Oh my God, girl. I can't stop laughing."

"Be serious, be serious." Berry was laughing too.

"Okay, okay." Jo was serious. Berry was serious, swallowing.

"I wanna be a lawyer, Jo. I always thought it was so cool. I saw a court on TV once."

Jo froze. Her expression went annoyed. "You took mine," she snapped.

"Took yours?" Berry scowled.

"You took my secret," Jo said. "Because that's one of mine. I wanted to be a lawyer."

"No way," said Berry. Their hands fell away, the warmth evaporating.

"Yes way, girl. I never told anybody, it feels silly. Who would let me? But I always did."

They stood there and stared at each other.

"Maybe it's something in the air," said Berry finally.

"I don't know," said Jo, shaking her head. "But that was my thing, it really was, and it was before you said it."

***

Hopes so high they were hardly hopes anymore. More like loose, wild fantasies. That conversation was forgotten for the time being. They were girls, laughing, talking, loving their new connection.

One day, Berry was walking into the house from the backyard, humming a little dancing tune, when Jo came skipping from the kitchen into the hall and blocked her way. She wore Berry's yellow apron and her hair was curling back to kinky under her headband.

They both giggled. They were always giggling now.

"Don't be a monster," said Berry through her giggling. "I have places to be."

"Check this out." Jo's voice was a sing-song tone. She held out her fist, and as Berry watched, as if it were some magical performance, Jo opened her palm. In it lay a skinny, pale brown toothpick. Jo picked it up with a flourish, and extended it to Berry.

"It's for your house," she announced. "Now you have all the lumber you need."

Berry took it and burst into full laughter, and kept on laughing as Jo went back into the kitchen, her laughter ringing out too.

That was the day that Berry fell in love with Jo. She watched her turn the corner of the house, still laughing, her lithe figure radiating with happiness, and Berry's heart did all kinds of things and fell down, down, down, down, down for Josephine Walker.

Chapter 8

Mr. Perscher blocked the way. The hallway in his house was much longer and more decorated down its length than the one in Berry's home. Matching mirrors watched them, the girl and the man. An empty white ceramic vase sat on the small corner table. Could Berry grab it and smash it over his head if it came down to it? Her heart raced.

"I'll just squeeze by you, sir," Berry said politely, trying not to sway with the heavy bucket. She hoped he could hear the seriousness in her tone.

"Don't splosh it now," said Mr. Perscher. He had a crooked, sun-weathered face that was currently smiling. His pale blue eyes raked over her, making her feel naked and wrong.

He let her pass reluctantly. She stepped quickly into the bathroom and locked the door, her fingers shaking as she did so. She stared at the knob, not seeing anything. There was no sound of his footsteps leaving.

She counted the tiles. She wiped the mirror. She flushed the toilet. Scrubbed a small square of grout. She held her breath. She did it all over again. There was still no sound of his steps.

She couldn't stay here forever. Anxiety and curiosity consumed her until she peeked out again. Mr. Perscher was picking at something on the table. He turned around immediately, catching her before she could duck back into the bathroom.

Fuck. Now it was awkward.

"Say," he said. "You get everything all done?"

She should have worked faster today. God, why didn't she work faster, before he got home?

"Yes, sir," she said wryly.

Mr. Perscher stopped close in front of her again, both hands in the pockets of his khaki slacks. His thin watch ticked loudly. She dropped the empty bucket. He dropped the pretense.

"Say, Berry," he said. "You got a boyfriend?"

If he was spiteful, he'd like that she did. If he was cruel, he'd like that she didn't. There was no right answer. Her heart beat faster. She was cold and hot at the same time, trying not to tremble.

"I don't do those things," she said finally, her voice hardly a whisper.

His throat moved as he stared down at her.

"How 'bout for an extra five dollars?" he murmured. "You'd let me have some for that?"

She took a step back, shaking her head. "I'm not that kind of girl, Mr. Perscher."

Her heart was beating so fast she was about to throw up. She peeled the gloves off without washing them and tossed them and the bucket in the closet. As calmly and as quickly as she could, she made her way to the side door. Screaming inside, her steps deliberate. And in no rush, he followed after her.

Justine's ride, the familiar red car, pulled up to the curb of the wide cement drive.

Berry glanced back at Mr. Perscher, who was standing right in the doorway behind her. And there was the other blue car bringing his wife and her friend, creeping up behind the first.

"You know," he said, with a dry laugh. "I could force you."

She looked at him incredulously. He still had his hands in his pockets. He leaned against the doorframe. The sun was as bright as ever. His dark hair was brown in the light.

"If I forced you," he said. "You wouldn't be able to do a damn thing. Would ya?"

***

Charlie blocked her way the next day, on the end of the sidewalk at the intersection. He asked why she hadn't come the evening before like she promised. He held the bar of his shiny green bike with one hand, shielded his eyes from the sun with the other. One brogued foot attached to a long leg steadied him on the ground. He missed her, he said, they sure had a lot of fun. What happened to her?

"I couldn't find the time," said Berry. She swallowed a feeling of disgust rising in her.

"Why not?" said Charlie.

A car pulled up to the stop sign. The head in the driver's seat turned to gawk. But it didn't matter if someone gossiped that Berry and Charlie were seen talking on the sidewalk today. Those kids got something going? There'd be nothing to gossip about after now.

"I guess I just don't want to meet anymore," Berry said finally. "Sorry, I just don't."

Both his hands gripped the shiny handlebars. The foot moved. He scratched his head.

"Really, Berry-berry? How come you don't want it no more?"

"I just don't want to." She felt bad for cutting him down, but she couldn't take it back now.

"So...nothing? Just nothing. Not even a kiss?"

"Charlie, I'm busy. I got a lot...to focus on."

"Hey, baby, alright." He was trying to sound cool, the way he said baby. Dumbass boy.

He sped off, and she walked on.

But as she went, her footsteps got lighter.

When she met Charlie, it was at a funeral—during the lineup to view the body. The grandmother of someone who was somehow connected to someone, a neighborhood person. Charlie was so tall and skinny and cute in his black suit and his tipped black hat, looking right at her. Afterwards he'd said to her as they stood side by side, looking straight ahead at the casket, "Dead bodies look so funny, don't they," not as a question, but as an observation. They were young, suffering through an event of old folks. And a statement like that, in that somber atmosphere, was so out of place and made her laugh and instantly like Charlie.

She wouldn't miss him now, though. She already knew she wouldn't.

***

At first Berry's heart was light with a good decision, but then her contemplation from earlier returned. What was this thing that she couldn't remember? There was some thought in the corner of her mind that she couldn't shine the light on. And no matter how hard she tried, she couldn't remember.

Eventually, it created a bad feeling in her chest, a feeling of dread, of fear. She was forgetting something, and forgetting wasn't good. Forgetting was being taken off guard. It made her so anxious that she took to taking deep breaths at the sink and counting to five.

Then it rained, and her half-completed tree house fell apart. Call it the builder's fault—if it were built right, it would've withstood the test of anything. Berry's fault. Mud and rain made everything sour, and Lucille had broken up with Zachary yet again and was crying at the table, mad. "Why won't he do right?"

In church, Grandma Maple walked Aunt Millie to the prayer line.

"Hallelujah! He's a healer!" cried Reverend Jackson, and promptly laid hands on Aunt Millie, who held her mother's sleeve. The two women were the same height, but Grandma Maple had the better, dignified posture.

"Do you believe?" said Reverend Jackson. "Do you believe that God can do this?"

"I believe," Aunt Millie whispered. "I believe I can be healed."

Reverend Jackson went off praying for her.

Berry glanced at her mother, rocking with her eyes closed. Lilah always got serious when she came to church, then, and only then. Lucille, on the other side of their mother, peered into a hand mirror at her puffy eyes. Jo was seated beside Berry. She was looking down, and she looked asleep. Until the tear streaks running down her face were visible.

Berry took her hand, and then they were squeezing, and Jo wasn't crying anymore.

Berry cried herself, later when she sat in the ruins of her project in the back-yard and imagined what it, and everything else, could have become. It would've been so good. But she didn't have the right tools. That was always the problem about doing things, the struggle of trying to do something—not having the right tools.

Chapter 9

Berry slept restlessly, dreaming of running over a large green hill and then falling off the side of it and careening down and down and down a thousand feet, but when she woke all she had was the odd curiosity of patchy memory. She lay in bed, staring up at the low white ceiling. What was it that her dreams were telling her? What was God trying to tell her? The uneasy feeling wouldn't shake.

"It's when you worry," Jo said, as they sat in the kitchen alone that evening.

"Everybody worries though," said Berry, rubbing the side of her face. "Mine gets so bad, like it lingers." Like a headache, she thought. A dull, nagging headache.

"I felt like that before we left the city," said Jo.

"Yeah?"

"Swear, I had a sinking feeling in my stomach every day."

Jo explained that it was all because of Aunt Millie and the husband's fights. He cheated all the time, but he got mad if she didn't sit there and patiently be a perfect wife. Aunt Millie shouted at him about bringing the drinking, gambling guy friends—and yes, the women he was cheating with, into the apartment! And then he started putting his hands on her.

"That's when it got scary as hell," said Jo. "I would lock myself in the basement. I called the police twice. That's how you get a Black man to pipe down. You call a white man on him." She smiled at Berry's loud laugh. "But," she finished, "You can guess they didn't stop. She was scared of him, and I was too, honestly. So yeah, I was worrying a lot."

"That's awful. I'm glad you got out."

"Me too. I helped her leave. I built her up." She sighed. "So that's done."

"That's good," said Berry. "Amen to that." Not wanting to feel queasy anymore, she added, "Hey, wanna make pancakes for a nighttime snack?"

***

Lucille and Zachary kept breaking up and getting back together, breaking up and getting back together. Whenever they broke up, nobody could ride the truck. For that reason and that reason only, the women generally wanted her to stay with him.

"You either get with him," said Grandma Maple. "Or down him and get from 'round him."

He'd been out at the club, dancing with other girls. But Lucille wasn't ready to let him go.

She was never ready to let him go. He made her cry her makeup off. He made her furious. He made her swear she'd never go back, and then she'd sit around chewing her nails and waiting for him and jump up and run into his arms when he came back again.

This time when they broke up he didn't call for days. The other women were tired of consoling Lucille, and went on about their way. Lilah turned on the blues and went to bed. Aunt Millie went to visit her mother's younger sister, Aunt Cora. Grandma Maple went off—she answered to nobody when she left. Wonder what the woman was getting up to? A man herself, maybe?

Eventually, Lucille scrambled after Zachary.

Jo and Berry were left alone, their familiarity growing like a palpable thing. Developing a consciousness of their bodies in proximity to each other. Hands, smiles, laughing, joking. Hated each other when they first met, just six weeks ago, yakking like best friends now. Every word, secret, whisper, laugh, shared.

***

Jo and Berry sat side by side on the porch floor in the mild spring weather. They had their legs tucked under them. In the dusk, bugs flitted around. The small outlines of surrounding houses were quiet. Everything was quiet, still as a cornfield.

"I still can't believe you already had my secret," said Jo, tilting her head to stare into a darkening, cloudless sky. Berry couldn't help but notice the soft rise and curve of her neat chest. Everything about Jo was self-sufficient and neat like that. Berry was aware that she was having strange thoughts of this other completely normal girl, but it wasn't bothering anyone, so she could have them.

"Great minds," murmured Berry.

Jo swatted her. Berry swatted her back. Jo swatted her again. And then she leaned towards Berry, Berry found herself moving towards her, and her body forgot its reservations. And the most remarkable, heavenly, unbelievable thing happened. Their lips met, touched in warmth. Berry got this buzz in her head, probably what drinking felt like. They pulled back and gazed at each other. Jo's eyes shone. That unmistakable, frank expression said: no regret.

Something took over, something came out that had been there all along. Berry leaned in, put her hand up, tentatively, but sure, to the back of Jo's head, and kissed her again, harder this time. And Jo kissed her back, her hand clasping Berry's cheek, and it felt so damn good.

Chapter 10

The kiss was broken by a dog's bark. This noise reminded them that they were in full view of God and the neighborhood. They looked frantically at the shuttered neighboring houses, but at least it was getting dark.

They jumped to their feet and went inside, they were relieved, they went to their bedrooms without stating an understood acknowledgement and agreement that this new, sudden thing did not have to be addressed right away.

Didn't even have to say the words. It was just there.

It was worthless anyway, Berry thought as she lay in bed later. Berry was a young woman. Jo was a young woman. Young women learned how to roll biscuits, hang clothes, and feed their families. Young women got married and raised children...

Berry was getting ahead of herself.

All that happened was that a girl kissed her. It could've been friendly, it might've been chaste. It didn't matter, it was just a kiss.

But with that, something in her just flipped. The center of her being awakened to something she'd never allowed herself to acknowledge. Her other kinds of desires.

Berry's dreams told the story. The space was a haze, and she was kissing Jo, and then moving her hands down to her chest, and kissing that, too. She could feel it. The plane of soft, bare flesh. A part of her consciousness was surprised that she could feel so viscerally in a dream. She felt Jo's lips on her neck, her belly, her warm, sleek body pressed against hers. When she woke, sometime past midnight, to turn over and flip her pillow, she had nothing but her empty hands, hot frustration, a subtle heartbeat between her legs.

***

At dinner the next day, Berry and Jo met eyes and melted into grins. Berry was floating in an enchantment of desire. Her whole body on fire. Where did last night come from? And why, more than anything else in the world, did she want it to happen again?

"What's all this about?" Grandma Maple said, catching them smiling at each other.

Lucille glanced up from biting a nail. Aunt Millie and Lilah's conversation halted.

"Nothing," Berry said quickly. "Jo burned her tongue."

"It's so hot." Jo put her hand over her mouth. Berry giggled again.

Girls were always giggling about one thing or another. That was what it meant for girls to be friends. Everything was so much funnier when there were two girls instead of one. And soon enough, people in town knew that Berry was best friends with Jo because they walked to the store together and they walked to church together and Jo wore Berry's fancy earrings and Berry wore Jo's best white-collared blouse.

Their friendship was always about exchanges. Secrets, advice, help, retorts.

Jo was looking out to see if she got anything on anybody at the police department. As far as she was concerned, the whole lot of them were KKK. Berry said of course they were, she'd already warned her. Didn't she know not to trust anyone, ever?

Jo said that of course she knew. "I'm an infiltrator," she said, standing on the steps as Berry leaned against the front door. "Do you know what that fancy word means? It's somebody that sneaks into somewhere."

"I know what it means," said Berry irritably. "Of course I do." The one could never feel that the other was older, wiser, smarter, or better. Those were not their morals. People might shelve them, but they would never shelve each other.

"I don't know if you can discern things about people," Berry continued, straightening. "But guarantee if I worked there I could tell you just who."

"You don't know if I can discern stuff?" said Jo. "Are you kidding? You think I survived growing up in Harlem without knowing how to tell things about people?"

So many little conversations like that.

The tension made it fun. They started sneaking here and there to kiss.

They never talked about it. They didn't need to. They were best girl friends, and best girl friends could do whatever they wanted to each other. Folks said, if they ever approached the very taboo, scandalous, and cursed topic at all, that two women had nothing to do anything with and it was a waste of time and that was that.

In a way, that idea did make it seem less serious. Not serious, never serious. So Berry felt less guilt. As long as nobody found out, she was going to keep on doing it. She could kiss Jo and look anyone in the eye. She couldn't look anyone in the eye right after she kissed a man. But this wasn't wrong in her head, not in the way it felt, it wasn't wrong one bit, it was the hottest thing in the world—it was only wrong when she thought of what others would say.

She'd stop when she had to. Of course, this couldn't keep going on.

They were kissing in the living room one day, just before everybody else came home.

"If we move to New York, we can do it all the time," Jo said as they lay on the floor together.

"God, yeah," said Berry.

The day before, Jo and Berry had decided they would move together.

But even then, Berry knew. This thing right here had to end, and no one could know. Other people would kill her if they knew. But other people must never, ever find out. And it had to end.

***

Lilah was expecting a letter from Social Services. She got up and plodded outside, walking on the backs of her shoes, with Berry following her. A little walk together. Perfect opportunity. It was so hard to get her mother alone, and so hard to talk to her, because Lilah listened only when she wanted to.

"Jo wants to go back to New York," said Berry, as Lilah collected the mail.

"Bet she do," Lilah said. "I feel sorry for her."

"Let's all go. Me, you and her. She knows people. It won't just be us two."

Lilah paused from sifting through the letters to look at her. "Berry, we've talked about this. You know how much that's gonna take."

"Everybody's moving, Mama."

"Millie can't go back, though."

"Aunt Millie gonna be okay with Grandma. Grandma holding everything down." Berry stopped in her mother's path, grabbing her sleeve. "I came in the house the other day, he asked me if I'll take money to sleep with him."

"What!" Lilah's face fell in horror. "You talking about the commissioner? He said that?"

"I'm not gonna come to anything if I stay here, Mama. There's nothing to become."

"Berry, oh, God. Be careful. No..."

"I just don't wanna stay here," Berry said. She didn't include the blatant threat of violence. No need to get her mother worked up over something that she couldn't do anything about. "Please Mama," she said as they walked back towards the house. "I need you to come with me. You know we can't survive alone. But if I'm with you, and you're with me..."

"I don't have enough money yet," said Lilah finally.

***

Mr. Perscher stood on the porch of his house while Berry watered the plants in the flower garden below. Sometimes Mrs. Perscher did it, sometimes Berry did it. She kept her eyes on the greenery, the white lattice of the deck, but she could feel and she could see in her peripheral vision. He watched her, hands jammed in his tan slacks' pockets again.

"She keeps a really nice flower garden," he said, stepping closer to the porch edge.

Berry duly agreed without looking up.

Mrs. Perscher was in the house now with a gal pal and the friend's little son. Her own children, a twin girl and boy, were off in college. One to find a husband and the other to make a career. What if Mrs. Perscher came out now?

"You like what she pay you?" Mr. Perscher asked.

For a moment, Berry considered saying that she didn't. Why not? Three dollars and fifty cents a day was no money at all. Mr. Perscher had plenty to give if Berry wanted to play that game. What if she negotiated, tricked? But then she envisioned herself on her back in the suede backseat of his truck, down a dark road, dusk—don't start something, can't finish it. Danger. Secrets, pain. His hands on her, vile. She'd choke.

She realized he was waiting for her because she hadn't answered.

"I'm grateful for whatever I get, sir," said Berry. She moved to the next pot.

He came off the steps and stood beside her. She gripped the pot tighter, not pouring.

"I didn't say I was gonna do it," he said, his tone lower. "I just said I could. Who'd believe you? Well, they would, but who would do anything?"

"Please don't say things like that," she said, shaking. "Stop."

"If and whenever you want that five bucks, girl, you just let me know, that's all."

He swatted her waist and was heading back up the steps and into the house before she could react. She gripped the pot, frozen, staring in anger and disgust.

Chapter 11

It would've never happened if Berry and Jo hadn't been laughing so hard that day. They were home alone. The house was clean. The clothes were on the lines. They were laughing and laughing, throwing suds, acorns, swatting each other and laughing. They kept on laughing, until they laughed themselves right into the house, and into the bedroom together, and they were kissing before they hit the bed.

Shirts and skirts came off, were tossed to the side. They met again, in a breathless kiss.

"Mmm, this is so fun," murmured Berry. Reality hit where she was then. Things came to a halt and they regarded each other. They were really doing this. "Have you ever...kissed a girl?" Berry didn't know why she'd never asked before.

"In New York," said Jo, closing her eyes briefly.

"You Yanks are something else," Berry whispered, her voice a giggle.

They started kissing again, same intensity, before Jo sat back up.

"Wanna see something?" Jo slid off her bra. And it was just like Berry's dream. Small and round, sit up so nice, dark areolas. Berry reached—Jo caught her hand. "No" accented by the tricky smile on her lips. "You gotta look first."

"Gosh, girl, they're so pretty," said Berry, excited. Mind racing already, comparing because she couldn't help it. Yeah, hers sat up like that too, and she had a dip in her own waist too, and Jo was gazing at her—

Jo started kissing her again and Berry kissed her back, equally hungry.

"Have you?" whispered Jo, moving back. Her eyes searched Berry's. "Did you?"

"No." Berry laughed dryly, feeling equally jealous and awed. Berry was jealous that someone had already kissed Jo, Berry was jealous that it hadn't been her. And awed because this all made her so, so in need.

Jo slid off the last piece. Then she took Berry's hand, put it right on her bare warm, plump, silky flesh, and Berry whispered, "Okay."

But then automatically, Berry rubbed softly. Her palm radiated with heat. The sensation was so much more noticeable, warmer on another body. Jo shuddered, and her chest rose quickly and fell. "Do it faster," she pleaded. Then, "Wait." And she flopped down, and Berry lay beside her, snuggled into her, and rubbed her in circles, and up and down. Berry couldn't believe she was doing this.

"You have to put your fingers on it," whispered Jo. Even lower. "Or in me."

"Yeah, I know," said Berry, softly. They rearranged to get more comfortable.

It was different from touching herself, but also not. She couldn't believe this: her face was in the neck of the naked girl next to her, and that girl was breathless, with her legs open and Berry's hand between them. It felt like touching herself, an extension of herself, except it was someone else.

"God, yeah," said Jo, closing her eyes. Her knees were shaky.

Berry started going harder, and Jo took deep, gasping breaths.

They turned and kissed each other more. Hands stroking and trying and teasing.

Jo was shaking and she was breathing faster, but she wanted to stop, she wanted to touch Berry. Another shuffle. Jo balled up Berry's panties and threw them on the floor. Berry laughed at the gesture. Jo grinned and smirked. She kissed Berry's neck, her collarbone, her breasts. Caressed her skin.

So much fun. Way too fun. Rubbed her. She moved back, gazing into Berry's face. Berry smiled again. This game was fun. They were really doing this. Then Jo slid her finger in. And Berry's giggle turned into a moan.

It was pure visual and physical pleasure. It was Jo's expression. The dazed yet focused expression that showed she was clearly so turned on doing it. Her two fingers and the steady pressure. Jo kept going just like that, just like that. And the house was so quiet, and Jo was so sexy and fun and equally hungry for Berry, leaning over her, with her pretty dark boobs, and perfect messy hair, her best friend, making her feel—

Oh God.

Berry tensed up suddenly, she forgot everything as something tightened deep inside her, and she came just like that.

Chapter 12

Heaven: when everything built up and collapsed into a hot, beautiful bliss. Reverend Jackson stood on the rostrum, snorting and hassling. Hell: What he would warn them about until his voice went hoarse. He was preaching about hell on Sunday morning, but Berry knew where she'd gone last Saturday night: Heaven. God, it felt so good.

Jo, beside her on the pew, stared at nothing in particular. Her legs were crossed neatly. She and Berry wore matching outfits: tucked dark blouses, neat white skirts, and saddle shoes. Green headbands over their pressed hair. Earrings. They always wore their best to church. Their lips were shiny with Vaseline. They had their hands in their laps. They looked so utterly girlish and innocent.

Somebody screeched in praise. Jo looked up and snickered.

"Pay attention," Grandma Maple said next to her. She rocked from side to side, but her face was sharp as she regarded Berry.

She'd been so picky at Berry lately. Why didn't she focus on Lucille, who wasn't even here today, laid up in bed because she was too sick to go to church? Lucille was probably lying, her cycles were never bad. Berry was the good one, the good granddaughter. They didn't know she'd slept with a man. They didn't even know she'd slept with a girl.

The deacon called the prayer line. Grandma Maple and Lilah got up, following Aunt Millie, with Grandma Maple putting a hand in the small of her back. The church was extra packed today. The next Sunday was Easter.

Reverend Jackson began his prayers. Sick members stood around the altar with bowed heads. Reverend Jackson went down the line, his prayers growing louder. Some members watched, while others closed their eyes and mumbled. Grandma Maple, lean and upright, kept her hand on the middle of Aunt Millie's back. Lilah, on the other side, added her hand.

Berry looked down and felt that old sense of dream creep into her soul again.

Then. A flash of something—a flash of something bright and harsh—flashed before her in an instant. She jolted and sat upright.

Her heart kicked up its pace. She sucked in a breath, trying to believe that she wasn't afraid, she wasn't shocked.

But that cut, that slice of light, it was so plain. What was it? Where was it from? The feeling behind it. It was bad, it was wrong. Something was.

Jo, beside her, moved her pinky finger across her hand as it rested on the seat. Berry looked at her and her expression softened and again, she forgot her fear.

***

Sex made Berry forget the doom. All over again. It made her forget that she was still discontented with her life. It made her forget that she was trying her hardest not to see what was right in front of her. And somehow everything turned into a blur.

All she could think about was that it was possible to be satisfied in life. It was possible to be happy, to feel good, to finish. That girl made her do what that man couldn't for a whole long year, but that girl made her do it in no more than two minutes, with her fingers pressed to the heart of her body. And she was so madly and wildly in love with that girl. It was forbidden, wrong, ridiculous, and nothing was going to ever, ever come of it, but boy this was just the way she felt, and damn, she couldn't help it.

Home alone, in bed, Berry and Jo were doing it again. They'd figured out the logistics of legs and how to slot against each other so they could enjoy each other at the same time. Soft, warm, flesh on flesh turned desire into flames. Berry was breathless, and Jo kept saying, God, over and over and over again. Both were shaking. Rubbing their bodies together, every inch of touching skin nothing but a map of electricity. Exploring. Touching. Berry was so horny she just might catch fire, until she was breathing calmly again after an explosive, triple orgasm. The white bed sheet warm against her back. It was hot in the room.

She turned to Jo, and gazed at her shuttered face, the black lashes against her cheek, kissed her warm shoulder. Jo looked like she was flat, worn out from pleasure.

"I love you," Berry said. The words came so easily.

"I love you too," said Jo, a smile in her voice. Berry listened to their hearts. She realized for the first time how special it was to hear somebody else's heartbeat. She closed her eyes. Their hearts beat in sync. For one extraordinary moment, they were one person. They were one. They could be one.

"Since we're talking love. I have something to confess," Jo murmured then. She didn't wait for Berry to answer. "You're my best friend, Berry. Like, best friend. I never had anyone before you." Her voice cracked at the end, like she wanted to cry.

"You're mine too," whispered Berry, and meant it. "It's the same for me."

"I love you with my whole heart," said Jo. "Everything in me."

"I love you just as bad. I said it first."

They moved closer, holding tighter.

What were they thinking right now? At any moment now, Grandma Maple would come home. Lilah's empty bed sat on the other side of the room. Five other women shared this house. The girls broke apart and sat up. Berry reached for her clothes. "She'd kill us."

"No kidding." Jo grabbed her t-shirt.

***

Later the next day, Berry and Jo knelt by the side of the house while Berry wiggled the board that had come loose. Next to her, Jo cupped the nails in her palm. They wore pants for convenience. As Jo straightened to take a break from crouching, Berry glanced at her.

Jo was so hot, she thought. She'd always thought it subconsciously but it came to her differently in that moment. Her figure, her eyes, her humor and her face. Why were girls who looked like her never in magazines, in books, on tv? Because she was so hot.

"Okay," said Berry, wiping her hair out her face. "I set it where it looks nice."

Jo handed her a nail. And Berry picked up the hammer—she was still clumsy with it, this just wasn't her line of work, but she managed to nail the underpin piece up again.

It had occurred to Berry that instead of building a new house that was small and insufficient, that she might instead fix up the one she was already in. That would make more sense. Fix up what she already had.

Sometimes, the truth was such a simple thing.

"This looks so much better," Jo said, as they both stood back.

"I'm just tired of it looking raggedy," Berry said.

"I'd help you paint too," said Jo. "Paint would look good."

Jo loved paint. Like Berry, she loved pretty things. Berry smiled.

"We could make all the shutters fresh, don't you think? Yeah?"

Lucille and Lilah tromped right by the fixed underpin. Aunt Millie never saw it. But Grandma Maple appreciated it. She surveyed it with a pleased eye and said that she was proud.

"I don't know why I didn't think to do it," Grandma Maple said, swinging the heavy cloth bag she carried to her other shoulder. "Being so busy, you skip right over this stuff."

"I know yeah," said Berry. "It bothered me, so me and Jo did it."

"Jo," said Grandma Maple, looking at the girl with admiration for the first time. "I see why Aunt Millie say you her standby. You hold your end up. That's real good."

Having a best friend gave Berry's life color. Made her world interesting. Gave her the future of real things to fantasize about. Her best friend. Who understood her and wanted what she wanted. Life improvements, fixing things and making them better. That night in bed, Berry fell asleep holding her pillow, imagining it was Jo. And this time she dreamed of a beautiful house. Never saw the shape of it or its colors or the location, but it was a beautiful house and hers that she owned.

Chapter 13

It was the Saturday before Easter. Berry, Lucille, and Jo sat at the kitchen table that morning after breakfast. Lucille was writing a letter, Berry was lounging, and Jo was asleep, her head on the table. Aunt Millie was home, too, napping. Grandma Maple and Lilah had gone over to a neighbor's house to prepare tomorrow's dinner.

For the past hour, Jo and Berry had been communicating with their eyes—when was Lucille going to leave so they could sneak into the bedroom and play with each other some more?—but Lucille was slow-moving.

Lucille was writing a letter to Zach. She'd already wasted two papers, and she was on her third. "I'm gon tell him everything he did wrong and make him cry," said Lucille when they first sat down. "Ima make him cry."

Berry had rolled her eyes. And as Lucille wasn't Jo's sister, Jo hadn't said anything.

Berry had said then, "Lucille, how you gonna make him cry when he the one doing you wrong?"

Lucille had ignored that. Scratch, scratch, her pen went across the paper on the table. And Jo had played with the salt and pepper shakers and her hands and her hair and then finally laid her head down and dozed off. Berry had her chin in her hand, bored. She really wished Lucille would leave. She was messing up the plan.

Eventually, Berry's mind wandered off.

She was jolted from her daze by a sharp rap on the door.

And even as her head still rested on the table, Jo's eyes popped open.

The rap was repeated, in forceful separations of twos and threes.

"You not gonna get it?" said Lucille. She was rereading her letter.

The rapping continued as Berry got up. She swung the door open, and the flash of light revealed a man. He wore a faded gray suit, a black trench coat, and he had a narrow, scowling dark face with a crooked nose and thick, uncombed hair.

"Hey," he said gruffly. It was clear he'd stepped back quickly just after he knocked. There was something nervous about his mannerisms.

"Do I know you?" asked Berry.

Berry didn't realize Jo was behind her until she bumped into her. Jo was looking at the man, and her eyes were wide as quarters.

"Wait, what?" she said, clearly shocked. "Clyde, what are you doing here?"

"It's chill," said Clyde. "It's chill." There was a grimace in his pronunciations. He had a raspy, distinguished voice. "I just wanna speak to Millie. Tell her I got her a gift."

"Huh?" said Jo. "What?"

He must've been doing it because he was so desperate to make up with Aunt Millie. That was the only thing Berry could think of in that quick moment. For a man giving a gift, though, he sure seemed unhappy. But that would explain the hands behind him.

She and Jo shared a look. Lucille was frozen at the table, halfway up in her seat trying to peer out. The only man they ever brought to the house was Zach.

"You go," said Jo. Her voice dropped to a whisper. "Tell her it's Clyde."

Berry rushed out of the kitchen and down the hall. She tapped quickly on Aunt Millie's door before coming in. Her aunt was a lump in bed, covered in an old multi-colored quilt. Berry shook her on the shoulder. Aunt Millie groaned and sat up. Berry told her that it was her ex-husband at the door.

She felt out of place, having to say the man's name. But Aunt Millie hardly seemed to hear her. She snorted and threw off the blanket. She stuffed her feet into her bed shoes and tripped out. Berry followed her.

Jo was still holding the door, her body tense. Lucille was looking back and forth at all of them with an alarmed expression. Clyde stepped forward, standing exactly in the doorway, and Jo stepped back, just to the side.

"Hey, Millie," said Clyde. His voice was gruff.

"Clyde," Aunt Millie said. And never was a wearier-sounding word than the one she spoke then.

It happened so fast that no one could have moved, even if they had the guts to.

As Berry stood rigidly backed against the table, Clyde whipped out his hand that held a sawed-off shotgun.

"Jesus rose, bitch," he said, and shot Aunt Millie point-blank in the forehead.

Aunt Millie sprawled on the floor and the front door was wide open and there was the sound of running steps, shrieks, and a loud engine scraping. There was an odd pause in Berry's senses where she could comprehend absolutely nothing, but as her vision cleared she realized she was still backed against the table, shrieking as she gazed at Aunt Millie's brains. And then she looked down at herself, at the blood all over her skirt and her socked feet and she shrieked some more.

When Berry got done falling apart, Aunt Millie was still lying there. And her brains and her blood and the bits of her skull were still spattered across the floor beneath her. One leg was flung out, her skirt up, revealing solid brown thighs and the ripped fabric of her dark nylon stockings. Berry couldn't take it. "Oh my God," she heard herself saying. "Oh my God, oh my God, oh my God."

Jo was on the phone, pure gibberish spewing from her lips. Except it wasn't gibberish.

She was saying, "He shot her, he shot her, I don't know but he shot her!"

Berry couldn't look at it again. She stared at Jo as if that stare would save her, but Jo wasn't looking at her. Jo hunched into herself as she stood by the wall, she gripped the telephone like she would break it, her expression aghast and her hands trembling.

Berry spun around. Lucille sat at the table, her eyes wide as silver dollars. She hadn't moved at all. And Berry took off. She ran straight through the house, out the back door, down the steps, down the path, across the street, running, running, and she didn't stop running.

Chapter 14

Her feet, her mind, her fear, her legs, took Berry to the steps of Mrs. Low's house. She was greeted, still in her devastated condition, first by her mother, who promptly passed out at the sight of blood on her daughter's clothing. Her mother was caught by her grandmother, who'd seen too much to faint and never lost control of herself. And Mrs. Low ran to the back and brought Berry fresh clothes to wear, all while Berry explained everything as fast as she could, not quite believing it all had happened.

They turned off the stove, shoved food into cases, and stuffed on shoes. They piled into the car and Mrs. Low raced them back to her church friend's house. As soon as they came into the yard, they were blocked off by an ambulance truck and a police car. A group of neighbors had gathered to witness the scene. Grandma Maple didn't wait, she jumped out before Mrs. Low could brake and rushed into the fray.

Berry took a look at her mother, whose own face was slack with dismay, reached out her hand, squeezed once, and was not reciprocated. Lilah just looked straight ahead, stiff as a board. Berry hit her on the arm. Nothing. Berry sighed and gave up. She got out of the car and crept gingerly down to the front of the house.

Lucille sobbed as she spoke to the cop, a white man with a thick blond mustache and a couple of blond nose hairs. His partner was jotting down notes. Grandma Maple was asking over and over, What had happened? People were crowding around her, she only had her eyes on the cop.

Like a memory, Berry's eyes found Jo. Jo sat on the steps, cradling her head.

Jo had called the cops. These were men she saw often and knew too well. She'd watched a man brutally slaughter her guardian. But she couldn't speak now. Lucille was talking. When Lucille's voice got erratic and high-pitched, they told her to calm down, calm down, miss. They made her repeat the story as it was, as she knew it, in chronological order. Yes, she watched a man kill his ex-wife. Yes, the girl on the steps was their coworker to some degree. No, they could not comfort her. Murder was business.

It was so surreal, so unreal. Berry paced, and in the background of all the noise and wailing and questioning and running and whispering, Jo just sat there and stared at the ground.

Chapter 15

Lucille and Berry stood at the window, peering out at the early morning of houses and the street and neighbors leaving their homes. Berry and her sister were still in their nightclothes. They weren't going to Easter service, obviously, or anywhere. Berry shifted and Lucille straightened, her face worried. Berry knew she and everyone else were worried about the same thing: what if Clyde, not yet apprehended, doubled back for them and blew them out too?

Berry exhausted herself that evening telling visitors how it happened. She had to do it because Jo wouldn't speak and people came to the house in streams. The visitors were stunned and horrified. A few were helpful. Aunt Cora, Grandma Maple's sister, left her husband and her sons and came twenty-five miles to stay with them—and also to help Grandma Maple clean up the floor, which couldn't be cleaned enough. Several neighboring women and two of their husbands sat with them for hours. Someone brought dinner.

When it was nearing night and only Aunt Cora was still there, they got a knock on the front door, and Grandma Maple wrapped herself in her shawl and went to answer it. The young officer stepped inside and licked his thin, chapped lips before telling them that the police found Clyde Varner close to the Virginia and Tennessee border at a gas station.

"Eleven hours?" Jo gasped when she heard. She was standing at the kitchen table. "He shoots her and it takes eleven hours just to find him?" She made a motion with her fingers.

"Josephine," Grandma Maple hissed, tossing her a glare.

Jo went quiet, her mouth a thin line.

"How quick will the trial be?" said Berry, coming to stand next to Grandma Maple. Her heart was erratic in the way it beat. The image stuck behind her eyes was ghastly.

"Well, now," said the officer, with a shrug, "I don't know all that. But they got 'im."

***

Berry, Jo, and Lucille huddled together on the single couch in the tiny living room after the officer left. Somehow, his news was a confirmation that what they witnessed last night was real. They couldn't blame it on a trick of the mind. Lucille had never liked being touched unless it was Zachary, but she didn't mind this time. Her head was heavy against Berry's shoulder, and Jo held Berry's other hand.

Aunt Cora, Mrs. Low and a third woman were in the kitchen discussing something. Berry couldn't listen, couldn't think, because everytime she blinked, every time she spoke, every time she breathed, she saw the gray and mushy matter of Aunt Millie's brains spread across the kitchen linoleum.

Once, somewhere during that long stretch of time, Berry got up and made her way to the hallway for the tiny bathroom, the only one in the house. As she came to the hall and stood before the door, she looked ahead and saw in the dim light Grandma Maple dragging a long white mop back and forth across the spot, the murder spot, her face a mask and her lean brown arms pumping.

Never going to clean that spot like it was before, before Aunt Millie's head with a hole clean through it lay there.

***

Gaines Funeral Home was crowded that following Thursday for the wake. There wasn't a single empty black folding chair in the room. Even if people didn't know the woman, they were eager to witness the grief surrounding her tragedy. Immediate family members held cinnamon-scented candles, and some stood in line to say what they remembered about Millie McKinley Varner.

As her mother, Grandma Maple had the floor first. "My daughter," Grandma Maple began, sighing. She stood in the front next to a giant white wreath on a stand that held a circle of photos of Aunt Millie, both young and more recent. Grandma Maple shook her head. "She was a beautiful, loving girl. She always tried to do right by everybody. Always."

People hummed and rocked.

"She never hurt anyone," said Grandma Maple, folding her black-gloved hands and staring down. At that moment, Berry saw that her grandmother wasn't old. Sixty wasn't old, just mature. The audience shook their heads. "Never." Grandma Maple's voice cracked.

She was trying not to cry. Berry leaned forward, surprised because she'd never seen the woman cry. But why wouldn't she cry? Berry thought then. Of course she'd cry. She'd probably cried a lot in life, if life was always like this.

"I remember when she was a little girl," said Grandma Maple. "And we had a cat named Pips. Pips caught a rat one day and brought it to her. He laid it on the step. She buried that thing, the rat, and put a dandelion on top of the mound."

A woman burst into sobs. And that set Grandma Maple off too, hands over her face.

Berry couldn't take that. She jumped up, squeezed past Lilah and Jo, and made her way to the front, conscious of her black pumps making the only noise as she moved. She'd just reached Grandma Maple when, out of the corner of her eye, she saw Aunt Cora also approaching from across the aisle. They put their hands on either of Grandma Maple's shoulders.

Grandma Maple looked up at her granddaughter with red eyes.

"Thank you," she said under her breath. And she squeezed Cora's hand, too. But her eyes were on Berry. Berry squeezed her shoulder and took her into her arms before pulling back to whisper as she stared into her face, "It's okay, Grandma."

Grandma Maple swallowed and resumed speaking.

"You sure you don't wanna speak at the funeral?" They all asked Jo, over and over.

"No," Jo said every time. And no was a complete sentence.

Sure enough, too, at the funeral the next day, Jo didn't speak. People knew that she came down there to help Millie Varner, that she was a nice girl, that she had no parents, a long life already at nineteen, they felt sad for her. On top of all that, she was Berry's best friend. They were curious about her.

The white casket framed in white flowers was shut. Berry and Jo stood at it together. Hands brushing, but not touching. And it wasn't because of the eyes, because it was perfectly fine for two girl best friends to hold hands.

It was them, their own silent, unspoken guilt driving a wedge between them. They should've had the sense not to wake Aunt Millie up and bring her to the door to a violent man, her death. One of them should've known better.

Berry didn't hear a single word she or anyone else said, as she sat in her seat. She played it again and again. He drew his hand from behind his back. Jesus rose, bitch. He pulled the trigger. Her brains are on the kitchen floor. She hated him, she hated that man.

Chapter 16

Berry went outside the morning after she heard the news of the conviction and yanked a loose nail from one of the boards she'd abandoned. Damn that lousy ass sentencing after a quick trial: the state gave Clyde life instead of the chair. She grabbed the hammer on the ground near the underpin and stomped to the small oak tree in the front yard. She nailed through it as hard and fast as she could. And then she curled her fists up and took a long, deep breath.

If she were a judge, she'd send a man straight to the chair for shooting a woman.

She re-entered the house through the back door, the same way she'd left. She hadn't used the front door since the shooting happened. Every time she stood on the steps, she ended up going around to the back.

She had to get out of this house. She hated the front door.

They coped. Aunt Cora helped with chores. Grandma Maple kept going to work and avoided looking white people in the eye when they asked about her daughter, but she couldn't hide when she was buckling. Lilah kept smoking and sitting moodily, Lucille kept disappearing, Jo started throwing things, and Berry went through the back door.

Their dinners were silent. One night, Jo abruptly left the table—without excusing herself. Grandma Maple didn't bat an eye. Usually, she made them excuse themselves. Berry stared at the top of her very white rice, thinking over and over and over. Clyde should've gotten the death penalty. She would've given it to him.

She shouldn't have woken up Aunt Millie. God.

Suddenly, Lucille started giggling, wiping her eyes. They all looked at her.

"It's just so stupid? Ain't it?" Lucille said. "It's all just so stupid."

***

That woman was her blood, Berry thought. Connected to her. Another woman, another human. These worthless, violent men. God, she hated them. Each and every one she had ever met. Sitting on the clean floor of Mrs. Perscher's bathroom, Berry rocked. Sobbing.

A door closed.

She wiped her face and got to her feet.

"How you been getting along, Berry?" said Mrs. Perscher five minutes later when they faced each other in the living room, which was now spotless thanks to Berry. Sunlight shone through the large windows and reflected a colorful ray across the beige couch. "This summer heat's gonna be something, don't ya think? Make sure you stay cool."

Berry didn't say a word, because it was pissing her off, this sideways approach. Mrs. Perscher just couldn't get it out, her heart was too hard. She was too cold, too evil, to even say simply: I'm sorry that another woman died. The county commissioner's wife muttered something else and went on out the side door.

Yeah, go the fuck away, thought Berry.

***

After a while, Aunt Cora needed to get back to her own family. Jo came in as she was preparing to leave, shoulders slumped. Aunt Cora, bag in hand, asked her why she was sighing. Lilah was stitching a shirt and didn't look up. Lucille exchanged glances with Berry. Berry shrugged. She hadn't said a lot to Jo since the incident.

She knew they were both thinking the same thing: Why did we escort Aunt Millie to the front door so a man could put a bullet through her head?

"You not gonna answer?" urged Aunt Cora.

"You don't wanna hear," groaned Jo. And when no one pressed further: "I quit my job."

"Why you do that?" Grandma Maple turned sharply from the stove.

"You never quit your job," said Aunt Cora. "Oh, noo."

"They didn't care about her." Jo shrugged.

"You already knew that," said Grandma Maple. She glared at Jo. "You been here long enough to know that. You go back tomorrow and get your job."

Lucille cut her eye at Berry again. Berry shrugged again.

"Whew, I need a cigarette," Lilah muttered. She balled up the shirt and dropped it on the table, jumped up, and went out the door.

"I'll find work somewhere else," said Jo.

"You telling me you want to go to the fields, then?" Grandma Maple asked. "Because the fields is all that's left."

"I don't want to go to the fields. I'm never going to no fucking fields."

"One thing you not gonna do, is keep doing that New York cussing in my house. We do not use that language. I told you before."

"I'm sorry, Mrs. McKinley. I'm so sorry, I really am. I just can't help the way I talk."

"Josephine, I know it's hard. I know it is. But you got to face life for what it is."

"I am facing it. I'm just sick of looking at it."

Life has got to be better than this, thought Berry. It has to be.

Chapter 17

Lucille, having seen that the worst thing that could happen to a woman was a man, ran into the arms of a man for comfort and married Zachary one month later. It all happened so fast. One day she was Lucille who sat at the kitchen table smacking her gum, and the next she was solemn, sitting in a white veil in front of Reverend Jackson as he declared her forever union to Zachary Wilson, who looked smart in a brand-new black suit and cufflinks. The church was empty besides Lucille's mother, sister, aunt, and grandmother. The couple's vows echoed across the large room.

There was no reception. Lucille came home afterwards, packed her bags, and rushed back outside to where Zachary waited. When the truck was gone and the dust had settled in the gravel driveway, Berry and Lilah sat at the kitchen table alone. Berry did nothing and Lilah sipped lemon water. Jo and Grandma Maple were who knows where.

"It doesn't feel right here," said Berry, cracking the silence. "I know you have to feel it. Well, I saved enough money to buy us both tickets. You just gotta say you're coming."

"You're a country girl, Berry."

"Everybody's moving. You don't stay where there's no purpose."

"We don't have family up there." Lilah stirred the water in the tall glass.

"We're the family, we're all we need. I'll make sure we're alright." Berry's voice went lower, trying to make a promise real. "We could have a better life."

Lilah's fist curled around the spoon. "My ma needs me."

"You mean you need her. She has Aunt Cora. And I need you more than Grandma do."

Lilah sat for a long time staring into her glass. She had long lashes. She was so fragile. Like a doll. A doll with a raspy voice and sad big eyes.

"I don't know, Berry," said Lilah. "Honestly. The world ain't like you think. You go from one place to the next, hoping to find something different, but you don't. It's the same old people and the same old crap, everywhere."

Berry sighed.

"She ain't getting no younger," murmured Lilah.

"Pfft. She's holding up better than some kids my age."

A horn honked across the street. They both jumped and glanced at the screen door.

"You're just scared of leaving your mama," said Berry after she caught her breath, and she wanted it to hurt like an insult. She really hoped it hurt. "That's all that is. You're scared."

Lilah seemed unmoved. "I left before. I left her when I married your daddy."

"Yeah, and you're right back. Ten years. With your mama."

"Berry, I had to come back. Where else you think I was gonna go? She was all I had."

"And you're all I have." Berry glared at her. Tears and a headache rose behind her eyes, threatening, throbbing. "I know what it is though," Berry said. "It's just like I said. You're scared to leave your mama. You're thirty-nine years old, but you have to have your mama."

"I could say the same about you," Lilah said reproachfully, throwing up her hands. "You're begging me to drop everything and go with you to someplace I never been before with no money. Why you think I want that? I could say the same thing about you."

Berry got up, kicked her chair, and went outside and sat on the porch and stared at the houses and the landscape and the fields around her until the kitchen light turned off. It had to be better than this, she thought, tears of frustration rising in her burning eyes. She had to make her life better than this.

***

Ideally, Berry would go to New York with Lilah and Jo. Then she'd have her mother and her best friend with her in the same place. And truly, Grandma Maple would be fine. That woman didn't need anybody to babysit her. She was smarter than all of them put together. Grandma Maple had her own little stash of money in a can, she had a tiny pistol hidden under her pillow, she walked fast, she thought even faster, and she was going to be just fine.

The next night, Jo and Berry inevitably collided in the kitchen. And what a relief it was when Jo said, "Hey, Berry," softly, bravely. But the feeling of ease was short lived because then Jo said that she wanted to leave for sure now. And that she wouldn't wait.

Berry leaned her back against the sink and cradled her forehead.

"I'm trying to get my mama to go with us," she said.

"Berry," said Jo. She stared at Berry directly. "You realized I only came here because of Mrs. Varner right? Like, I didn't come here because I was oh so in love with corn fields and segregation. I came here because your aunt needed me."

"I want to go, Jo. I've been, been wanting to go. It's just my mama."

Jo shrugged. "I don't know her story but I know I'm not staying in this crap place."

"She's stubborn. And scared. She's locked down."

"Well," said Jo. "I'm going, and I hope you come too."

"I am," said Berry, feeling defensive. "I'm going."

They stared at each other with a thousand thoughts running between them. Jo turned to leave, then she stopped suddenly. "Berry," she said quietly, firmly. "You know I have to go. Like, I have to. I have to go."

But by the end of the week Berry made up her mind. And when her mind was made up, not a thing in the world could stop her. Not her mother's troubled face, or her grandmother's squint of concern. Not even her own apprehension. Berry bought a ticket to take a train to go to New York City.

She was washed with a strange sense of relief, holding that ticket. And it was all going to work out because Jo knew the woman Aunt Millie knew, the woman who would take them in when they arrived in New York. Mrs. Helen Crew was extremely religious, but just as fine a person as she could be. Aunt Millie had said so. And just as of now, Helen Crew had a room open in her Harlem apartment.

Berry didn't even tell Mrs. Perscher she was leaving. She owed her nothing.

All these young people like them escaping the South, the fields, cruelty, hopelessness. Going North, like following a beacon of light in the darkness. Berry and Jo weren't unordinary. They were running from something just like everybody else. Searching for something better, determined to find happiness.

Chapter 18

This? Berry's jaw dropped as she walked. New York City was big, filthy, and smelled just like pee—a far cry from glorious imagination. This musty ass place was supposed to be the capital of the world? Everything was so dingy, gray, and trashy. What. The. Hell. New York.

Berry couldn't stop looking around. At the buildings. At the people. So, so many people. So much busier, louder, dirtier, and brighter than clean, quiet, North Carolina. Her neck hurt from looking around, and then she realized that it probably made her look like she was out of town, so she resolved to stop staring.

She picked up her pace to keep up with Jo's quick gait through the train station and on the sidewalks. Jo always moved so fast. Berry kept her head straight, the blur of dark pavement swimming beneath her tired eyes.

***

Helen Crew was a thin, serious woman who always swallowed before answering a question, and who wore her dark, heavy skirts to her ankles and her white shirts buttoned to her throat. Her hair was covered with a round, black hat and pulled into a small bun in the back. She was as deeply religious as she had been described, and the wrinkles in her light brown cheeks were severe. But she was also very motherly.

"You and Josephine can stay free for the first two months," she said to the girls as they set down their things in the living room of her Harlem apartment. "After you find a job and work some, alright?"

They thanked her profusely.

Crew didn't want thanks. Each time they thanked her, she said, "Give it to God."

***

The new environment was jarring. In a matter of hours, Berry was no longer in a tiny house, but somewhere in a massive building of hundreds of apartments—in a room that she and Jo would share. And she was exhausted and anxious. Six hours after arriving in New York City, Berry woke in a strange bed covered in a strange blanket to the sound of doors closing and men's voices. She bolted upright, her heart pounding. One of the men was speaking very loudly. More laughter.

Berry glanced at the locked door, and then at Jo's still sleeping form.

Then a woman's voice. "I put your suit jacket right over there, yeah," said Crew clearly. "See if they cleaned it enough for you."

Berry relaxed at the sound of the woman's voice.

Twenty minutes later, she met these other tenements. Three men sat at the table, leaving two other free high chairs. Crew was at the stove. The kitchen opened right to a modest living room, where a second woman sat on the couch drinking from a mug. She was dressed in long clothing like Crew. They were probably Holiness, Berry realized. She'd seen them in North Carolina.

"Come eat," said Crew. "No strangers here." New York community competed with Southern hospitality, thought Berry, okay, that was relieving. Berry followed Jo to the table.

"I don't want to take your seat," said Berry.

"No, no," Crew waved her hand. "I'm sitting with Dorothy."

Dorothy was slim like Crew, early forties too, and had an inquisitive expression in her dark smooth face. She'd probably look nice if she'd take off all those extra clothes.

"So, you just got here yesterday?" said the man closest to Berry. He had a thick mustache, thick brows, and long, capable hands folded. His brown eyes were kind.

"This is Bernadette Smith," said Crew, answering instead. "She's the new tenant. She's from North Carolina. Josephine bought her."

"Nice to meet you," said the man, nodding. "I think I met you, Jo. Several times."

"Nice to meet you," Berry said, giving a friendly smile. "Thanks."

"I'm sorry about your godmother." He turned back to Berry. "And your aunt. I'm sorry."

"Thank you," said Berry again. Jo only nodded.

"I'm Friday," said the man. "You can just call me Uncle Friday like everybody does. I was happy to tell my wife she could take you all in." He gestured to the two men. "And this is Ernest and this is Ike. They're cousins, they're from Virginia."

The men, who looked alike with their deep set eyes and skinniness, nodded to her.

No matter how friendly everyone was to her, Berry still felt out of place. She chewed so slowly the food was tasteless in her mouth. She was conscious of Uncle Friday laughing with Ernest and jostling Ike, talking about the day, the work, the news. She felt every time Jo shifted in her seat and laughed politely at something that made the conversation general. She noticed Dorothy frequently whispering to Crew.

Those two women were clearly best friends. They kept whispering.

As for the men. The jarring pitch of their male voices. Their casualness, their jokes, their ease with one another—all that made her uneasy. As Berry sat there, she realized that she didn't like being in a house with men. After everything she'd seen, she didn't want to be around them.

But it would have to do for now.

***

Berry and Jo weren't talking a lot. It was hard to talk because of Aunt Millie. Berry felt so bad for waking her up to tell her to go to that door. She walked her to her death. God, why'd she do that? It was her fault.

She knew Jo must feel the same way. They had the same emotions all the time.

But despite not speaking much, the girls stuck together. Wherever Jo went, Berry went, and vice versa.

They went looking for a job. They'd go to school, but they needed to find jobs first.

Berry half dreaded finding one. She'd have to walk the street alone. In North Carolina, in her town of tall trees and small roads, that was so easy. She'd walked without thinking, walked in her daydreams. But could she walk out there, with all those scores of people flowing by at every moment, and not trip over her own feet, not get lost, breathe?

"Don't rush yourself," Crew said the third night. "You're in a big world now, and I don't want either of you to get hurt. Your people back home would kill me, if I let you get hurt."

Uncle Friday worked at a shoe factory and Helen drove a bus. The brothers Ike and Ernest did odd jobs here and there. Nothing was too stable in Harlem. There could never be total stability in these great waves of moving people.

All these people from all these places, coming to New York.

They were looking for the same things that she was.

There was stability in that.

Jo and Berry walked the street one evening, looking for work. They'd seen an ad in the newspaper for cleaning at a hotel. Maybe one of them could score the job. Whoever could get it. It wasn't a competition, after all. They were best friends.

At the hotel, they were told the job was taken.

More looking. They were tired. They'd come hundreds of miles and changed their lives in a matter of days, and who really needed a job immediately after all that?

"Let's try tomorrow?" said Berry, and Jo sighed and said yes.

The two of them wandered home together. They were two young women walking, attractive in their slacks and fitted shirts showing their narrow waists—and men eyed them as they passed by. Near the steps, on the railing actually, they saw him. The man who could've been any age, v-neck striped top, thick shiny black hair, loitering presence. A cigar hanging from his lips. His partner, or maybe two other men—Berry didn't look long enough to see. Never look too long at strange men, or any men—leering across with him.

"Hey young lady! Young lady! Young lady!"

It didn't matter that it was in the singular. There was a demand for the attention of either one of them. They were faceless, young, female shaped—targets. A long wolf whistle pierced the air, and then another. The fear grew palpable, thick.

Jo picked up her steps and Berry followed close behind. They were almost running when they came to the end of the street. And then turning the corner, crossing swiftly and headed to the direction of Graham Court.

Chapter 19

Helen Crew was a member of Refuge Temple, the church she attended four times a week. Religion was her life. She blasted gospel music on the record player in the living room. She said a prayer each time she entered the apartment when coming in from work. She didn't drink coffee because that was a drug, or Coke sodas, because they'd been made with cocaine in them. She didn't watch the TV because it was worldly, even though Uncle Friday did.

But most of the time, for her sake, the TV was off.

Although R.C. Lawson was her bishop, her favorite religious leader was S.C. Johnson. Crew would be seated on the edge of her seat beside the radio, faithfully listening every time his broadcast came on. Bishop Johnson had a ringing, distinguished tone, and there was his unforgettable broadcast theme song, One Way to God.

"One, one, one—one way to God, I know there's one, one, one, one way to God—"

And Crew would shout out, in a deeply melodious voice: "Baptized in Jesus' name!"

One time, Berry was in the kitchen while the broadcast blasted.

Try as she might, she couldn't tune it out.

"You going to hell!" Bishop Johnson shouted. "If you don't repent and be baptized and receive this gospel! You going to hell and you're going to burn forever!"

Berry froze, the dish towel slipping from her fingers onto the floor. She didn't want to burn forever. She blinked as she rested her hands on the sink, she swore she saw dancing orange flames against an eternal blackness, and then, when she closed her eyes again, she felt a dizzy, swooping motion, as if she were hurtling towards the very pit itself.

The only way to avoid Hell, preached Bishop Johnson, was to repent, be baptized in Jesus Christ's name, and then receive the gift of the Holy Ghost by speaking in tongues. Reverend Jackson preached salvation, but he never said a person needed to be saved by speaking in tongues—receiving the Holy Ghost. And he'd talked about Hell, but he hadn't made it sound anywhere near as scary and chilling as Bishop Johnson did. That message cut her so deep, it paralyzed her.

Deep down, Berry was always afraid of something. She was afraid of lack, of uselessness, of being broken. Afraid of death. And now, she was afraid of hell, too.

She was tired of being afraid. She gripped the counter. It was all so thoroughly exhausting. She wished she didn't have to be afraid anymore.

***

"Nah," said Uncle Friday to his wife in the living room as they stood before the radio one evening. Johnson had just finished his litany on the fires of hell and Berry was sweating. "Johnson got his collar buttoned up too high. You don't need all that to be saved."

They disagreed about their faith frequently. Crew was only growing more religious (how was that even possible?) but Uncle Friday was content with Refuge Temple and Bishop Lawson. Crew felt it was time for her to upgrade her holiness. She wanted something to pierce her, to shake her, to make her tremble. To crucify her flesh, as she always said.

Uncle Friday wasn't zealous enough for her.

"You got to do everything that book say," said Crew.

"But the Book don't say all that," said Uncle Friday. He shook his head and headed toward the kitchen where Berry stood at the open drawer looking for a teaspoon.

"You better listen to these true men of God," Crew shot back. "How many can you say bring the Word like Bishop Johnson does, the pure unadulterated Word?"

"But, Helen," said Uncle Friday. "God just don't give it all to one person."

"He gave it to Johnson," said Crew. "He gave it to Johnson if nobody else." Uncle Friday didn't say anything.

Crew must've been waiting for him to respond and she must've not liked that he didn't, because then she got up and stormed out, slamming the door behind her. Berry turned around in shock, but Uncle Friday was already rushing after his wife.

What in the world? Berry thought, confused. Was faith that serious? And then she felt out of place again, here in a strange city, in a strange home, witnessing a strange couple's even stranger fight. She sat down at the island, put her head in her hands, and sighed.

***

Refuge Temple was only a ten-minute walk down the street. It was a beautiful church—tall, elegant, spacious, and jumping with swathes of new members every year. But one thing stood out to Berry: all those women in long clothing headed to its doors.

"If you stay here," Crew had told them, "you have to go to church. Those are my rules."

At the very least, the girls had to wear skirts, and if God led them, said Crew, they would put on head-coverings too. So Berry and Jo stuffed their pants at the bottom of their suitcases, never to be worn again while here. "You girls need to get your souls saved," Crew told Berry and Jo as they headed up the church steps, in a line.

"I'm Baptist," said Berry automatically.

"Baptists going to hell just as fast as the sinners, baby," Crew said.

Berry's stomach flipped. Hell was so much more visceral after everything she'd seen.

"I want you to be saved," said Crew, looking back at her. "That's why I have to tell you the truth. Jojo knows. When your aunt was up here, I was trying to recruit her, but she didn't go, and that's why the wrath of God fell on her."

"What—" Berry began, absolutely stunned that someone could say that.

"When you serve God. He keeps you in perfect peace. Murder is his destruction."

Berry didn't get the chance to reply, because then they reached the doors, and a couple approaching at the same time greeted them.

Sitting on the pew, Jo wept and hit the side with her palm. Somebody else might think she was crying because of the prayer, but Berry was sure it was because of what Crew said about Aunt Millie. It was a cruel comment to an ear that didn't understand—but deep, deep down, Berry was superstitious. She sat staring forward, thinking.

She had dreams. She had sparks of intuition. It had to come from somewhere. She believed in otherworldly things. In the pulpit ahead, Bishop Lawson rose to his feet, pompous and determined, pushed his glasses up on his nose, and began his sermon. The clergy seated on the rostrum behind him, all black-suited, called out in various deep tones, "Amen! Preach, bishop!"

Berry's eyes were glued on him. Then this new, hushed, holy feeling descended on her, the warm desire to know and believe that religion would save her, free her. She started thinking that maybe because there was only hell on earth, her safe, happy place could be heaven.

***

After that day, Berry was sucked into the world of religion at Refuge Temple. These people prayed hard. It was impossible not to be swept away in the spirit of the energy. Berry sobbed on the floor many nights, crying so hard her voice left her. The next thing she knew, she was dancing in those perfect, rapid circles that she used to only watch other people dance in. Her feet were so light, it was like something else was spinning her around.

"You have to tarry until you get it," they told her. They said that would happen when she spoke in tongues. Then she'd know she was saved. Berry hadn't done that yet. But at this point in her life, she wanted to be saved—to speak in tongues—more than anything else.

Jo wandered into her own world of silence. Often she sobbed, curled over in her seat, but she never danced. And she barely spoke to Berry. But Berry didn't want her. All Berry wanted was this good feeling of deep, deep prayer. She wanted to receive the Holy Ghost, as they told her she had to have in order to be saved.

***

Berry came home one day from the job she had just gotten at a restaurant a few blocks away. It was July 4, 1960. Suddenly overwhelmed by this powerful feeling of sadness and worship, she dropped to the floor and started crying again. Somewhere during that moment, she went silent and she relaxed like she was dying, sprawled on the floor. And she gave in to it, this unnamed and indescribable feeling of belief. Before she knew it, her tongue was moving on its own, moving and speaking, and she wasn't doing it.

She felt it burning all the way through her. This thrilling, frightening ecstasy. Blackness before her closed eyes, on another level, another plane—out of this world. At some point, a door might have opened, but Berry was absolutely transported. No words, and she couldn't stop, because she was not the power moving through herself, this was something different.

She was lying on her back on the gray living room carpet when she came back down.

She wasn't going to go to hell! She couldn't believe it! God had saved her! Saved not just her body, but her soul. Heaven. One day, she'd have heaven. She felt a sensation of soaring above the world. Delight flowed through her veins as she relaxed.

She opened her eyes to see Crew above her. Even in Berry's state of absolute, stunned ecstasy, she could see the pure, frenetic joy in the older woman's eyes. Crew threw her bag on the floor and ran to her.

Berry scrambled to her feet, and they embraced as they jumped together in circles. This was what she needed. To feel safe. Now she was safe! She was safe!

"Sister," said Crew, pulling away to touch her cheek with a loving thumb. "You are one of us now, baby. You are a child of God now." Crew shivered, suddenly weeping.

"Thank you, Jesus!" whispered Berry. Her whole body trembled. "Thank you, Jesus."

They submerged her that weekend in a baptism pool of water so heavy she couldn't say her own name when the deacon asked her to confirm. They brought her up, jumping and dancing, and just like that, Berry found religion and safety.

Chapter 20

It was the first day of class at City College in Harlem, and Berry sat next to Jo.

Sitting there was a victory after phone calls, transcript requests, essays, and pleading. But Berry and Jo had good grades, and nobody could keep them out.

Berry had abandoned her premise after the tragedy. She forgot she had dreams. Maybe that was how it was to be always running in fear of something, to be reacting to something, a person forgot their premise, their purpose, their dream. But now she was back on track. She wanted a beautiful house. And she needed a better education and a better job to get it.

She ignored the gazes of the white students around her. There were a few Puerto Rican students sitting towards the back, who also stared at them. Berry was glad she had Jo, and by the look on her face when Jo looked over, Jo was glad she had Berry. The hour flew by as they took notes. Berry was determined.

She had somewhere to go, and God help her, she was going to get there.

***

Jo was majoring in political science and Berry was majoring in English. Work in the day, classes in the evening. But while Berry was wrapped in her faith, Jo was lost elsewhere. She went to Refuge Temple with them, and she prayed. But something was different. Aunt Millie's death and what they'd done together. They shared the same room, different beds. Wanting to spill secrets, tongue-tied because God changed everything, everything was a sin now, even those fifteen cent Harlequin novels Jo kept buying that Crew didn't like.

"It's a crazy story," Jo said, sitting up in bed with a yet new book. "Berry, do you really think true love is real?"

"God loves," said Berry. "And everyone can love through God."

Jo didn't say anything. After a while, she turned over and read with her back to Berry.

One book did look interesting: *Island of the Blue Dolphins* by Scott O'Dell. "Is it any good?" Berry asked Jo another night, leaning forward to study the cover.

"I just started it," Jo said. "But I think it's gonna be."

Berry still wanted to kiss Jo sometimes, but she didn't allow herself to dwell on it. She wasn't supposed to have those sinful, lustful thoughts now that she was saved.

She must be faithful to God, who saved her. He was the One Who gave her that intuition. And if she'd only listened to him before! Aunt Millie wouldn't have died. It occurred to her as she sat at the counter in the apartment alone, staring at nothing. If only, if only, she would've understood the dreams, the feelings. Could've warned Millie.

When Crew nitpicked about their hems or the novels or what time they came in from studying at the library, Jo always had a response. Jo couldn't shut up to save her life. Of course, she'd known Crew longer than Berry had.

But Berry held her peace. She was trying to be saved.

There was also another important reason for why Berry was as polite as she could be to Crew and Uncle Friday. Berry had to be here to finish her degree. Where else would she go if she didn't have them? She didn't know a thing about New York and she only had a little money. So she'd better please them, because she had to be here.

***

But how long would this be a safe place?

"Just talk to them," said Crew. It was a sunny Sunday morning, and she, Jo, and Berry were walking down the street, Bibles in hand, headed for Refuge Temple. "They're nice men."

Crew wanted Jo and Berry to reciprocate Ike and Ernest's interest. They were of the same faith, and they were single, so obviously, they should be together.

Ernest and Ike were a few paces ahead. Ernest glanced back just then and caught Berry's eyes. He smiled. She smiled quickly and looked away immediately, across the street.

"They're nice, they got jobs," pressed Crew. The men couldn't hear her.

The girls said nothing.

They tried to please Crew for a little while. They went to Sunday dinner with the men, as a foursome, at the restaurant right up the street. But far too easily, Ernest and Ike irritated them. Ernest made an annoying comment to Berry when she complained about hard jobs, that she was 'soft like a white woman.'

"So is a Black woman supposed to like it?" Berry asked, narrowing her eyes.

At another time, Ike told Jo that she had a lot of growing to do in God.

Everything those men said was the wrong thing.

Berry and Jo gave them no energy. Yet Ike and Ernest continued to pursue them. Or rather, Ernest stalked Jo, and Ike trailed Berry. That was actually how it felt, with his constant following of her. It was either his steps or his eyes. She felt the intense claustrophobia of being unable to escape either. When he shook her hand after service, it was always a few seconds too long. Berry didn't like it, but she wasn't sure how to avoid it.

Chapter 21

The car was parked on the street, some distance away from Graham Court. It was loaded with things Crew had taken out of the apartment. Uncle Friday dropped to his knees on the hard kitchen floor and begged her to stay.

"I have to save my soul," said Crew. She stacked plates into a box. She walked the perimeter of the little kitchen with its yellow wallpaper and took things to load. Uncle Friday followed her.

"Helen, you can't be serious, baby. Helen, Helen," he pleaded.

"Why you doing this to me? Why? Why you got to take it this far?"

"I don't want my soul to be lost. I am not going to be lost." She shook him off. Something powerful, convicting, and religious had come over her. Her light brown eyes were wild. They were actually wild, it was scary. She slung the bag on her shoulder, lifted the box, and marched to the door.

"I'm going," she called. "And Josephine and Bernadette, I'm coming back for you."

And she was out.

***

They thought she was joking. They thought she was joking, so they sat on the couch, Berry and Jo, and they looked at Uncle Friday, holding his forehead, slumped across from them in the armchair. Crew was going to return, her anger would blow over and she'd march back here in a day or so and everyone would sigh in relief.

Crew had gone to her best friend Dorothy Carver's place in Philadelphia. Dorothy was also a member of Bishop Johnson's church. Crew had finally made up her mind to choose Bishop Johnson over Bishop Lawson and heaven over hell.

"Man, what I'm gonna do?" said Uncle Friday.

Berry got up and went to the kitchen. She didn't have the heart to do anything grand for dinner. She boiled hot dogs and put them on bread and warmed up a can of peas. When she set the meager meal before Jo and Uncle Friday, they didn't complain. Jo for his sake, and Uncle Friday because he was still too stunned.

The doorknob turned. With all her heart Berry prayed that it would be Crew. Her eyes burned with rage when Ike popped around the corner, followed by Ernest. They took off their caps and hung them on the nook by the door.

They knew something had changed immediately. Ike asked, "What's wrong?"

"Helen left," replied Uncle Friday.

The men looked at the girls. They sighed and looked away.

"Hey, Friday, man," said Ernest. He sat next to Uncle Friday and shook his shoulder roughly. Uncle Friday didn't budge.

"I don't even know," muttered Uncle Friday. "I don't even know."

"She'll come back," Jo mumbled. She put down her fork. "She will."

Uncle Friday was never good enough for Crew, he said. When they started Refuge Temple she got saved first. She always questioned, always stopped doing worldly things first, always had more faith and zeal.

"Heck," he said, with a bitter laugh. "We even went seven months without the marriage bed when she said she wanted to consecrate herself to God. And guess what, I didn't leave her then. I didn't leave her then because I loved her."

He swiped under his nose. "But yeah, oh, she was always deeper than me. And I guess it's come to a head now, huh?"

Such a strange thing to see a grown man cry. Uncle Friday sat with the phone receiver to his ear, tears on his face. "She's with Dorothy," he said, half under his breath. "I know it."

Three days later, Crew still hadn't come back, although Uncle Friday did make her return the car. That was his, at least. She returned it without letting him know and Dorothy must've sped away with her.

Time to go home, Berry thought.

But to what? Because there was nothing there, and she couldn't live in that house.

And if she went, she'd have to leave Jo.

That was unthinkable. Jo was her family outside of family now, and Jo only had her. They had to take care of each other.

Berry was also taking classes and she had a job. She'd just started the things she needed to finish in order to achieve her dreams. She couldn't go back.

But neither did she want to stay in this house of men.

***

Berry and Jo stood in front of the phone in the living room. Berry leaned against the wall, shaking her head at Jo, who was extending the receiver.

"I don't want to get disrespectful," Jo said. "You talk to her. Please, Berry." When Jo got mad at people, she'd explode on them. She hadn't exploded yet on Crew, which meant that it was simply an outburst waiting to happen. She'd rather let Berry handle it.

But Berry refused to call up Crew and ask her why she'd left her husband. That wasn't her place. And frankly, none of her business. Jo didn't have inhibitions about that sort of stuff, but she'd grown up differently.

"I'm gonna say something mad, Berry. You know it."

"No thank you, Josephine."

"We need her. You know we do. She brought us here."

With a sigh, Berry grabbed the receiver and put the call through.

"You wouldn't understand it," said Crew once she was on the line. They had a back and forth. "I can't be with him in adultery."

"Adultery?" That stunned Berry. "You were in adultery?"

"I had a husband before I met him," Crew said. "Yes, adultery. And he had a wife. I got two grown sons, Bernadette. Friday has a daughter." Her voice grew sharp. "You know the Bible, you read it yourself. We were living in sin."

Berry started to say something but Crew interrupted. "When will you and Jojo be ready for us to pick you up?"

"To come to Philly?"

"Why would you stay in Harlem? Put her on the phone. We're gonna get you all up here."

"I just can't leave and go to Philadelphia," Berry said.

"I'm the one taking you in. I can't leave you. You know I'm not gonna do that. I said you could stay with me and that's what I meant. I'm a woman of my word. Put Josephine on the phone. I know she's right there."

"We go to school!" Jo exclaimed when she held the receiver. "We just can't go. We have jobs." Back and forth they went.

"It doesn't make sense. No, I know it's the Bible. I went to church with Mrs. Varner, you know. No! Yes, but why can't—"

A pause. Jo rolled her eyes and smacked the wall.

"Okay, this is just silly. No. I'm not being disrespectful. I'm not. I just said I think it's crazy. Fine. Fine. I'm sorry. Sorry."

Berry and Jo told Uncle Friday as they sat at the table for dinner that they'd spoken to his wife. He gripped his fork like it was a lifeline as Berry described the talk.

Uncle Friday admitted that yes, he had another family that he'd subsequently disappeared on when he met Helen Rutherford. She was dancing in a club, he was singing in a club, they were all drunk. They left their spouses for each other. Then one spring day she decided to clean herself up and change her life around. And she was never the same again, and try as he might he was never holy enough for her. And now she'd jumped and left him.

"She was always quick to change her mind," he said ruefully.

Chapter 22

"Jo," Berry said, as they lay in Berry's bed that night, shoulder to shoulder, fully clothed. "Do you think we should go up there with her to Philly? If she won't come back."

Jo looked like Berry had just announced she was a clown. "You know we can't."

Berry stared into the distance and said no more.

"Jo," she said again the next day. "Are you sure?"

"Berry, we can't leave! We just got things going for us!"

Berry's unease crept up to a suffocating level. She didn't know this city. Jo and Crew were her only bridges here. She couldn't be exposed up here like this, alone. Her chest hurt, her skin itched, and every sound in the apartment made her jump.

Living in a strange place with strange people, she was always breathless, always looking over her shoulder to see nothing.

***

Helen Crew held that house together: the moment she left it all fell apart. Friday evening, Ike stood at the kitchen counter and cracked open a tall can of stinking beer. Uncle Friday looked at him in disgust and told him, "Man, take that crap out."

But the conversation fizzled to nothing. And Ernest didn't check his brother. Ernest left. Ike drank, burped, and opened another tall can.

Jo and Berry immediately went to their room. Berry tried to study, sitting on the bedroom floor, while Jo slept, curled up in a depressed-looking lump.

Ike left the apartment and came back.

Berry heard the woman laughing in the hallway. She peeked out the door. The woman wore little white pumps, bright purple lipstick, and a sparkling red jumpsuit. She had very light skin and freckles across her wide, overly happy face. Ike and the woman went out and the door clicked. Everything was quiet.

The fear was a hold, but the need to know pushed her. Berry slipped out of the room. She flicked on the light again. There was no sign of Uncle Friday anywhere in the house. Her college geography textbook sat on the counter. She poked around in the trash can and finally saw the empty beer cans. Four.

Her head went light.

And that was when she knew she had to leave.

Prayer could possibly make a man stick to his morals. But when his head was all spun around with alcohol, who knows what he would do? Aunt Millie, sprawled on the spotted linoleum floor. Clyde was a drunk, and now he was in prison. Her father was a drunk, at least on the weekend. Mr. Perscher liked his ice cold beers, stored deep in the refrigerator. He wanted to drag her somewhere dangerous and use her and ruin her life.

She didn't know any of these people.

***

Jo was in tears. "You can't leave."

But that morning, Berry had already packed.

"We're just getting started!" said Jo. "Where else are you gonna go to college?"

"I'm not doing it," declared Berry. "Not here."

"No, Berry. Berry, for real? For real?" Jo grabbed Berry's suitcase, started going through the things Berry was laying out.

"I refuse to be in the house with a drunk. You already know what that spells."

"We were just getting started here! We just got started here!"

"Pack up," Berry told her. "You come too."

"I don't want to move, I—"

"You have to. We can find something in Philly. We can do something there."

"I don't even know if they would let us into any of those schools. We just made it into the one we're in. How can you just throw it away?"

That hit Berry, stopping her in her tracks. Because where else would she go to college?

But she couldn't stay here. It still wasn't safe enough.

They were pushing against each other. Berry refolding her things, Jo taking them out and shaking her head. Jo was on the verge of panicking. There was this look in her eye. And no matter what, Berry couldn't make Jo calm. But Berry herself wasn't calm . Her heart raced and her eyes hurt.

"I'm not doing it again," Jo said, her voice high. "I already did that with Mrs. Varner! I threw away everything and went with her. I almost got killed. He could have shot me, Berry!" Her voice went so high it ended in a broken shriek. Her eyes were full of tears.

Berry kept rushing around the room. "This is not her. This is not that."

"I don't care," Jo cried. "I'm tired of people dragging me around like a faithful servant. Breaking up my fucking life!"

Berry spun around. "This is me trying to protect you! How did you come up with 'servant' when I'm trying to care for you, my best friend?"

"If you cared so much, why are you leaving?" She started crying again.

"Oh my God Jo-se-phine-walk-er-can you just try not to be stubborn all the time?"

Berry didn't realize she was shouting until she paused. But that didn't deter anything. "You won't listen to me," she said through gritted teeth. "We have to restart, we don't have a choice. Crew's all we have. We gotta go, we gotta stay with her."

Jo set her face straight. "I have cousins here."

"Yeah, that ain't worth two cents. You told me about them."

"Don't you talk crap about my family."

"Baby, your family is drunks and molesters."

"I don't give a flip, Bernadette Know-it-all-Smith. I'm not leaving."

"Okay, go be with your creepy cousins then."

"Oh, you bet I will. They'll look out for me better than you."

Berry grabbed her bag and stormed out, slamming the door so hard the pictures rattled.

She was sobbing and couldn't stop. She walked right down the street with her bag, tears running down her face. In the broad daylight. That was acceptable in New York City anyway. Everything was acceptable in New York City. As of today she had no job, she was going to a house she'd never been to before, and the whole world felt like one giant trap and she was sweating.

"Where's Josephine?" Crew asked, stepping out of a different car parked on the corner. Her collar looked like it was choking her throat, and her shiny eyes still had the glare from days ago. She looked crazy, but at least she was safety. Swallowing sobs, Berry explained.

Chapter 23

Dorothy's house was a decent-sized place in the middle of other similarly sized and equally plain white homes, no yard to lounge on and a narrow sidewalk just a step outside the front door. Cars were parked along the street, including hers.

Dorothy was divorced, so there was no man in the house. But she had a grown son who was in and out, she said with a wave of her hand. And the son, a big strapping man in his early twenties with a loping walk, soon made an appearance. He stalked in, grabbed something off the end table, and made a beeline and was on his way out the door without a word.

"You coming to church tomorrow?" Dorothy called after him. He grunted something.

Berry, seated stiffly on the couch, followed his movements with her eyes. Please, she thought, Don't let me have to share a house with a strange man again.

She was uncomfortable about everything. It wasn't that Dorothy hadn't welcomed her. Dorothy had wanted her, Jo, and Crew to come up for the longest time. In fact, Dorothy had told them before that they could stay. Berry just felt out of place.

Hopefully, Jo would come to her senses. They should be together. No matter what, Berry and Jo should be together.

Berry was vaguely conscious of the women's conversation. She hardly had the mental lucidity to focus on other things after her fight with Jo. Crew was going to get a bus job, just like the one she had in Harlem. Dorothy was excited. She was acting like Crew moving in was a sleepover party, but maybe it was for her.

Clearly, neither woman cared that Crew had left Uncle Friday.

"I'm so glad you're here, Nell," Dorothy kept saying. "Oh, girl, you made my day when you told me you were coming—"

They had their backs to her as they stood at the table. They were awfully close.

Berry suddenly pictured herself and Jo. Were they like this? Fawning over each other like this? Did they look besotted like this? Because yes, there was a story behind it all, but the surface presentation was remarkably questionable: a woman left her husband of fifteen years to move in with her female best friend.

Berry had a sudden image of Crew and Dorothy kissing, touching, taking their clothes off and doing things she and Jo had done. It was so disgusting that she had to block it out by clamping her eyes tightly and fixating on the color gray.

***

Berry had the same need: a safe, comfortable place. She gratefully took the cramped bedroom next to the kitchen with the one off-colored pink curtain covering the window. The bedroom used to be the storage room, but Dorothy moved all the boxes she'd had in the room out into the narrow hallway.

There was a limp mattress and a lousy frame already waiting, which Crew had brought in when she thought both girls were coming with her to Philly. Crew herself slept in the bedroom that Dorothy's son no longer stayed in. Dorothy's room was adjacent to hers. Often the doors closed and the sound of the women's voices drifted down the hall. They had each other, but Berry didn't have Jo. Berry felt isolated, unsure, and like a burden. She was by no means complaining. She was lucky they even let her be here at all.

Berry wrote home after she found a restaurant job, which was the next day. After that, she went to a nearby thrift store and bought a quilt. It was purple, green, and patched, and she needed the softness. It spread so nicely on the bed, and she loathed not having a lot of money to buy all kinds of beautiful things and spread them around the house.

Pining turned to slumber, and then, crazy evening dreams.

In the dream, she never saw the outline of the place that was hers. Instead, there was a moving, swirling haze. There were wide rooms, long hallways, and an upstairs. Warm light streamed through large white windows. This place was beautiful, and it was real. But more visceral than that was the emotion, the feeling: secret happiness, hidden away.

When she woke, she lay on her back, staring at nothing, awash in a sense of wonder.

She'd do everything she could to get a good education and a job that paid her more than all these little sorry pickings so far, and one day she would own that feeling of having that house. She had to hold on to that feeling.

***

Berry called Jo the next day. Her nerves were still high, so high that reality hadn't set in. After speaking to the operator, Berry was put through to the apartment, clenching and unclenching her fist as she waited for the pickup.

No one answered. She should ask Crew or Dorothy to take her back to Harlem to talk to Jo, who by now must have come to her senses.

Everything had changed so suddenly, and Jo would soon realize that the changes couldn't work. She and Berry always had the same mind. Jo would certainly agree with her on something this important. Jo was her best friend. They had to be together. They had to.

They had to be together—one recurring thought. Berry was sitting at dinner with Crew and Dorothy, not listening to them gossip about their day. She picked at food that was nothing as good as Grandma Maple's dishes, which nobody could compete with anyway. She thought about Jo and how they had to be together because best friends couldn't leave each other. Her best friend, her only friend, the only girl in the world who mattered.

Suddenly, Berry felt short of breath. A choked gasp escaped her. She pressed a palm to her mouth and glanced with watering eyes at the two women laughing and talking. They were gossiping, oblivious to her.

Crew only looked that happy with Dorothy. Her stern face was lit with a smile. Berry knew that happiness. Once a person found it, they couldn't let it go because it was life itself. On the verge of tears, she jumped up from the table and said with a breaking voice that she was going to bed early.

***

Jo called instead—the next day. Dorothy held the phone and said, "It's Josephine."

Berry raced to grab the receiver. "Hey you're coming?" she said breathlessly. Dorothy stepped out of the foyer and left her to it. "When are you coming?"

"Uh, I was going to ask you that," said Jo quietly. "When are *you* coming back?"

Berry stopped, sighing. "Don't be so stubborn."

"No, don't you be so stubborn. It's not funny anymore."

"Funny? Girl? What? You think I left to be funny?"

"Berry, I can't stay here with all men. You have to talk to Crew."

"He can't get her back." After what Berry had seen, she knew for sure that Crew was never going back to her husband. "You're just going to have to come up here."

"He can't get her back because he doesn't even know how! If you'd help them they'd listen. We could be back together."

"They're not my business."

"How come? You're living with them? They're the freaking reason you left in the first place!"

"Jo, please." Berry was getting impatient at them going in circles.

"You're giving up," said Jo. She sounded disappointed.

"No, I'm moving smart," said Berry. She knew she was making the right choice, and it was ridiculous that Jo couldn't see it. "I'm not staying in that place with those men."

"And so you leave me here by myself." Jo sounded sarcastic.

"I told you to come! I told you can come right with me. You could be here tonight if you just said so." She rubbed her forehead, exhausted with this bull-headed girl. It was so crazy that Jo couldn't see.

"I'm not changing my whole life just because of them."

"Well, you can't tell her anything either. She made her choice."

"She's crazy, saved and crazy. You shouldn't have left me."

"I didn't leave you, you left me."

"Just come back, Berry." Jo's tone went to pleading.

"No," said Berry. "You get some sense and come here." She took a deep breath. "What you gonna do if they hurt you?"

"We'll be fine together."

"But we won't," said Berry. "That's what I keep telling you. We're not gonna be safe living with a group of men we don't know and one of them started drinking again."

"You don't care about me."

"You'd know I did if you listened."

"Girl," said Jo, and slammed the phone down.

Chapter 24

Berry went through the operator and called back. Jo didn't pick up. Berry rang again. Still no answer. She walked away, feeling panicky. She couldn't get her face together. She felt crooked inside. She was going to call back, or come, or Crew was going to go back to Uncle Friday. This couldn't be this. Everything would be alright. By the weekend.

But it wasn't alright. Berry couldn't straighten her face out. She ate a spoonful of dinner. Dorothy was an awful cook. Her stuff tasted like salted cardboard. Berry ate it anyway. It didn't matter. Her stomach felt like jelly.

***

Berry followed Crew and Dorothy through the brown double doors of the church. A hush fell over them and they filed in silently. Bishop Johnson's first church had a somber feel that was different from the enthusiasm flowing in Refuge Temple in Harlem. Berry was heavy with a deeper sense of restriction, piety, and solemnity. As she sat on the pew, she asked herself: What the heck am I doing? In North Carolina only a few months ago, she was crooked. Now she sat here with her skirt to her ankles, knee-deep in the straight and narrow.

The front row containing the leaders of the church consisted of men in dark suits wearing stern faces, but Berry didn't get to see the famed Bishop

Johnson. She was disappointed, because she wanted to see this controversial man in person. Apparently, he was on tour preaching the gospel.

Bishop Johnson's members looked like they'd gotten dressed in the curtains. Berry eyed them and remembered Uncle Friday saying, "Bishop Lawson call 'em happy hooligans!" and laughing and slapping his knee. At least Bishop Lawson's members looked normal in their modesty. These women were covered from head to toe.

Women. There were so many women! There were always more women than men in all the churches Berry went to before, but this one had the most. Bishop Lawson versus Bishop Johnson. One let his wife pray during the broadcasts, the other didn't even let the women sit on the front rows of the congregation. Women still loved them both anyway, made their churches full and their ministries run. Berry looked around, suddenly wondering why.

***

Berry was home alone after work, so she called the Harlem apartment. Twice.

The third time, Ernest answered. She hung up without speaking. She wanted Jo.

She had Jo. Three days later, standing in front of her after she opened the door to incessant knocking, Jo stood there, wearing pants again. So she backslid, then. But she looked good in those pink pants and that flowery shirt, her hair held down with a hair band. And for a moment, Berry wanted to wear those kinds of clothes again, too.

Uncle Friday's car was haphazardly parked on the curb behind. Jo was driving?

Berry hugged her without thinking. And they held each other. Berry loved her, so she loved this girl so much. Just seeing her, holding her, and lying against her warm, soft frame suddenly made her breathe normally again. They pulled back, facing each other at the same height.

"You came all the way up here by yourself?" Berry said softly. "Are you alright?"

"Are you coming home?" Jo got right to the point.

Berry sighed. "I told you I'm not coming back."

"Berry—"

"Those men still there?"

Jo's face turned. "I don't want to be with them by myself, Berry. Please. Please."

"I already told you." It was so hard to tell her no, but Berry knew it was right.

"It won't be as bad if you come back." Jo looked desperate.

"They're still there."

"You had to drop out of school." Jo looked bitter.

"School don't matter if I don't have a place safe to sleep at night. And I got a job. You didn't even look around."

"I didn't come up here to look around, I came up here to get you."

Berry shook her head.

"We need each other," said Jo. "You know it."

"Yes," Berry said. "So you move here. You already came here. Now you just stay."

Jo sighed. Berry glared at her with crossed arms. She didn't know how many times she'd have to tell this hard-headed girl, but it was getting tiresome.

"Jo," she said then. "You're not listening. I don't want us in that house alone with three men. One of them is drinking. What don't you understand?"

Jo stared at the ground. She kicked aimlessly at the bottom step and said, in a quiet voice, "My whole life, people made me move." She looked up at Berry, her eyes shining with pain and something else, something defiant. "It never mattered what I had going on because I always dropped it. You can't take roots if you keep digging them up. How am I supposed to grow if every time I get settled, something tears me up?"

Berry didn't know what to say. Her chest constricted again.

Jo looked on the edge of breaking down. Her shoulders heaved.

Berry's voice lowered when she spoke again. "What you gonna do at night when one of those men gets drunk and comes into your room and tries to get on top of you? Because you know they'll try that, don't you? What's your other option?"

"You just want everything your way."

"Shoot, girl. I'm trying to help you. I try to help you, you don't wanna listen."

Jo stomped off. Berry stood at the edge of the step. They stared at each other.

"You can't just leave!" Berry said. "Wait, listen."

"You don't want to be reasonable!" Crying. "I'm not coming here. I told you I can't."

"Well, I'm not going back there. And I told you."

"I hate you."

"Feeling is shared, Miss Rude."

Jo got back in the car. Berry watched her speed off. Jo was so ridiculous. Why couldn't she see that Berry had made the better choice?

School and little jobs weren't going to save them if they had nowhere safe to live. So what if Jo had to move not once, not twice, but three times in a year? She should care about being safe. Because how else could they live?

They'd watched a man shoot his estranged wife point-blank in the head. The man whose house Berry used to clean had told her he could rape her and she wouldn't be able to 'do a darn thing'. She wasn't going to sleep where she had to keep one eye open all night. Jo would be back. She had to come to her senses. Because Berry was right. She hadn't lied to Jo, not once.

Uncle Friday's car was finally out of sight. Another car turned down the street. Berry caught a glimpse of a yellow daisy growing near her feet. She bent and ripped it and a handful of grasses from the ground. She flung them, watching the spray of soil and plants. The dirt was cold on her skin as she rubbed her fingers against the doorpost. She retreated into the house, slamming the door as hard as she could.

Chapter 25

When Berry got mad, she let her rage grow and steam until she boiled over. Jo was the opposite. Jo would blow up right then and there, and then she'd go silent afterward. So when Jo wouldn't speak to her, Berry thought that was it. Jo was baking in anger.

Let Jo come back down to earth, back to her senses, then they could talk.

But as the time went by, Berry grew anxious instead of angry enough to boil over. Her functions were automated. Church was a motion, her job a routine of meaningless actions. Nothing would be right until Josephine came. She waited and waited and waited.

Days turned into weeks. She had a few dollars to put away and Dorothy didn't make her pay much of anything. Life was better here, why couldn't Jo see that?

The women worked hard. Crew took a second job, working weekends too. Dorothy worked at a grocery store, cleaned homes on the side, and also worked as a custodian at a bank. Berry took extra hours at the restaurant. She told herself over and over that she needed to go back to school, but life pushed her away from anything outside bare necessity. Her concern was a job to support herself, keeping this place where she was graciously being allowed to stay, staying sane, and not losing her safety—this house to stay in.

And she waited for Jo.

***

Eventually, Berry decided to give in. After all, Jo could be unbelievably stubborn when she was upset. That was one of the things Berry had loved about her, how stubborn she could be. Girls like them needed to be stubborn to live. It just hurt when Jo was being that way against her. Berry couldn't take it any longer.

Berry rang the apartment, holding her breath and tapping her fingers against the receiver.

"'Lo?" said Uncle Friday after she was put through, sounding tired.

"Uncle Friday, it's me." She sounded shaky.

The more he spoke, the clearer it was that he was very down, but he talked to her.

Eventually, he said, "Please tell me, Berry. Tell me she changed her mind now."

"I don't think she's coming back," she told him glumly.

After that statement was made several times and she tried her best to comfort him, then it was Berry's turn to ask, earnestly, hopefully, holding her breath: "Have you seen Jo? Is she gonna come over here now?"

"Oh, Josephine moved out," said Uncle Friday.

"Oh," said Berry. God, she must've gone to those cousins. Who else? Berry rubbed her forehead, trying to think. Her mind ran through a million possibilities as her heart's pace increased and her stomach flipped and curled.

"Did she tell you where?" Berry asked finally.

Uncle Friday said he didn't know. Jo just got her bag and she was gone one day. He didn't know much about her. Maybe Crew knew all about who her people were—he wasn't too certain. She'd gotten to know Crew distantly after she met poor Aunt Millie.

"So you don't know anything?" Berry said. Her stomach was now in knots.

"I don't," he said sadly. "You know I'd tell you if I could. I knew you were close."

"If you see her can you tell her to call me?"

Crew didn't know either. She'd met Jo through Aunt Millie. She knew her mother was in the crazy house. No more on that. But maybe Jo was with some of the mother's people. Jo was all over the place. Jo never stayed in one place too long, came from a broken home.

Berry asked if they could drive back over to New York to look for her.

Crew didn't think much of that.

"The thing is, Berry," she said. "If the girl don't wanna talk to you, she just don't wanna talk to you. You can't force it."

"I'm not tryna force it," said Berry. She felt sicker with each passing moment.

Dorothy, sitting at the table, just looked at her. Berry thought she saw Crew and Dorothy exchange inquisitive glances, but her eyes were blurred by threatening tears.

Chapter 26

Berry's waiting turned to agony, and then the realization that her friendship with Jo was over. For all she knew, Jo might not even be alive. No one had a trace of her, and Berry couldn't look for her. As the realization deepened, depression kicked in. Berry would go to work and come home to cry. She stopped eating.

"Little sister, service is tonight," Crew told her one evening. Dorothy stood behind her friend, holding their black Bible cases by the straps. Berry was curled on the couch under a blanket.

"I don't feel good," Berry mumbled.

"You been feeling not good for a long time," said Crew. "You're gonna be alright."

"What if something's wrong with Jo?"

"Not everybody want this truth like we got it. She chose to leave."

But they let Berry stay there without any more urging. And she cried to her heart's content, until she fell asleep, her face drying and itchy against the gray suede material of the couch, the lamp still on.

Coworkers never said anything to Berry. Struggling in the city, she found no solace from strangers. Berry couldn't have come around other people anywhere in the South with bags under her eyes without being pulled aside and asked: What's going on with you, child?

She didn't care. Let them look. If they had this pain, they'd feel the same way.

***

Heartache was more than a word. It was a physical sensation. So damn tight in the chest, vise on this place Berry couldn't touch with her hand but she could feel in her soul. When she found out that white men hung her father and stuffed his privates in his mouth, that made her bitter. When she saw Aunt Millie laid on the kitchen floor with a hole in her face, that traumatized her. When she looked out into the world, that made her bitter.

When Berry thought of Jo being gone, that broke her heart.

In bed at night, while everything else was silent and asleep, Berry grieved, her face pressed to her pillow, her knees drawn up against her chest. The world was colorless, worthless, meaningless. It didn't have Jo.

Berry took it so hard, she eventually couldn't get out of bed. Everything ached, most of all her chest. Crew sat at her side one morning, pressing a hand against her forehead.

"You're not hot," Crew said, frowning in bafflement. "I don't know what it is."

Berry tossed and turned. She groaned.

"You gonna have to tell your boss you can't come in," Crew said, shaking her head. "Lord, Bernadette. Lord. You take it easy, life gets better."

Berry's chest ached. Ached so bad she had to be on her way to have a heart attack.

"When you're crying a lot," said Dorothy, who was standing in the narrow doorway. "That can make you sick too."

Dorothy was dressed for work, poised to leave. Her oversized son passed by, glancing into the room, ever a fleeting malevolent shadow. He never spoke to any of them besides his mother. Dorothy said something to him and followed him.

Berry was too tired to even care that a man had stayed in the house last night.

"You think you need some water?" Crew said. They didn't believe in doctors no matter what illness. God was a healer. Berry wished God would heal her.

Berry just shook her head.

"Berry, talk. You want me to call your mama and tell her? Grandma?"

"They can't help," Berry mumbled, and began to cry again.

Crew seemed puzzled. And all Berry knew was that her body refused to let her sit up and go about her day. Her stomach felt hollowed.

"I think you better get some rest," Crew said. "But now, I can call your mama."

***

Later there was Berry, crumpled at a different angle on her bed. She'd attempted to get up. Then it all felt meaningless and she laid down again. She couldn't breathe, she couldn't get the beastly grief demon up off her goddamned back. She was kicked, she was broken. She wanted Jo. All she wanted and needed was Jo.

Remember how they giggled? Held hands, swapped clothing, secrets? Those times they sat facing each other with their legs tucked under them, so close their knees touched. And the thrill of sneaking to secret places to kiss. Their bodies were made one. Their friendship was a secret world where only they existed. They told each other they loved each other! How could Jo just leave and not come back?

She couldn't know. That was the worst part. She couldn't know where Jo was, what she was doing, what she was thinking. If she felt as alone as Berry did.

Or even if she was safe.

And everything was ruined. Berry had dropped out of college. She left New York City. She undid all the things worth living for, and now no more Jo, to get through life with.

And the worst part was that she couldn't even tell anybody the truth.

She couldn't say why she was crying. She couldn't say: I broke up with my best friend and I loved her too, yeah, in that way. She had to endure that part of the pain silently.

Crew just stood next to the bed. The glass of water sat on the table.

"Bernadette, you pray," said Crew. "Your grandmother says you can come home, and I told her that you wanted to stay. But why you letting the devil get you down?"

Chapter 27

"These really are the last days," Crew muttered to Dorothy as they sat at the kitchen table, in a voice like a broken, pained wonder. Berry, who hadn't worked in six weeks now, stood at the sink staring at nothing. Ten days ago, Bishop Johnson had died suddenly on a preaching trip in Jamaica. His churches were falling apart. Bishop Johnson, the greatest man alive, was dead. Berry was crying solely for Jo, but Crew and Dorothy had been crying for Bishop Johnson. Crew's voice had been all wrong since it happened, and Dorothy kept randomly sniffing.

After a period of silence, Berry realized they were looking at her. She glanced back.

They asked her if she was coming to service at Brother Sidney's house.

Berry squinted. Brother Sidney's house? Brother Sidney was just one of the people they went to church with, what did he have to do with actual sermons?

"He's playing Johnson's tapes," said Crew, looking at her impatiently. "We're keeping the Word alive at home. You should be trying to stand with the faith."

Berry shook her head no. And the cross way Crew and Dorothy eyed her made her eventually find a reason to leave the room and retreat to her own small one.

***

They stopped going to the Philadelphia church after that. They didn't trust the new leader. No one else could preach the Word like Bishop Johnson. And since Brother Sidney had the former leader's sermons recorded on several hundred tapes, they decided to gather in his house to listen to those instead.

The whole idea sounded a little silly, but Berry didn't really care what those people were doing. She checked out completely. She spent her time on the couch. She'd cried a lot of tears, and now she felt even dry on that. She was numbed.

Then Dorothy came to her one Saturday morning as Berry curled up in the living room. Dorothy opened the blinds to let cloudy sunlight in and crossed her legs. She sat across from Berry in the armchair.

"Berry," Dorothy said. "You know I don't mind you staying here. I want you here."

Berry looked up at her, drearily.

"But you gotta do something while you're here."

"Sorry," Berry said, sitting straight. She was too tired to even be ashamed. "I know."

"An idle mind is the devil's playground," admonished Dorothy.

"I understand." Berry sighed. She looked down.

"God is greater than all of us," said Dorothy. "If you're sad about your best friend, all I can say is that you give it to Him. I had a lot of girlfriends who didn't wanna join this straight and narrow way, and guess what, I lost them. You can't save her."

That evening, Crew stepped into Berry's room and sat on her bed. Berry had the covers pulled up to her chin, two pillows behind her head, and a balled up tissue in her hand.

"Berry," Crew said. "Did Dottie talk to you?"

Berry said she had. Crew made a pleased noise. Berry glanced up at Crew staring at her. Even at home, Crew was covered from head to toe. Collar to her neck, skirt to her ankles, cotton stockings. Crew didn't blink or move. Berry closed her eyes, opened them again, and Crew was still looking at her. Berry stiffened with the blanket clutched closed.

"That girl is not a believer," said Crew finally, her voice like a knife so sharp that the cut it makes is undiscovered until it bleeds. "She shouldn't have you down and out like that. She doesn't even want God. She rejected her only hope."

"She was my best friend."

"Humph. Friend but threw you away. Soon as it got hard, poof, she gone." Crew made an indignant flicking motion with her hand and shook her head.

"I could've gone to her," Berry whispered ruefully.

"But you chose Christ. You chose Christ over the world."

Berry stared at the tops of her covers.

"You'll be glad you did in the end. Your soul will be saved, hers won't."

"I don't want anybody to go to hell."

Crew snorted. "Well, child, most of them are going, right down the broad way." She got to her feet, fixed her skirt, patted herself, and then tilted her head ever so slightly.

"Berry," she said. Her eyes were pinpoints. Her stern face was full of suspicion and curiosity. "How deep did you go with this girl? Is there something else going on? Because you sure are broke up a lot. The way it's going on, Berry, it's almost unseemly."

Berry went hot like she'd been stung. She hid a physical jerk. "What do you mean?"

"This ain't no funny business is it?" Crew murmured. "What happened between you two that's got you all like this? You seem pretty hurt."

"Don't say that," said Berry vehemently. "How could you even think that?"

Crew just fixed her with that piercing stare.

"No! It's not! Don't say that. I hate that you even said that." Berry shook her head vigorously. The pain broke just like that. She felt stabbed awake.

"Forgive me," said Crew, not with a hint of contrition at all. She kept her gaze locked on Berry's, searching. "As long as it's nothing crazy."

"I don't want anybody even thinking something like that about me."

"I was just making sure. I mean, as long as it's nothing weird."

At that, Crew went to the door without looking back and closed it firmly behind her. Berry pressed a hand to her chest and let out a deep sigh, shaky but her tears were gone and her eyes were wide. She had to stop grieving. For her own sake. Her own safety.

Because what if they found her out? Then what would they do to her?

Chapter 28

After that conversation, Berry forced herself up. She went to the next church tape service with them. Even if she didn't feel like it, she resolved to look productive to keep them from critiquing her. She even took it upon herself to cook dinner one evening.

When the women sat down and tasted the baked BBQ chicken and seasoned greens she made, they looked at her with pleased, wide eyes.

"Good Lord, girl!" said Dorothy. "This you, Berry? You cook like this?"

"This is delicious," said Crew. It was a surprise to see her stern face so delighted.

"It's my grandmother's recipe," said Berry humbly.

"Well, gracious, she taught you! She taught you well." Crew actually smiled at her.

Berry, digging in with her fork, tentatively smiled back.

Berry still felt the guilt of their earlier conversation. Crew had a sharp nose. She'd come so close to discovering the truth of Berry's real feelings. And by the way she looked at Berry at that moment, Crew still felt mildly wary, but she was giving Berry a chance.

Berry would have to be more careful. More helpful. Walk the line straight. Stay undetected. What would they do to her, if they found out her secrets?

***

Berry was young, slim, with nothing but a dead end job and a broken heart. For many men in church she might've been perfect. She wanted none of them. But other women wanted her to want a man. "God gonna bless you with a nice husband, child," Dorothy kept saying.

"Don't you turn the good men away," Crew often insisted.

It was ironic that they pressured her to entertain a man when they never did themselves. The only man they liked was their deceased bishop. Crew had hung up a large picture of him in the living room. She and Dorothy liked their dresses, their prayers, and going to work and coming home. But alive, attainable men? Those were kept at arm's length.

It was a strange world of women—with men posted only at intervals of benefit and power. The women did the planning, organizing, the work, and turned events into shows. The men, in the pulpit that was reserved to them, enjoyed the fruits of their work.

Berry didn't want a man. Especially not if it meant having to do all the work.

She'd rather hide in plain sight.

And she couldn't have found a better place. Two forty-something, devout women who only enjoyed each other's company in their nice, quiet house. All Berry had to do was be holy.

Chapter 29

Lincoln University was a historically black university and a half-hour drive from Dorothy's house. Berry got her driver's license so Dorothy let her use her car. On the days Berry had class, Dorothy and Crew carpooled with a friend. Berry asked herself sometimes how she even got here, but she was living what she'd asked for. Not in the way she thought, but it was just what she asked for.

Every day, she reminded herself that she'd better not mess this up.

But really—she was at Lincoln University. She was at university!

Classes were interesting. Modern history was fun. The study of insects was icky and fascinating. English literature—that was beautiful. So many niche and cool classes. That year, Berry realized she liked learning. She made A's. She loved making A's.

It was also hard. She was sad and lonely. She wrote letters home. She called there, too, ending the calls whenever Grandma Maple or Lilah irritated her. Calls ran the phone bill up anyway. She went to church. Lucille had her first child. Berry wanted to go and see her, but had neither the time nor the money. She resigned herself to waiting for a picture.

"You find a nice man at college?" Crew asked her many evenings. "When you gonna find a nice man and settle down?"

"When I find one," Berry would say, making a show of sorting through her bag to hide her expression and nervousness. Was Crew picking her or just making conversation? It was hard to say. But it reminded Berry that she'd better stay on the straight and narrow, that was what.

Berry prayed. She prayed it all away. Prayer was a transportative, blinding state of emotion. In the deepest prayer, there was faith, love, hope, and resolve. She prayed away her emotions every night, every early morning, and every church service.

Old thoughts crept into her mind as she lay in bed at night. Need made her toss and turn. Memories of freedom kept her from falling into peaceful sleep. These clothes were so long and ugly. She missed dressing up on Sunday. She missed looking good. She missed being sexy, having sex.

She lived in a house that wasn't hers, though. She drove a car that wasn't hers. She needed to finish her degree, she was afraid of dying and going to hell, her family was states away and their place was limiting. Sometimes when Berry closed her eyes, she heard the gun go off. God had saved her. She couldn't go back. She had to stay with this, no matter the temptation.

***

And the temptation came. It appeared in the form of Janette Matthews, who was Berry's age, had recently started attending the same tape church, and sometimes hung out with them at Crew's house with her mother and sister. The sister, Adie, was light skinned and snooty. Janette was darkskin and quick to show her pearly teeth. Everyone preferred Adie to Janette regardless. Everyone except Berry.

Janette wasn't that kind of girl, obviously. She wore her skirts long. She only showed that dazzling smile for holy things. Janette was very, very devout. And no doubt, her family wouldn't let her be any other way.

The father Herbert was stern and quiet, dark like his daughter, while Adie and her mother looked and acted just alike. So holy they were stuck up. Skirts to their ankles, Bibles under their arms. Couldn't have a conversation with them about anything other than God. Thank God. Thank God, thank God.

Adie was so, so holy. She'd tip her head up and not speak. She thought she was more beautiful than she was, and she was so holy.

Janette was warm and friendly.

Berry wished they could be friends, like she'd been with Jo. She wanted friends.

Jo wasn't here. The thought was still a fresh wound.

Maybe Janette could replace Jo? Make it hurt less?

Funny that everyone liked Adie while Berry wanted to befriend Janette. Adie always acted in a hurry, like she was on her way to do something for the Lord, whatever that might be. She was so modest in her long cream dresses and carefully wrapped headscarves that revealed a peek of hair that they all called good, because it was shiny and easily slicked down with water and Vaseline. Adie was perfect.

But Janette, it was Janette for Berry.

Berry wouldn't dare. Daring was inconceivable. Even though it lingered on the edge of her thoughts. But Janette wasn't that kind of girl.

And Berry wasn't either.

But wouldn't Janette make a nice friend?

***

Janette smiled at Berry one evening during service as Janette sat next to her father, Herbert, who was standing up testifying. The group sat in a circle on brown folding chairs. A thought occurred to Berry as she smiled back. If Janette looked nice, and Jo looked nice, and Berry was the same looking kind of girl as them, then that must mean that was what people saw when they looked at her. The same kind of girl. It was an interesting realization.

Janette looked up. What an angelic, finely structured face.

"We have to keep this straight and narrow way," said Herbert, pressing his broad hands together. His forehead was lined. "That's what I tell my wife and my daughters."

Janette caught eyes with Berry again.

Berry smiled again, tentatively. Janette smiled back, fully.

***

Berry hadn't talked to her mother and grandmother for weeks. When she finally called them, Grandma Maple asked her when she was coming home. "Don't wait too long," she said. "We miss you, baby. Come down for the holidays!"

Berry hesitated. She'd wanted to go home every time she was sick or sad, but whenever it was finally an option she never did.

"You got money for a ticket?" Grandma Maple asked, quieter now.

"I can get it," said Berry immediately. "But I just—I have a lot to do. Exams."

"Please come, Berry!" Lilah said. "Come whenever you can."

"We wanna see you," said Grandma Maple. "We really do."

Berry didn't go home that year, though.

For the Apostolics, Christmas was a pagan holiday. It involved idols and dates no one could confirm. Berry didn't want the others thinking she'd gone home because she was celebrating Christmas. She had to keep up the appearance of complying.

She focused on finals. Before she knew it, winter break was over, and it was January and time to go to school again. So Berry never found the time or reason to return to North Carolina.

Excuses. Excuses.

The truth was that she didn't have the guts to go back into that house.

Chapter 30

Janette with her pearly smile, perfect posture, and clean steps. She strolled towards Berry as they crossed the lawn from opposite directions, headed to the green and white house just off the corner of the street. Janette's mother, Mary, and Dorothy followed. Janette waved. The church was doing prayer partners at each other's homes and tonight they were at a sister's place. Wasn't that so nice? One to keep the other strong. Iron sharpens iron.

Janette was Berry's prayer partner. They stood in a circle in the dim living room, all holding hands. Janette's palm was soft. She was soft. Perfectly soft. Such a ridiculous thing, these backwards thoughts Berry had. Berry bowed her head and prayed it off.

She was determined to do right. She was determined to one day be free of this thing plaguing her. She'd never asked to desire women. It just happened to manifest in her personality one day and never left. She hadn't asked for it.

Yeah, she thought as the prayer went on, so maybe she'd looked at girls growing up. Compared her body to theirs, relieved that she looked like who she looked at. She'd wanted to be friends with them, was frustrated that they all were so crazy about useless boys. But all that was normal. She wasn't crooked until one day when she was nineteen years old.

Jo corrupted her. If they hadn't started giggling that day, they would've never started to fool around. But they'd been laughing. Laughing so hard they got naked and put their hands on each other and did things Berry had never explicitly imagined doing. Laughter was of the devil. She should've never laughed.

Berry was always willing herself, promising herself—This is who I'm going to be. I can do it. Trying to force something to be, force herself to be—something she wasn't.

Prayer ended and the group sat on the circle of chairs. Janette never crossed her legs at the knee. She only crossed them at the ankles. Berry also crossed her legs at the ankles. A brother read the Bible and they listened. Their poses matched each other's.

That was the problem. Berry was perfectly feminine. Female. Her style of dress was utterly decent. Her mannerisms were proper. Her thick, coiled hair was neat and covered. Her black lashes were curved upward. When she looked into the mirror, a young, smooth, well-carved face gazed tenderly back at her. So orderly and specific and holy on the outside, but she just couldn't get her heart right.

She'd prayed so hard for the feeling to go away.

But Janette's hand was soft, and Jo had unforgettably broken her heart.

***

"You and Janette are close," said Crew to her that night as they did laundry in the living room.

"She's spiritual," Berry replied quickly. She paid great attention to smoothing the sleeves of a blouse. Her fingers shook.

Crew leaned down to place a stack of towels into the large empty basket on the floor. "That's good." The 'for you' was silently attached. "When you hang with people who love the Lord, the Jesus in them influences you."
Berry humbly murmured her amen.

"The enemy snares the youth," said Crew. "You need strong people of Christ."

Berry hadn't made any friends in college. She dressed and carried herself so differently. And having friends outside of the faith wasn't particularly acceptable. Two other young women had tried to be friendly to her in English class, but they fell off soon.

Berry had to look holy before Crew and Dorothy.

"Make sure you stay strong," said Crew, "So you don't pull her off either."

Berry humbly, once again, said amen.

Pretending to be holy and her own brutal self-conviction paid off. Berry finished her second semester at Lincoln University on the Dean's List. And with everything in her account, she bought the cheapest car she could find. It didn't sound reliable the way it started, it was an ugly lime color, but it had a nice shape and would take her places she needed to go.

She'd do anything to get to the next place.

Chapter 31

Berry had been in the Holiness movement since she moved to New York. But she still wasn't interested in most of her fellow church members. Berry thought so differently from everyone else. She thought hard about things, other people stayed on the surface. She tried to learn, others were happy with their small container of knowledge. She wanted to be, others would just do. She would never be one of them, a seamless puzzle piece. It vexed her.

The more she read at college, the more their devotion unsettled her. Often, Berry looked at her fellow members' laps during services and observed their closed Bibles. Why didn't they study their own acclaimed book?

Berry was able to see these things because she still felt distant from her religion. It was as if she never really belonged anywhere or with anything, no matter how much she needed to for her own sake, or even how much she wanted to.

And when people at church stared at her, Berry worried and wondered: Can they see who I really am?

***

The prayer partners became close friends and visited each others' homes. The women spent a lot of time at Dorothy's house. One evening, Adie and Janette sat with Berry, who was doing her homework, while the older women talked.

"How's school, sister?" Janette leaned forward, smiling at Berry. "I finished last year. If you need help, I wouldn't mind." Janette had taken up English, too. It was a good major. And now Janette had a part-time job as an admin assistant at a local black office and she worked at a daycare. Berry was so appreciative of her.

"Adie did psychology," said Janette, obviously trying to bring her sister into the conversation. Adie was sitting next to her, knitting a cap and humming.

"That's nice," said Berry.

Adie gave her a tight smile and focused on her knitting.

Whenever she spoke to Berry, Janette would try to include Adie. Berry wondered why she bothered. Adie never had a lot to say. It almost seemed like she expected Berry to strive and clamber for her attention. Adie was going to be waiting for a while. She was a nurse, acting snide like that. Was she kind to her patients?

But in church, Adie always had a testimony. Adie's light skin got her smiles when she was passionate, and nods when she was indignant. They loved that light skin because they craved it for themselves.

All Berry could think when she looked at her: she didn't get that skin on her own. And that hair she brushed till it lay flat under her cap. Somewhere along the line is a white man. Great grandfather? Something, it was somewhere. Some kind of violence.

Adie and Janette were half-sisters, too, of course.

***

Time and time again, Berry had variations of the dream. Always that feeling. In her dreams she floated through a house that was her own. The curtains were gold, sometimes they were red, or gray. It was a living room or something like that in the dream. And she was just so happy. So at peace.

Berry sat up in bed one morning after one of her dreams, and realized that she needed to get married. If she wanted a house, then she needed to get married. Women didn't buy homes because who would sell to them? Marriage was the only way it was likely to happen. Crew and Dorothy got their freedom in separation and divorce. Berry needed to find a man.

She needed to make a change quick, because she was getting restless.

Restless in every way.

Berry had to lie down alone at night. Her warm body was alive, her hands inevitably creeping to the place between her thighs. Remembering. Her desires couldn't die. She was only twenty-two. Other girls her age got married or sneaked around. She worked and came home. The tension in her body climbed to the top of her head.

What should she do?

***

Crew and Dorothy watched Berry endlessly. If she sat at the table and sighed, they eyed her knowingly. If she stayed in her room too long on a Saturday, Dorothy would knock on the door and ask if she wanted to come out and join them for prayer, or breakfast. If she walked too fast or hummed to herself, they stared at her.

Berry came back one Saturday evening from a shop, carrying a handful of bags. Dorothy and Crew sat in the kitchen, gossiping and laughing. Berry passed them coming through the foyer. She peeked through the doorway, raised the bag and asked, "Can I put these up?"

"What's that?" Crew answered first, even though they were in Dorothy's house. The women were sitting across from each other at the table, and Dorothy turned slightly, a smirk on her face from something Crew had said a few seconds before.

"Just some decorations," said Berry. She suddenly felt ridiculous.

"Oh," said Dorothy with a little smile. "To decorate what?" She leaned forward to see inside the cloth bags.

"I just bought—" Berry dug inside one of them and retrieved a small, white, clay elephant figurine. "Thought it would be cute," she explained. "In the living room. Maybe?"

Crew and Dorothy exchanged glances.

"That's if you want it," she added quickly. "You have it so nice."

Berry had other things in the bag. Decorations for her room, fake green and white and fuchsia flowers, a small square mirror to set on a dresser. Little neat things to make the place feel more like home. To make herself happy. She'd been so sad since Jo and coming here that she'd never decorated.

"I don't prefer all that junk on my end tables, baby," said Dorothy finally, smiling again.

Berry's face went hot. "I wasn't gonna put it up and not ask," she said.

Cew raised a thin eyebrow and sipped whatever was in her mug.

"If you want to put up something," said Dorothy, still smiling gently. "You can do it in the room but don't put tacks in the wall. The landlord hates that."

Berry didn't even know she was renting. She walked off, embarrassed.

Who would buy something for somebody else's already furnished living room? What was she thinking? She sat the bag in the corner in her own room.

If only she could be in a place where she could truly be herself. Where she didn't have to worry about how much water she used in the shower or if she looked holy enough or if some man was going to come in and terrorize her. Where she could put up things that looked beautiful, and lay back and gaze at them with pleasure. A house.

Not just any old house. She wanted a nice house. A beautiful house. A beautiful house with a nice, clean yard and a white fence and a cement drive with a clean new car parked there that didn't shudder when it started. The kind of homes in the magazines. She would walk through all the rooms and stand in the kitchen and smile and know that no matter what sad, chaotic story was on the cover of the daily newspaper, no matter who hated her or abandoned her or traumatized her, no matter what this sick, dangerous, suffocating world punished her with, she could be happy and safe in free in these walls that were hers.

She needed a man.

She didn't want a husband, but she needed him for the house. She could try to get it herself, but that was just a dream. She worked, she paid her portion of the rent. She kept the rest. Never getting there at this rate: no man, one penny, two dollars, in a glass jar. Wanting anyway.

Chapter 32

Janette and Berry sat at the kitchen table one evening. Janette was a big help, quizzing Berry before exams and giving her college advice. She was educated, so she spoke very well.

"There's one thing you should do to study," Janette said, her soft voice crisp. "And that's to understand your concepts in your own words as a story."

Berry nodded, fascinated.

"Have you ever had to recite a poem?" said Janette. "It's like that. You won't remember that poem if you try to remember the lines. But try instead to remember what logically follows the next part of the story. Sister, those lines will come right back."

"Wow," said Berry.

"Think of all your learning as a concept. Not just something to know for the sake of memorizing. Think about why."

"Janette, you're so smart."

"Oh no," Janette said, putting her hands together. "All credit to God."

But that advice helped Berry on her exam that next week, when she got stuck on a math course problem that she was able to answer correctly eight minutes later. Thank God for Janette.

***

Berry didn't go home that summer. She worked overtime in June. Her car broke down in July. It took her three weeks to get it fixed. She then decided that home was too much of a hassle to return to, after she spent her money fixing the car.

The trouble started with the stupid magazines. She loved pretty things. Pretty things hopelessly snared her heart. She couldn't resist walking past the magazines in the store, at first only staring, then finally plucking the interesting looking ones. It was one thing to stare too long at forbidden paraphernalia, but it was another thing to take it home.

She laid the one with the extremely skinny woman on the front cover in a bright dress, some British model, on the table. Berry had savored the pages on interior design and fashion descriptions.

"When did you start looking at these?" Crew held the magazine up when she and Dorothy sat Berry down later.

The judgmental, piercing looks on their faces answered the needless question.

"I bought it without thinking," said Berry. "I didn't know it would be offensive."

"You know we don't look at worldly magazines, sister."

"I apologize. I'm sorry." Berry cursed herself for being careless.

"We only want to help you in the spirit of meekness," said Dorothy solemnly.

"Again, I'm sorry and I'll throw it away." Berry half-rose and reached for it.

Crew pulled it out of reach and studied the cover. Berry remained standing.

"Lemme just toss it," Berry said, her hand still out. Her face burned. "I'll throw it away."

Crew finally surrendered it to her, sighing as if she had been soiled by even having to touch the sinful item, and Berry chucked it in the trash.

***

Berry's resentment grew. All that over a magazine. She bought another one the next week. This time she read it, relished it, and hid it underneath her pillow.

One Sunday later, Crew stood up and said, as if Berry wasn't right in the room, "Pray for our young sister, the devil desires to sift her as wheat."

Even Janette's empathetic smile was annoying. And Adie's side glance made Berry seethe. She hooked her fingers in her lap and kept her ankles crossed.

"Do you fast a lot?" Janette asked her in the yard after the service. "I don't judge anybody, sister. I hate to see them call you out for things when you never meant any harm."

"I fast with everyone else," Berry said calmly.

"That's good." Janette nodded quickly. "Fasting helps you develop discipline. I know you're trying just like us." Janette squeezed her hand. "Don't you let anything defeat your strength. You're a beautiful person, Bernadette."

"Thank you, Janette."

"God loves you," said Janette, and embraced her tightly.

Chapter 33

The more Berry obsessed over having the right thoughts, the more powerful her wrong ones became. Now she couldn't look at Janette without feeling an irrational tug to touch her. To be near her. Janette smelled like peppermint. Fresh, airy. She was always there.

Berry felt terrible. Her mind violated her. She was going crazy checking her every move. Lust must be burning on her face. If she so much as smiled kindly at the other girl, in her guilty mind it was a leer. A wave was a come on. A glance was a wink. Her countenance felt obscene.

It was all in her head. She looked normal.

It wasn't even so much Janette as it was a memory. It was really a memory of Jo. If only Berry hadn't done those things with Jo, then she wouldn't be sitting here now trying to relive them on the next girl who came along.

But it was far more than carnal, even though her own shame made her fixate on that aspect of the attraction. The real pull was her longing for connection. Berry wanted a best friend, she wanted a girl who knew her better than anyone else, who would stand beside her and look at the world out of a similar pair of dark eyes.

Berry wanted Jo back.

***

Then there was the stocking incident. Berry took her stockings off at work because she got grease on them from cleaning the restaurant kitchen and Adie and Mary walked in while she was barelegged, wiping down tables. They said nothing to her, neither of them, but their eyes scanned her. Later that night, Crew confronted her in the hallway.

"Do you have two dress styles?" Crew said, staring at her pointedly as they stood six feet apart. "You know we have to be one way, sister. One way before God. All the time."

Berry explained what had happened, keeping her tone even. The audacity of Adie and her mother to report her, she thought as she fumed. But for the sake of a place to stay while she earned her education, she kept calm.

Crew sniffed. "Our modesty is how we show others our belief, sister."

"I understand," said Berry.

"Good, good," said Crew. She moved to her bedroom door.

Berry turned on her heel and made her way to her own bedroom, forcing herself to shut the door instead of slamming it. She was furious. So furious but she had to hide it. Because she had no other place to stay.

Sometimes being holy made people mean. Prayer partners switched to Mary instead of Janette, who was forced to move a seat over. Now Crew, Dottie, and Mary split Berry, Janette and Adie.

Berry felt exhausted. She was tired of Crew, Dorothy, and church. She prayed so much and it felt like nothing ever happened. Sure, she'd never forget her beautiful, otherworldly experience of the Spirit on July 4, 1960. But she was weary of the faith that rescued her and made her afraid all at the same time.

Here was the only safe place she knew.

But she didn't know how much more of being here she could take.

Chapter 34

Janette went over to hold Berry's hand during the prayer. Berry didn't miss the surprised looks from the other women when she stole a peek. But the gesture warmed Berry to the core. It was sweet, kind, and selfless, just like Janette.

Janette had been told to stay away from her. Berry had read between the lines. They thought Berry was shaky in her religion. But Janette didn't care after all, and Berry was surprised.

"I understand you," Janette said later when they were walking to the cars parked on the street outside the house. "It's hard. People judge. They scolded me one time, too."

Sweet, holy, Janette, in trouble? "What happened?" asked Berry.

"I was at the bus stop coming back from seeing my cousin. And I missed it. A young church brother happened to be coming by there and he gave me a lift. He left Johnson some years ago, you didn't know him. Anyways, everyone criticized me for taking the ride, saying I gave the appearance of evil, that I was a stumbling block. My mother was one of them."

"Really?" said Berry.

"Yes," said Janette. "But what was he supposed to do? Leave me there, get a chaperone, then come back? I'd have already walked home by then."

They laughed. They reached the cars and stopped.

"Sometimes good intentions get read wrong," said Janette.

"I'm so glad you understand." Berry felt so relieved.

"I sure do, sister."

***

Their friendship grew. Janette asked Berry if she wanted to hang out more often. Berry happily agreed. She drove over to Janette's house around four one evening. The family had a nice, medium-sized house on a street of similarly built homes. In the foyer, Berry handed Janette a brown bag with the tallest burger from the restaurant and a note that said, 'Thank you for being my friend'.

"Aww," Janette gushed. "You brought me food?" She read the note and looked up at Berry with the most touched smile. "No, this is so sweet! Berry, you're the best." She grabbed Berry and squeezed her, laughing as she pulled back. "You won't believe this! I got you something too, and I was going to give it to you at church!"

Berry was so excited. Janette rushed to the back of the house. Berry looked around, realizing no one was home but Janette. A minute later, Janette came hurrying back. She gave Berry a blue square notebook.

"Oh, this is so sweet!" Berry exclaimed. She hadn't been so happy in a while. Laughing and talking, they sat in the dining room while Janette ate. After Janette finished her meal, they wandered to the living room and sprawled on the floor.

Finally, after a few hours of lounging, listening to music, and talking, Berry prepared to leave.

As she stepped to the front door, there was a moment of quiet.

Berry knew she needed to relax, knew she was being too needy too soon, but she couldn't stop herself. She reached for Janette. There was nothing inherently sexual about the touch. She simply reached for her arm and rested her hand there.

"I just love you," said Berry, her voice almost a whisper. She was drunk on the excitement of having a friend again. "I'm glad we're close. I just love you. So much."

As soon as she said it, she realized that it came out wrong. Berry flinched.

There was a horrible, immediate understanding between them.

Janette stared at her, seeming to see her for the first time.

Berry quickly moved her hand. "I sound weird," she said, trying to laugh it off. "Sorry. I meant—"

Janette blinked, confusion lining her features. She stared at Berry.

"Please don't think I'm strange." Berry's voice was a whisper, begging.

"You're...being strange, for sure," said Janette. Her eyes were wide, as if she couldn't believe what she was thinking.

Berry was frozen.

"It just felt strange," said Janette quietly. "I'm sorry. I can't help, you know. My feelings. It—it felt strange..." She looked nervous, even more confused.

"I'm not like that," Berry said. "I promise I'm not like what you're thinking." She put her hands on her cheeks. She was talking too much.

Janette looked like she couldn't decide if she should believe Berry or not. Berry couldn't believe herself. What had she done? How was one touch so different from all the others?

Janette looked as frightened as Berry felt. Her voice was small when she whispered, "What do you mean you love me?"

"I...love like Christ," lied Berry, her voice small too.

"I won't judge," whispered Janette. "I just want to know what you meant. I won't judge."

The foyer was dark and they were still home alone. And Janette and Berry were the same height and slim size, standing close enough to kiss. A million things went through Berry's head as they faced each other. They were really going there. How was this bad dream happening? What was in Berry's heart was being revealed. But she couldn't just stand there because Janette was pressing—and the weight of the secret was so heavy.

It was a burden Berry never wanted to have alone.

And maybe, maybe Janette would understand. She clearly wanted to know.

"Sometimes," Berry stumbled, trying to gauge if she should continue. But Janette's expression was open, soft, astonished. "The enemy...tries to trick me into feeling...things...when I...all sorts of things. But I'm not. Like that."

"Are you sure?" Janette whispered back.

Berry hesitated.

"I won't judge," promised Janette.

"I feel confused," conceded Berry. "Haven't you ever felt...confused?"

She might as well have punched the girl in the face.

"Absolutely not," said Janette, abruptly passing her to get to the door. "Jesus. I can't believe you meant it."

"Wait—" said Berry, spinning around. "You asked me if I—"

"You're like that, Berry? You're like that?"

"Janette, please, you—"

"If you're really like that, I don't want you around me. I'm sorry. But I can't have something like that around me. That is foolish."

Janette opened the door. Berry stepped out.

They looked at each other for a few seconds. Visceral hate shone in Janette's deep brown eyes. Her smile was converted into a glare. The sun was bright before Berry, making Janette glow. She looked like an angel—a dark, beautiful, angry angel. The disgust in her eyes, though, made Berry recoil and then pause in indignation.

"Just because you touch somebody," said Berry, suddenly thinking to speak. "Doesn't mean you want them." Why, of all times, did she choose to be logical? She plunged ahead. "Even if I was like that, it wouldn't mean I wanted every other girl I saw. And that's just the truth."

Janette jolted as the words sank in. Her glare radiated disgust. Just the idea of those words must've made her feel vile. She smacked the door in Berry's face.

Berry walked to her car with her heart in her shoes.

She drove home in silence, replaying the interaction and cringing. Stupid, she was so stupid. Why'd she go and say all that and make things hard for herself? Trusting, admitting, hoping she'd get understanding.

Was it really understanding she wanted, or a touch in kind? Either way, so stupid.

Parked on the street, Berry banged her head against the steering wheel as she realized. Oh, God. No, no, no. Janette definitely was going to tell Crew and Dorothy.

Chapter 35

"Tell me the truth," said Crew. Berry folded herself on the edge of a chair across from Crew and Dorothy in the living room. Dorothy looked horrified, like she'd aged overnight or not gotten enough sleep. All three women had their ankles crossed. Berry clutched herself, heart pounding. Her stomach roiled. If she could evaporate, she would have, right then and there.

"Are you a homosexual?" Crew asked directly, icily.

"No," said Berry, shaking her head vigorously.

Dorothy looked on in amazement.

In any other situation, Berry would have had time to be shocked too. This was really being brought to the surface. They were using that word. Asking her this thing. They were saying this out loud, cutting her. But the hum was too loud in her ears.

"It's something not right about you, Berry," said Crew. "She said you said you was fighting something. I know she didn't make it up. She said you admitted it."

"She took it wrong," Berry insisted, voice shaking. "Janette took it wrong."

"You told her though," hissed Crew. "You said the devil was trying you."

"I was talking about loneliness! I get lonely."

"What was you and that girl? The fast smart talking one. Josephine."

"I had nothing to do with her."

"Bernadette, I asked you. I asked you did you have unnatural desires back when you first came here and she wouldn't come with you."

"Because I don't! I don't!" Hot tears spilled down her cheeks. The dam had broken anyway, she might as well let it flow. "I don't."

There was a long silence. Dorothy was rocking again in disgust and disbelief. Crew sat rigid on the edge of her chair, observing Berry with her bald, hard light eyes. She worked her stern mouth, studying Berry.

"Janette wouldn't say something like that for no reason," Crew said.

"I didn't do anything to her."

"Why you keep going back to that? Nobody said you did anything to her. That ain't even the question. I'm saying she think she can see that you have something going on in you, possibly towards her, that's not right."

"Well I don't," said Berry. "No. I don't."

"Yes, you do," said Crew suddenly. "I know it because when Millie was living, she told me they caught Josephine kissing and rubbing up on a girl at school one time. And I didn't want to believe it. But that's what she told me."

"What's that have to do with me?" said Berry. She hid her shock. A girl? At school? Was this the girl Jo had mentioned? So Crew had known about Jo all this time?

Crew got to her feet. She seemed to be searching for something. Dorothy was still shaking her head, looking floored. Berry wiped her face with the back of her hand.

"I don't believe you," said Crew then. Each word was a thud of judgment that shamed Berry to the core. "Something in me just won't." Crew turned to Dorothy for support, her eyes demanding that Dorothy speak.

Dorothy just shook her head. "It's messed up," she said. "Folks are messed up. What is the world coming to? Girl, I didn't know you were like that."

"I'm not!" Berry protested. "I'm not like that."

"Janette say she knows it," said Crew. "Dorothy knows it, I know it. And you all but told Janette. So tell us. We're waiting."

"But it's not true," said Berry. "I'm not like that."

Crew huffed, looking triumphant and disgusted. "You see that, Dottie. You see?"

There was a long moment of silence. They weren't buying her. She didn't know what she had to do to convince them, but they weren't buying her. Her skin was soaked with sweat, her eyes hurt, and she thought her heart would jump right out of her mouth. She felt nauseous. Sunlight turned the room gold and there was only the sound of the ticking clock—

"Berry," Dorothy said firmly, drawing a deep breath. "I can't have that in my house."

Berry looked up sharply at her. The worst was happening. Oh, no. She couldn't believe it. The world was falling apart. She got to her feet, her head spinning.

Dorothy squared her shoulders. "I let you stay here because it was on the belief that we would live a certain way and serve God and all get along. But I see that's not where you wanna go, and I can't tolerate that mess. You can fake being holy somewhere else."

Berry was speechless.

"You gonna have to leave," said Dorothy. "You gonna have to get your things and leave."

Berry couldn't say a word as she went to the door of her bedroom. Dorothy was right behind her. She dragged her suitcase from under the bed. She told herself not to panic. She turned to Dorothy standing in the bedroom doorway, hands on her hips.

"You don't mean it," said Berry. Her voice sounded young and hurt to her own ears.

"Child, get your stuff and go."

"I don't have anywhere else. I don't have nowhere else."

"That ain't my business, Berry. You gotta get up outta here, that's all I know. This is not a sin house. Or a sodomy house—or whatever it is they call what women—"

Eyes blinded with tears, Berry threw the suitcase open. She yanked open the drawers and pulled out all the few clothes she had. She stuffed them haphazardly into the suitcase. She trembled as she took down the one small candle on the bedside. She left the mirror. She shoved her Bible, case and all, into the suitcase too. Then she remembered her backpack of textbooks.

Dorothy was already holding it by the strap. She'd left it in the hall.

Berry took it from her without looking at her. Dorothy folded her arms.

"I swear I'm not crooked," said Berry in a trembling voice.

"Don't keep talking, child," said Dorothy. "Lies don't get you nowhere."

Berry walked to the door with her arms full. Two pairs of shoes in her hands, the suitcase, and the backpack on her shoulder.

From the living room, Crew prayed loudly, nearly screaming. "Lord Jesus keep us clean! Purify us, Lord! And don't let us invite your wrath with our sin!"

That infuriated Berry. These people were actually crazy. They were crazy, and how hadn't she realized it before she jumped into their crazy religion? She stopped on the threshold and gave Dorothy the dirtiest, nastiest look she could muster.

But Dorothy had steeled herself.

"Don't come back round here no more," said Dorothy. She laid Berry's car keys on top of the bag in her arms and shut the door firmly in Berry's face.

Berry looked around on the street. Her arms were still full. In a few weeks it would be cold. The drying tears stung on her face. Her vision swam. She looked all around. She was alone. Nothing but the things in her arms. Somehow, on this Saturday afternoon, even the street was empty. There was no one.

Chapter 36

Berry sat at the table in the dingy back room of the restaurant, furiously wiping away relentless tears as they fell. Everything she owned was in the back seat of her unreliable car. She was several states away from a home she could never bring herself to return to. She had no one, and nowhere to sleep tonight. She choked out a gasp.

Someone laid a heavy hand on her shoulder and a deep voice asked her what was wrong. Reginald's kind brown eyes stared into hers when she jumped and looked up through her haze at her restaurant manager's face. She didn't trust men, but anybody could do you wrong. "I—" she started.

"Take your time," said Reginald. "Take your time, baby girl."

At the end of the shift, Reginald drove her to his apartment. Berry was nervous the entire ride, but what choice did she have? She was down to the bits. At the doorway, Berry faced a suspicious looking wife who reminded her of Adie, and three small children.

"I had to help her," said Reginald, throwing out his hands. He was a sturdy man with a kind face, but he looked wilted in front of his wife. "I had to."

Berry repeated her new story for Minnie, the wife. Her adopted mother threw her out because she wouldn't pay her twice for the rent.

"Humph," said Minnie. Her light cheeks were dots of red.

Dinner was a cold, awkward affair at a table where she didn't fit so she had to stand. And Berry wished more than anything else that she had a place where she belonged. Her chest hurt so badly, her eyes stung with tears she refused to shed.

She slept on the couch with her belongings at her feet. At midnight, she heard Reginald walk by to the bathroom, his footsteps slow and heavy, and after that she didn't sleep again.

***

The next morning, Minnie handed her an apple from the counter and informed her of the nearest homeless shelter. Berry rode with Reginald to work. When they reached the restaurant, he parked next to her car, which had stayed overnight in the parking lot.

"You gone be alright," Reginald said in his deep gravelly voice. His eyes studied her.

"Thanks," she mumbled, for lack of all other words.

She considered hugging him, but that might be too far.

She drove herself to the homeless shelter. She missed English, her favorite class.

***

The shelter was surprisingly not crowded. She was shown into a large, open room filled with twin beds on severe looking frames. She looked around at the gray trim, the too-white sheets exposed by thrown back pale blue covers, the scrubbed raw cement floors. Her shoulders dropped as her bags dropped. At that moment, she felt that she was the only person on earth who was alone.

Homeless. It was such an awful, embarrassing word, and that was what she was. She laid her Bible on the bed as she emptied her backpack. That stupid book mocked her. God will always be with you. Where the frick was He now? More items fell out.

Berry hadn't done laundry. Half of her clothes were left in the bathroom at Dorothy's house, and the few she had from the bag were worn from last night or not complete enough to make an outfit. She needed new clothes, too. She almost lost it, but she had to hold it together.

Thankfully, there was another room with a pile of donated clothes in bins.

She pulled out several pairs of pants. She put one pair on right away. These long ugly dresses. She rolled up the skirt and tossed it in the bin of donated clothing. Who cared?

As she headed back to the room, she thought again of her mother and her grandmother. Since yesterday she'd been debating whether to call. Then she decided not to. They'd only discourage her—You better come home, you shouldn't be out there by yourself. That wouldn't do any good. She couldn't go back there and she knew why.

A look at the wall clock showed 2:45 PM. Anthropology class was starting now. She was going to miss that too. By the time she got there it would be halfway over. She sat on the shelter bed, stared at the hard gray floor, and tried to think about what to do next.

She was starving, that's what.

Besides the small dinner at Reginald's place, all she'd eaten for the past two days was an apple and a hotdog. She should go back to the restaurant and eat there, but for her pride's sake she didn't want to see Reginald anymore than necessary. She didn't want to become even more vulnerable by relying on him.

Ignoring the growling of her stomach, she took out her backpack. Absences could be explained, but when she returned to class, she wanted to have her homework done. And most of all, she didn't want to think about where she was now.

She sat cross-legged on the bed and started to write.

"Young lady, are you okay?" the shelter worker asked her, leaning around the doorway. A friendly woman in a blue uniform, but could anybody be trusted these days?

Berry said she was okay.

"Where's your family?" said the lady.

"I don't have none nearby," said Berry. She corrected her speech. "Any."

The woman looked at her curiously.

"Did you see the clothing in the donation room?"

"Yes, thank you, ma'am."

"There's some places for rent over on Askew Street. You might need to check them out. For young people, poor students, struggling families."

"I will—thanks," said Berry.

"Let me give you a paper," said the lady. "And you can go over there and check it out tomorrow. We can help you. Low-income housing."

Berry tried to drive over an hour later, but the car wouldn't start.

"Fuck you, God," she said under her breath, and that was when she broke up with Him. She punched the steering wheel and burst into tears at the pain that radiated in her knuckles, or maybe in everything.

She got out of the car and went back into the shelter.

Chapter 37

Late evening of the same day that she arrived at the shelter, there was a plastic tasting dinner served in a small room off to the side that was classified as a kitchen. Berry picked over the grayish colored meat and watery canned vegetables and then went to write more homework answers. She distracted herself with studying until nightfall.

Four other women had moved in by then. They were all older than her, haggard looking, but she stopped noting their appearances quickly. She had her own problems. And when the lights were out and Berry lay alone in an unfamiliar bed, in a state that she still didn't really know, her chest ached again.

They kicked her out, she thought. They really kicked her out onto the street.

It was so cruel that it was unreal. They really kicked her out.

How come she couldn't see how controlling they were until they tossed her out on the street? But she'd put up with them in exchange for safety. She flipped to her back, gripping her pillow as tears spilled out. She let them roll down her cheek, her neck, her chest, as she shook in silence. Her heart squeezed and her throat closed.

She ought to go home. And as clear as a picture, a crossroads appeared in her mind. With her eyes closed, in her mind's view she stood before a forked path. Home, North Carolina, retreat and poverty lay down one road. Forward on the other road, was the pursuit of her desires and the life she still believed she could have. It was hard either way.

She turned to her side, still clutching her pillow and sniffling. She missed her mother, she missed her grandmother. She missed the comfort of their narrow worlds and simple answers. She missed their hugs and food and care.

But that was a path that led to nowhere. And she hadn't been safe, not after all.

If she went home, she'd have to live in that house. She couldn't do that again, not after what happened that day in the kitchen.

Such a simple, massive thing she'd never admitted to herself: she could never live in that house again. It wasn't just the front door she didn't want to walk through. It was the house itself in the world it sat in. Cramped. Limited. She could never go back to it.

Soft sounds of the women's snores around her brought her to her full senses, from the mode of lower consciousness and grief. There was no sense in crying. Nobody was coming to save her. No one ever had. All she had was herself, so she would save herself.

She wiped her face. She'd been to her lowest, finally, and now she knew there was nothing to be afraid of, nowhere to go but up from here, and in that moment she decided: whatever she had to do, whatever it took, she would not stop until she held the key to her own sanctuary, her safety, her made world—her beautiful house.

Chapter 38

Berry called Lilah and Grandma Maple at a phone booth. Their voices were worried, excited, and relieved all at the same time to hear from her, as they always were. But she hadn't called in a while, or taken their calls, it had been too long. Was she alright? Lord, they were wondering. Berry had to calm them.

"How's the two women you stay with? Miss Dorothy and Miss Helen?" Grandma Maple asked when she and Lilah settled.

"Good, I guess," said Berry emptily.

"You don't know?" Grandma Maple sounded immediately suspicious.

"I don't go to that church anymore. And I moved out."

"Oh," said Grandma Maple. "Why you move out?"

Lilah was saying something in the background.

"I just wanted to be alone," Berry answered.

"Well, you be safe," said Grandma Maple. "Be safe." Berry could tell the gears were spinning in the clever old woman's head. "I'm worried about you, Berry."

"You sure you okay?" Lilah asked, finally audible.

Berry's heart skipped a few beats. "Yeah, Mama," she said quietly. "I'm okay."

"My stomach started hurting really bad some nights ago," Lilah said, her tone airy. "I figured it was something wrong with you. It always did when you were a little girl and you cried."

Berry didn't know what to say. Before she could say anything at all, Lilah had moved from the phone and Grandma Maple was carrying the conversation again. "So what you been doing, Berry? You sure you're alright, daughter?"

Berry told them half-truths. She was just busy, that was all. She'd walked a mile down to the auto shop and gotten them to tow her car there to fix it. She arranged to pay for it on credit. She'd missed a week of classes. Oh, and the new apartment was a dingy hole in the wall, but it was all okay. It was all okay.

"So why you drop religion?" Grandma Maple eventually circled back. "I thought you said you got saved."

"They were too strict, Grandma. Too strict."

"Well, you were heavy in it one time," said Grandma Maple. "Sounded like to me."

"I'm still saved, I just don't go there."

If she told them she didn't believe in God anymore, they'd think she was crazy.

"I'm glad you left that," Lilah interjected. She was close to the phone again. "Because the way I see it, there wasn't never nothing wrong with being a Baptist anyway. Me and Mama are Baptist and we're saved."

"Mhm," said Grandma Maple. "We sure are. Berry, you sure there's nothing wrong?"

***

Two of Berry's new professors, Dr. Moses Gladwell and Dr. Amber Kelly, were fond of her. They understood her absences. She still received high grades for the late homework she submitted. That was the consequence of sticking things out even when they were hard, see? Berry was proud of herself. And Dr. Gladwell always complimented her papers.

"I mean," he'd say, "The intelligence is there. And you have good handwriting."

And she would smile.

"Have you thought about grad school?" Dr. Kelly asked her after class once. She was a six-foot-tall, broad-shouldered white woman who wore glasses and a brown clip in her short hair. That, and the fact she only ever wore pants, distinguished her. Dr. Kelly was different, and she always went out of her way to show that she was kind.

"I'll think about it," Berry told her. "But I have to finish my undergrad degree first."

"Think about it," said Dr. Kelly. "I think you'd be amazing!"

Dr. Kelly was unusual. She'd never married, had no children, and was working at a historically black university. Berry looked at her quite often, trying to figure her out. Clearly she had rejected all the roles and structures that would've made her the typical white woman Berry was used to knowing. There was a reason Dr. Kelly appeared different. And why did she want to teach at a black school?

Dr. Gladwell, whose estranged mother was herself white, thought a lot of Dr. Kelly for how hard she tried to be decent. He said he knew the kind of work that went into her practice to be open-minded, because his white family, including his own mother—she was a typical, hellish white woman—his words—and his mother's side of the family was just like the family Dr. Kelly had been cut off from.

****

Dr. Kelly talked a lot about politics. She taught Introduction to International Relations. After a few classes, Berry hung a map up in her apartment. Now she could visualize other places. Ghana, Cuba, Israel and Italy.

Berry now had a stack of articles on the March on Washington, which had happened only a couple of months ago. It was everywhere when it happened. And Dr. Martin Luther King's "I Have a Dream speech" was apparently a big deal, but it didn't feel like that to Berry. She was too busy sorting out her life.

Chapter 39

Berry sat on the couch of a friend's apartment, her eyes glued to the television. Her friends sat around her. Louise Hall was a philosophy major at Lincoln University, and her boyfriend Arthur and his sister Delanie were studying mathematics. The ceiling fan ran on the highest setting. Arthur fanned himself. Berry clutched a pillow. They watched as the anchor delivered the news of President Johnson signing the Civil Rights Act.

"Boy, this is big," said Arthur. "This is monumental."

Delanie and Louise started talking. Berry was still staring at the television.

The Civil Rights Act legally banned segregation. Legally banned discrimination because of sex and race. Berry felt breathless as the channel focus went to the next segment. North Carolina? So North Carolina was now a place where she could walk in anywhere and be served? Those signs saying COLORED and WHITE were now illegal. Those signs had vexed her every single day she went into town. And now it was illegal.

Was this how the ancestors felt when they heard the Emancipation Proclamation?

No more outright discrimination in employment. No more segregation in public places.

But the red and white store, if she were back home right now, she still wouldn't frequent.

"Hey, Berry, you from NC aren't ya?" Arthur looked past Louise at her.

"Yes, it must be amazing now," she said, with a sarcastic smile.

She still didn't want to go home. It'd all be easier said than done. Just as the plantations trapped them into sharecropping. There was always another trick following the promise of equality. Always something new to tip the scales so that they never hung balanced. She hated the world, she felt it in her chest. She'd never go back to the South.

Nor did she want to see the house.

She preferred her distance.

Later, she bought a copy of *The New York Times* and took it up to her apartment and sat on her own couch to read more about the new law. There was an opinion-ed done here. Of course white people wanted to repeal it. They just had to be evil all the time. So damn tiresome, she was so damn fed up with them.

She thought of her father. He usually never came to her. She wondered what flashed through his mind in his last moments. She'd always hated him for being weak enough to die when he had a wife and two daughters who needed him.

She still looked down on him. But so many people like him would never see this.

"'Civil rights' bills have been enacted against the South before...and they have been beaten back..." was the paper's reported statement on a conflicting group. A terror group, they ought to call it what it really was.

She folded the paper, tossed it to the side, and put her feet up. This damn world, screwed-up place. Her homework lay on the floor, stamped up with high grades.

It didn't matter what they'd try to do to upend it all and force the Southern Blacks back into their position of absolute dejection, poverty, and submission. This thing was on. They weren't going to stop. And Berry was building her life.

***

The summer of 1964 was all about new things. At Louise's suggestion, Berry joined the NAACP chapter in her Philadelphia county. In a Methodist church backroom, the score of them met around a table. Berry, feeling refreshed in a new black skirt and white blouse, shook hands as Louise introduced her to a circle of new people.

Later that evening, Berry and her friends were dancing in the club. The lights blared and the music bumped, and Louise, Berry and Delanie swung with each other. These girls had never been tempted by other girls. Lucky selves. None of them were Berry's type. Louise was also dating Arthur and Delanie was boy-crazy. And no matter the stories they swapped or the secrets they shared, Berry had resolved to keep her most important one buried.

They pointed out guys to her. Always the same kind of man—He was tall, he was dark-skinned, his body language screamed arrogant. Every Black girl was supposed to be into that type of man, you know. What did she think of him? Berry made excuses. She had to focus on school. She couldn't tell them she only wanted a man because she needed a house.

But tonight she was bored, the liquor was hitting right, and she'd told herself that if the world could be better, then so could she. They could still have this paradise on Earth. Where everyone treated everyone equally in their governments and institutions and systems and where people did things the right way for the good of everyone, including themselves. And she too could do right—do right by herself. She'd kill this stupid idea that she wanted another woman, once and for all. She'd get herself a man and house.

Then she could fit in and be like everyone else, all the other normal people.

And as she danced, he approached her. He was just like the men her girlfriends always pointed out to her. But he might just be her ride. Delanie and Louise giggled. And Berry didn't turn her back to him, because the liquor was hitting.

"What's your name, baby?" he asked her.

***

Tommy Westfield was twenty-seven to her twenty-three. Tommy was from Maryland, but he'd moved up here to live with his cousins. Family row, he said. And his urge to get out and see the world.

Berry wasn't physically against men. Not entirely. Her fear of them was greater than her hatred. It was complicated.

And anyways, Tommy had a great smile, straight teeth and even lips. And a nice grip when he tucked his broad hand around her slim waist as they stood on the sidewalk outside the club. She swayed against him.

"You a sexy little thing," he murmured near her ear. "You know that?"

"Tommy." She laughed, drawing the last syllable out in her soft voice. The liquor was really getting to her brain.

"Nah, I'm serious," he said. "You a fine ass chick. Where you stay, baby?"

A cab took them to Berry's small, rinky-dink apartment.

And honestly, Berry hadn't had sex in so long. She hadn't had sex since 1960, and she was a young woman. Tommy helped her up the stairs. He wore a stylish leather jacket and very shiny shoes, which when she almost stepped on, he straightened her to protect. He grabbed her arm and she laughed. He smiled.

She was wearing chunky strap heels and a mini silver dress, clothes she would've never worn in her dowdy hometown, with her strict grandma and her easily scandalized mama. She felt as amazing as she knew she looked. She went to the couch and kicked off the heels. She tucked her nyloned feet underneath her and observed him.

Heavy steps came from the floor above. Sounded like people were breaking things. Tommy slumped in the armchair across from her, his legs thrown out. "Heck is that?" he said.

She rolled her eyes. "You know when you live in these little screwed up places, you never get no peace."

"Thank God my cousins got the house," he said.

"Oh, you're a lucky dude."

He grinned. He really did have a nice smile.

"I want a house," she blurted. "I get sick of having to live with other folks."

"What you gonna do when you get married?" Tommy said. "If you already got a house?"

She shrugged. She felt mysterious and sexy, but she'd just told him her secret.

He just smiled at her. Didn't he know women couldn't just up and buy houses?

After a few minutes her racing heart slowed to beat at a normal rate. Her vision swam less. The drunk was wearing off, not quite. And he still wanted her. Finally, he sat beside her and kissed her. She hadn't kissed a man in so long, she forgot their power and their forwardness. She put her hand against the side of his face, urging him to gentleness. He kissed her harder, she kissed him harder. And then he picked her up—scooped her up like she was nothing, and carried her to her tiny bedroom, where he laid her on the bed and hit it so good she screamed his name.

Chapter 40

Instead of doing homework alone at her own tiny place, Berry had Tommy's cousin's house to go to. The two-story home on the corner of Roxy Street was big enough to house ten people. It sat in a row of similar rented homes. Tommy lived here with his cousins, their girlfriends, and the multiple people who came and went. Berry should've wanted silence while she worked, but it wasn't about having silence. Not right then. And because there were other women at the house, it felt safe. And look at Berry, she actually had a life and a social circle now. She felt so optimistic.

Tommy and his cousins were raucous. They drank, they joked, and life was a day-by-day thing for them. "My girl is a smarty pants," Tommy would say, catching her by the waist when she came to sit at the table with them, books in her arms—usually while he and his boys were playing cards. They'd swipe away hats and cigarette packs and half-finished liquor glasses to make space for her and the textbooks.

She'd toss her hair and laugh. He was describing her right.

***

"Reading the Bible through?" said Tommy's friend Chester one evening when she took it out in the middle of their card game. "Dang!" He was a young brown-skinned man with a crooked smile and droopy eyes.

"I'm searching for something," said Berry, looking up. "And it's gotta be in here."

"The Bible got everything in it," said Chester. "I would know, my daddy was a pastor."

"That got kicked out of his church," Tommy laughed. And Chester guffawed.

Tommy's cousin Judas, a dark man with a cheek scar, was quiet as he shuffled the cards.

Tommy said he didn't know a damn thing about any of that theology stuff. "When I die, he said, "Ima just ask God not to let a black man have hell on earth and in the afterlife too."

The men burst out laughing.

Tommy always seemed proud of what he didn't know, what he didn't care to know or try to know. The brick. That was the codename Berry used for Tommy when talking to her girlfriends. He was handsome, and he was a brick. Both in build and personality. He had nice biceps, he was stubborn as a goat, and dumb as a wall.

She was usually annoyed by not smart people. But his nonchalance made her feel smarter, and there was nothing Berry loved more than feeling smart.

***

As Berry approached her final year of university, being smart became her personality. Her grades told her so. What would she do with all that smartness after college?

She forced down her inner qualms about the fact that Tommy worked at a grocery store. She decided it was fine because she was making her life for her, and he was making his life for him. As long as they were kind to each other and had fun, that was all that mattered. Right?

She went to monthly NAACP meetings with Louise. She read *The New York Times*. She followed Dr. Martin Luther King Jr. a little, but she preferred listening to Malcolm X.

Tommy spurned that kind of stuff as "what the white man is doing."

"It just never changes, Blueberry," he said. They were sitting in his car one evening. Hers was still unreliable. "They let you have one thing, and then take something else."

Berry was quiet, staring moodily at the clear blue sky.

"You never get too happy. This cage ain't being opened no time soon."

Her hope sat at the bottom of her belly. She hated when he said things like that.

But was he wrong? He couldn't be faulted for the way he felt. Everybody took things in different ways, she thought.

***

It was an early Saturday evening when Berry laid the tiny photo on her bedside table. Her sister Lucille looked glowing in it. The picture had come with her most recent letter. Her pregnancy wasn't visible in the photo, but of course, no woman wanted her belly bump showing. Lucille sat on the couch next to Zachary, who held their little son. They looked clean, happy, and sane. Berry had been asking how North Carolina felt since the new laws. And she was right, things were slow to change. But Zachary was doing well in his contracting job, and Lucille didn't have to work.

Outside, Berry heard a woman's high-pitched laugh. She swirled her gaze around Tommy's room. It needed the touch of someone like herself. Those blankets were a dull in-between gray and blue color, the blinds were coffee brown, and the center beige rug, even after she'd vacuumed it twice, still looked worn. The floor was wooden. Her suitcase lay on it, open and empty. The woman's laughter tinkled out again.

She was one of the men's girlfriends.

The men's women were the main reason Berry felt comfortable enough to move in.

She missed her family, she thought, staring at the photo. She kept telling herself she'd go back down there, but going back felt just like heading back into a burning place. And what would her heart do if she stepped back into that haunted house?

So she was here with Tommy. Tommy who made her laugh, and worry when he got annoyed, and Tommy who lulled her into a sense of safety.

She deserved a normal life. She'd have one. She'd marry Tommy if he asked her, and he'd get them a nice house. And she'd have a couple of kids in that nice house with her husband and finally, she'd fit in just like everyone else.

Chapter 41

Berry did marry Tommy. They went to the justice of the peace and made it official six months after they met at the club that Saturday night. She was thrilled by him and the prospect of living a normal life. What she loved about the man himself—not him, but other things: one, the sex. Two: that he was always there. Quite literally. She was never alone.

Even though he sometimes got on her nerves, she was certain she could tolerate him.

Tommy loved eggs. She'd never seen a man love his eggs so much. Eggs, ketchup, and potatoes. He made them for her. And insisted that she eat them. She wanted to keep that grin on his face, so she ate them. She kept it to herself that she didn't think nobody's food was as good as Southern food. She made the mistake of saying that once at the table.

"What do you mean?" Tommy said. "You think one region own good food?"

"I didn't say that," she said. "I just said I've never been anywhere that topped it."

"Blueberry," he said. "You only been to one state. Pennsylvania."

"I also lived in New York," she said. "You forgot New York."

"That's still not enough to say that one state got the best food."

"I didn't say that either," she snapped.

"You just did," he retorted.

"Ya both stop fussing," said his cousin Judas, who was also at the table.

Berry and Tommy argued often now. Never serious arguments, but back-and-forth exchanges. Now that they were married, they were free to express themselves. Tommy never quit, and Berry never gave in. The cousin Judas always told them to knock it off.

***

"We need our own place," Berry told Tommy, over and over. When she held his hands and said "I do" she was hoping that it meant they'd soon get a house. Because that was what married people did.

"We don't have kids yet," said Tommy. "When we get kids we can move."

But Berry wanted to move now.

"Don't keep asking me that," he snapped once, spinning on her as he stood in the bedroom door. And that time, he actually scared her a little. That was the first time she backed down. She felt shocked at him and herself when she went and sat back down on the bed and actually dropped the conversation.

She didn't know why her request irritated him so much.

"When you have kids," he told her later when they were lying on the floor in front of the TV in the dark living room, and all the cousins and girlfriends and house-goers were away or in bed. "Then we can get some place and move out."

"Alright," she whispered. But she wanted to do it now, not later.

***

Bernadette Westfield. That was a mouthful to say. She held the phone, standing in the living room, rolling her eyes as her grandmother repeated it in shock. "Married? Married, Berry? Girl, you could've told us. You could've at least told us!"

"It just happened," said Berry. "I don't know, it just happened."

"You didn't tell us nothing," said Grandma Maple. "Nothing! You skip every holiday with us, you get married, and then you don't tell us nothing. Girl, you don't like us or something?"

Berry sighed, but she couldn't keep the smile out of her voice. "I was in love," she said, wincing at that untruth even as she continued to smile. She was smiling because she was so proud to announce it. It made her feel normal.

"When you gonna let us meet him?" Lilah asked.

"Soon!" she said. "Soon. I promise, I won't surprise you like that again."

"Girl, you'd better not!" chided Grandma Maple. "You'd better not. And you bring that man home and let us see him! Stop living life without us, girl!"

Berry promised she would.

***

Louise and Arthur hadn't seemed surprised that she got married, but they were surprised there was no wedding. Arthur and Louise were a well-put-together couple. They went to church. They were educated. Both good looking people. Louise listened to Arthur, and Arthur catered to Louise. He got a good job balancing the books at a black shoe business. Louise was on track to be a nurse. Louise had told Berry that they were going to start having children in three years after their own wedding.

It was embarrassing for Berry to fuss with Tommy in front of them.

But Arthur and Louise weren't the type to say anything. Their eyes would just go wide.

"When you get married," Berry told Louise at lunch in Louise's apartment. "Don't rush it like we did. We just went downtown. Do a real wedding."

"Oh, I am," said Louise primly. "We will. Mrs. J is sewing the dress."

Louise's mother, who Louise referred to as Mrs. J, was a very good seamstress. And again, Berry envied their very normal, middle class lives.

"It's not too late," Louise told her, digging her fork politely into her lettuce and radishes. "You and Tommy only just did it. You two can still have a wedding."

"I don't know, it just won't feel fresh," said Berry.

"Yes it will," said Louise. "Why wouldn't it, Berry?"

"I don't know," said Berry, shrugging.

She stared at her plate, her mind running back to five years ago and sitting at a table across from a girl named Jo. Flashbacks didn't stop there. They were lying in bed together, and the love they had was pure and raw and desperate. Their friendship was transcendental. There would never be anything like it.

And she still wanted it. Even as Berry Westfield, with a simple gold band on her finger, she wanted the wrong thing. She didn't love Tommy. She found things to make her feel better about herself by being with him. She could appear normal to the world now, she could fit in. She needed him to get herself a house.

What was the point of a wedding when she had a heart like hers?

Chapter 42

Berry's grades were so good that she won a scholarship. She was absolutely thrilled when her advisor called her into his office to tell her. She called it getting paid for being smart. It paid to be smart, being smart paid off. Her grin split her face. She couldn't believe it. That was the first time she was recognized for her work, and it was satisfying.

College was cheap, but now she could save even more money, and she'd been paid for being smart! She burst into the house, where Judas and Tommy sat at the kitchen table, overflowing with the good news.

Judas said, "Ahn ha, that's good." And nodded. He was painting something on a white paper. He made art whenever he wasn't playing cards.

Tommy was eating a pork chop sandwich and drinking a grape soda. "Huh?" he said.

Berry was expecting him to jump up with excitement. Tommy never reacted with excitement when she really needed him to.

"I was one of the first to get one," she squealed. "And it all came from my grades!"

She dropped into the chair, barely able to be still.

"Aren't you guys happy?" Their lack of enthusiasm would've rained on her parade in any other instance. But she was too happy because of that check.

"You something else ain't ya," said Judas, chuckling.

"I think I'm pretty good," said Berry, rolling her eyes. She'd never bragged about herself before. But it felt good to brag.

Tommy got this stony look. He chewed ferociously at his sandwich. "You know what that mean," he said. He clutched the soda in the other hand, denting the side.

"What?" Berry said.

"You can't start slacking up just because you feel you got there quick."

"What?" said Berry. "What are you talking about?"

"I don't know. Sometimes people start feeling comfortable."

Silence.

"That doesn't even make sense," she said finally. "If anything, I'm gonna work harder."

"I hope so," said Tommy, grunting.

"God," said Berry, tsking. "Stop being weird!"

Judas laughed and drew a swish of blue with his brush.

***

Berry and Tommy prepared for bed. She was reading a book and he was standing at the bedside, taking his sleeping pills. Lately, he hadn't been sleeping as well. His job made him surly, he hated his boss, and he complained. She often told him that if he changed jobs, then he wouldn't feel so anxious and irritable. She didn't say that tonight.

She was reading the book she got from the library. It was nonfiction, as usual, about fauna in North America. Extremely bland, but reading about things that had nothing to do with people was how she entertained herself and shut out the world.

Out in the hall, Judas was saying something to Fan, his new girlfriend. Another man's deep voice came from the living room, which temporarily wasn't really the living room at all for a week or two since it had been divided into a bedroom with a curtain. Someone needed it between apartments.

"What you reading tonight?" Tommy asked her, settling in beside her.

"Just something to pass the time," said Berry.

"You always reading or studying."

He was so dumb. "It helps me make those good grades."

He muttered something.

"What?" she said, trying to keep the edge out of her voice. She'd rather not fight tonight.

"Nevermind." He turned on his side to face away from her. She turned the page.

"Are you happy for me?" she asked.

"Why the hell you ask that?" he snapped. "Of course I'm happy for you."

"Thank you, baby."

"You trying and that's what matters," he said.

She frowned. Today hadn't been a failure by any means.

"I think I want to go to law school," she said suddenly.

He stirred, but didn't say anything.

As always when he didn't reply, she wanted to talk even more.

"I know that sounds crazy," she went on, more to herself than him. "A Black woman, lawyer. But one time I had this friend. We said that's what we wanted to do. We were always talking. And we laughed. We laughed."

"You know that's gonna be difficult," he said.

"I know, Tommy, you know I know that. But if I'm the best. If I'm the best they'll take me. They can't keep us all out, not the best."

"Just don't get your hopes all high and get hurt."

She was quiet. He was always so gloomy, goddamn.

Who was to say she couldn't? If ridiculous, bad things could happen to her, then unbelievable, good things could happen to her too.

Thurgood Marshall, he was a Black lawyer! And he went to Lincoln University, too. Sure, he was a man, but she was good enough of a woman.

She said so to Tommy, who simply grunted.

She went back to reading about the plants. But at length he rolled over to face her. His warm hand came up to her knee. And she looked at his rising chest and into his eyes. She sat the book on her bedside table. Slid down until she was level with him, or maybe he tugged her down.

Chapter 43

"Tommy," Berry kept saying. "We're married, why can't we have a house?"

It made him so mad that she kept asking, but she was serious. They needed to have their own place. There were too many people here. This was a fast house. And they were married! The other people here were girlfriends and boyfriends.

She'd gotten the husband, so why couldn't he give her the house?

She'd always wanted a house. Always. The house was the center of her dreams.

"You not gonna stop nagging me 'bout that, are you?" Tommy said.

"But it's what we need, Tommy. It's what we need."

"We don't rent here. You gotta learn to be grateful when something is good. You want to move out to pay rent when Judas let us stay here free."

"I am grateful."

He gave her the silent treatment for two days after that. No matter what she did, he refused to respond. Berry was almost in tears by the time he finally spoke to her again. Of course that included another round of sex. Maybe sex could fix anything. If a man got his rocks off, then he just might calm down and be nicer.

But instead, now she was angry. She got up from the bed feeling awful. She was angry because he'd been angry with her and he hadn't apologized. He hadn't even talked it over with her. And then they'd had sex when they should've had a conversation. She slammed the bathroom door.

She considered calling her mother and grandmother, as she often did, but then changed her mind. They'd just tell her the same old things they told other women. He's a man, he's a dog, what else can you expect?

Besides, that was just the way it was. Berry and Tommy got over it by the end of the week.

***

"I want a son," said Tommy, lying next to her in bed one evening while she read.

Tommy had mentioned twice that he wanted children. But she wasn't ready. She wanted to teach for a year or so after she got her degree, have two children, and then go to law school. She reminded him.

"That's what I don't get," he said. "You want to move but we don't even have a family."

"Because Tommy, we can't start one here! You think I'm gonna get pregnant here when we don't have a house?"

"You worry about everything. If there's something to worry about, Blueberry, you gonna worry about it."

"I'm careful! I think things through."

"I'm the man. If you can't trust your man, I don't see what you need me for."

"Don't say that!" She was cut. But no, she didn't trust him. He hadn't done anything for her to trust. He couldn't even give her a simple thing: a house.

He dug in. "What you need me for if you already got it?"

She turned her back to him.

Berry tried taking the pill soon after that, although it made her throw up so much she had to stop. But she didn't want a child and she meant that. And Tommy couldn't guilt her into having one, either. She always made him pull out. She kept close track of her cycle, which was regular without fail.

If he couldn't give her a house, why should she give him a child?

Chapter 44

Berry graduated from Lincoln University in fall 1965 with a degree in English. Tommy didn't come to the graduation, which damn near ruined the day. For all she'd done, for how hard she'd worked, her own husband didn't care to show up and see her accept her diploma. It was already bad enough that her mother and grandmother couldn't make it because they didn't have the funds and couldn't get a break from work, and they'd all cried over that. But Berry understood them.

But not the husband.

"You could've come." She was sitting on the couch, tears staining her cheeks. Judas was playing checkers with a neighborhood boy, and Tommy was watching TV. Or had been interrupted watching it. Berry had a lot to say.

"I told you I was sick," Tommy said, wiping his nose with a towel. "You know I would've come if I wasn't."

Berry glared at him.

"Stop crying like that," he said. "You know I would've come if I could."

He patted her shoulder. She shook him off, got up, and stormed to their room. She lay on her back in bed, staring into the silence. Her mind went back to years ago and New York City when she walked into her first college class one bright morning with her best friend right beside her. Where was Jo now? Jo would've been happy for her. She and Jo would've celebrated together. Just imagine how they would've laughed if they'd spent a triumphant day like this together. She reached for the black-cased diploma she'd laid on the bedside table earlier. She flipped it open and gazed at it, and then she kissed it.

Berry went cold on Tommy. He couldn't justify not attending her graduation. A moment like that should've had his utmost respect. Her mother worked odd jobs. Her grandmother was a cook. Before her father joined the Army, he was a sharecropper in Texas. The sharecropper's daughter grew up to earn a bachelor's degree, and in English, nonetheless. Berry resolved not to forgive her husband until he did something grand to make it up to her.

Berry wouldn't speak to Tommy in the kitchen. She avoided him in the living room and at night when they climbed into bed. His warm hand sliding up her midriff meant nothing. She wouldn't turn around. She hated him.

The jackass was pining for sex with her, for acknowledgment from her. He acted bewildered and annoyed with her rejections until he gave in and brought her a pair of heart-shaped earrings and a fake rose.

She hated heart-shaped things, but that brought her temperature down. She put the rose in a clear vase on their bedside table. He begged.

And they were civil again.

***

Berry got hired to teach English at a Black middle school that winter. Around the same time, her sister Lucille phoned to tell her that they were moving up to Maryland, expecting their third child, and she would love to see Berry soon.

Because it wasn't the state of her trauma, Berry decided to meet.

She and Tommy drove two and a half hours. Lucille and Zachary lived in a fairly neat neighborhood in Prince George County, a decent sized brick house with two white rocking chairs on the porch and a playset in the yard. Tommy and Berry jumped out of the car, surprised to see Lucille in a flowing burgundy dress, already waiting on the step.

"Berry!" Lucille cried, and waddled to her as fast as her legs would take her.

Berry ran to close the distance and hugged her as hard as she could.

"You look so good!" Berry told her, pulling back. Lucille was flushed and bright-eyed, happily cradling her bump covered by her coat.

Berry introduced Lucille to Tommy. Zachary had come out of the house. The men shook hands politely. Zachary looked so different. He'd filled out and had a thick black mustache that complemented his clean-shaven, square face. He and Berry hugged each other like siblings.

The children, a boy and a girl, clung to their mother once they were all inside.

"Berry!" squealed Lucille. "You went and got your degree!"

"I did," said Berry. She couldn't help but smile.

"That's just amazing," said Lucille. "I'm so happy for you."

"Yeah, yeah," said Zachary, looking awkward for some reason. "Congrats, Berry."

Tommy was quiet.

"I knew you could always do something," said Lucille.

"Well, you two are living good, too," said Berry. Zachary did look the part of husband and father now. Berry hardly knew what to make of that. And Lucille, so mature! Berry couldn't stop looking at them. And looking all around at their kitchen. They had a house.

Lucille seemed content to be a homemaker. But that was most women. Most women Berry met weren't going to say, I never wanted to get married and I'd rather have a girlfriend than a husband. And this marriage and children did seem to have given Lucille joy.

"Zachary got in the church," Lucille told her when they were alone in the kitchen. It was a nice sized kitchen, with pale green cabinets and brown chairs, and a matching green telephone. The men were in the other room. "We go every Sunday now. We really love it. We—"

"Sit down," Berry told her, interrupting her story and jumping up. "I know I'm in your house, but I can't let you work like that, girl."

"Well, thank you, Berry." Lucille sat right down, jiggling the youngest child.

Berry started mixing up flour. "So what church?"

"He joined the Seventh-day Adventists," said Lucille.

For precisely that moment, Berry got the urge to tell her sister everything, and then it vanished just as quickly. Lucille had never had an inkling about who she truly was.

"I can't believe you left yours," Lucille said. "I thought you were deep into Johnson."

"I couldn't keep up with all that stuff they were doing," said Berry dismissively.

While Zachary and Tommy went out to do whatever men did, Berry helped her sister. Berry easily played the aunt. She sat with little Beatrice and Robbie. She cut apple slices and made peanut butter crackers. And when she was done with their many questions and sticky fingers, she let both of them sit on either side of her and hummed to them until they fell asleep. Lucille came back from the supermarket later.

"Thank you so, so much," said Lucille. She sounded like she was going to drop on the floor in exhaustion—or gratitude. "You don't know what you did for me."

"It's okay," said Berry. "I wish I were around to help you more."

She didn't mean that. What she meant was that she wanted everything to be easier for Lucille. This was hard work.

Lucille put the TV on for the children. She and Berry sat side by side on the couch, talking through a kids' show that wasn't interesting to them.

"It kicked," Lucille gasped, turning to smile at her. Berry put a hand on her sister's belly. She felt it kick too. Something went all through her. Her eyes welled up, her chest tightened, and her throat constricted.

She wanted what she weanted, that she still didn't have, that was wrong to desire, but at that moment, she also wanted this too.

"Oh," Berry said. Flesh and bone, her sister's own design, and an experience that she would create too, if only there were different circumstances. And she felt that little tiny kick again, breaking her heart beyond words.

***

Tommy thought she wasn't talking enough on the ride back to Philly, so he got fed up and turned on the radio. But Berry couldn't talk. As the roads spun before them and stoplights came and went, she thought about the feel of that baby kicking. Shouldn't she have the chance to experience that? Every woman in her line before her had done it. Every woman alive before her daughter knew what it felt like to grow a child and birth it.

Was she thinking wrong? She imagined most of the women's lives before hers hadn't been easy. Even her mother and grandmother hadn't had easy lives. Was her life any better than theirs?

An emptiness sat inside of her. It wasn't because of her empty womb. That was both good and sad. She still planned to have a child in a few years. It was the emptiness of knowing she couldn't make two opposite decisions at the same time. What would she make of her life, if she didn't make the right choices? There must be some reason everybody did the same things. Were they being fulfilled, she wondered? Was she missing something?

Lucille's shining face. Her protective hand over her belly. Her two children. Her family. The safety of her house and her husband. Did Zachary love her? He'd run so many girls when they were dating and made her cry all the time. But now they'd made a life together. There was no point, really, in trying to figure out if he did love her. Lucille was surrounded by things she had brought into her world that she wanted. That had to mean something.

At the same time, there was her hairline shining with sweat. Her heaviness. Her dependency on Zachary. Her express relief that Berry helped her with the clamoring, sweaty, sticky children. Too much noise of everything, too many clothes, too many hands, too many requests. Lucille was tired. Berry had a feeling she was more tired than Berry could ever comprehend as a childless woman.

Maybe Berry would be the one rare woman who could have it all. She'd teach for two years, she'd go to law school, she'd have the children. And maybe by then things would be so different. If they could end segregation, then maybe by the time her children were two and four, there'd be so many Black female lawyers, that her going to law school wouldn't be so odd. Maybe by then, Tommy would be a better man, a better husband, and a good father.

And they'd have a house.

She really wanted to go to law school. Every year, she knew more of why she wanted to. At first it was because it was important and professional, the opposite of her world. Then it was because she learned she was smart. Now it was because it seemed like it would make her truly happy, the only straightforward decision about her future.

Chapter 45

The children at school adored Berry. The boys had crushes on her. The girls saw her as an older sister. Berry was younger than the older teachers sending students to the principal's office for minor offenses, and more lenient too. As long as a student was polite, neat and well-dressed in Berry's English class, she wouldn't send them to Mr. Lane for chastisement. She didn't like to see children crying after getting whacked with the paddle.

"Stand up straight," she'd say crisply, and everybody would stand up straight.

The money was finally good enough to live on. Not a lot, but just enough.

And she put every extra dollar and cent she had into the black safe under the couch. They still didn't have a house, and she still wanted one.

If Tommy wouldn't save for it, then she would. She'd been saving off and on for years anyway. She was going to get that house somehow.

***

"We ought not wait on having kids," said Tommy at the table.

"But you know I'll have to quit teaching when I do," Berry told him.

"You gonna quit anyway," he said. "And I'm making enough to support us. You know I'm not gonna have you out working when the kids get here."

She didn't believe him. He hadn't even gotten her a house.

She wanted it all—eventually. She wanted a child, a little girl specifically, so she could style her hair in ponytails and dress her in pink for photos. But she also wanted to ditch the teaching and the rest of the plan and go straight to law school.

Why did she always want things that were strange? Why were her wants always different from normal wants? Other people lived simple, formulaic lives. She went for brave, open ended things, things women like her weren't supposed to desire. Something was wrong with her.

"How about when we move out?" she said.

Berry and Tommy had both been influenced by Zach and Lucille. There was a hunger in them both. To have a family, raise it, be normal. Play their respective roles required of them to fit in. But they weren't very good at it.

Grandma Maple had asked in a roundabout way—"When you think you gonna tip the scales from Lucille? She can't have them all."

Berry still hadn't come to see them. They didn't like that, but she kept saying: Soon.

***

Berry and Tommy finally moved out of Judas's apartment. He was sad to see them go. Tommy and Judas were in a close family. Somebody always had to be with somebody: the cousins had to be together, or the remaining siblings, or grandchildren with grandparents.

The one bedroom apartment that Tommy and Berry rented was closer to both their jobs. So that was a good thing. The bad thing was that it felt empty, bereft of male voices and women's laughter. And the TV ran unless one of them got irate and shut it off.

Berry put up cheap green curtains and moved the sagging brown couch so that the room looked bigger. But she still felt restless. This wasn't nice enough. Because this wasn't the house she dreamed of or the life she really wanted.

She lay down to sleep with Tommy. As usual they rolled together. She needed something. So did he. They both had their reasons. They started. She was under him. He wasn't looking at her face. But that was okay. She wasn't looking at him either now, she closed her eyes. It felt good. So deep.

"I'm gonna come," he gasped.

She stiffened, looking sharply up at him. He should pull out now. But he wasn't. She pushed against his arms and struggled to move herself back.

He held her there and kept going.

"Tommy," she whispered frantically. "What are you doing?"

"Shit," he muttered.

"Stop, stop," she said frantically. "Stop." She pushed him.

He didn't stop. Stilled over her, and came in her. She took it in disbelief.

A second later he flopped onto his back.

She looked down between her legs in shock. Her heart was racing.

"Why didn't you stop?" she gasped, voice breaking.

His eyes were closed. He said, "Sorry. I couldn't."

Horrified, she leapt up and raced into the bathroom.

Five minutes later at the door, one hand over her chest and different underwear on, she glared at him. She wished she could stab him with her eyes. She wished she could tear his out.

"Why didn't you pull out?" she sobbed.

"I couldn't stop in time," he muttered.

"Yes you could! I told you to stop. What the fuck is wrong with you? I told you to stop."

"I was already coming."

"You still could've pulled out, you idiot!" Her voice was so high it shocked her.

He glared at her.

"You should know when you're about to! You always pull out before!"

He sat up, reaching for his white t-shirt.

"I seriously think something is wrong with you," she said, shaking. "I don't know what the fuck it is, but something is wrong with you."

"Stop bitching. I told you I didn't have time."

A hot rage came over her that had never taken her before. She grabbed the fake rose from the bedside and flung it at him. It landed lightly and uselessly on the floor a few paces before her. She reached for the clock—

"Cut that shit out," he said, jumping to his feet. "I told you I was sorry!"

His loud deep voice stilled her.

"I hate you," she hissed. "You're sick. You're evil. You beast."

"Fuck you too, Berry," he said.

He went into the kitchen. She slammed the bedroom door, locked it, and flung herself across the bed. Oh God, she'd have to take something. She couldn't get pregnant. That idiot. She felt so dirty and angry. Hot tears streamed down her face, wetting the pillow.

His footsteps came back to the bedroom door. He beat on it.

"Stay out there!" she yelled.

"Berry pie, let me in. Come on, Blueberry. You get mad over the craziest stuff. You know you said you want a baby! Hey!"

He beat harder on the door.

"Come on, Berry. Man."

She buried her face in the pillow. Tears racked her.

"Fuck you, alright?" he said. "Fuck you."

His footsteps sounded as he went to the living room.

Chapter 46

They were never quite right with each other after that. He kissed her and brought takeout. She graded papers, and he watched TV and didn't disturb her. They even slept together again at his insistence. She was relieved she wasn't pregnant. She went to the doctor and got a different pill, a second option out of the new brands available. She felt a little better.

But they weren't right.

She hated him. She still felt she needed to have a child, because that was what normal people did, and she was so convinced she needed to play normal, but she hated him. He'd pinned her down as he finished inside her against her will, and she hated him.

***

Now that Berry knew for sure that she hated the man who was supposed to give her the house and a normal-looking life, her gaze went back to wandering. And fixed itself on was the perfect physicality of Nora Anderson, Berry's colleague.

Nora taught the wanna-be-rowdy sixth graders. Nora wore perfect pencil skirts and jackets every day, complete with glossy, pressed hair and a watch on one wrist and a bracelet on the other. She was about thirty-five, a decade older than Berry, and she had a mischievous glint in her eye and a bob set so perfect it looked fake. Her dark skin was so clear it looked glassy. Her English was crisp as a fresh morning, and her students in perfect order.

Nora and another teacher, the heavyset Mr. Donald Pell, liked to stand in the hallway and talk between bells. Berry's room was right beside hers, but the way the door was set up put Nora at more of a distance from her than closeness.

Sometimes, Nora would look at her and smile and wave. That fluttering of her fingers did something to Berry.

Nora was so feminine, so sleek. And Berry was hopelessly attracted to her.

This wasn't a regular attraction. Nora made her hungry.

Berry hadn't been that attracted to someone in a long time.

She wanted to be friends with Nora. She wanted to know everything about her. She wanted to swap stories with her. She wanted to sit with Nora in her kitchen and laugh about stupid things with her. She wanted to bake a cake and let Nora rate it. She wanted to put her lips up to that perfect, smooth, done up face.

She wanted to *be* Nora.

Nora started speaking to her when they encountered each other in the teacher's lounge.

"How's their papers coming?" Nora asked her once. Berry sat at the table eating the lunch she brought from home. Berry put a hand over her mouth and finished her bite before speaking. She had to be as polite and perfect as Nora.

"They're doing well," Berry said finally. "But you know how they are. I have to remind them to work on it every night."

"Honey, I know," said Nora. "My kids are the same way. You just have to stay on them."

"They don't want to work unless you make them."

"Exactly. That's why you have to press them." Nora paused at the refrigerator, debating between items. "But I think what's more important is that you be a steady guide for them."

Berry was listening.

"I don't raise my voice," said Nora. She put her food out and sat. "So then they know that if I ever have to, it's real trouble. And that what I say needs to be done the very first time."

"Wow," said Berry. "You sound serious." And they both laughed.

Nora's dark eyes sparkled when she was amused, and the twinkle in them was even brighter.

***

There was really something about Nora's eyes. Something about her eyes that was so, so interesting. So beguiling. Eyes that made a person stop and think—Who is that? What's she thinking? Something else there, too. Interest. It didn't need to be said. Berry felt the ripple of energy flowing from her to Nora. This was not a Janette situation. Berry was not reading this wrong. She couldn't be.

Nora came by her class door to give her a poster. It was for the upcoming talent show.

"Encourage the kids to sign up," said Nora. And, being always prepared as she was, she even had an extra wall tack to go up.

Berry's kids were out for lunch. Nora's class was just about to come in.

"You keep a nice room," said Nora, and tapped her playfully on the arm.

They laughed. Berry's gaze snagged on hers.

And she thought, It has to be.

There is no way it can be. Because no one is like that but me.

But it has to be.

She was disheartened to see Nora after school, walking to the car with her twin sons, little boys in cuffed blue jeans with pressed white shirts, who were second graders and went to the elementary school across the street.

Chapter 47

Berry and Tommy argued constantly. Nothing he did pleased her, and every word she spoke annoyed him. The only time they weren't in blinding rage with one another was when they were having sex—although that was happening far less now, hardly at all. She'd been on edge since he didn't pull out in time, and she didn't desire him anymore.

He hadn't done it again, though.

She'd honestly have to kill if he did that again.

But it didn't feel right engaging with him.

As their marriage increasingly fell apart, they spent less time at the apartment together. Tommy had a new hobby besides being useless: gambling. Judas had opened a nightclub, and now Tommy spent his weekends drinking and spending money. He wasn't good at gambling, but who was, because a gamble is a gamble.

Tommy wasn't a mean drunk, just an annoying one. He called a list of wrong numbers instead of the one for the taxi, that's why he got home so late. He'd beg Berry to make him some eggs or hamburger patties, which she would. Being drunk made people hungry. He'd fall asleep on the couch. And she'd glare at his broad back with disdain.

What was the point of a man having a big, strong back, but not using it to build her a house?

Tommy was at his worst when he was hungover. That's when he turned mean. Saturday or Sunday morning was a guaranteed brawl.

Somehow, in the midst of all that, Berry finally finished reading the Bible. She sat it on the table in the living room, right behind the TV, and made up her mind about it. God could never be a man, because there was no way a man could be God.

***

Berry hated Tommy, but she stayed. The apartment was in his name, and she'd still need him when they finally bought the house she was saving for. And maybe by then, he'd be better. Because she needed him for the mortgage and the normal life. Things she couldn't get on her own. She couldn't believe there was a time when she'd dreamed of her own beautiful house without a clue in the world about what she actually needed to get it: a man's name.

However, there was one new decision that she would stand on.

She wouldn't have a child. Tommy's child.

Tommy wasn't father material. She'd ruin her life having one by him.

And maybe she wasn't ready either. She liked her freedom. She liked her flat stomach. She'd rather not stretch it. She didn't want to spend her free time doing laundry and wiping up snotty nosed children. She'd rather tire herself out from studying, not making chicken soup and changing diapers.

Let women like Lucille have it. Berry had to pass on that for now.

With that decision, another naturally came forth. Berry sat on the couch to write a letter to the two professors from Lincoln University who'd always encouraged her. There was no need to wait. Now was the time to go to law school.

Chapter 48

Dr. Gladwell told her in a meeting in his office, "Try to find another man to write you a letter, too. Mary's word can only go so far." So Berry went to her boss, the school's principal, Mr. Lane, to ask him to write the third letter.

When she got home, Tommy was already there. He was watching TV, or the TV was watching him. He was asleep on the couch.

Just the sight of him pissed her off. She wished she could kick him.

She sat at the dining room table to study. Later, he came into the room. She took a deep breath. They greeted each other civilly. He asked her if she was grading work. She said no.

"What you doing then?" he asked, noticing the LSAT book at the same time. "I thought you said you were waiting to start that," he said.

"I changed my mind," she replied crisply. "I don't like teaching."

"You always getting those fast ideas, just like a woman," he said.

She started to say, At least we think. But she didn't want to fight him today.

He tromped back into the kitchen.

He wasn't going to stop her. Nothing was. She was excited. She imagined herself saying, I'm a lawyer. It sounded so smart. Sleek. Perfect. She'd be so proud of herself if she could do this. She deserved to be proud of herself. And neither he nor anyone else could stop her.

***

Berry volunteered to help with the new school event because Nora was leading the program. Anything to be around Nora somehow. Berry had no idea how to move forward, wasn't sure if she was ready not only to cheat on Tommy, but to cheat on him with a woman—and—

She was way ahead of herself. She didn't even know if Nora was really like that.

Mr. Pell and Mrs. Armstrong were also helping Nora. Now those two were definitely like that—involved. Mrs. Armstrong swatted Mr. Pell with a paper cutout and he grinned at her. They were gluing fun pieces to cardboard in an empty classroom. They had to get all the decorations done this week.

"We should've made the kids do it," said Mr. Pell, laughing. He was heavyset, kind, and harmless. And definitely sweet on plump Mrs. Armstrong. Perfect match, since both of them were married. Berry and Nora exchanged knowing glances when the two other teachers laughed, standing too close.

"The kids can't do it right," said Mrs. Armstrong, whose idea it had been for them to do it instead, and who had somehow won over the very straightforward Nora. "We can't have it botched when we put it up. We want it to look all nice and pretty." She had a very soft voice, almost like a child's.

"Well, let's not take all day," advised Nora, with a sophisticated smile.

***

Later, Nora and Berry sat across from each other at the table in the teachers lounge.

"Law school," said Nora. "Ambitious!" When Nora said that word, she made it sound so utterly magnificent. Berry beamed, gazing at her deeply.

"Well, James Meredith got into Columbia and a bunch of them got into top places," said Nora. "Just keep believing it, Berry, and you've got it too."

"Thanks, Nora."

"Your husband and kids prepared for the big change?" Nora asked. "You know how it is for us women with all these responsibilities."

"Oh," said Berry with a laugh. "No, I don't have any kids yet. But my husband, well, he's got to get used to it, you know. It's different. I'm different."

"Right," said Nora sagely.

"Right," said Berry. She cringed at herself. What she was realizing lately was that whenever she talked to Nora, she couldn't help but imitate her gestures and tone. She hoped Nora didn't notice. "I think Tommy will be fine though," Berry added.

"Do it before you get any kids," said Nora. "Once you get kids, honey, you won't have time for anything." She got to her feet and reached for her green lunch bag at the end of the table. "I need to clean this darned thing out. These bags just hold the worst stenches!"

Berry and Nora grew more familiar, talking in the lunch lounge and speaking to each other every day now. At the science fair, Nora said that she was just so glad that Berry was there to help her along with the others. In Nora's words, Berry could 'get the ball rolling.'

Mr. Pell mocked envy and said, "What about us?"

"You already know how to show up and show out," Nora said, rolling her eyes, and they all had a good laugh.

It was a good thing she had nice, normal co-workers who didn't carry on. Lots of the teachers had drama, but not the four of them. They were all great friends, laughing, flirting. Teaching was awesome if only those things counted. It wasn't so good though when summer break meant no pay, when winter break also meant no pay. Berry could do a lot better than this. She had to go to law school.

Chapter 49

In the dining room, a small opening with a table and two chairs that was connected to the equally small kitchen, Berry's stack of nonfiction books sat in a space carved out for her. Berry sat there when she wanted to get away from Tommy, which was often.

Tommy came into the dining room one evening, carrying a fork and a plate stacked with three large chocolate donuts. They looked yummy. She didn't bother asking him for any, though. He didn't like to share with her.

Reluctantly, she moved her feet so he could get the chair. She had to share with him.

"What you doing?" He dropped the plate on the table as he sat.

"What I always do," she said, picking up her pencil.

"You always talking smart."

She didn't say anything. He started on the donuts. She kept writing. She was working out the answer to a logical reasoning question, drawing a diagram for conditionals.

The pencil scratched across the paper as he munched. Berry glanced up. "Tommy, I can hear you chewing. It's—" She made an irritated gesture.

"Huh?" he said. "The hell wrong with you?"

"Nothing," she said. "But you're chewing really, really loud."

"I can't eat my fucking food?" he said, voice low.

"I didn't say that. I'm trying to study. And you're chewing. That's all."

He went silent again, just dead staring at her.

In the living room, the TV was loud. A man's voice and a woman's laughter.

She shouldn't have continued, but she did. "I have to study somewhere. I need quiet."

And why'd she say that for?

"I know you ain't tryna tell me where to go in my own daggone house," Tommy said.

"I'm not. I was just asking—"

He threw down the fork. It clattered to the floor.

Berry went rigid.

"Don't try to backtrack." He jumped to his feet. "You said what you said. You said you didn't want me in here and I heard you."

"Tommy, I didn't say that!" She pushed the book aside.

"You did. Stop lying. You said—"

"I didn't! I—"

He got up to her and loomed over her as she sat. "Don't you try to tell me what to do in my house," he shouted. "This is my motherfucking house."

She was as frozen as a cold piece of fish.

"If I wanna eat a motherfucking donut in my goddamn kitchen and I wanna smack it like an ass, I can!" Tommy yelled.

He stormed back to his seat. He finished the donuts, while she kept her eyes on her textbook. Her body was too stiff for her mind to comprehend the black and white lettering of the page. She had one thought: This was turning worse.

***

Berry and Tommy openly despised each other. Casual conversations always ended in fights. She could never say the right thing to him. Something always ticked him off. Her shaky feet tiptoed on eggshells. Many times, she threw up her hands and marched away. More often, she snarled back.

All the while, she packed more and more resentment towards him. He never gave her anything, he wasn't smart, he was only kind to her when he wanted her to sleep with him. Mean all day long, but 10 P.M. and his caressing hand was as soft as a lover's. Sometimes, and grudgingly, she submitted, because if she turned her back, he'd be rude to her for the next two days. Best to let him have it instead of enduring his sulking.

And now there was fear. The fear was frustrating. It put its hand around her throat and took her back to days when she was always, always afraid.

Sometimes she brought her frustration to school. She was quieter, teaching without a smile.

A wave from Nora would lighten her up. Often, sitting in the lounge, they'd laugh and talk for the whole hour. She'd forget everything, sitting in the lounge, laughing and gossiping with Nora.

***

Coming home was a dreadful thing now, because he was there. Inside the front room of the apartment, Berry set her bag on the floor. Those few peaceful hours before he got off work were heavenly. She made a quick dinner and decided to take a nap before grading papers. Her law school application was ready for six schools. She deserved a rest.

Berry slept later than she'd intended. It was past six when she woke up.

That strange intuition that came and went at times told her to get up. She moved without thinking. The TV was blaring. Tommy must be home. She opened the door and peeked out. He wasn't in the living room.

Curiously, she tiptoed to the kitchen. The lamp that sat on the edge of the table was on, yellow light draping the small room and casting a tall shadow.

She watched her husband cut pages out of her LSAT textbook with a small pair of black scissors that seemed too delicate for his big hands. Ridiculously evil, but she could believe it.

With a sigh, she walked right up to him. He jumped like he'd seen Jesus. The scissors clattered on the tabletop. The papers scattered to the floor.

"I was pranking you, Berry. I was just teasing." He threw his hands up and laughed.

She scooped up the papers. She took the LSAT book. She didn't say a single word. She put it all in her book bag and took it and went back to the bedroom, where she closed the door and firmly locked it.

***

"You should go to church," Berry told him later. She was sitting cross-legged on the couch, working as usual. It was Friday night and he'd come in from the club. He slumped beside her, reeking of liquor.

"Ain't nothing to that mess." He reached for the TV remote.

"Could be for you. You sure need something."

He turned the channel, not answering her. She studied his side profile. Why did he have to be so ornery when he could just listen to her and be a better person? She was far smarter than him, and she had only their best interests at heart.

"You need a purpose, Tommy," she said. "Your life needs a purpose."

"I don't want your pity, Berry."

"Oh, I don't pity you, Negro. Your state of life is your own fault."

They glared at each other before she turned away.

***

Berry did laundry one quiet evening. She was shocked at herself, standing as she did over the hamper, studying the collar of his beige shirt with a furrowed brow and a racing heart. This was ridiculous. She didn't love this man. She didn't even like this man. She wasn't heartbroken. She threw the clothes back into the hamper and slammed the lid closed.

She hadn't seen any other signs of other women, although there was a call that came in last night? But no, that was just Judas's aunt.

Fuck, Tommy. He was ruining everything. Did he have a single good quality?

There was no time to worry about that, not right now. It would upset her life too much. She had goals to achieve and then she'd figure out what to do with him.

Chapter 50

"Guess you gonna be uppity now," Tommy said, as they headed downstairs out of the apartment to the car. Berry held in her hand the crisp white letter of acceptance from the University of Pennsylvania to study law. The best letter of her life. And Tommy was ruining it.

"What?" she turned to him, glaring. "I'm not allowed to be happy?"

"Of course you're allowed to be happy."

"I don't see how that's uppity," she said. "You don't want me to be happy."

He was so annoying and stupid. She stuffed the letter into her coat pocket and rolled her eyes. They reached his car. He got in the driver's seat, and she got in the passenger side, but he didn't start up. His hands gripped the steering wheel.

"Berry," he said. "It ain't about you being smart. I don't give a fuck how smart you are, because you still need a man."

"Where's all this coming from," she scoffed, turning to stare out her window.

"You want to know what I'm thinking, so I'm telling you." He cranked the car.

"Right," she said sarcastically.

"Here's the thing," Tommy said. "You stay in school all your life, when you gonna find time to have children?"

"Tommy?" she said, swinging to face him. "I got into Penn Carey Law. An Ivy League school. Ivy fucking League. And you're talking about some damn kids."

He grunted and backed up so fast it made her head spin.

***

Tommy was even more riled up when he found out about the scholarship she received. Now she had free money! Not fair! She could pay for things better than he could at this rate. She tried to explain to him that goddamn it, Tommy, the money was for tuition and would all be put towards that. He was having none of it.

He made her angry then. She hissed, standing in the hall across from him, "You know what, Thomas? Why don't you do something, then? Why don't you do something that matters, then, instead of always worrying about what I'm doing?"

That started an argument of raised voices and him punching a wall. It ended with her running back into the bedroom, slamming the door and locking it, and sobbing.

She cried. When she wiped her tears, she realized she hadn't even had the chance to be happy for her wins, because she was so busy soothing and battling his insecurities.

She closed her eyes, put her head back against the bed and breathed. Reaching over to the bedside, she pulled the acceptance letter out of the envelope and reread it again with a smile, her chest gradually rising and falling more softly.

Chapter 51

Berry spent her time with Louise and Delanie, and Tommy spent his time at the club with Judas, spending up his money. Berry talked down to him whenever she felt like it. The labor it took to birth him was worthless, she said, but it didn't occur to her to leave him. He was simply a disappointment, just like pretty much every other man she'd ever met.

Everything was a disappointment sometimes. Lilah and Grandma Maple didn't know what "Ivy League school" meant, so it had little effect. Dr. Gladwell was sick when she phoned him to tell him and got into a coughing fit trying to congratulate her. And when she called Dr. Kelly and told her with a smile in her voice that she got into Penn Carey, Dr. Kelly said, after a very long pause: "Wow. I didn't think you could do that. I knew you could do something, but I didn't even get into a school like that myself, Berry."

Berry stilled, slightly confused. "What do you mean?"

Dr. Kelly went quiet. And suddenly, despite her short hair and her lack of a husband, her near-manliness, and her willingness to immerse herself in the Black world, Dr. Kelly was not a soul different from Mrs. Perscher.

Then, the woman hung up on her. Berry looked at the mouthpiece in shock when she heard the hang-up. It was actually unbelievable. So she encouraged Berry, praised her, and wrote Berry a letter of recommendation, but when Berry succeeded, then it was too much for her?

She tried to call again, but Dr. Kelly didn't answer.

Berry wasn't imagining things. Her success was quite literally making people angry. If she said it out loud she'd sound crazy, but she was staring right at it. Oh fucking well.

***

"Honey," Nora gasped. "No, honey, no, what's wrong?"

Berry was crying in her empty classroom, feeling overwhelmed by everything.

Nora sat on the desk and touched Berry on the shoulder.

"Man, life," said Berry, looking up at her and smiling through tears staining her face.

Nora poked out her lips. And squeezed Berry's shoulder.

"It's just so much," said Berry.

"I was overwhelmed when I started, too," said Nora. "You're not alone. Daniel helped me, thank goodness."

"You're so lucky," said Berry.

Nora stared at her with those piercing dark eyes.

"My husband hates me," said Berry. "I feel like a wildcat when I'm dealing with him." She smiled sadly again.

"What did he say about you getting into law school?"

"It's an Ivy League, Nora. An Ivy League school. And he can't just celebrate with me for once. Think about it. I'm an African American woman. Who got a scholarship. To a top school in the country. And he's talking about some stupid babies."

"Don't you let nobody stop you," said Nora, sitting next to Berry and shaking her head. "He can be mad all he wants. Everybody's mad when you try to do something good."

"I know," said Berry. "I know. I'd think my own husband would celebrate me, though."

"Berry," said Nora. "You've achieved a lot. A lot. More than most of us will do. Ever. You be happy for yourself. You be happy for you."

***

There was a week when Tommy was suddenly madder than a hatter. Berry avoided him meticulously all while wondering. Was there something wrong at the club? Was he upset because he was simply growing into a more unpleasant man? Was that even possible?

Then one night he came into the bedroom after she was already in bed. Although it wasn't an invitation, he climbed in beside her and moved close. Her back was turned and stiff. He put a hand on her side. "You sleep?" he said. His voice reminded her of the days when they were swinging and happy and going to the club together.

"Yes," she said. She still hated him.

He kissed the side of her face. So gently.

When she didn't respond, he flipped her onto her back. Their eyes met for a few seconds. She hated him so much, but she just wanted to be normal.

Chapter 52

A random, uncomfortable experience was the catalyst for the end of Berry's marriage. Women could get yeast infections from soap, jeans, wrong underclothes, new laundry detergent, or practically anything, but nothing that white nurse said was wrong, nonetheless. Always practice safe sex. Berry was sure it was because of Tommy.

That was the moment it all clicked. She was relieved it was nothing serious, but it was the bigger picture. Berry could've avoided every fight, frustration, everything, with Tommy if she simply hadn't slept with him. That was all she had to do. Not sleep with him. Right from the beginning.

She drove home resolved. No way to really know, it could've been the soap or the food or the seventy other things that could interfere with a woman's delicate body, but really, she might as well pin it on him. She was ready to leave him anyway, long before today. She took the stairs two at a time.

***

Berry was waiting for him when he walked into the apartment.

"Tommy," she said. It was the severe, final tone of her voice.

"What?" He draped his jacket over the chair.

"Tell the truth," she said.

He looked at her, his brows knitting in contempt.

"Did you sleep with anybody else?"

"Did I what?" His sneer deepened.

"I think you heard me."

"Why the hell you asking?"

"I think I have a right to ask, as your wife." Then she mentioned her doctor's visit.

"That's just women's things," said Tommy dismissively.

He went to the refrigerator. She came up behind him.

"You know what," she said, when he turned around, holding a cling-wrapped bowl, staring down at her. "It doesn't matter, because I'm leaving you," she whispered, her voice icy and sharp. "I just needed only a million reasons to."

His lip quirked up. His shoulders bristled.

"And I'm taking everything," she hissed, feeling a powerful urge to humiliate him. She wanted him to feel like shoe scum. "Out of this apartment. All my motherfucking things, please and thank you and fuck you."

He decked her before she saw it coming.

It took all the wind out of her. Her cheek burst into flames. She might've screamed once, and she certainly did again, when he half lifted her and then slammed her, this time into the side of the stove. And slammed her again.

"You got a smart, smart mouth," he hissed through gritted teeth, and they were grappling now because she realized that she had to fight for her life—it flashed before her eyes—she was absolutely useless against him, he was strong out of this world, and he shoved her one more time right back down where he'd lifted her up.

She tried to get in a strike—

The floor was cold. There was the sound of a door closing. Another door closing. And then the apartment was silent. Her face felt like a rock, and also pins, and also burning, all at the same time. Her arm was trapped underneath her. Her shoe was off. A strand of hair crawled into her mouth. And as her eyes moved, her gaze landed on the linoleum of the kitchen floor.

A flash before her. It all flashed before her.

Aunt Millie lying on the kitchen floor, a gaping hole in her skull. Pieces of her brains splattered. That could be Berry. Berry could be lying on the floor like that right now. Instead of pain, she could be as dead as a doorknob. Those brains could be her brains. That leg up and the skirt flying up could be her leg and her skirt. Her pain. Her murder. That could be her.

Standing over every fallen woman, there was a man.

Berry went down to the county clerk and filed for a divorce that very same evening.

Chapter 53

Louise came inside when Berry went back to the house to get her belongings. Delanie sat in the car and watched to see that Tommy didn't come by.

Bunking in the living room of Arthur and Louise's two-bedroom apartment (the second bedroom was like their storage and had a lot of things in it), Berry was starting over again. At some point before they crashed and she filed for a divorce, Tommy had reached under the couch and stolen the safe that kept her cash stash.

Four hundred dollars. Unbelievable.

Because Aunt Millie's story loomed, Berry didn't argue. She didn't go to the police either, because how could she prove she'd ever had the money? Also, she wanted the divorce to be as quick as possible. She'd be happy if she never saw Tommy again. She'd be happy if he died.

But the robbery cut deep. That was supposed to be her safety. Her plan. Her trust.

And he'd taken all that from her just like that.

So dumb to bring that fool from the club with her that night. That was an error of her own judgment.

Louise held Berry as they sat on her couch and let her cry. Berry wanted nothing more than her mother right then, but Louise held her. Louise, who was smart enough not to marry a man she met in the club. Louise married a man she met at university.

"Dear Jesus," Louise prayed, rocking Berry. "Please help us all. You see the wrong that man did, and vengeance is yours, Lord."

Berry's drying eyes focused on their intertwined hands.

In the same way she'd given up on God, she'd given up on men.

***

This was a nice setup, Berry thought as she looked around. Maybe, when she one day had her own house, her bathroom would be neat and bright like this with a pale blue trim and matching mats and little dots of the same on the white ceiling. She lay in the tub with her head resting on the rim, the water turning her skin pruny as she counted the time on the clock. Never let another filthy male near her body.

She was always right about these men, starting with her father. She should've never given them a try. She hated Black men, if she were honest. The thought made her laugh out loud, the sound echoing on the bathroom's clear wall.

Some of them were better than others, she supposed. Arthur, for example. Not that his exception was enough to convince her to change her judgment about the rule, but he was trying. At Louise's request, he'd swept here tonight before Berry came in. This whole apartment felt like a mansion, it was so clean. And Arthur helped Louise without grumbling.

Berry kept counting the ticks on the clock.

Why'd she get married? Because she was trying to be normal, trying to live the life that everyone else lived, trying to fit into a narrow system with everyone else.

Women got husbands because men had things women couldn't get. A man was a ticket—that was the whole reason for getting him. A man was supposed to provide a shelter, literally, a relief from the world. Tommy hadn't given Berry a thing. In fact, he'd taken from her. Joy, and four hundred dollars.

She'd often heard men and even other women making fun of women for saying they didn't need a man. Their mockery was dishonest, designed to guilt.

She'd never heed such lies again. She understood clearly now where she'd gone wrong. She'd signed herself up for pain. Honestly, she could probably get what she wanted on her own. Because what did men like Tommy have? All they had—mean words, small envious hearts, and flat wallets. No respect from their women, and no respect from the world. Absolutely useless.

Damn right she didn't need a man—not one like that.

Chapter 54

Nora lived in a beautiful, quiet neighborhood. Berry observed the square brick houses and the well-kept greenery as she rolled through the streets, going slowly so she wouldn't miss her destination. She had the right address, which she double-checked now on the wrinkled note lying beside her in the passenger seat. She pulled slowly into a dark cement drive and braked in front of the two-car garage, stopping on the side, just in case someone came up.

Hopefully no one came up, though.

So much freedom. Berry had been happily divorced for half a year.

The driver's window could stay cracked for the heat. Berry glanced in the mirror. Nora was so classy and perfect, Berry couldn't be any less of those things in her presence, or else she'd hate herself. She always critiqued herself on how well she performed before Nora when they chatted at school. Right now, her clear lip gloss gleamed, and her keen dark eyes stared back at her under lashes blackened even deeper with mascara.

Berry got out of the car and took a deep breath. The setup was as appealing as Nora. Clean-swept steps and pavement. Bright, soft flowers framed the porch rails. Dark brown shutters and a dark pink door. God, Berry loved that contrast. It reminded her of chocolate, of strawberries, of something tasty that she wanted to try.

Berry rang the bell. A second later the pretty pink door flew open.

"Honey, come in!" Nora held the door wide for her, allowing Berry to step into the foyer.

"Do you take off your shoes?" Berry asked, immediately noticing the shoe rack.

"House rule," said Nora. "Ever since I got Daniel to obey. I almost forgot with you!"

They laughed. Nora waited as Berry placed her sneakers on the rack. Berry felt delicate, tiptoeing behind Nora across her squeaky-clean wood floors.

Berry secretly wanted a tour, but Nora took her straight to the living room, where they sat on a cushy gray couch at opposite ends.

"Make yourself comfortable," Nora encouraged. "Be free here!"

Berry studied the scenery when Nora went to the kitchen. The curtains were a lovely shade of lime—remarkable because God knows that phrase was an oxymoron. A large glass end table sat in the center and two on the side. Two black mirrors hung beside a painting of a valley. The darker green reached out, somehow, to complement the curtain's green. Berry was awash in a powerful feeling of conscientious comfort. It felt as if someone had said, Let's make this more than a house, let's build it with love. The little pieces of art decor. The bravery to depart from a theme and return to it in bits. Berry loved it.

She was sitting with her legs drawn up when Nora returned with a tray of sugar cookies and two cups. "Lemonade," said Nora, winking. "I know you have to drive back."

Berry felt stung. Did she really have to drive back? There was time. She glanced at Nora with a pang. Daniel was out, Nora had said before Berry came over. He was in South Carolina visiting his family. Nora never went. She detested her mother-in-law. And the kids were away.

"Thanks." Berry took a cup.

"So what do we have? Do we have any plans for the summer before the big event? Or should I say, the big series of one event. You'll be in law school for three years."

"If you can call my plans working in a laundromat," said Berry, getting over the small, silly feeling of being slighted. "Then yes, that's something."

Nora laughed. "I know," she said. "Every summer I get so restless. I try to do a little something, but Daniel says, Don't worry about it, sweetheart. But I'm thinking, I'm used to that check, and I need it."

"Exactly." Berry nodded vigorously. She finished the lemonade.

Nora had turned on the TV. They watched in silence for a while, heads resting against the couch. Neither of them ate the cookies.

"I try to limit my television," said Nora after a while, looking at her. "But every time I sit down, it's like I fall into a black hole. And there I go, boom, for hours." She flicked her fingers out. Berry laughed.

Nora turned the light down several shades and made herself comfortable with a plush cream blanket. Berry relaxed completely. Neither of them had expressly stated the meaning of the visit, but there was a feeling. It was always important to sense the spirit of intentions. Berry felt this spirit heavy.

Daniel in South Carolina. The twin sons, Michael and Matthew, at summer camp.

Nora rocked herself. That was her little tic. She smoothed her hair as they watched TV. The time seemed to pass by so slowly, and so quickly, equally, and in the best ways.

A sense of lull. Drinking lemonade, chatting casually.

They were closer together. Berry had moved and Nora had moved. It was the right time. Berry leaned in, and Nora leaned in. Their lips met. Berry couldn't believe she was actually doing it, but she was. Nora smelled divine, like cinnamon. She became more forthright in her kisses, and then she took the lead.

Her hand slid up Berry's side, a gentle but intent press. Berry undid a button. And Nora's hand went in and cupped her breast, feeling over the bra. Then she did something that was too cool. She slid her hand across Berry's back and undid the bra. It fell quickly, easy. And only a woman could do that.

Their lips met again. Legs and knees and thighs collided. Berry didn't want to rush it and seem inappropriate, but all the same, the woman had her whole perfect mouth on the skin above her breast. Her skin burned and she was filled with need, need, need. Her hand found the tender, bare warm flesh of Nora's hip. She moved left.

Berry hesitated, because she'd only ever done it with...

She couldn't think about Jo now. Berry stroked. Nora gasped.

"Not here," said Nora, pulling up breathlessly. "We can't do it in the living room."

And Berry just couldn't believe it was happening, still couldn't believe it. They got off the couch. She and Nora crossed the hall, and Nora reached back, grabbed her hand, and led her into the bedroom.

Nora turned on the lamp and yellow, comforting light rushed in as Berry sat on the bed. Berry was aware of her cuffed jeans. Why had she worn them? That's what doubt brought—complications. Her bare chest, she covered with an arm over herself, which Nora came to and kissed again. They moved back onto the covers.

"I always thought," Berry said in a reverent whisper, "That you were so, so sexy."

Her hands brushed Nora's arms. Nora's knee wedged between Berry's legs.

"We gotta get you out of these jeans, honey," whispered Nora. Berry was already electric. Her palm smoothed over the delicate, hardened nipple under Nora's t-shirt.

Chapter 55

Sex was supposed to be fun, and indeed they did have fun. They did it over and over and over—and over, and over again. Lying on her back on the heavy, luxurious mattress, Nora patted a towel between her legs and said, "I can't even feel it anymore." Beside her, Berry dissolved into soft laughter.

"It's ridiculous," Berry said breathlessly. Her hand rested on her pattering chest. She held her drawn up knees together. Her whole body trembled.

"Heaven is a place on earth," Nora murmured dreamily, her arms above her head.

Nora was pristine in public. It was so jarring and stunning to gaze at her naked body now. And the things she could gasp and say when her legs were apart. Berry felt emptiness, awe, and satisfaction all at once. This fun, crazy game.

She closed her eyes and turned her head to Nora. They kissed slowly.

"I think there's enough feeling back for us to do it again," Nora whispered after a while.

"I only needed two minutes," said Berry, and they tangled themselves again.

***

One could not party all night, alas. The sun really did have to come up. Or, in this case, the day had to go on. Nora went into the bathroom and stayed for a long time. When she came out, she wore a simple white shift and her straightened hair was flat again. Berry was curled up on the bed, covered in the plush blanket. She'd dared not go back to the living room because who knew what good things could happen if she stayed nearby and waited for round number whatever?

She'd needed this kind of sex so badly.

"This is just too hard to have on, ugh." Nora scooped up Berry's crumpled jeans, shook them, and folded them. Berry sat up suddenly. Nora laid the folded jeans on the bed.

"Let me find you something easier to wear for this weather," she said. "No jeans in the summertime, honey."

But they were such cute jeans! And they'd revealed her nice ankles. Berry had fine, slender ankles.

Nora slid her closet door back to reveal a jaw dropping collection of color coordinated tops, skirts and dresses, complete with racks of various colored and designed shoes. Berry forgot that she was topless and leaned forward.

"Nora, you are living it up," she gasped in wonder.

"Hm?" said Nora. She was swiping through things on the hanger.

And then Berry had a chance to really see the bedroom for the first time. It was spacious, the bed was large. and the sheets were crisp white. There was a stark white rug on the floor, too. Everything was beautiful, including the woman looking through her closet. Longing tugged at Berry like a rope.

Nora held up a white shirt and a pale cream skirt.

"I think you can fit this," she said and tossed them. Berry caught it. It would be embarrassing having to dress in front of Nora—why was it more embarrassing to be seen dressing than undressing? But Nora had already turned around to re-tidy her selection.

Berry got into the clothes. They even smelled like Nora, like cinnamon.

They faced each other, shared a smile, and exchanged a quick kiss.

Berry was going to have a closet like Nora's one day. Organized, categorized, colorful, and full. Well built. She was going to be pristine and fancy. One day just like Nora.

"Good thing you don't have to worry about driving back," said Nora, as they left the bedroom, squeezing Berry's hand. "We only drank lemonade."

Chapter 56

Having to leave so soon stung a little. Not that Nora explicitly rushed Berry away. They'd talked more in the foyer. But it would've been nice to have sat around and played with the art in the living room, and tinkered at the kitchen table, and watched TV, and had each other one more time, or three more times, before having to leave.

But Nora wasn't free. It didn't matter how much of a kind friend she was outside of the bedroom. Nora had a life already. Nora had a husband and two children.

Not that Berry cared. She didn't give a damn about anybody's husband. A man could go fuck himself, for all she cared.

Maybe she and Nora would do it again. That, she looked forward to.

So much to look forward to, really. She'd start Penn Law this fall. She was really Ivy League bound! And she'd divorced that useless user, and slept with a woman so fine and hot they burned the bedroom down. She had no husband, no god, and no money. She didn't mind not having the first two things. She could work for the money.

Her life was on the upswing. She moved out of Arthur and Louise's apartment, which was greatly relieving. Her new place was small, and her savings were meager, but she promised herself she wouldn't stay there. One day, she swore to herself every day, she'd have a closet like Nora's, in her own beautiful house.

Chapter 57

Eight years ago and a girl named Josephine Walker. Often Berry wondered, where was that child now? They'd fought like their hearts depended on it when the two of them were forced to break. In hindsight, their situation made complete sense. Berry had to do what was best for herself, and Jo had to do what was best for herself. It would've been nice if they could've stayed together, but life wasn't always convenient like that.

Berry remembered like yesterday how she'd felt for Jo. She was a gagging, drowning fish out of water when taken from any world that lacked Jo. That was how she felt those next months, when Jo refused to come to Philadelphia with her and tore her heart to pieces.

It was a shame they'd gone so long without talking. Emotions were high as the sky, and they were girls. They were crazy. They were immature. She knew now. It was all so foolish. Their situation was impossible, but she wished they'd at least stayed in touch.

They'd been so, so close, and it happened so fast. No wonder it went all wrong.

Berry purchased six gigantic phone books and started looking.

She sat on the tiny couch in her tiny living room, flipping the pages. Variations of names in dark ink on faded paper swam before her eyes until she fell asleep, night after night. No Josephine Walker. Maybe Jo changed her name? What if she got married too? Not everybody's name was in the phonebook.

Twice, Berry sat in the new used car she'd bought and thought of driving to New York.

Twice, her fingers tapped the steering wheel.

But what street would she drive to? And she got out of the car and went back inside.

She didn't know where to look. Because Jo might still be in New York, but the phonebooks said she wasn't. Not that the phonebooks had it all correct. Maybe she was in Virginia, Maryland, California, or Texas. It was impossible to find her in lists of all these people.

After weeks of pondering and searching, Berry gave up.

But she sure would've liked to find her best friend. She thought about that a lot after her affair with Nora. She thought about Jo.

She needed that kind of friendship. Nothing and no one else could compare.

***

Yes, Louise and Delanie were wonderful to her, absolutely wonderful. No, Berry told her mother and grandmother on the phone, they didn't have to come up, she was alright. When Berry moved into yet another tiny apartment closer to the university, her girlfriends helped her set up her things.

"Girl, I am so, so proud of you!" said Louise. Bangles jangling, she grabbed Berry and kissed her on both cheeks. Delanie set out red wine for them in glasses. And their conversation was wonderful and hilarious as usual.

But they weren't Berry's best friends. They couldn't know her biggest secret. And they weren't obsessive. Berry needed a friendship that felt so real it made her heart hurt. She needed a love so deep that it shook her soul.

No, no she didn't. She'd had that before and it almost killed her, in 1961.

But she still wanted it. She still wanted Jo.

Chapter 58

There was nothing like law school, and maybe there would never be anything like it. Because law school was where Berry learned to think.

In law school, Berry also learned to speak. In classes full of mostly white and male students, heads would whip around if she said, "Nah, I don't think that's true."

Instead, Berry learned to say, "Actually, I disagree with that sentiment."

By the time she was near the end of her first semester, she was nearly unrecognizable to herself. She'd ruthlessly discarded her former casual speech. And she had even less faith than she ever had in the goodness of other human beings. She'd always hated most people, and now there was one more confirmation for her hatred: the unethical ones in her classes.

In conlaw class, they always ended up off topic somehow, talking about poverty, war, crime, greed, human rights. Berry's thoughts were generally the opposite of whatever the others said.

"Why would you say that starvation due to inflation is not an issue of a country's leadership?" Berry asked once.

She was in a back-and-forth exchange with Grant Thurston, who always said the cruelest things in the most casual tone. It was almost fascinating, how ridiculous he was.

"No," said Grant. He was a preppy white boy who always spoke very quickly. "I didn't say it wouldn't be an issue for them. I said that they have no moral obligation towards those citizens who are hungry, because that's a function of hegemony. If the citizens prefer the leader to be their leader, they also accept the situation of that leader's leadership."

Berry stared at him, and people stared at them.

People always stared at her, like she came from some other planet.

It didn't matter one bit. She'd come this far. There was no turning back.

Soon, she was no longer baited into conversations about politics or ethics. She realized after a few conversations that she didn't need to comment on everything. She wasn't the representative for justice. She was here for a good education so she could get a better job and a beautiful house.

She'd only speak now to earn a grade, as everyone was required to do for participation.

She worked, went to class, studied, and slept, over and over again. She was so busy that she forgot that giving up was an option.

***

Nora quit their affair after a few more rounds, although Berry still wanted to sleep with her. But Nora was going on a sex cleanse. She'd told her husband that she was devoting her body to God. Nora was tired of sex. Berry still wanted her. The woman was a god.

Nevertheless, Nora and Berry hung tight. Nora introduced Berry to her unsuspecting husband and Berry was allowed to visit as if everything were perfectly innocent. She came to the house one Saturday, walked right past Daniel, who was standing on the bottom step, and waved gaily at him. He waved back, showing a big smile. He was a broad shouldered man who wore glasses, and he looked like a sucker, because his wife had sexed Berry in his house, right in their bed, right behind his back.

Berry and Nora sat at the kitchen table to have lunch. Daniel came back into the house and passed the kitchen, then came back wearing a blue baseball cap. He was headed out to whatever men liked to do. The boys were at their grandmother's. Nora's mother-in-law had moved from South Carolina to Philly that month.

"You ladies have fun," Daniel said, without a touch of irony.

Nora burst out laughing and Berry smiled, feeling her expression turn into a smirk. She hid it by lifting her glass of lemonade and drinking. Daniel looked perplexed, but kissed his wife on the cheek anyway. She tittered louder. And then he was out the door.

When he was good and gone, Nora turned to Berry over their sandwiches and chips.

"I have something to share," she said, her eyes sparkling as they always did.

"Tell me," Berry begged. The way Nora dangled it was so thrilling.

"You're going to love it," said Nora, grinning.

"So tell me!" said Berry.

Nora finally told her: it was a poetry club of 'like-minded women', and Berry was invited tonight. "You'll love it," promised Nora. "And they will like you."

***

A few hours later, Berry walked into a nearby apartment living room, following on Nora's heels.

The space was full of women. Three sat on the floor on pillows, two were on the couch, and another two occupied armchairs. There was room on the carpet where a handful of other women sat, and Berry paused near the door as she stood behind Nora, taking it all in.

Illuminated theatrically by the lamplight, one woman was already reading as she stood at the front of the gathering, near the bay windows. She had dark skin and was willowy, dressed in a long black skirt and a cream cashmere sweater. Fashionable too, wearing deep burgundy lipstick and a perfectly circular afro. Berry immediately wanted to stop straightening her own hair, looking at her.

"And if my black is beautiful," said the woman. "Why am I changing it?"

She concluded the poem. The women clapped and there were some murmurs.

"Say hello to our new arrival," said the woman in the first armchair then, turning to Nora and Berry. All eyes went to them. Nobody had heard them come in.

"Ladies, this is Berry Smith," said Nora, stepping closer to the group. "She's from North Carolina." Nora snapped her fingers. "And get this, ladies. Berry is a law school student at Penn Carey." Oohs went around the room. "Right? Fancy pants girl. Anyways, she's good people. Like-minded."

All eyes were on Berry. She waved.

The women just kept on looking at her.

"You told her the rules?" said the leader, Eris, in an aside, when the others resumed talking. Eris was the one in the armchair. She was a thick light skin woman wearing a black, witchy looking dress. Her hair was curly on top and tapered at the temples. Her gold hoops were massive.

"You know I wouldn't bring anybody I didn't know, Eris," said Nora.

"Alright," said Eris. "Welcome, Berry." They exchanged a few pleasantries, Berry leaning down to shake her hand because Eris didn't stand up for her. Eris had a hard look in her eyes. This was swinging the pendulum from Helen Crew to Eris Howard.

Someone bought pizzas and set them on the floor. Everyone was free to dive in. Ringed hands and jeweled wrists moved forward. It was such an amazing, unifying experience, it was like coming in from the cold. And yet Berry couldn't stop worrying. Would they judge her, would they dislike her?

"Ivy League," said Amara, the woman who'd been reading the poem. She leaned over. Her face was kind. "So you must be smart. Smartypants."

"You don't get in being dumb," said Berry. "If I say so myself." She laughed.

"Where are you from again?" asked the last woman sitting on the couch. She had bald eyes, deep skin, and a shawl on her shoulders. She regarded Berry coolly.

Berry told her.

"Oh, yeah," said the woman, never smiling. "I can hear it in your accent."

Everyone got quiet on that number. Then movement resumed. So it was things like that.

***

One dusky evening, Berry smoked her first cigarette. She and Amara stood next to the street light at the end of a road near the poetry group's apartment. Out of the new tribe, Berry had clicked best with Amara. Amara was closer to her age, not as sharp as Nora, had a funny, blunt side, and Berry was utterly relaxed with her. Their friendship felt like a sisterhood, or a cousinhood.

"Once you stop coughing," said Amara, as Berry sputtered. "You get the hang of it."

Amara had work in the morning, and Berry had class and work. Nonetheless, here they were.

The tobacco was oddly soothing. Berry watched the white smoke she exhaled float in front of her face and curl up and fade away. She felt marvelous, odd, and cleansed. She took another puff and blew out again. She was mysterious, sexy, marvelous, with a cigarette between her fingers and her eyes half-lidded.

"Have you ever tried drugs?" Amara whispered.

"Drugs aren't for me," said Berry. "It's sick, people get addicted."

"Yeah," said Amara. "Don't do drugs. Drugs are shit."

And they blew out again.

Chapter 59

Joseph Goldstein had a second semester class with Berry, and he always sat next to her. The others kept a cool distance. Nothing personal. No need to be anything other than professional. But that was where Berry liked to keep it too, because she had very little to do with most people, white or black.

But Joseph was alright. The first time in her life she'd ever had a long, genuine conversation with a white person was with Joseph, who just so happened to be Jewish and Southern. He was from Birmingham, Alabama, and his accent was deeper than hers. He had a mop of brown hair and a serious face with a squinting, thoughtful gaze. He was only a few years behind her, but the way he carried himself made him look older.

"The work's hard," said Joseph, as they left the class together. "But I think we're also gonna pretty much coast along until finals."

"You think?" said Berry. "I'm not so sure." She was overwhelmed by studying, but she had no idea what to expect from the first year, not even from a single class. She'd done her best regardless. Hopefully he was right.

"So how are you liking it here?" Joseph asked. They stopped on the ramp facing the parking lot.

She looked him in the face. "Amazing and crazy," she said honestly.

He smiled.

***

"You must like me," said Joseph as she passed him one of her cigarettes. They smoked together in the Biddle Law Library after they ran into each other there that evening.

"I like people if they're nice," said Berry, shrugging. She felt so good, smoking. The nicotine went to her head. So amazing. It soothed her nerves and made her whole again.

"We should make a study group," he said. "Me, you, my buddy Max and David."

She looked up in surprise. She'd never hung out with white people before. She couldn't help but narrow her eyes. "Study together?"

"Hey," said Joseph, turning a slight shade of pink. "It's all good if—" He spread his hands, put the cigarette back to his lips. She looked away at the row of shelves, and she suddenly realized that it was as awkward for him as it was for her. And that he'd taken a huge step, even to offer.

She did need to study. And it would be nice if she didn't have to do it alone.

And they were humans, it didn't need to be this hard. Did it?

"Thanks for the invitation," Berry told him, taking her cigarette out and shrugging again. "I'm down to join. When do you meet?"

Chapter 60

The white men at the table looked at her like she sported a horn, but otherwise no one commented on her. Introductions were made. Joseph was nice, David was good-looking, and Max was cocky. White people looked alike at first. Upon closer inspection, there were differences. And certainly in personality.

Joseph was down-to-earth, David was interesting, and Max was standoffish, which was the most familiar of all the white personalities to Berry. Her life just got stranger with each new chapter. Here she was, in a study room of the library, wearing a fro because obviously, black was beautiful by now. And these were her new reluctant, curious, and accepting study partners.

***

Determined to make a good impression, Berry went out of her way to prove that she was smart. She didn't want to lose the group because she'd found, after all, that she did indeed need other students.

Joseph and David were just people. Every time white people behaved like normal humans, Berry was shocked. In terms of personality, they were actually two of the kindest people she had ever met, which was greatly confusing to her, for obvious reasons.

Max was different. He rarely spoke to her or looked her in the eye. And he never, ever wanted to listen to her. Let Joseph or David say it, and it might be true, but never Berry. Max always squinted at her, like she'd said something confusing even when she said nothing at all.

"It's answer A," he said, refuting her once at the library table.

"I still believe it's going to be D," she said calmly.

Max shook his head. Berry resisted rolling her eyes.

"Let's just look at it and see," said David neutrally.

"I could see it being D," Joseph said.

"Alright then," said Max.

The answer, of course, was D.

Outlines, papers, cases, and practice exams. They stayed immersed. The boys had other connections, but Berry only had their group. That was probably why Joseph took pity on her.

They found out where they stood academically at the end of their first year in law school. Berry was clean ahead of Max, who had acted like he knew the most.

She had an edge over Joseph, who didn't jump to conclusions.

And she was neck and neck with David, but she'd still done better than him, too.

Berry was at the top of her class.

***

Berry was smarter than them. A big wall came tumbling down in her head. Nobody was better than anyone else just because of the color of their skin or their size of their money or the shape of their parts or the location of their hometown. But if anyone was better after all, it was her, the Black woman. She was smarter than the men in her study group. They just so happened to be white. And she just so happened to be smarter than them. That gave her a new found confidence.

She wouldn't have had that new confidence if she hadn't made that observation.

All year long, she'd worried. Worried that she wasn't good enough, that she didn't fit in here, and that she couldn't handle the program. Worried because there were so many whites and she was one of the few blacks. Because so many people stared at her and walked around her.

All her life she'd worried. Worried that deep down, what if all those things they said were true. About her hair, her skin, her mind. Amara showed her that her afro looked better than any burned straight style. Joseph, Max, and David taught her that their supremacy was a lie. All these things she'd had to unlearn, and she didn't even know she believed them, that was the scary part. Those messages did one heck of a job, making people feel that God made some people greater than others. But it wasn't true, it wasn't true, and she was living proof.

Chapter 61

If law school stressed her, the poetry club entertained her. Berry herself never wrote. She wrote enough in pursuit of her degree. But Amara, Nora, and the others were prolific. Sometimes, they'd get into disagreements when one critiqued another. Their sophisticated voices flung rapid, sharp words. Berry watched and smothered laughter.

Countless discussions on men and the patriarchy were also interesting. Berry also told the story of her ex-husband, which earned her points. Oh, the woes of tying oneself to a man. They'd all realized at some turning point in their lives that they were simply signing up for slavery, taking up with a man.

Phyllis, the woman who'd challenged Berry's accent, talked the most. Phyllis had something to say about everyone and everything. The women let her have her way. She was not a person Berry would like to have a run-in with, seeing as Phyllis had recruited half of the members on Eris's behalf.

The group had cliques. Berry and Amara. Selena, Phyllis, and Cokey. And so on.

Eventually, Berry found out Nora was sleeping with Eris, and that Nora was in love with her, and that Eris had made Nora tell her husband Daniel that she was on a sex-cleanse, her words. Berry saw the love note from Eris to Nora in Nora's glove compartment when they were parked on Berry's street one day. She read it before Nora could snatch it.

"You know, why don't you leave him?" said Berry. "Why don't you just leave?"

And why'd she say that for?

"You think I want to be a single mommy?" Nora snapped.

Berry threw her shoulders up, but she'd said the wrong thing to Nora.

"It's already enough of that," said Nora. "I always told myself I'd have a man for my kids, and I do. I'm not raising my kids alone."

"You have your friends to help you," said Berry. "You have tons of girlfriends who'd do anything for you. I'd do anything for you."

"None of you could raise my kids."

"Okay, and I thought that's what we all said was possible? That women could have their kids and raise them together? You don't believe your own ideology then. I knew no one really believed that, because nobody's doing it in our group."

"Be so for real, Berry. No one wants children after you get them. I had them before I learned who I was."

"No, I am being so for real." She did air quotes. "Eris loves you."

She was so jealous of Eris. Berry also didn't believe women should have children without their husbands, which was part of why she'd never had any by Tommy, who deep down she always knew that eventually she would leave.

"Get out of my car," said Nora. "Now you talking mad. And with that trifling smoke."

Berry, cigarette in hand, crumpled the note, got out of the car and glared through the window at Nora. She stuck up her middle finger. Nora waved her hand in front of her face, wrinkled her pretty nose, and put the car in gear and sped off.

***

Berry grew away from Nora and closer to Amara. Her new friend's name hadn't been Amara when she was born. It was Mary. But Mary just sounded so boring and old lady-ish. And like Berry, Amara had rejected men, gods, and traditional culture. When she graduated high school, she changed her legal name to Amara. Amara Watson. She was from Virginia. She had a record breaker on Berry—she was married all of seven months to her ex-husband Hugo. She'd had two abortions and no children. She'd always known she was a lesbian. But she'd married a man to get out of the house. And slept with a few rich ones too, in hard times.

"Did you always know you were gay?" she asked Berry, when they were casually lying on the floor of Amara's living room.

"I'm just who I am," said Berry. She'd never, ever been comfortable with the label. When Amara looked mildly disappointed, Berry added, "I guess so. Yeah, I did."

"You're so cool," said Amara.

"So are you," said Berry.

They kissed each other lightly, in a friendly way. A kiss meant nothing. Any woman could kiss her friend. That was just kindness.

They weren't attracted to each other. They were just great friends. Berry gave Amara a bracelet with charms, a sweater, and a record. Amara gave Berry books on radical feminism, holistic healing, and geology. "I know you like theory and knowledge!" said Amara. Berry did. She promised to read them when she had the time.

***

Amara and Berry talked about their ex-husbands until they were tired of talking about them. They made retroactive discoveries about the wickedness of the men they'd foolishly brought into their lives. They uncovered the secrets of the world, race, and the falsehoods of religion. They talked about things no one could understand but them. Berry loved every moment. Pouring out her heart cleansed her soul.

Amara always wore her splendid afro. "Black was always beautiful," she'd tell Berry.

And Berry would nod. "They didn't want us to know because they're jealous they can't grow what we have…" And she'd think of the first time she realized the beauty, when she looked at Jo Walker. But now she understood it even more, not out of desire only, but logically, intellectually.

Amara said that healing was from within.

"Teach me your ways, Amara," Berry always said, laughing.

Amara said she would, if Berry stayed around her long enough.

"Sisterhood comes first," Amara always said.

***

But sisterhood didn't mean liking every woman ever. Amara and Phyllis hated each other. They'd cussed each other out multiple times. Phyllis had control issues. When she gave Berry a sniffy look for walking in with Amara, Berry glowered right back. There were so many cliques in this group, but everybody kept on coming.

Fights couldn't break them up. They wanted to be around each other. They had to be around each other. No matter how much they fought, they longed for each other. They found safety in each other. They loved each other.

Regular clubs were nice, gay clubs were better. In the summer, Berry took an easy job just like before and spent the rest of her time hanging with Amara. Everybody wanted to get down. Nobody wanted to get down more that summer. They were sexy in chunky heels, big hair, and bellbottoms. Hurrying to escape black men who whistled at them and white men who gazed at them. Berry smoked more than she drank. She was in love: with cigarettes.

Chapter 62

Berry sat in a circle of red plush library chairs, waiting for Joseph. They were friendly enough with each other to be interested in catching up before classes started again. She quite liked their association.

She didn't have to wait long before he appeared from the stacks. He walked towards her with his hands tucked in his jeans, shoulders somewhat stooped as usual. He was such an old man. She smiled.

"Ready for the next beatdown?" She was in a good enough mood to joke.

He sighed and rolled his eyes. "I never got a break. My internship felt like class."

Internship? She stared at him. "Oh? What did you do? Who'd you do that with again?"

He named some firm, said something about business. She nodded because she didn't know what he was talking about. And then he told her that David and Max had also done internships, both of them in corporate firms. She was confused as she listened. Was this something she was supposed to have done?

"What about you?" Joseph asked. It was an innocent question, but they came from different worlds. And suddenly no answer was right. He was looking expectantly, and maybe just a little hesitant as he asked. He had to know she didn't know what he knew.

"Oh," she said, thinking fast. "I took a holistic break." It was the first thing that came to her head. Holistic sounded rich, edgy. His face cleared, and he nodded like that was wonderful.

"Yeah, oh yeah," he said. "That's good too. Did you travel?"

"I had surgery," she lied. "I should've told you. I had to get my appendix taken out. So that put me out of commission for a few weeks. And then I needed to get my head together, so I did a religious seminar and just relaxed."

"Berry, no! You didn't tell me. How are you feeling?"

"Well, I'm awesome now."

"That's good, that's good. Gosh, that is holistic."

The conversation moved elsewhere, to her relief.

She felt like a fool after he left. She hadn't even thought about the possibility of doing an internship. She was, after all, doing this alone. No one was going to drag her by the hand and tell her, Here's how you go about setting up your life and paving the way for yourself. She didn't know any lawyers. Meanwhile, Joseph's father was a lawyer, David's father was a lawyer, and Max's uncle and father were both lawyers.

But if she couldn't do research for herself, her ignorance would be her own undoing.

And dang it, hadn't she heard professors mentioning internships, too? She never paid it any mind. She hadn't felt brave enough to walk up and inquire about that anyway. She was tired of people snubbing her when she spoke up or asked questions.

Excuses. This was so embarrassing. She needed to get her act together.

***

Joseph invited her to a get-together at his apartment. She readily accepted. She decided she'd better start hanging out with white people if she wanted to know what they were doing. Then, when someone mentioned some obscure and important rule she needed to know but didn't, she could glean it.

She'd moved into a different position in her small academic circle, and it wasn't because of charity. She was smart, indispensable to the group. And Joseph truly liked her.

The apartment was in a quiet neighborhood on the second floor. In the living room stood several of her classmates, including David and Max, but there were also new faces—one with color. There was an Indian law student, Adam Singh. No way his real first name was Adam. He was probably trying to fit in. He wouldn't even look at her. Whatever, she thought.

There were two other girls, one of whom was David's girlfriend. David and his girlfriend stood outside on the ground floor arguing for the first ten minutes of the party. Max whispered a joke about them to Joseph, who just shook his head. Max was smiling, but as soon as he met Berry's gaze, his face turned blank. She turned her back to him.

The other girl and Adam Singh were having a conversation.

"I'll just have to prove to them that I'm not there to bring coffee," Tricia said. "They seem to think that's what female interns are for. But overall, it was a learning experience."

"I'm glad you liked it," said Adam Singh. He was very talkative with Tricia.

Tricia asked Berry what she did. She gave a similar answer to the one she gave before.

David came back without his girlfriend. He'd taken her home and they were fine, he said, but his handsome face looked annoyed. The group occupied a circular couch to watch TV, which had been playing all this time in the background.

Meanwhile, Tricia chattered on and on about her ski trip that winter before. She had no time now, law school took all her time away! Joseph, between her and Berry, entertained her. His girlfriend complained about the same thing as Tricia, he said. Tricia laughed at that, she had a bright, irritating laugh.

That same question again, this time from Adam, who finally decided to acknowledge her. What had Berry done this summer?

And again, Berry answered the same: a holistic break.

"Her appendix died," said Joseph.

"What?" said Adam.

"It's okay," she said easily, hoping to get away from the subject. "Happens."

They broke out drinks. Max arranged neat lines of pure white powder on a small square mirror and took a long snort. He sighed, got up, and went to the other room, with Tricia on his trail begging him and David following. Eventually, the trio returned, looking happier.

Someone increased the TV volume. Berry lit up. She passed one to Joseph because, like her, he could never stand to see a cigarette without smoking it. David, sitting next to her now, looked over. Their eyes met and caught.

"Can I have one too?" he whispered. She gave him one, their fingers brushing. He lit too, and the three of them blew smoke all over the room together.

***

People liked coke, alcohol, or prayer, and Berry liked cigarettes. It was all about what could carry a person through. Often, it was a good piece of nonfiction. Berry started a book about the Russian Revolution and couldn't shut up about it. She found it so fascinating. Eventually, she brought it to the poetry group.

"People revolt," she said. "When they don't like something."

She'd always felt isolated in the Black American experience. And it was unique for them, wearing their identity on their skin and faces. Double or triple that for the women. But cause and effect was happening everywhere, all the time. And everything was connected. She'd never realized it. She wanted to talk about it.

"The Russian Revolution isn't poetry," Eris snapped, from where she occupied her arm chair. "Let them do what they do over there. Whites are wacky everywhere."

"You have to look at other people and learn from them," said Berry.

"Berry is a second-year law student," chimed in Amara. "Let her speak."

"Never drown out your sister's voice," Nora added. She and Berry were cordial again.

"I'm not drowning out her voice," said Eris. "I'm just asking everyone in the group to stay on topic."

"But it is on topic," said Berry. "We can look at it and ask, what can we as Black women develop or learn from others?"

"Exactly," said Amara.

"Fine," said Eris. "Tell us more."

***

"We have to talk about this," David said, visibly excited as he trailed Berry down the hall of the main campus building. "In great detail."

She looked over her shoulder and grinned at him.

David appreciated Berry's obsession with the Russian Revolution. Her study partner had been a fan of historical conspiracies for a long time. David Heigl was from Europe—Switzerland, to be exact—and he'd seen all the famous landmarks on the continent and had an opinion on all the major events there. He was pretty sure Grand Duchess Anastasia was still alive.

"I think she died," blurted Berry. "I really do."

"I don't want to believe that, Berry! Ah! No."

"But there's no way they would've let her live. They would've made sure everybody was dead, dead. When I read that story, I get this feeling they made sure." She shuddered.

That weekend, when she joined the group in their library study room, David reached for his bag and pulled out a thin book. She took her seat. "Oh? What's this?"

"Thought you might like it," he said.

She took it and read the title: *The Eighteenth Brumaire of Louis Bonaparte.* Karl Marx.

"You want me to read it?" she said, uncertain.

"I'm giving it to you. It's yours."

"Oh, thank you!" She hid her surprise.

"No thing. Tell me what you think."

She finished it the next day and called him to tell him. He was so delighted to hear it. They began talking more, always about class or international events. Once, David walked her to her car, where he stood, fervently disagreeing with her about the French philosopher Voltaire.

"He was preposterous sometimes—" He made a gesture.

She laughed. "Yes, but the satire of his style..."

It wasn't about who was right. The truth was that Berry liked to argue. Going back and forth made her feel smart. God, she loved to feel smart. David liked to feel smart, too. Back and forth. Finally, she got into the car, he closed her door, and waved at her as she drove away. When she glanced into the rearview mirror, he was standing with his hands in his pockets, looking thoughtful.

***

David was fun. Born and raised in Zurich, David had split his time between there, New York City, and London. He didn't have that tainted spirit of American bigotry. He'd observed it from a distance and decided how much he wanted to engage with it. His foreignness was refreshing.

David's family was extremely well off. The guys said his family was loaded, but each one said that about the other one. It felt like they were all rich and Berry was the only poor one, the only one descended from maids, fieldworkers and sharecroppers, hiding her roots behind her back.

But never mind all that. Back to David. His distant background intrigued Berry. It didn't absolve him, but it certainly didn't condemn him. She liked that he wasn't American and raised in its mire of open, heavy racism that enveloped everyone's consciousness all the time. And he had an open curiosity about Berry. She'd noticed that from day one but never paid it any mind because she was so nervous about them mistreating her.

David had pro-Marxist ideas. An extremely unpopular sentiment in Switzerland, but he believed in it anyway. His family was so wealthy though, and hadn't capitalism been the answer to his good life? She'd never tell him, but Berry couldn't understand that. Money was good and necessary. She'd never had enough of it. What was wrong with money?

Soon, she realized he had this opinion for the sake of having a cause. Because he was literally pursuing a field to make a lot of money, and he was very ambitious.

"So, who's your family?" David asked her once when they were sitting together alone in the library. "What about them?"

"Oh, they don't live around here," was all Berry said. She knew how to answer to end a conversation, and she had no intentions of telling anybody here about her people. They were poor, they didn't speak well, she stayed away from them. They embarrassed her.

Chapter 63

No matter how much distance Berry put between her family and herself, they were always calling or inquiring, wanting to visit, and she was always declining. Her family knew she was running from them, but they couldn't catch her. Then Lucille called Berry one morning, crying. She'd left Zachary, she'd taken the kids and gone back to North Carolina.

"Oh God, 'Cille," said Berry. Her old accent came out. She leaned against her bedroom wall, holding the phone. "What happened?"

"He won't act right!" Lucille was a racket of tears. But she managed to calm herself down to explain everything. Zachary had confessed to having an extramarital affair—and fathering a two-year-old son by a much younger and unmarried woman.

Berry damn near rocketed out of her white tennis shoes. "Girl, what!"

"Berry, I walked past her lots of times in the store and had no idea I was walking past my own kids' half-brother. A whole child. And get this, the mother's barely grown. Letta is like twenty-two or something. All this time, people wondering who the daddy is and he's right in the neighborhood, and he's my husband."

Berry's eyes grew wider. She was speechless.

"Her parents were mad when she got pregnant," said Lucille. "She's trifling too, because she knew about me when she let Zach put a baby in her."

Berry rubbed her forehead and sighed. Lucille went through all the details, and Berry just listened. At the end, all Berry could say was, "I'm so sorry, 'Cille. That's low, he had a child on you. That's low on everybody involved. I'm sorry."

Lucille still wanted the man. She got through listing all his misdeeds, and then she said, without a hint of irony in her voice, that other than those things, Zachary was a good man and she still loved him.

Lord, spare Berry the torture of ever having loyalty to a man.

Lord, free women from their hopeless love of men.

"What do you think?" Lucille asked. "Grandma and Mama don't know what to tell me. I figured I'd call you."

"'Cille," said Berry slowly. "You know what I'm gonna say."

"I can't raise these kids alone, Berry." Her voice sounded like it was breaking again.

"Is he raising them with you, or are you raising them anyway?"

"He bought me a car, Berry. It's a brand new car. I drove me and my children to Grandma's with this car he bought. And we can't stay in this little house. This place is cramped."

"I don't know what to tell you."

Every part of Berry wanted to say: Don't go back. But also, look at all Lucille needed and how much easier it would be if she went back. The right decision was so easy in theory, but practice was reality. Or maybe not. Lucille could probably find her own way. Probably. The whole thing was mind-boggling. Berry just held the phone.

"He regrets it," Lucille said quietly. Like she wanted to, needed to believe. "And he says he really loves me."

"So when you found out and he confessed, he tried to make it up to you?"

Lucille said yes. Zachary calmed her down when it all first came out, and now he was begging for her to come back.

"What would you do, Berry? I know you divorced, I know you hate men."

"Who said I hate men?" Berry said. She added, "You're damned right I do."

"Berry!"

"Okay, fine. Listen. This one is your choice. I can't call it for you." Talking to family brought out her Southern drawl. "You gotta look at what you want to do and have in your life. What's gonna please you, deep, deep down? That's all I can say."

Lucille was silent.

"You ask yourself if you're okay with that, or if you can make another way."

"Yeah," said Lucille quietly.

***

Berry and Amara sat on the bedroom floor of Berry's little apartment. Berry had her books open, while Amara crocheted a sky blue mini skirt.

"My sister left her husband," muttered Berry, shaking her head.

"Good girl," said Amara. Her hands moved deftly with the hooks. "They all learn eventually."

"She's going back," said Berry. "If I know Lucille. It's a mindset. She's locked in."

"You're so right!" said Amara. "But you have to break it. You have to break it."

Amara had always been headstrong. Things were easier for her because she'd lived her life freely since she could walk. But most people never got to that point. Lucille never had that courage and frankly, someone like her didn't need to be alone. Lucille always needed someone, or something to cling to, even if that thing made her cry.

If Lucille left her husband, her problems just might become Berry's own. And Berry really didn't need Lucille's choices interfering with her ambitious dreams. Suppose Berry had to end up taking up for her single mother sister? That would certainly hinder her. Maybe Zachary would learn to keep his junk in his pants. And at least he was paying for things. How many broke ass Negroes could do that?

"I'm just saying if she leaves," said Amara. "She'll be happier."

"She will," agreed Berry. "But she doesn't believe that. She's gotta believe it."

She understood Lucille, Berry thought as she stared without seeing at the page of her book. For a long time, Berry had wanted to fit in. And she still could, if she abandoned her own premise and lied to herself.

She could go to church, worship an egotistical black male behind the pulpit, and a fictional white one on her knees. Run after unruly children. Keep a house for her husband and complain about his abuse that she still tolerated. There'd be steady supplies of endless gossip, nonstop sandwich making and diaper changing, and a sisterhood of its own fucked up sort. She could go back to slavery, fear, and fitting in.

She was glad she was brave enough to live her life.

Although—she couldn't help but hope she wouldn't regret her decisions later. Would she be lonely in old age with no children? Were her choices some trick to bring her to a grievous ending? Berry stood before the bathroom mirror later, palming her flat, smooth belly. Always rethinking, always overthinking. At the end of the day, everybody was alone.

Chapter 64

Certain individuals made Berry rethink her conclusions. David was growing on her.

David's staple outfit was crisp, white button down shirts tucked into starched dark jeans. His style was efficient and simple, and there was something so masculine about him. His long legs reminded her of Charlie, the first person she'd ever slept with. Berry found herself watching David walk. Those long legs. Long strides.

David started going with Berry to places besides the college library. Dinner, the park, movies, skating, museums. The check was always on him. Everywhere they went, people stared. Judgment, shock, curiosity. But she learned something while walking with David. When he stepped forward and asked for a table, waitresses responded quickly with pearly smiles. He cut through crowds when he walked, hands in his pockets like he didn't have a care in the world. People nodded to him, saw Berry at his side, and then gawked.

The whole thing made Berry's spin. She damn near envied him.

People living in the same world could live such vastly different lives.

It was also nice. She let him do the talking and let herself enjoy their outings.

She had a lot of hangups about men, but she liked David fine enough.

David and Berry started pairing off at his apartment to study. David's recent ex-girlfriend, Nina, also in law school, was tall with long brown hair and a bland demeanor. They'd dated for three years, but they broke it off because she was going back to California. She'd transferred there. David stayed alone now. He had a nice, spacious apartment—a luxury apartment, although Nina took most of the fancy decorations with her.

***

Berry was at David's apartment one night. David lay on the couch while Berry curled in the armchair with her legs tucked under her. The lamp was low and warm, and the windows' dark shades were drawn. He was smoking. She was smoking. The scent of smoke filled the room.

"So they make all our chocolate in Switzerland," she said.

"Yes." He exhaled a gray cloud. "Swiss chocolate. Lindt. Toblerone. Nestlé! I can't believe you didn't know where they were from, I'd have told you when I gave you that bar yesterday."

"There's a lot of things I don't know," she said, sadly and philosophically.

"That's true for all of us, though," said David. "You could teach me about the things you know that I don't know."

Berry agreed.

"So chocolates, cheese, watches." She listed them.

"Correct." He put his feet down and sat up. "What's your state—where are you from again, Carolina?"

"It's called North Carolina, yeah."

"Ah, right. Because then you have one called South, too."

"Yes. You remember." She smiled. "There's two states."

"Sometimes you go in and out, a little bit. With your voice." He gestured to his throat.

"Everybody keeps saying that," said Berry, feeling wistful for home at that moment. "But everybody has an accent. They just can't hear their own."

"Do I have one?"

"It's different from people here and where I'm from."

"So I have an accent then."

She smiled. He put the cigarette in the tray. She held hers between her fingers. He looked at her. She looked at him, trying to figure out where he was really coming from. He had really nice eyes, so warm and brown. And she wondered what his thick dark hair felt like.

"Berry," he said, gazing back at her. "I would lick the chocolate off your ass."

"David," she said. "I'm actually not opposed to that."

***

In his room, on his bed, they kissed slowly. He put his whole heavy body between her legs. She hated men. And their slowness. And heaviness. But not this. She'd make an exception this one time. Because she felt good right now and it was fun. And why not? His dark brown hair was silky. She'd never touched a white person's hair. He touched hers too, and it didn't even matter that her fro would be smashed in the back when she sat up.

"It's so nice," he said, grinning. "So soft. I always loved your hair."

She kissed his jaw, pulling him in again.

She was naked except for her one last piece, and he had his shirt off. His jeans were still on. He went on down kissing her. She stopped thinking about it and just let it be. She giggled at his kisses, giggled at herself, took another drag off the new cigarette he stuck in her mouth. She started giggling so much she started coughing. He pressed a warm hand to her stomach and asked if she was fine. But she was only throbbing with need. She stubbed the cigarette out in the bedside table ashtray. He was philosophical and smart and a smoker like her, and right now they weren't male, female, black, white, they were just humans.

She lifted her hips to let him pull her underwear off. He draped the pink material on his wrist like an oversized, polyester bracelet.

"Oh my God—" she whispered, when he licked her pussy from the bottom to the top.

She put her feet on his hard shoulders. She let herself enjoy it. The things he did with his mouth made her squirm and moan. And then when he rubbed her, moved his two fingers in and out of her, put his head down again and licked her clit in swirls.

"You're gonna make me come, you're gonna make me come," she gasped, wanting to be there so badly. Every lick went down to her feet and made her nipples ache and her core burn. They smiled at each other when he came up. The open fly of his jeans showed an intersection that made her curious. And she was going to let him put it in. He could put it in right now and have her any way he wanted. They could just do this and get it over with like they never knew they wanted to do, all those meetings in the library, refusing to acknowledge what was there.

He pushed down his waistband, grunting. Jeans sucked for sex.

"Do you have a condom?" Berry murmured.

"Oh, shit." David made a pained face, ran a hand through his messed hair, hopped off the bed, and looked into the drawer.

He rummaged around for some time while she waited, knees pressed together. There wasn't a condom in the drawer.

"I forgot to buy more," he said, straightening. "I thought I..."

Berry sat up, her back against the headboard. "You don't have any?"

He started looking again. "No. I forgot that I ran out. Shit."

Tommy vexed Berry. Her last experience had to be good.

"We can't finish it without protection," she said miserably.

"Wait." His voice was muffled as he leaned down. He bumped against the drawer as he pulled something out from between it and the bed. "Wait. Think I found one."

He came back to the bed.

Chapter 65

Bright blue light wafted over the auditorium, and Berry was high as she marched across the stage. She accepted her law degree, shook the proffered hands, and posed for the photographer, triumph surging through her being in a glorious wave. She came down the steps, striding the best walk of her life. Her feet barely touched the ground as her heart soared. She took her seat in a row next to a fellow black-robed graduate and remembered Nora's words: You be happy for you.

Bernadette Smith, J.D., her cap pinned precariously to her afro. She did it! She did it! Today was real. It was 1972, and she had just graduated from law school. She had graduated. *Law school.*

She gazed at the booklet in her hands in wonder.

Lilah, Lucille, and Grandma Maple were all seated somewhere in the audience, but there were too many people to see where. Zachary was with the kids, Lucille had said on the phone before they headed up, and she didn't want to bring them anyway. Berry didn't look around at anyone, kept her head straight and her eyes half closed, enjoying the bliss.

Berry didn't wait for her family to greet her after the ceremony. Her girl-friends were in the crowd too, and the lesbian poetry club must never, ever interact with her God-fearing, old school people. She'd get up with Amara and the rest after today. And she expected lectures from her grandmother. Why had their daughter dodged them all these years? Why?

Berry was at her apartment by the time the family arrived soon after. In the living room, she was engulfed in hugs, congratulations, and looks of awe, as if she were some kind of exotic creature now. The women surrounded her, touching her, shaken that they had her again.

"When you coming home, baby?" asked Grandma Maple. She hadn't aged one bit. Her skin was still taut, and her eyes were still clear and sharp. That woman was never going to give in and actually get old. She'd held Berry for a full two minutes before letting her go.

"I don't know," said Berry, sighing. "I have to figure everything out."

"What are you doing, Berry? You don't like us anymore? You know how long we've been trying to see you? By the time you said we could come, I had actually saved enough money to visit." Grandma Maple laughed at her own joke. Berry just smiled.

They didn't understand. If she let them live in her spirit, she'd never own this black book with her name on it that said *Bernadette Smith, J.D.*

Grandma Maple opened the blinds. Lilah stared at her daughter, lip quivering like she wanted to cry. Lucille was smiling at Berry. All of them were dressed well, and looked well, even Lucille with the hint of mature sadness in her eyes. She had set a vase of white and pink flowers for Berry on the end table.

"You a smart girl," Grandma Maple said solemnly, sitting down next to Lilah. "You get you somebody by your side, somebody good this time, and you figure it out."

"Pfft," said Berry, rolling her eyes. "Not men on my graduation day, Grandma. Can't it be about my degree?"

"I'm just so proud of my baby," said Lilah, dabbing at her own eyes with a handkerchief from her bag. "I never thought I'd see the day."

"Aww, Mama," Berry said, truly touched that her mother was saying it.

"Times changing." Grandma Maple shook her head in wonder. "Berry, we really are proud. We really are. I told the people back home, they said, What?

Really? Just couldn't believe it. Nobody's ever done that, you just different. We really proud of you, girl."

"I worked my tail off," said Berry, sighing with a smile. "Thank you, Grandma."

Grandma Maple nodded to her booklet. "So what's that called now? The law thing? What they call it? A J.T.?"

"J.D. Juris Doctor. It's a Latin word."

"Oh, alright," said Grandma Maple. She repeated it, testing it. Then came the inevitable question: "So well, what you gonna do with that? They actually gonna hire you somewhere?"

Berry was thirty-one years old. She'd asked herself those questions every day in the weeks leading up to graduation. But calmly, she explained to her grandmother that she wanted to pass the bar exam first—and also explained what the bar exam was.

It wasn't the time for that draining conversation about future plans. Thoughts of whether she'd get a job in law would ruin her celebration. Lilah, merciful mother that she had the capacity to be at times, saw Berry's expression and brought the conversation back to the present.

But that was why Berry left them in the first place.

They talked for hours, having dinner and catching up on everything. Grandma Maple kept saying she was proud of her, that she hoped that they would let Berry in somewhere—where? Because you know they don't hire us, tuh—Berry internally rolled her eyes each time Grandma Maple said that. She'd rather not be discouraged by the truth today, of all days. Lilah bringing it back again. Lucille told her there was a card, too, tucked in the flowers.

***

When they left two days later, Berry sat alone, clutching her black-booked diploma in her lap and thinking, Well, there's that. She'd done an internship with a nonprofit civil rights organization during the break before her final year, but she couldn't go back because the position lost funding. She'd have to work somewhere else in the meantime while she tried to pass the bar.

But she was still so happy. She floated in a haze because it was still so unreal. And as she sat alone on the couch, staring at nothing, she remembered. Nineteen years old and standing at the lopsided clothesline beside a lopsided house, holding warm tender hands and staring into the laughing dark eyes of the closest and truest friend she'd ever had.

"Doctors and lawyers," Berry had said, and they'd both laughed.

"We'd be so cool!" Jo had said, bouncing up and down.

Berry even remembered her voice as she said it. The sweetness of it, the sharp giggle accompanying it, and the girlish squeal Berry herself had made. She missed Jo, damn. Imagine what Jo would say to her, how she would congratulate her, celebrate with her, understand her. Even back then, Jo was the only person Berry felt comfortable enough to tell her dreams to. Because everyone else said, You can't have that dream, how dare you dream, don't you know you're a Black girl and you're not supposed to dream?

They had the same dream. Jo had wanted to be a lawyer, too. Did she make it?

Tears welled in Berry's eyes. Before she knew it, they were falling on her hands, her sleeve, her diploma. She was overjoyed because of her win, and she was sad because the one person who should've been here wasn't. She was smiling as she wiped her face. Jo, she wanted to say, I did it! I did it!

Chapter 66

Berry failed the bar the first time she took it. She came back to her apartment after receiving the news, her heart feeling like a brick. She slumped on the couch with her knees drawn up and a blanket around herself.

The devil started talking to her. Told her she'd never get a good job now. Nobody was going to hire her, because first of all she wasn't even smart like she thought she was, and second of all, the devil whispered, who would hire a woman like her at that?

***

But the devil was a lie. Mr. Paul Henley was Berry's former manager at the nonprofit firm. Mr. Henley, in his early seventies, had given his life to civil rights activism. He marched in Selma with Dr. King, and was one of the founders of the NAACP chapter in his tiny hometown county in South Carolina. He was a slender, straightforward man, sometimes a little stern. His wife Joanna, willowy and sharp eyed, was equally active in the organization where he worked, maybe even more than him. The wife had gone to Tuskegee Institute before she met Mr. Henley and they moved North, which was an interesting bit of history.

Joanna and Paul spoke for Berry to get a receptionist job at a Black pediatrician's office, a small building in downtown Philly. The receptionist job paid little more than the last job Berry had delightfully quit, but at least Berry could wear a white-collar shirt to work now.

Berry revisited her studies for the bar, and phone calls came.

The others in the study group were heading to amazing places. They'd passed the bar, they were thriving in the appropriate next steps, they were working jobs in big law that they all got just before graduation. Conversations with them threw her into a tizzy of comparison, self-loathing, horror, frustration, and more frustration.

She graduated at the top of her class, for Christ's sake, and yet they all had jobs and she didn't. What was she doing wrong?

Berry needed a revamp. She had to pass the bar, and she had to figure out what image to create of herself, how to present herself so well that no one could turn her down.

Chapter 67

"We can not have this bullshit in our midst," declared Phyllis. "We can't!"

The voices in the living room were high that evening. The lights were dimmed and instrumental music played low on the record in the corner, but no one was relaxed.

Nora's secret was out, and Phyllis had discovered it.

Phyllis had exposed Nora with a copy of Nora's marriage certificate—Nora protested and tried to shout her down, but Phyllis just kept on talking and then she opened the floor for everybody to discuss how hurt they felt about the deception. Eris, who should've responded by now, just sat with her head back and her feet on the divan, watching with narrow eyes.

Crashes always came after celebrations. Only last week they had a highlight of sisterhood: a Black radical feminist event in Philadelphia with all the group members attending, including Berry, who'd carried a sign with the words "WOMAN IS A HUMAN". A speech to recruit new young women. Connection in the spirit of shared goals. This week, drama.

"That's just wrong," somebody said, her voice scathing. "That's just plain wrong." They were passing the evidence around. Nora sat on the couch with her legs crossed and her hands folded in her lap, looking cool as ever, elegant shoulders stiff, staring straight ahead.

"You don't see yourself?" said the woman next to her, scooting away from her with a scowl. The two women on her side shifted to accommodate. Nora had tired herself out protesting Phyllis's presentation, so she said nothing.

"And Eris," said Cokey, another group member. "How could you lie to us like that?"

"Everything doesn't have to be everybody's business," Eris snapped.

"But something like that is!" said Phyllis, voice rising. "She had a whole entire husband!"

Berry, sitting on the floor with her legs tucked under her, was quiet through it all.

Cokey spun around and looked down at Berry. "So who side are you gonna pick?"

"I was unaware of this entire situation," said Berry, shrugging.

Nora cut her pretty dark eyes at her.

"You didn't know Nora had a husband?" said Phyllis. "Oh, you really are lying like a lawyer now. Just like a lawyer."

"You think she tells me everything?" Berry retorted. "She doesn't tell me everything."

Nora started laughing. But it wasn't a happy laugh. It was that 'laugh before cussing somebody out laugh'. She started hugging herself, rocking and humming.

"Tell you what," said Phyllis, snapping her fingers. "If you two wanna start lying, then you can lie all by yourselves. Consider yourself uninvited to my group."

"Excuse me?" Eris went erect. "I brought them here. And this is my house."

The women were silent. The music played on. Their other fireball, Rose, wasn't here today. Thank goodness for that, at least. Amara lit a cigarette and Berry reached for one, too.

Ten minutes later, Nora grabbed her handbag and stormed to the door. She stopped on the threshold and whipped around to face them, her face angrier than Berry had ever seen before. "You ladies act like bigots sometimes," she spat.

"Hell no," said Phyllis scornfully. "We have standards. Standards don't make us bigots."

"We love you!" Eris called, hands cupped over her mouth.

"Eris," Nora told her. "Grow a backbone, honey. Grow a backbone."

Berry called her afterward, standing in her own apartment. When Nora picked up and heard Berry's voice, she hung up immediately.

When Nora called her days later, Berry had cooled off, had already had another phone call with Lucille about Zachary, and had changed her mind about some very important things. When she picked up the phone and Nora's voice said hello, she lightly laid it down again.

Berry didn't want anyone who had a man in their life to close up on her. She was an exception, obviously. It was fine when it was her because she knew what she wanted. And hers was clean. The times she slept with David was different. It was holistic, artistic. The orgasms he gave her rocked her soul, and she was still in control of herself when she got up from under him.

But when other women messed with men, they got confused and they ended up sabotaging everyone else for him. There was nothing more of a turn-off, and an unpleasantry, than a woman who was emotionally gagging on dick.

Not that this described Nora. But nevertheless, she did have a husband.

Berry stopped going to the group, so Amara dropped too.

***

David called. They hadn't spoken in a while. He'd gotten engaged and he was living in New York City. She'd really rather not go back to that place, but some people found it to be a major appeal.

"How's life, Berry?" asked David.

"I'm sorting it," she told him, pleased he'd called her.

"I hope that means it's all lining up then," he said. He told her about his own exploits and his new job at a big law firm. They hadn't hooked up since graduation. Sleeping with him was a law school affair. Or at least if she never got the feeling again.

He was well worth it, though, and she wanted to remember it that way.

"I'm proud of you," she said sincerely. "And it sounds like you're doing great."

"It's a good year," he said. He had an infuriatingly optimistic tone in his voice. Were only white men ever this happy? This confident? "Let me know if you need something."

"I appreciate it, David."

"Hey," he said. "Let's keep in touch." There was a pause—and then— "I love you, Berry, you know. I do."

"You say crazy things," she said quietly, after a while of silence. She was American and he wasn't. He didn't understand how bad hate could be, living on the other end of it. But she couldn't help but smile, something warm reaching to the bottom of her. And her voice was softer. "I like that a lot, David, that you love me."

"Thanks, Berry. I'm glad you like it. Look. Take care of yourself, alright?"

She could imagine what he saw. Berry who never let any man get too close for reasons he probably had an inkling about, Berry who was always working twice as hard as her colleagues who seemed to have it so much easier compared to her.

He held the phone. He thought she hadn't said everything. And she hadn't. She wanted to say, I haven't passed the bar yet. I still need a job. But there were a lot of things going through her head at the moment, about his confession, her future, how she had to figure out all these confusing things on her own.

Chapter 68

Berry didn't figure it out on her own. Joseph called her, said David had talked to him, and asked her straight out if she had a job. Berry realized that they felt sorry for her. She'd gone through the arduous task of proving herself to them, so now they felt sorry for her.

"No," she admitted. "I don't have a job. Not yet."

"You know Dr. Ashbury?" said Joseph. "Dr. Wilson Ashbury?"

Dr. Ashbury was one of their old professors. She spoke with him in his office later that week. "You graduated at the top of your class at this school," Dr. Ashbury said, emphasizing 'this' in reference to Penn Carey Law. He shook his head as if he was irritated with her. "There are plenty of resources you should have known to utilize."

White men could be the devil or a door. He gave her some snappy recommendations and made some calls. Aided by Paul, Joanna, and Amara, Berry moved to Virginia. She'd already driven down once to take the bar exam for the state, results she was still awaiting.

She took a bakery job for the time being—one that would not be included on her resume—and waited for her upcoming interview at the big law firm she'd finally been connected to. She felt like she was striking a rock with a butter knife, but she really had to get the mineral out of the mud. She had to make this work.

***

Schwartz and Hagan was a commercial law firm in Arlington, Virginia. Berry had been told through her network of contacts who set up the interview that she would be speaking with Mr. Peter Hagan and Mr. Richard Schwartz. Berry scrounged around for photos and information on them. There was nothing to find besides the names and numbers in the phonebook.

She talked on the phone with her mother and grandmother the night before the interview, and then when she got sick of them asking questions and filling her with doubts, she hung up and called Amara.

Amara breathed life into her: "Give it your all, Berry. You can do it."

Louise and Delanie also encouraged her.

Berry was so nervous that she threw up once, her stomach cramping furiously, and smoked half a pack of cigarettes. She sat on her bed, holding her chest. If she didn't get this job—then what? She'd gone to a top school, for God's sake. Even if this didn't work, she'd make it work some damn where. She'd make it work. She always made things work.

***

In the morning, Berry woke up as composed as a sunrise. She stared at the ceiling of yet another tiny, cheap apartment and remembered Nora. Nora was so graceful, confident. Nora was a picture, an inspiration. Berry had always wanted to be like her.

Berry was smart. She was sharp. She was Ivy League. She dressed in the fitted black skirt and black jacket she'd set out. She pulled on hose, she tugged on heels. She sprayed and sprayed until her hot-combed hair was so set firm even the wind couldn't blow it astray. She dabbed a little cherry perfume on her wrists for good luck. She recited her potential interview answers. And she could've sworn she saw a sign from God—her version of the supernatural intelligence that was—flash right before her eyes as she locked the front door to leave.

The voice told her: Call yourself a new name.

"Bernie Smith," she said as she stepped into the large, oak-brown paneled office, and shook the taller one's hand. Richard Schwartz was the first partner. And shorter, rounder Peter Hagan was the second partner of the firm. Richard was younger, probably forty-five, and Peter was older, closer to sixty. They stared at her as if she had dropped right out of the sky, like she was an exotic specimen that had tiptoed into a church—but they were also trying to hide it.

They knew to expect a Black woman. Her contacts had stressed that point. And that was also one of the reasons she was here. Black law students must be placed, and this exceptional young woman with exceptional grades could not be ignored. She was one of the best.

Richard and Peter sat on opposite sides behind the desk in chairs. Peter laced his arms across his large belly. He was almost Southern. Virginia was almost Southern. Richard leaned forward. His pale blue eyes glared like lights as he smiled. He had sharp canines. He looked like a wizard. She forced herself to hold his gaze.

He said that it was nice to have her for the interview. "Are you from Virginia, Bernie?"

She told him she was originally from North Carolina.

"Beautiful state," murmured Peter. His eyes kept going from the top of her head to her chest and back again.

Berry agreed.

"Well," said Richard. "Let's just jump right in." They had pens and paper out in front of them. "What led you to your interest in pursuing law?"

Berry, who had hung her purse behind her chair and crossed her legs, sat very straight. And looked them in the eye.

"My interest was a culmination of effects," she said sturdily. "But I was always interested in learning the way things work. And I felt that being analytical, law was the perfect field for me to exercise that part of my capabilities. And you do learn quite a lot about the real world."

She ended with a quick smile. They kept staring at her, like they just couldn't believe it.

I'll be damned, they were probably thinking. Well, she'd be damned too, because she deserved what she desired.

Her heart wasn't even pounding. Because she was so, so smart, and if anybody didn't want her, then they were blind, and dumb.

Chapter 69

Bernadette Smith, associate at Schwartz and Hagan. She was sworn into the Virginia Bar in her second month of working as a clerk at the firm, and subsequently, had her title changed to associate.

Berry had been used to making small amounts of money. Three months into her new job, she still wasn't over how much more money she was making now. She didn't even let the intuitive knowing that she was probably being paid less than her colleagues get her down. She was making so much money.

Damn, she thought when she held that first check and eyes watered at the number. This was how life was supposed to be! A person was supposed to be able to get an education, get a good job, and make a good, comfortable living.

She molded herself. There couldn't be a single thing undone or awry with her. Not in this world. Regimes demanded that people conform for survival. The American regime was the most adamant about conformity. Berry was crisp, smart, on twenty-four-seven. Her hair, her dress, her voice. Nobody could know her unpolished background. She didn't even let herself think about it.

"Berry, really?"

"Mama, just call me Bernie now, please."

"Why Bernie? That sounds like a man."

"No it doesn't. It just sounds more professional."

"Alright then, Bernie. Humph. Ma, you hear this?"

And Grandma Maple: "Yeah, I hear it. But I guess she gotta feel like somebody new."

"It's not that," said Berry. "It just sounds better. Berry sounds like a little cornfield girl."

The second time she said that, Grandma Maple said, "Don't start that now. Don't start dissing where you came from."

"I'm not dissing it," said Berry. "I just don't prefer it."

"Let her tell you," said Grandma Maple, smile in her voice. "Gal got up and got fancy in the world."

Berry refused to be ashamed of her new preference. Bernie was so much sleeker than Berry. Berry was running around, making mistakes. Bernie could stand on her own. Bernie could break barriers, Bernie could create anything in life she wanted for herself. Bernie was an accomplished woman.

***

"You're married?" Richard asked her, standing on the eleventh floor in the kitchen.

Richard was curious about her. He talked to her more than her direct manager did. Her boss, Stanley Turner, was a bland-faced man who treated all his hires the same—blandly. Richard couldn't figure out where to put Berry in his mind, she knew. She was supposed to be a simple stereotype to drop into a box, and it fascinated him that she wasn't. She read him like a crystal. She'd seen many, many variations of him.

"I was," Berry said.

"Really?" said Richard, raising his brows. "So where's the guy?"

Berry tried to keep it simple. "We parted ways in 1968."

"Wow," said Richard. "I bet the guy couldn't keep up with you. No kids either? Are you lonely?"

"I work too much to be lonely," said Berry, thinking of all the research and drafting she had to do. "Work is life!" And then they both laughed.

Sometimes people asked questions to set up a series of them. Berry learned to look like she was answering while dodging all the while. She wasn't at work to talk about her personal life. In fact, she'd rather her colleagues believe she had absolutely no personal life at all. She would like them to see her as a blank, but incredibly smart avatar.

***

Berry was the second woman in a firm of nearly seventy attorneys, the only Black woman—or Black person, for that matter—out of all the people there. There was a man, but he looked mixed race. The only other woman, Madeleine, was white. She was on another team, but they wouldn't have spoken regardless. On Berry's first day, the receptionist, a young white woman chewing on her pencil, looked up from the front desk and told her: "The cleaning crew isn't here yet."

And Berry replied: "Oh, I'd have no idea. I'm an attorney here."

The receptionist looked like someone had yanked an invisible string at the bottom of her pale jaw. And grudgingly gave her the instructions to the ninth floor.

These small trifles, they weren't things to worry about. She didn't care if one dumb receptionist thought she was housekeeping. Guess what? Once upon a time, she was a cleaner. If a black woman spent too much time worrying about all these silly little instances of insults, she'd have no brain space left to do the things that really mattered, such as her work.

Small things. Could she bring everyone coffee? Which she learned to decline. Gawking at her. Excluding her. She was five foot five, neither short nor tall, and elevated in heels, but these white men, always taller, loved to turn their backs to her in conversation. They loved to close ranks and show her their broad backs. She sat in her car and stressed every morning and took deep breaths, and in the evening she said fuck all these people, as long as she got that sweet fat check on payday.

***

Now on the positive side of things. The housekeeping crew, all black employees, immediately took note of her. A woman stopped her in the hall, threw up an arm, and squealed, "You made it, sister! Yes, Lord!"

Berry smiled warmly at her. Her chest rose to the sky. "Yes, we did!"

The first custodian's coworker greeted Berry as if she were a breath of fresh air.

"Thank God for you," he rasped, stopping his bucket to stare at her. "God bless you."

"Thank you," she said. "Bless you too."

"What's your name, young lady?"

"Ms. Smith," she said crisply. She was leaving the women's bathroom, wiping her hands with a tissue. He looked so reverently at her as he grasped his mop and rolling bucket. He had a hard, hard face and weathered, dark skin, like he'd lived a hard, hard life.

"God bless you," he said again.

But Berry didn't want to live in a world where she made it. Where she was a representative to people like the astonished and reverent black housekeeping crew. She wanted to live in a world where she was just another face, expected to be there. She always wished for a world for her, it was her deepest longest.

Chapter 70

Old anxieties returned, her abusive exes. Berry looked all around for a face that reflected hers. She knew before she turned in her seat she'd never find it. Her associate colleagues did their research and wrote their drafts and acted normal. She was uneasy in her own skin. She couldn't afford that! It would start to bleed out her pores, they'd smell her weakness and kill her, or she'd lose her mind and kill herself.

Her grandmother's voice ate at her. They let you in.

She knew her grandmother didn't mean it that way, but things like that...

No matter her hard work, figuring it all out at every step as she went. At the top of her class. They let you in. They did her a favor and allowed her into a place she worked her ass off to be. Was she good enough? Of course she was good enough. She was at the top of her class.

She worked six days a week at the firm, staying after 5. Litigation was busy. Strategically placed cigarettes helped her cope. She had a pack for the apartment and one for the job. She took smoke breaks whenever she could, hiding to smoke.

Her colleagues watched everything she did. She was under an inescapable microscope, where every action was assigned some value. She could rub her face, and somehow Richard would appear out of thin air to say, in his gravelly voice, "Bernie, holding up?" And give a thumbs-up. She could walk to the bathroom twice: pairs of eyes would watch her return. She hid the cigarettes. She didn't want them thinking she was a slattern.

Peter already had the wrong intentions. Peter Hagan was just so typical. Somehow he acted exactly how he looked. A little petulant at times, but mostly well-behaved. His new indiscretion towards her was walking to her desk to squeeze her shoulders.

She hated that.

"Girl, how are ya today?" Peter would say. And then he'd pat her shoulders. He had thick, short fingers. They looked like little pink sausages. The last one was adorned with a gold pinky ring.

"Every day is a different day," Berry always said, with a polite smile.

He'd never call a male colleague "boy", but quite a few times she was "girl".

Stanley only looked at them and looked away. He didn't care.

Peter's touch made her wary. His hands went from her shoulder to the flesh of her upper arms. She didn't correct him because he was partner. And she was making all this money now. She dared not fuck up her own goals because of her discomfort. So shoot, he could squeeze her all he wanted to, as long as she got that sweet check on payday.

***

Berry had an enormous task. She had to show her colleagues that she was none of the negative judgments attached to those of her color and sex, and that she was all of the things they respected professionally and more. She had to do it, both for the sake of her own ego, and for the sake of her dreams.

She still wanted a house. She wanted a place to retreat from this world she hated, tolerated—this world that wasn't made for her—a place of her own where she could be safe.

She was saving her money to buy the house of her dreams.

Women could do more now. Berry applied for a credit card and got one as Ms. Bernadette Smith, no man attached to her name to sign for her.

***

Despite how much Berry worked, she managed to go out again—and reconnect with the Black lesbian scene. Amara told her about the secret club she'd sneaked to many times when she lived in Virginia. By the end of one Saturday night, Berry had met Winnifred Jenkins, who was stylishly sporting her fro. Berry hadn't worn hers since starting her big law job. She couldn't find the courage, even though in the mirror it was as stylish and as perfect as it was last year. Straightened hair was flat and didn't look as gorgeous as natural, but...

Winnifred missed her taxi because she was in the bathroom reapplying her lipstick when the driver stopped at the club curb. So she went home with Berry. Winnifred was twenty-one years old and an English major at Howard University. She still had the tender, confused eagerness of youth in her eyes. Berry didn't want her.

They kept talking, though, and by the end of the night they were having sex.

"Oh my God," said Winnifred, when they were kissing on the couch. And she said that a lot more times.

Winnifred's dorm was about fifteen minutes from Berry's apartment. Winnifred was so fun, and Berry could only look at her with wistfulness because she reminded Berry of being that age, so Berry let her come back and hang out with her again.

***

Winnifred had this swinging way about her. Every moment was wide, girlish, flirty. Her books were haphazardly thrown on the couch but the sprawl was artful. Her beige cardigan slung over the back of the dining room chair. Her bracelets sparkled across the living room floor. She was in awe of Berry for being a Black female attorney.

"You must've had such a hard time," said Winnifred as they lay on the couch one night.

Berry didn't want to talk about it, so she said nothing. Work was the last thing she wanted to talk about in her free time. She was resting, watching the TV.

Berry moved to change the channel and sat back down. Winnifred snuggled up next to her. The eyes that looked up at her—it was going to be hard to sleep with Winnifred later if Berry had that image in her head. Berry looked away. Winnifred rose up and kissed her, taking her chin in her fingers.

Berry kissed her back before drawing away. "Please, Winni," she said, laughing irritably. Winnifred liked her name spelled with 'i' and not 'ie' on the end. "I'm trying to watch this, girl."

"You know I need lots of attention," whined Winni.

"Okay," Berry said flatly.

They finally snuggled, but Berry kept her eyes on the television. She and Winni were never supposed to have had a relationship of any sort. And she was too old to go to the club, Berry decided then. No more. Time for fancy hobbies.

***

Lord, Winni was so damn suffocating. Berry always had to throw her out. Because Winni never knew when it was time to leave. Winni hated her dorm and was avoiding her house.

"Why don't you want to be home?" Berry asked her. They were sitting on Berry's couch again, curled up at either end, facing each other. Winni loved Berry's couch.

"I hate my parents," Winni sighed, rolling her eyes. "They're overly controlling. Exacting. Religious. Draconian." Winni loved big, colorful words.

"Oh God," said Berry. She thought about Crew and Dorothy.

"It's bad," said Winni. "I don't even want to speak to them."

"What did they do?"

Winni sighed. "Don't get me started. I'm of legal age, Bernie. I'm twenty-one. And they want me to sleep with my bedroom door open."

"That is draconian," agreed Berry.

"Isn't it though? And I have to go to church every single time they go."

Berry shook her head.

"Exactly," said Winni. "And I have to wear a skirt and a head covering when I'm home."

"Are they Apostolic Holiness? I was in that myself. We did all that."

"They're Pentecostal, but not the Johnson kind. You were in Holiness?"

"Yeah. But that's bad enough. All of it's bad."

"It is," said Winni. "It really is!"

Winni's father was a pastor. Winni showed Berry the picture of him that she kept in her bag, pictures of her family and their numbers in case she was lost. He was a stout man with an equally severe tie and hairline. Her mother looked like she called other people sinners. Her lip was turned up even in the photo. Berry almost laughed. No wonder Winni was running.

"So you get out next year," Berry said. "And what are you gonna do then?"

Winni wasn't sure. Berry couldn't blame her. Sometimes, when she walked into the office and looked around, she asked herself if it was all worth it, although surely it had to be. But did she know what she was doing?

She was always so wound up. She worried so much about work that she started to dream of it. That a report wasn't submitted. That she was late. That she'd walked in wearing an apron and sneakers and everyone laughed at her and then Stanley came with a red face like the devil and fired her with a pitchfork-shaped finger pointed in her face.

Berry had all kinds of nightmares. She held onto that one dream, though.

Because she was making real money now.

She made so much money that there was enough to cover the rent and other expenses of the house down South that she had never returned to.

"Thank you, Bernie!" said Lilah. And Grandma Maple said, "Baby, you are a blessing to us." They thanked her over and over again. She'd never witnessed them be so touched.

"Just send me all the bills," said Berry matter-of-factly. "Don't worry."

She also got herself a new car.

Those expenses set her back a few dollars, because ideally, every cent would have gone towards her dream, but she was still making a crap load of money, more money than probably any Black woman who wasn't a singer was likely to get her pretty dark brown hands on, and Berry was going to get her beautiful house no matter how long it took.

Chapter 71

Berry had money to splurge on her looks, too. She had to stay beautiful in lovely clothes, high heels, and fine, classic jewelry. Winni wanted to shop, also. Berry drove them to Macy's one Sunday. Three hours later, they were ready to check out.

Winni followed Berry to checkout. When they got to the register, Winni dumped all of her things on the counter and looked expectantly at Berry. The cashier rang up Berry's stuff as Winni watched. She didn't move or let the cashier know the items were separate.

"Are you getting these?" Berry asked her casually.

Winni nodded. But she made no move to the bag on her shoulder. "I don't have enough," she blurted then, in an undertone.

"Alright," said Berry. She opened her purse and took out her credit card.

She didn't mind paying for them. She wasn't stingy.

But every time they went anywhere, she ended up paying for Winni.

"I'm just a broke student," Winni said once, kissing her on the cheek. "Thanks, Bernie."

Something about that rubbed Berry the wrong way. It felt like Winni was trying to make Berry into something she wasn't. Berry wasn't into that. She'd never assigned herself to be anyone's guardian or provider, especially not of a romantic partner.

***

In bed, Winni wanted to lie back the whole time. She barely wanted to touch Berry. The few times they'd done it, it was always the same. Berry was disappointed by that. She didn't want it to be a one-sided action. She wanted it to be fun, shared pleasure with zero power dynamics or imbalances. What was the point of two women being together, otherwise?

Berry felt like Winni wanted a man. Winni had once said, "You're so in control." And, "I just love how you make me feel."

Berry hated that. Winni couldn't project a male and female dynamic onto their woman and woman relationship. Winni could just go get a daggone man if she wanted to play roles.

They were the wrong ages, honestly. It was Berry's fault.

She avoided Winni for two weeks.

***

Ding, ding, ding. The phone rang off the hook one night. Berry had just fallen asleep after a long day at the office. It was one of those days that wore her out to the point of coming home and collapsing immediately on the couch. Until she roused herself and got into bed. Who was calling this late? Berry finally answered, groggy and mad as hell.

Winni was sobbing on the other end. "I'm locked out of my dorm," she said, hysterical. "I don't know what to do! Bernie, what do I do?"

"Locked out of your dorm?" said Berry, rolling over and sitting up. The phone line got caught under her arm. She ignored it. "What do you mean you're locked out?"

"My roomies are gone and I lost my key. I don't know how I lost it," said Winnie. "But I was coming back from the club, and—"

"Call your father," said Berry suddenly. "Call your daddy, then. And tell him."

Winni's voice went frightened. "I can't do that. He'll find out I was out!"

"You're gonna have to tell them. They're gonna find out anyway."

"Bernie, please. I can't. You have to help me."

"No," said Berry. "Call your dad and tell him." Her voice turned even, final. "Winnifred, I have work in the morning."

Winni started crying again.

"Who's there with you?"

"Nobody."

"Well then you'd better call them," said Berry. "Call your daddy."

Winni slammed down the phone. Berry rolled over and went right back to sleep.

But a month later, Winni called again. She wanted to come over. But Berry had met Angela Key, who worked at a civil rights nonprofit. Angela had a nice-looking face and was down-to-earth. But the tailored suits she wore should've been a giveaway. And Angela wanted to be the man in the relationship.

Berry didn't want that either. If Berry wanted a man, she'd just go get one.

Angela would also call Berry in the middle of the night—after eleven, which was a no-no.

"Are you sleeping yet, baby?" Angela would ask.

"Girl, I am in bed. I do not stay up like that."

Angela didn't like being called 'girl'. Berry called every woman friend 'girl'. It was just a natural expression when they were familiar. Angela tried to walk like a man. It wasn't really Berry's cup of tea, but at least Angela did have a nice stride, and she was tall.

Angela never took her bra off. The poor woman acted like her breasts were the work of the devil. Sometimes even her shirt stayed on.

"It looks silly," Berry told her, sitting up in bed. "Take it off, Angie. Let me kiss you."

"I never liked these two big heaps," Angela told her as they sat on the stairs later. "Don't ask me next time to take my shirt off."

"I had mine off. You don't like to touch yourself."

"Yours are pretty. And they suit you. They sit up. Mine don't suit me."

"We're women, Angie," said Berry, sighing. "Our bodies always suit us."

***

While Berry was seeing Angela off and on, and billing long hours at the firm, she somehow found the time for another dalliance. Yvetta Green was Berry's hairdresser. Yvetta had a son who was almost grown and she was divorced. She was a friendly, sweet woman, and after any glance or stare, no one would assume that she was—like that. But so many women were like that. It was just a secret game for them.

They wouldn't have known the two of them were like that if Yvetta hadn't held Berry's chin in her hands one day as Berry sat in the salon chair and said, "Baby, ooh, I could just kiss you, I think I got you right with this look."

And Berry just said, looking in the mirror at the hair, all shiny and fluffed after a simple, elegant curling, "No, I could kiss you!"

And then they did kiss.

***

No one could ever tell. Berry loved it. That was her privilege.

Her personal style was smart. Her entire image was smart. She wore fitted skirts and expensive shirts. A thin watch. Sometimes a necktie, depending on the season. Her nails were always buffed and clean. Her hair, perfect and shiny. Her walk, riveting. And she would come clicking down the halls.

Berry walked a thin balance. Being attractive won her favor and courtesy even from initially dismissive colleagues, but she couldn't be too sexy for a corporate environment. She must also never, ever present as matronly, because she understood intuitively that they would immediately disregard her. So she kept herself carefully curated. Attractive and professional. Professional and attractive.

Chapter 72

Berry stood outside the office, smoking. She surveyed the wide cement parking lot and the cars and surrounding tall buildings. These folks drove her mad. She let it all out through the smoke. She clutched her handbag in the other hand.

Richard came walking towards her. She pretended not to see him, but he stopped right beside her, the top of his shiny black shoe visible from the corner of her eye.

"A woman is too fine a creature to smoke," said Richard, and plucked the cigarette from her lips, his thumb brushing the side of her mouth. He threw the butt on the ground and scrubbed it with his polished black brogue.

"Richard!" She gave a snort-laugh of shock. She looked at him, aghast. Irritation and anger flared in her. How dare he!

"How many times a day do you have these things?" he asked, lounging beside her. It wasn't actually a question. He loomed over her with his height of over six feet. Her heart picked up speed, but she didn't look up. "Peter's having a bad day," Richard continued, without waiting for her response. "You'd think when he has a bad day that he'd go off somewhere, get it off him, and then come back."

"Uh-oh," said Berry softly.

They made casual conversation, with her mostly nodding and raising her brows at all the right times. Richard was always trying to get her to talk, always trying to figure her out. She let him know what she wanted him to know, and kept it right at that. He couldn't read her, and that enticed him. He pried and pried, trying to force her open.

Recently, she'd started wondering if she should open up to him, though. Because he could be an advocate as well as an enemy, and if he was the former, wouldn't that be an excellent risk to have taken and discovered?

***

Berry did have to talk to him. When she got a phone call from Grandma Maple, telling her that Lilah had throat cancer. Berry said she worked too much to take a day off. But really, she was afraid. She was terrified of seeing Lilah like that, of facing herself after running for so long. Grandma Maple asked her to please come home.

Berry sat on the secret for two more months, calling every day and asking about Lilah. Berry spiraled into worry. Lilah wasn't getting any better.

"Baby, come home," begged Grandma Maple. "Your mama is dying, Berry."

And Berry couldn't hold out any longer.

She talked to her manager, Stanley, and then to Richard.

"I'm sorry about that," said Richard finally. "You'll have to see about her."

Chapter 73

As the highway turned into the two lanes of a small road and the trees grew thicker, that same old heavy feeling came over her. For the first time in over a decade, Berry was back in the South—back in North Carolina. God, it was just something about this place that haunted her and embraced her. And almost nothing had changed. All these years, nothing had changed. When she hit those even narrower two-lane roads and the green fields expanded and the little brick stores came back into view and she got that tight feeling in her chest, she knew she was home.

She drove right to the house and parked. There was an orange child's toy upturned in the yard, the same yard where she'd sat and tried to figure out how to have the beautiful house she still didn't have, thirteen years ago. Her heart constricted. Her throat tried to close. She swallowed and checked her face in the rearview mirror.

The door swung open. Grandma Maple came out of the house. She was only marginally slower. She couldn't stay young forever, but God was she holding up. "Lil' girl!" said Grandma Maple. And she hadn't called Berry that in years.

Berry got out of the car and they embraced. They held each other in silence. Not even a bird chirped in the sunny background. Finally, Grandma Maple pulled back and looked at her.

"You don't want to come in?" Grandma Maple asked, her voice low.

"Oh no," said Berry. "Let's just get on straight over there, yeah?"

Grandma Maple was looking at her like she had shed her skin and returned as a lizard. She'd been looking at her like that since she graduated law school. Berry got it. She was something strange and different now. Hardly knew herself.

They got into the car and headed to the hospital.

***

It tore Berry's heart to pieces to see Lilah laid in the hospital bed, hooked up to all those things, tubes running from her. Thin black plaits peeked out of the corners of the dark red cotton scarf tied on her head. "Bernie!" Lilah rasped.

"Mama." That was all Berry could say.

Berry leaned down and hugged her mother tight, tears coming to her eyes. She wiped them away. "Mama, how you feel? Tell me you gonna get better, Mama."

Lilah looked at her sadly, with her mouth turned down, and held her arms out for another hug. Berry laid on her again, not caring about the tubes, the cords, all of the hospital crap, just wanting to hold this woman and make her whole right now.

All her life, she'd wanted her mother. She wanted Lilah to see her, to embrace her, to be with her. But she'd never really had her, not even when they were living in the same house.

"Bernie," Lilah whispered. Lilah didn't forget the name she liked now. "I missed you."

"I missed you too," Berry said and just lay against her, her back aching from bending so far down. She fought back tears that threatened and burned her eyes. "Mama," she said, like a prayer that was more for convincing herself than anything. "You're gonna be alright, Mama. You're gonna be alright."

She squeezed Lilah's hand again, holding back tears, and sat down to be by her side for as long as necessary.

***

Lucille and Zachary came later that day. Lucille first, without Zachary, and then later, with him. Berry cut her eye at her brother-in-law, thinking of everything he'd done to Lucille. But he belonged here, Berry wouldn't deny that. Zach had known Lilah since forever.

They held hands in a circle while Zachary prayed. Berry, holding her mother's hand while Lucille held the other, kept her eyes wide open, staring at Lilah and then out the hospital window. The blinds were half-opened. The sun was still bright.

"I'm too sad for this," Berry told Angela on the phone later at Aunt Cora's house, her voice cracking. "I just can't do it."

"You can talk to me," said Angela. "I'm here for you Bernie and you know that. You helped me through my pain." Angela had talked to Berry about what the older neighborhood boys did to her when she was thirteen and they held her down in the backyard of her house.

"Thanks, Angie."

But she hung up. Whatever she wanted to say, she didn't want to say it to Angie.

She was always alone, somehow.

Chapter 74

The doctor was a white man in his thirties, a little older than Berry. Maybe just out of residency. He was kind, but solemn. Three days later he was honest. Lilah didn't have long to live. She was in the final stage and there was nothing more they could do for her.

Berry felt like the world had shrunk in on her. At the same time, flung her out again.

She held her mama's hand. They were alone. The blinds were closed at noon.

"Everybody got to do it," Lilah whispered, squeezing her.

"I know, Mama," said Berry, shaking. "But not you. Not right now."

"Bernie..." Lilah closed her eyes. "Tell me you gon be alright."

"I should've taken you with me, Mama. I'm sorry I didn't. I'm sorry."

"You had to live your life."

"No, I was selfish. I never thought about you. It was me, me, me. My life. My career."

"I wanted my ma, Bernie. You know I did."

"I know you did. But you're mine."

The two of them stared at each other as Berry sat on the bed, still holding Lilah's hand.

"Have some kids," Lilah whispered. Her gaze pierced Berry. "You won't be alone then. Why you didn't have no children, baby? None. You liked being alone?"

There was a silence that stretched. And stretched.

"You still got plenty of time," Lilah said, in the same low tone.

Berry stroked her hand.

"I kept smoking, you know. So I got sick. Everything you do, is a choice."

"I don't know," said Berry, and immediately began to weep. Her shoulders shook, her head ached, her heart ached more, and she regretted everything and she was tired and she was afraid. Lilah let her weep and sat quietly. That alone was a comfort in itself.

When she finally wiped the tears with the back of her hand, Berry got up and got a tissue from the counter. She sat back down beside her mother. Grandma Maple was down in the lobby with Lucille, probably on the phone talking to Aunt Cora, who was also coming up. And Lilah had her attention solely on her.

"I get that you couldn't have 'em," Lilah said then. "You had a career. And I'm proud of you. You did what I never could've done. I couldn't. I didn't know to dream like you."

Berry swallowed and sighed. "I didn't have a choice. I couldn't stay where I was. And when I hit the big world, life chased me, so I had to run. What else?"

"What else, Bernie?"

"Would you hate me if I told you the truth?" Berry steeled herself. The woman was going to die. Berry had to accept that. But whatever Lilah took with her to the other side would be hers to keep.

"What else, Bernie?" said Lilah, evenly, softly.

"I never wanted kids, Mama. That's the truth."

"It's okay. It's okay." Lilah sighed and closed her eyes. Her brown skin was ashen.

Berry gazed at her face. Looking for what she needed to see. Lilah looked up again.

"I never wanted kids," Berry repeated, holding Lilah's gaze. "I never wanted a man. The one I had was so bad, I said never again. I didn't get what I needed from him. So I certainly couldn't have kids. If I didn't want a man." She let the silence fall. Then she said as quietly as she could, "A man was never what I wanted. Not what my heart wanted."

Lilah didn't move, head straight. "You're like that. Those kinda women."

"I guess I am. I'm like something."

"You're just who you are, then."

Berry's voice was shaky and low when she spoke again. "I was expecting you to call me everything but a child of God and throw me out this hospital room."

Lilah took Bernie's nearest hand. "I wouldn't call you that, baby. I would never call you that. I had you, carried you, fed you. I accept you, because you're mine. Any way you are. I grew you, Bernie. Nine months, in me. You always mine."

Chapter 75

Berry came this close to cussing out the funeral director. She was irritable, as people get when they oversee their families and are paying for everything in the aftermath of their mothers' deaths. Lilah didn't have a life insurance policy, Grandma Maple didn't have the funds, and well, forget the others taking up the slack. There were also leftover hospital bills to be paid. That was the thing about having a poor family, they needed everything. But Berry was going to supply it, because this was about her mother.

Zachary did offer to contribute to the funeral costs, but Berry insisted she'd handle it all. She didn't need his fingers in it. She wanted the funeral to be exactly as she dictated.

And they lowered Lilah into the ground.

Then Berry sat in the car outside of Aunt Cora's house and cried. She cried, and cried, and cried, and cried. Nothing had hurt like this since before her first heartbreak.

After she wiped her eyes, she thought.

She thought about Josephine Walker and how bad that hurt. Where was she?

She thought about becoming a lawyer and how she had serious chops to make it to where she did. She thought about how much work went into this life, and how at the end, it was extinguished like a simple flame. She thought about happiness, and how much she deserved it. She just sat there and thought.

She sat there until Lucille came outside and got her.

They went inside and sat at the table. The wake had been a mess. The food was terrible, Berry shouldn't have hired that caterer. She and Grandma Maple could whip up a better meal than that in their sleep. The dry, uninspired music crushed what little heart she had. The sight of the house made her feel awful all over again, even though it was years ago. Just spooky.

And now, being at Aunt Cora's house was putting her in a worse mood.

"Carl didn't do that right," said Lucille. She was mad, too, about the way the director laid it out. Berry looked over at her with red eyes.

"He was supposed to have engraved the name on the casket, too," Lucille said. "Because I remember you told me that's what you said we was gonna do."

Berry snorted. "I don't remember now." She was exhausted.

"No, but I know you said it because I took a note down for you."

"They're sloppy anyway," said Berry. She grabbed her purse and started rummaging.

Grandma Maple came in, followed by Zachary, Aunt Cora, and her husband, Jimmy. They sat at the table. Aunt Cora sighed loudly. Jimmy asked if anyone wanted a beer. They could knock the edge off. They were all adults here.

Everybody shook their heads. Except for Grandma Maple. Jimmy went into the refrigerator and got out two beers. Lucille sat with folded arms and watched.

"I've got to get back up North," said Berry, sighing. "Old job waiting for me."

"You still at that law firm?" said Jimmy, scratching his head.

"Indeed. And working like a dog."

"Girl, you gotta take it easy."

"No taking it easy in this life."

"Humph!" Grandma Maple conceded. She drank her beer slowly.

"Is anybody else still hungry?" said Aunt Cora. "Cus I was just thinking this whole time—"

"That the food wasn't right?" said Lucille. "I know. I got the kids burgers and cookies."

Berry just shook her head. She went back to digging. Past a notepad, sanitary napkins, lipstick and hairpins. She got out the things. And lit up a cigarette and took a puff.

"You gotta be kidding me," said Grandma Maple, slamming her can to the table.

Berry inhaled, and blew out again.

"You just watched them put Lilah in the ground for that, and five minutes later you lighting up too?"

Everybody gaped at Berry.

"My mouth, my choice," said Berry.

"Yeah, a daggone bad one," said Grandma Maple.

"Oh God, Berry, no..." Lucille began.

"You don't want that cancer crap," said Jimmy, lacing his hands on his large belly and shaking his head. "Cancer is a bad man. Bad, bad man."

"She know," said Grandma Maple. "She know, the girl just watched her mama die."

"Y'all," said Berry. "Get off my back. Relax. And you see my perfect teeth?"

She bared them to her family. They were indeed straight, cleaned rigorously by her dentist every few months. She blew gray smoke in their faces, narrowing her eyes.

Chapter 76

"You're not going back to that haunted house," Berry told Grandma Maple firmly. The woman had scared her, scolded her, and cared for her when she was five, thirteen, and eighteen years old in just the same way, but Berry was grown now, and the one with the money.

Grandma Maple's jaw dropped. But she looked so pleased.

"Get your stuff," Berry told her. "We're gonna get you something better."

Berry secured a nice, decent place for her grandmother, closer to Aunt Cora.

Berry still wanted her own house. She had to buy one. It was what she deserved, working hard like she did. All she did was work and make that money. No time to grieve. She was at her desk again on Monday morning, working.

She had this recurring thought that Lilah's death made apparent to her. Life wasn't meant to be complicated. It was supposed to be as simple as a person could make it. That meant get a good job, buy a nice house, and enjoy living itself. It wasn't supposed to be about people's skin colors or whatever the funk between their legs.

There was nothing wrong with Berry. She just so happened to be born into an age when a lot of people had made up a lot of stories about what was right. That was it, that was all. Maybe in another two hundred years, everyone would be forced to conform to her image. Imagine that, they'd have to tease their hair and darken their skin. They'd be drowned in and pervaded with her opinion, her perspective, her gaze and point of view.

Lilah was dead. Berry had grieved driving home. She lay in bed, staring at the ceiling, grieving. Staring at the plaques on her wall, grieving.

It was all fake. Her colleagues' ambitions were fake. Sure, they wore shiny black brogues and expensive suits and thick watches and felt more important than everyone else. But they were just in the right place at the right time. Schwartz was a German last name. Hogan was Irish. The Irish hadn't been White until a hundred years ago. The Germans were barbarians a few hundred years ago. The whole world had once been connected.

Berry would've never been in this land, if not for history.

Living. Dying.

Everybody got to do it, said Lilah.

Berry loved her mother. She saw her point of view more and more, it was interesting how much clearer it became to her, the older she got. All over the world, Berry, her mother had once said, You find people are the same.

She didn't even hate men anymore, now that she understood everything. She simply knew what was what about the world, and moved accordingly.

Life was so, so short.

She had to get that house. She should have what she wanted before she died, too. If she couldn't have her best friend back, she could at least have the material things. She gazed at the degrees on her wall. If she couldn't do that with this, then what was the point of having done that?

Chapter 77

Later that year, Peter Hagan started preparing for his retirement. His secretary, Karla, was involved in most of the proceedings. Lots of talk swirled about what was going to happen with the firm. And who would attend the retirement party. Several associates crowded in a circle in the kitchen near the coffee machines.

"Do you know her?" the one named Wells asked. He worked a lot alongside Berry. Karla had seen the picture and thought maybe Berry and the subject knew each other. After all, they were "of a similar background". So Wells brought it up to Berry.

Of course her—was Josephine Walker.

It should've been exciting, it should've made her feel something, anything. It didn't. It was so utterly strange that Berry just stood there.

It made her mind stutter so badly that her thoughts skipped to the next natural question:

How on earth was Jo on the invite for Peter Hagan's retirement party?

Oh, well, here was the thing, one of the associates explained. The retirement party was also for attorney acquaintances connected to Peter. Peter knew a lot of people, half of Virginia. Wasn't that something?

"Your competition's in town, Bernie," said Richard, coming up to her desk. He hadn't known about the earlier conversation in the kitchen. He smiled his wizardly smile at her. The colleague next to her whipped his head around.

"I don't compete," said Berry silkily. "Must not be enough space for two Black ladies."

"Bernie, don't be like that." Richard laughed at a misinterpreted glare. "Tell you what," he continued. "Just wait till you meet her and then you tell me what you think of her after that."

"Oh," said Berry, setting down her pen. "I've known her since 1960."

Berry feigned disinterest, but inside she was a maze of confusion. Was this real or was she walking in a dream? Jo was right here in Virginia, nearby, almost back to her, just like that? And then Berry couldn't help but wonder if Jo was still mad at her. If Jo would speak to her. Suddenly, a pure emotion came back, and it was a strange one: rage.

She'd cried so much. She'd wanted Jo back at every interval of her life. But now, when that was going to be a reality, she was filled with an overwhelming, pure, red rage. She hated Jo suddenly, even more than she did when they had those angry words on the steps.

This was going to ruin the event for sure. She was going to be pissed off all evening.

Josephine Walker was also a lawyer. She worked for the Department of Defense. She'd moved in from California a year ago, but it was a few months ago that Peter met her boss at a gala. The boss was bringing Jo, because he liked to go places with his favorite employee. She was always with him. What was up with that, Berry thought? But yes, Jo was coming. If Berry wasn't sitting down, her legs would've given out and she would've crashed right to the floor. Again, Richard mistook her expression for a smirk.

"Oh," said Richard. "She's a tiger."

Another man standing nearby laughed. Virginia seemed big and crowded. But some people knew everyone, and some people everybody knew. Jo Walker was bound to stick out. Just as everyone knew Bernie Smith, the sharp young Black female attorney at Schwartz and Hagan. They knew Josephine Walker. She had only just arrived on the scene, but they already knew her.

"Just wait 'til you meet her," said Richard.

"I already told you I know her," said Berry

"Right," said Richard. "Right. What, you two grew up in the same neighborhood? How old were you in 1960? Thirteen?"

"We were grown, and neighbors. Or something like that."

Chapter 78

The retirement party was at Richard's house in a fancy neighborhood. Tall houses and all of that. Cars were lined down the street when Berry pulled up. People from the firm who'd been invited. Other friends. It was more of a moment to socialize, she realized, than a retirement thing.

Berry got out of her car and straightened her jacket. She had already checked her hair and face. She was tiptoe-clean. She made her way across the street, half nervous that somebody would come out and ask what she was doing in the yard and if she was trespassing, but also reminding herself that everyone here knew her.

She had two packs of cigarettes in her purse and many words on her tongue. She was ready.

Richard's gazebo could hold all forty of his guests. Peter, sporty in a bowtie, saluted and grinned at people as they arrived. Peter's wife had declined to come, but Richard's wife, blond and angular, was there, talking to two other men the whole time.

The curiosity about Berry was heavy enough to bury her in. She was always the only one, or one of two. Currently, going on an excellent number, the second. There was a narrow-built Black man with his back turned, nodding zealously as he talked to two white men. Would she and the first man interact? Didn't matter.

She visualized smoking a cigarette and rode over it.

There were covered trays of some kind of food. She doubted it would be any good. She eyed it suspiciously. Every time she ate somebody else's cooking, she found herself inevitably judging it. Nobody could prepare things the way she did.

A man removing lids revealed the contents of several dishes. This was a light party, an affair of cake and hotdogs. Well, she thought, sometimes simple stuff was more edible than a failed attempt at a real meal.

She stood near a seat at the end as more people approached. That was when Berry saw Jo in the midst of them. She was walking behind Richard and a tall, dark-haired white man with bushy brows. That must be her boss. As they approached, somebody brought beers from the cooler. Beer tasted disgusting, and thankfully Berry was a woman, so she didn't have to drink it. Jo, Peter, and the others reached the table. Some of them sat, and some of them picked around, going here and there making conversation.

Berry was still watching Jo.

Richard leaned across the table and gestured behind him. "Bernie, I got your twin. Look."

"Well long time no see!" said Josephine calmly. If she was surprised, she didn't show it.

"Hello, hello," said Berry evenly. She wanted to scream, for what she wasn't sure.

"Come on," Richard goaded. "You girls say you've known each other for thirteen years and don't speak any livelier than that." The other man laughed, enjoying the spectacle.

Berry just smiled. Jo looked mostly expressionless.

Richard turned to Jo's boss. "Glenn, you already know Bernie. Bernie, this is Mr. Glenn Hadley. Glenn and I met a few months ago. Private charity event. We're a small circle with a lot of figures, you'll find. You don't know us out of work, really."

Glenn nodded, assessing Berry. He had a craggy, crooked look but he wasn't ugly. He had something in his eyes that read, player, and dirty. Berry knew that look.

Glenn whispered something to Jo. She nodded and sat down quickly, her face masked. Berry took a note to return to that later. Something was there, something quite twisted, just like Glenn's hard, sharp nose and his hand on Jo's shoulder, but she couldn't place what.

Richard and Glenn walked away. The same Black man converged with them and exchanged a few words. Three of us at the whole event, thought Berry. That was actually a decent number. And she was used to it by now.

People sat down soon. Madeleine was still up, picking at the slices of strawberry and vanilla cake. Her hair was dangerously close to the cream. One of the problems with open parties.

"Everybody, attention!" called Richard.

Berry and Jo looked at each other. Berry's eyes narrowed automatically.

Jo regarded her coolly. Her expression was set, still.

"The man of the hour is Mr. Peter Hagan," Richard began. "Almost forty years in and he finally came to his senses and got enough of this crap."

Some of the men laughed. A few women smiled.

Jo wore a fancy skirt suit. Three gold bracelets adorned one arm, over sleeves were cuffed and lacy. Her skin was as smooth as butter. She looked remarkably well for thirteen years of growing up. Actually, the woman looked better.

"Berry, how you doing?" said Jo. Almost in an undertone. She didn't smile.

"I go by Bernie now," said Berry. "Bernie. I'm doing pleasant."

"Oh, right," said Jo. "Bernie. That's interesting. Well, I sure haven't seen you."

"And I haven't seen you."

They smiled at the same time, tentatively. Jo stared into her eyes. Jo's own looked wide and striking, framed as they were by the touch of mascara and her brows dainty and sharp. Berry's breath caught. They looked away at the same time, at Richard getting to his feet to offer some remarks about his former firm partner.

Berry felt strangely warm. She got another look at Jo. Who was also looking again at her.

Berry hardly heard the rest of what Richard said. She clapped when everyone else clapped. And then she took a bite out of her hotdog and ate. Josephine, across from her, opened her soda, and their eyes met again.

Chapter 79

As Berry walked to her car, someone stayed right on her, almost moving parallel. In that split second, Berry turned and went to her. The rage, the pain, everything drained away in an instant. All that was left was the good that had been. And they threw out their arms and hugged each other. Jo was as soft as she was before—her clothes were soft, her hair was soft, and her presence was soft. They embraced for what felt like eons, simply holding each other.

"It's good to see you," Berry said as she looked into Jo's face, deciding to be honest.

Jo held her hands. "You look amazing, Bernie."

"You do too. I had no idea you knew Peter or that you lived here."

"I came back last year. California. I prefer the East Coast more, though."

They released each other. Berry couldn't stop looking at her. All the time, all that story of them being apart, just sat there, existing, being what it was. Her best friend.

"Is it nice out there?" Berry asked.

"It's not all like they say. But we made a living for sure. I stay outside D.C. now."

"Oh, D.C. Alright, alright." Berry searched for words.

"Where are you?" Jo asked.

Berry told her she was renting in Arlington. "When did you go to California, Jo?" She added, "I thought you were in New York for the longest time."

"Actually, Cali was more recent." Jo blinked, then she reached into her purse. People were getting into their cars. "You can call me?" she said, her voice just a little warbly. And she gave Berry the card and another tentative smile. They waved at each other as Jo turned away and Berry got into her car.

Chapter 80

The breakfast diner was the perfect place to meet an old girlfriend and catch up on life. Keeping it simple. Berry wasn't mad anymore, not at all. But Berry didn't trust Jo. She'd laid on the floor and cried after their breakup. She really didn't want to get tangled up with her again. That had been so bad. And she still wasn't over it. Because no one ever truly gets over the pain of a first heartbreak.

Berry steeled her nerves before she got out of the car. She'd be careful. Jo was a wild card. She had mascara on her bottom lashes and a smirk on her face like she'd do you in. Women like that could kill you in love or friendship. Friendship might be harder, because friendship was deeper and truer than love.

Berry gazed into the mirror. She'd reapplied her Vaseline. Her lips were shiny. Her dark eyes gazed back at her. She thought she looked very kissable, not that it was necessary to be thinking such a thought at the moment.

She was earlier than Jo. She was stopped off to the side of the front doors when Jo rounded the corner, walking swiftly. They embraced again, not as long as at the retirement function, just a greeting. They both pulled back respectfully, quickly. They were older now.

Jo was still attracted to her. Berry was certain of it by the way Jo looked at her. Not in some base, carnal way, but drawn to her deeply as a woman she had told all of her secrets to. Berry ignored that, because she was ignoring her own attraction. She didn't want to get into all that. They went inside, where Berry asked for a table for two.

The host seated them near the back. But that was good because they could be alone and talk freely. The dim amber light enhanced the ambiance. Their purses went over the backs of chairs. Their legs went crossed. Their menus sat unopened.

Did Berry break Jo's heart, or did Jo only break Berry's? Clearly, it had gone both ways.

"I'm so glad we get to meet again," said Jo, after she swallowed. "I tried to call you when I first got in. But I don't know if that was your number."

"You called me?"

"Yes, I looked you up. But I don't know, I didn't have your address."

"When you came in from California?"

"No, this was years ago. But you know, I didn't have a way…"

"Oh. So I thought it was just me. I wrote you a letter in 1965."

"Oh my goodness, no."

"Yes. To New York. Our Harlem address."

"See I wasn't there in 1965."

"Right. Oh well."

"Wow, this is news to me."

"Yes. So you have to tell me everything about what you've been doing."

They were avoiding mention of the last fight. And thank goodness the waitress was there. They needed to discuss it, but the restaurant wasn't the right place. The girl, white and blonde with pigtails, seemed annoyed at having to serve them.

"What do you want to eat?" the waitress asked baldly. She didn't introduce herself.

Jo ordered. "Thank you!" she said politely, crisply.

The waitress turned and glared at Berry. Berry ordered and also said thank you.

The waitress stomped away.

"They'll never get used to that," said Jo, grinning wickedly.

"Always acting the fool," Berry said, rolling her eyes.

"I should've brought you over to my place. It would've been better. But Leonard hates when people are over too early."

"Leonard?" said Berry. And then as the realization dawned. "Oh, you're—?"

"Yes," said Jo matter-of-factly. "Married for ten years."

Berry felt like the chair had been knocked out from under her. Her spine ached.

"It's a sham," said Jo bluntly. "We married for reasons. Not because we love each other."

She leaned forward, and Berry did too, until Jo was near her ear. "He's like us."

The world slowed, and sped up again. The pressure in her released somewhat. And Berry started laughing. "That kind of thing."

"Yes. Berry, you are still? Right..."

"Be for real. What else would I..."

"Just checking!"

They straightened, both smiling. "But yes," said Jo. "All that. Anyways, I try to get out on Sundays because otherwise, I'll never go anywhere but work and home."

Jo's speech was so beautiful and proper, Berry thought. But her own voice had also changed drastically. Sometimes still, she heard herself say words in ways she didn't recognize.

They talked for about ten minutes, waiting for the food. Finally Jo moaned that she was starving, and Berry went to the counter to investigate. The other pair of people had been served. The waitress leaned against the stand, flirting with the young white male host, one hand on her hip. She said she'd bring the food, she said she forgot.

Berry got back to her seat, shaking her head. Jo rolled her eyes.

The waitress brought the food after another five minutes, and then over pancakes, eggs, bacon, and ham, Jo started to catch Berry up on the past years.

Chapter 81

"I went back to my cousins," Jo said as the food sat between them. "That's why your letter didn't get to me. And then…"

Berry took the time to speak. "Would you have replied?"

"I would've written back," Jo said seriously. "I wanted nothing more than to hear something, anything, from you."

Berry made a little laugh, pleased in spite of everything.

"I was pissed at you, Berry. You left me." Jo squeezed her napkin, smiling but her eyes still serious as her gaze held Berry's.

"You left me!" said Berry.

"I was forced to go to my cousins. And I'd said, I never want to move back in with them. You knew that. I was hurt."

"How do you think I felt, all the way from North Carolina with no family? I'm a little country girl from the sticks, scared to death to walk the streets. With no you."

Jo sighed.

Berry shook her head, slicing into her pancake. This was pissing her off all over again. Best friends didn't drop each other and lovers didn't stay away for over ten years and act like nothing had happened. She wanted to slap the makeup off Jo for all the missing years.

And kiss her too.

She still wanted this woman. That couldn't be.

But she did. She'd always wanted her.

"Let's talk about something else," she said. "Because you get on my nerves with that."

"I don't know what you want me to say," Jo said simply. "I have my side of the story too."

"I know you do. But let's talk about something else."

"I was trying to tell you what I did before you butted in."

"I'm sorry. Excuse me." It took everything in Berry to be humble.

Jo continued. "I moved in with my cousin's friend's mama. I'd live with anybody then. She was nice. That's how I finished school. Her son was a fat creep, though."

"Oh Lord," said Berry. "Another one, huh."

"It's always the sons," said Jo. "So, I met Leonard eventually, he was studying to be a teacher. And he sorta just stuck around me until I finished City College."

"You have to let me meet him." Berry was so horridly jealous of this man she didn't even know, who'd stuck by and done life with her old best friend. And it all felt so futile, and hopeless, and maddening, the years they lost. She actually wanted to cry.

"I'll let you meet him," said Jo. "He's my little plus one."

"Hm," said Berry.

"So we did that. I hopped around quite a bit, but mostly we bunked with friends and his mom. Then he started work, he did his thing. And I went to New York University, and then I went to Columbia. And that was, wow! Whole life changed. I don't need to tell you. You know how this works, good and bad. Anyways, we moved to California after I'd worked for a while. I was scared." She laughed. "I know it doesn't quite make sense. But I never wanted to go to California, it was his idea. He was a principal in an affluent high school. So that's why I went. And then I said, we're coming back. So it was his turn to give in."

They talked like that for an entire two hours. They covered it all. Jo even told her that yes, her mother Elaine was most likely alive, and that no, she wouldn't go see her. The last time she had, the woman tried to kill her with a plastic fork and called her a 'dirty black bitch'. The waitress circled the other tables just then, but didn't come to theirs. It was good in this case, because who needed to hear this?

The waitress came around two more times, never once asked them about their food.

At the end of their meal, Jo and Berry fought over who would get the check.

"I've got it," said Berry. "This one's on me."

"No, no," said Jo. "I can take it. Let me get it."

Berry was going through her purse, but Jo had already laid out cash. Berry gave Jo's cash back to her. "Really, no. Let me get it this time. Don't be stubborn. Take a gift."

"Alright," said Jo. "But I'll get it next time."

The girl waiting on them came back and took the money and went to the register.

"Such a bad attitude," said Jo, wrinkling her nose.

"And I ain't leaving her nothing," said Berry. "I'll leave her a dime." She threw it on the table. It went noisily spinning in a shimmer of silver and landed flat. Jo burst out laughing—the same fun, mischievous laugh of years ago. Berry grinned. They got up and left.

Chapter 82

Try as she might, Berry couldn't take the renewed friendship slow. It wasn't possible when so many emotions were involved. She was shocked to see Jo, but also extremely pleased, and equally uneasy about getting involved with her again in any capacity. Anything related to their relationship stirred Berry's swirl of feelings. Jo could be sweet, she could be rude, she could be quick, all whenever she wanted to. And she was married.

But Berry looked forward to being friends again regardless. Who else could relate to her the way Jo could? They'd lived the same lives, even if the details were different. Jo was her twin, her sister, her spirit, her doppelganger, her soul in the flesh.

Jo had returned, bringing with her a resurgence of color to this gray world. They could talk like they'd never stopped. And as long as they didn't talk about their falling out, which made them both irritable, they were fine.

The way it hurt Berry before, boy, this couldn't be good.

But man, she just loved Jo.

***

"You two get along?" Richard asked her.

This dick was always trying to start something. Smiling, Berry said it wasn't hard to get along because they were already friends.

"That's pretty convenient," he said. "I thought you and her would have a catfight."

He loved picking her! There should've been so little for him to say to her, given their positions at the firm. He rarely acknowledged her colleagues. But she stood out. Every breath she took, every blink she made, was a source of curiosity, interest. He couldn't help himself from coming all the way down from his office just to peer at her.

Men gossiped like women, too! She'd been wrong to think they didn't. There were so many cliques in the office it made her head spin. They managed it all with a professional front.

The office politics took an exciting turn when senior associate Carl Williams was promoted to partner. Berry watched them all grappling with each other. She turned her head, smoked her cigarettes and focused on her work. There was always too much drama at work.

Besides, she was distracted by all the new things happening in her personal life.

***

Jo started calling at night, always around 10:30 PM. Berry learned to wait for it, thrilled when it arrived. She'd grab the phone and lie back on her bed to talk. Jo worked just as long hours as Berry did. But she still found the time to call. She must still love Berry, fancied her a whole lot at least, right?

After a twenty minute rant about work, the topic would move to their personal lives, which were mostly nonexistent. They hardly did anything for fun besides making money.

"We should do something," said Berry. "I don't know, something. I'm learning golf."

"You'll be playing that a lot."

"I don't get the obsession with it though. It's boring as hell. You just stand there."

"They like slow games. You always said that."

"I did, didn't I? I don't wanna talk about them. Jo, what are you doing right now?"

"Stretching. I always stretch before bed."

"Is Leonard in the room?"

"Nope, I'm in the living room. Why?"

Silence, and then Jo laughed. "You don't like him and you've never even met him."

"I told you what my ex-husband did to me."

"I know. I'm sorry. Typical. I should be grateful Leon's different."

"He doesn't even do you, Jo. 'Course he's different."

Jo started laughing again.

"Not in a crass way," said Berry, smiling. "I'm just saying."

"I hear you. You could do me. If you wanted to." She'd stopped moving.

The last time that happened, the last time they were something more than just friends, Berry cried so hard she thought the world was going to end. She didn't say anything.

"I still like you, Berry. And you know that. When they told me you were coming to the retirement function, I said, Oh God. And I didn't know what to think until we were face to face." Jo was holding the phone to her ear now. "And then when we talked at the diner. You know I couldn't help the way I saw you. I just saw what I saw."

"You're not in any...groups?" Berry asked.

"Meeting other women?"

"Yes."

Jo paused. "Not for a while. And not that it matters. I have my friends but...No woman I've met was my best friend in the worst year of my life. My best friend of all time. Did you love anybody? I know there's all kinds of love, but did you love anybody deeply, deeply, deeply in our way?"

"You know I only loved you like that."

"So let's get together then."

Chapter 83

Leonard wore a white sweater with flared pants, had a black mustache, a short afro, and very light skin. He leaned against the counter as Berry and Jo walked into the house. It would take only a glance at him to see that indeed he was one of those men whose wrists were delicate. This unopposing fairy. And the reason Berry couldn't have Jo.

"Well hello," Leonard said, smiling widely at Berry. Jo had told him beforehand that Berry was her old best friend and that they'd recently reconnected.

Berry said it was nice to meet him. She held a case of lemonade cans. She didn't want to come to dinner empty-handed.

"You've done incredibly well for yourself, then," said Leonard, as they talked. He sat one side of the rounded dining room table, and Berry and Jo sat adjacent to him, across from one another.

"Someone's got to be first," said Berry.

"Jo talked about a lot when we first met. More than a lot. She was still devastated."

Jo smiled bashfully, Leonard laughed. Berry raised her eyes.

"You broke her heart, Bernie, shame on you."

"I did not—" Berry gasped.

"It's alright, because she comforted me when Dennis ripped me apart."

"You poor thing," said Jo. "Dennis was too fast for you."

"I'm sorry," said Berry.

"It's all over now," Leonard said. "I fell in love with Michael after that and was subsequently wrung apart again."

"And I comforted him again," said Jo. "After that we decided to get married."

"Yeppers," said Leonard, smiling sweetly.

***

Leonard had bought tequila. They could chase it with lemonade. After the meal, the three of them toasted and started drinking.

"I hate D.C.," sighed Leonard. "D.C. is nothing like L.A."

"What's the difference?" Berry asked.

"Well for one thing," said Leonard. "It's this big." He put his hands a few inches apart.

"I missed the East Coast myself," said Jo. "I don't know."

"I've never been out there," said Berry.

"It's just a feeling," Leonard told her. He turned his plastic cup up to his face.

"Ima be drunker than a bum on Tuesday," said Berry, taking a sip.

The two of them broke out laughing, Jo swatting Leonard on the arm.

"You still have your Southern accent sometimes," Jo said. Her eyes were aglow as she met Berry's. "You know I loved your twang."

"Stop saying twang," said Berry. "It's drawl. Leon, why is she always picking on me?"

"I see, I see! But it does come out!"

They carried the alcohol to the living room and made themselves comfortable on the couch before the TV. The more drink Berry had, the less annoyed she felt about the husband. And after a while, Leonard slipped into the hallway and put on his overcoat.

"Where are you going?" Berry asked him.

"Someone's picking me up," he said, buttoning up. "Only lame people stay in on Friday night."

"Are you calling us lame?" said Jo.

"Not necessarily," he said. And they all laughed again.

Berry stood at the door, staring at the car parked on the street. Even in the dusk, it was clear to see the profile of the older white man in a suit who had pulled up to collect Leon.

"That's just Ben Schultz." Jo stood behind her. "They break each other's hearts every other three months and then get back together. They have no business being together at all."

"Sounds awful," said Berry.

"A little bit like us. You did break my heart, you know."

Berry stepped inside and shut the door. They faced each other, Jo leaning against the counter where Leon had stood earlier.

"I'm convinced you only say that because you want the moral high horse," said Berry.

"I begged you to come, Berry. I'd never left you. You left me."

"Right, and anything could've happened to me when I was homeless. I was actually homeless, you know."

Jo sighed. "I just don't see why you can't admit it."

"Why can't I admit what? That I'm still mad as hell that you don't want to say you're sorry for leaving me alone?"

"I'm never saying that, so you can just forget that."

"Ooh, you really, really do piss me off. It's like you do it on purpose."

Jo stormed away to the living room, Berry right on her heels. They sat on the couch side by side, as close as they could be without touching.

"I hate dealing with you," said Berry. "Because you make everything so damn difficult."

"Not half as hard as you," Jo said. She grabbed the tequila bottle and put it to her face.

Berry watched her in shock.

"What?" said Jo, lowering the bottle.

"You can't be a normal person doing that."

"Do I look like a normal person to you?"

The TV was playing a soap opera. Berry watched it for a while, and Jo put ice cubes in her lemonade. They were melting now. Jo grabbed some pads for the water stains.

Berry got her purse and found a cigarette and lit.

"Ew," said Jo, coughing.

"What's wrong with me? You drink."

"I'm not blowing smoke all over the place. I could never stand that."

Huffing, Berry held it away.

"You'll destroy your lungs," said Jo. The words were slurred.

"You know what?" said Berry. "You're drunk, baby. You don't count."

Chapter 84

By the look of its fine gilded interior and arching white ceilings, the hotel was definitely five stars as advertised. Jo had booked it. She wanted Berry to feel treated in response to the meal. Jo insisted she didn't want anything, even when Berry insisted. She was treating Berry. Women with lots of money having lots of fun.

The lady at the desk wore a long-sleeved, beige, high-collared dress and a head covering that concealed all her hair. Berry knew by the outfit that she was Apostolic Holiness. And Berry slipped into faking before she realized she was doing it.

"The church conference is coming early," Berry heard herself say. Jo, beside her, resumed a face of humble neutrality. That was new. Younger Jo had never worn that expression. Berry glanced over at her to study it, but the lady was already speaking.

"Got to be there on time," said the lady. "That's important." Then she eyed them. Berry could pretend to be Baptist, but definitely not Holiness, by her sleek, glamorous look. "Coming from out of state?"

"Yes," said Berry. The truth was that they were here because she and Jo thought it would be romantic to have sex in a hotel instead of either of their places. The strange scenery would be fun.

The lady started counting the money Jo had given her.

"I hate the ones that go on for three days," said the lady then, looking back up. "Now that's my secret. You get tired of a hotel after three days."

"I hear you!" Berry said.

The woman nodded, smiling, and gave the keys to Jo.

Jo and Berry waited in the lobby hall for the elevator. They grinned at each other.

"Can you imagine?" said Jo, her voice hushed with the joy of getting away with it.

Jo didn't have to say what. Berry started laughing, her hand over her mouth.

She could be herself in the broad daylight. All she had to do was wear a skirt and heels and have perfect hair and makeup, and she and the woman who was dressed as prettily as her would never be suspected. They were girlfriends, but not *girlfriends*. They could kiss each other, probably on the lips even, standing right here, and still nobody would think—Are those two women...?

They got off the elevator and headed down the carpeted hall to the room. Both Jo and Berry carried a single duffel bag. They weren't planning to stay for more than a night. But it would be fun. Berry's heart pounded with anticipation as Jo unlocked the doors. Doing this was wading back into trouble, but Berry couldn't resist. They were such good friends, it couldn't hurt to do it just one more time with each other.

Neither of them had made moves at the apartment that night after Leonard left. They were older now, less impulsive. When they were young girls, they were overwhelmed by desire, by the longing to be close. Now they were tentative because so much time had passed, they couldn't decide whether they still had a grudge against each other or not, and these fancy clothes could take some time getting out of. They were proper, smart women. It felt disrespectful to just lunge. Berry didn't want to put Jo off by rushing, and Jo probably didn't want to put her off by rushing, either.

There were two queen-sized beds draped in white comforters. The TV looked new, sporting a few extra knobs. Jo went straight to the thermostat and started fiddling with it. Berry checked mirrors and vents, peered into the spacious bathroom. There was a black radio cassette player and a gray Bible on the bedside table. She dropped the Bible to the floor and chucked it under the table with a foot.

"I'm excited," she said, spinning.

"Me too," said Jo. They sat on the left bed, facing each other. Jo dug some tapes out of her bag. She'd recorded all kinds of songs on these tapes, she said. She presented some to Berry. "What do you want to hear right now?"

Jo put on a tape. She lay back with her eyes closed and her feet up. And they were just girls again at that moment, listening to good music together. They let the tape play until it stopped.

Berry put in a second tape and turned the volume up. Jo went outside and stood in the hall, on her tiptoes. She shook her head. Berry turned it down. Jo went back out into the hall again. This time she nodded. The music was perfect now—loud enough so no one could hear it, loud enough so no one could hear them.

"Happy vacation to us," Berry said, smiling. Jo grinned. She went into the bag, pulled out a bottle of wine and plastic cups. She poured a cup for Berry and gave it to her, poured one for herself, and they drank.

They were talking about hobbies. Berry wasn't really listening, just responding and nodding happily. They were happy and warm, but not drunk. Berry stacked the cups and said that she had enough, and then they kissed. And the music in the background grew louder the longer and harder they kissed and the more they touched, hands in hair, on cheeks. So warm, so happy, so perfect.

"Can you believe," said Berry, when they drew apart. "We haven't kissed in years."

"We should've done it again before then," Jo whispered, and kissed her again.

Chapter 85

Berry had stopped her visits with Yvetta for anything besides hair, so she wasn't seeing anyone at all, and she could sleep alone if it really came down to it. But she'd gotten involved with Jo again, and just like that, her feelings were spinning out of control.

She wanted Jo to stay at her place, which turned into an argument.

"I have a life," Jo said as they sat in the car one evening. "And I'm still married, so you can't expect me to spend every night with you. Plus, your spot is too small."

"Your place is also small."

"But it's still bigger than yours," said Jo. "And we're used to it."

"It doesn't make sense, Jo. It just doesn't."

"Leon doesn't mind if you sleep over."

"It feels weird."

Why could they never have it just the way they wanted it? Everything was edgy between them and it didn't take much to set it off.

Another argument next week. Berry had hung out with Amara, who came down from Philly to visit, and Jo didn't like it, even though she'd gone out with her own friends the week before.

"You're acting like one of the straights," said Berry, as they argued in her apartment. "You don't want every woman you see either, do you?"

"You could've just told me who she was," said Jo.

"Well, I'm telling you now!"

"You would've wanted me to tell you, Berry. But when it comes to me, it was too hard to just say, Amara is this and that."

"Because she's literally just a friend! She doesn't even check for women like us."

"Alright," said Jo, calming suddenly. She took a deep breath. "Fine. But I think you could just tell me who's who so I know."

"Okay," said Berry simply. "I acknowledge how that may have come across to you."

When Jo left, Berry thought, That was very different! Jo as a girl would have exploded and stormed out. Jo now was able to be upset and still not act extremely emotional? That was certainly new. And Berry had expressed herself then and there, and then conceded. That was also new. They both had changed. Maybe this could work?

***

Berry and Jo sat in the car in the mall parking lot. Leonard had wanted her to go with him for groceries, but Berry's invitation came five minutes later. Jo had no loyalty to the man of her lavender marriage when it came to Berry. Berry hoped Jo had no loyalty to any men. Jo always denied that she did, and today she did again.

"We tried to do it one night," said Jo to her then. "When we first got married. We tried to be straight. We got so drunk. I said, Okay, I'll see what dick is like. He couldn't do it, though. I honestly don't think he knew where to touch me."

"Bless his heart." Berry studied Jo. "You've seriously never had dick?"

Jo looked away immediately. "I haven't."

Berry smiled. "No woman our age hasn't, Jo. I don't believe you."

Jo was still looking out the window. She shrugged.

"Your boss," said Berry. There, she'd said it. She'd said it without waiting. She'd been wanting to say it since they met again.

"What about him?" said Jo, cutting her eye at Berry. But the shift in her body language was clear.

"You've never done it with him once? You travel with him. Work closely with him."

Jo smiled like the Sphinx, staring ahead now. "I don't like men, remember."

"But you've never let him dick you down. Not once. Just once, he made a pass at you and then you went all the way with him." Because that was just what she'd done with David. And she knew about the undercurrent of attraction that ran in these situations.

"If I had it, baby, I don't remember it."

"Jo, you are a fool."

They had a good laugh, but Jo's face went serious again as she fell silent in thought.

That's how Berry knew Jo was lying.

If Berry had to bet, she'd say Jo and Glenn had done it for a year or two in a toxic, passionate mess and then stopped. She could tell by their body language that they'd been doing it, really. It was hard to avoid men, especially when a woman worked with them everyday, and sometimes a man just happened to a woman.

***

"I saw you," Richard came to her desk on Monday morning. Berry was swamped in papers. Her colleagues whipped around.

"Saw me?"

"You and Jo Walker. Was that you two on 15th Street? On Sunday?"

Berry had to think. She conceded that it was.

"Gal pals," he said. "What'd you do? Go shopping? Talk about how you hate working with a bunch of white men?"

"Richard, please." She laughed. He was so, so annoying.

"We went shopping," she said. "Work hard, play hard, right?"

"I can't argue with you on that," he said.

***

Jo drank heavily, as did everyone in her and Leon's circle. She drank her tequila and vodka with no chasers. Occasionally, an ounce or two of orange juice or soda. She enjoyed her vice, but she wanted Berry to stop hers. These cigarettes would be pried from Berry's cold, dead hands. They had another disagreement.

"Berry, it's bad for you," said Jo.

"It's no worse than you washing your liver up."

"Every time I see you, you're smoking."

"Who cares, girl? Who really cares?"

"You should, because you're killing yourself!"

It was almost midnight on a Saturday, and they were on the couch together at Jo's apartment. After the fight, Jo got so drunk she started crying, because what if Berry really died like Lilah did at only fifty-two? Berry said she wasn't going to die. Jo was just crazy. Jo said don't call her crazy.

Then they went into the bedroom that Leonard and Jo were supposed to share—and they had crazy, hard sex. And then they held hands and promised they would never be mean to each other again.

And then they had sex again.

And then again.

And then one more time.

Finally Jo curled up, half-asleep, while Berry stared into the dark, wishing time could halt here: right here at 3 AM, in a bed in a house together. She closed her eyes for one brief moment and saw behind her lids a dream of that forever.

What was the point of working and struggling like she did to get where she was if she couldn't live her dream life in a dream house with her dream best friend?

Leon had come in at some point, and from the sound of now quietness, Berry assumed he was now sleeping on the couch. The bedroom door was locked.

Really, he just couldn't stay, Berry thought suddenly.

What was he going to do with Jo Walker anyway?

Berry had to get them apart.

Chapter 86

Berry's first strike to get Jo away was Christmas later that year.

"You don't want to do the Christmas party we always do?" Leonard asked the two women. They were getting dressed in the house on the day before Christmas Eve. Jo was wearing Berry's black heels. Berry was wearing Jo's silver earrings. Both of them wore simple, cute short dresses. They were going to hit the road soon for North Carolina, but they never went anywhere not looking good.

"We do the same thing at every party," Jo told him lightly.

"I know," he said. "But all our friends will be there. And I was counting on you to do the decorations. You put them up better than me."

"Leon, they're always in the same place." Jo sounded exasperated, like she was talking to a child.

"But you know how we always did it. I would do the drinks and you would do the decorations."

"I don't know, Leon. But I don't have time to sort it, babycakes. I don't."

When Jo was irritated, she repeatedly called people by their names.

On the steps, Jo gave him a quick hug, Berry gave him a wicked, smug smile, and they went on out to Berry's car, put their things in the trunk and got in.

Jo was driving. Berry could tell the directions if Jo needed them. The roads had changed, but they didn't need the map. It was almost entirely a straight shot. And they made their way to the interstate.

Berry was so satisfied. Jo should've always been hers. From the first day she met her and hated her, she wanted her to be hers. Wanted them to be together, a thing, exclusive, a secret.

"This car can go now." Berry looked at Jo and smiled.

"Oh?" said Jo. She pressed her sexy, heeled foot down, and the car lit onto I-95.

Chapter 87

Women were so lucky, and so not taken seriously.

"I brought my gal pal, Jo," Berry said to the family when she and Jo arrived at Grandma Maple's new place in North Carolina, and no one batted an eye. Nobody questioned that her husband was still in Virginia, no one even cared what he looked like or if she had one at all. And because Jo and Berry looked innocent, the family welcomed them.

They would've put them on the street if they knew.

But the things they did didn't even count in the dictionary's definition.

A part of Berry could almost deny it. The thing that happened in bed was just a game.

They really were just friends. She hadn't lied. Jo was her gal pal. Just with a few extra, unnecessary and private details.

***

Grandma Maple remembered Jo. Aunt Cora remembered her too. Aunt Cora couldn't believe that was the same girl that came to the house that spring in 1960.

"Wow," she said, as they all stood in the living room. "Black folks really going up in the world."

"They better watch themselves," said Grandma Maple.

"You don't have to remind me, okay," said Berry. She could talk back to Grandma Maple now, since she paid her rent. And she made more money than probably everyone else here put together, so she really wasn't with all the yapping.

"I just try to help you out," said Grandma Maple. They all sat down. There were wrapped gifts underneath the large tree near the window, especially for the kids. Jo remarked on them, smiling. Berry lit a cigarette.

"Won't you put that thing out?" Grandma Maple said.

"I need it," said Berry. She blew out smoke.

Grandma Maple shook her head. "Stuff killed your mama."

"Everybody got a vice. That's what they tell me."

"Okay, Bernie. But you willingly know it's hurting you."

"I just don't see how my cigarettes are a problem, Grandma."

Grandma Maple couldn't say much. Her granddaughter paid her rent, which had once seemed expensive, but was not much at all to take care of. Grandma Maple should just be old and happy. People were always so damn worried about things even when they didn't have to be.

***

The rest of the family arrived on Christmas itself. There were Zachary and Lucille, nieces and nephews, Cora, Jimmy, his brothers, and more cousins. After eating, they gathered to watch TV and drink. They passed eggnog, dessert, beer, and wine.

Talk of politics. Zachary had this new weird thing with Berry that just wouldn't quit. A strange resentment because he seemed to feel that she, a woman, had outdone him as a man.

They used to be so friendly, so casual. Not anymore, since her job.

He said the world was getting worse ever since women started trying to push men out and take over. The world was alright when men had everything under control.

"Push them where?" said Berry. She didn't even address that comment about control. "We want the same life you have."

"Who's gonna care for the kids?" he said.

"Whoever cares for the kids," said Berry. She didn't like this conversation. There had to be better ways than whatever was being described. And no amount of intellectualizing could answer real, complicated problems. She'd rather not, not on Christmas Day.

"I don't have kids," she said. "And that's my final word on that. Those that have them, figure it out." Naturally, sometimes, she still did wonder.

"It's rewarding," said Lucille.

"Good," said Berry without any underlying snark. "I'm glad."

"You got any kids, Josephine?" Grandma Maple asked.

Jo was drinking, cozy in her seat with a blanket over her lap. She shook her head.

"What is going on?" said Grandma Maple. "When did women stop having their children?"

"I don't think they did," said Jo evenly. "It's just us. I think we're just the odd ones."

"Well you can still have some," said Grandma Maple. "I bet you can. Esther Lee, she was a neighbor. She had twins at fifty-two."

The others sitting around expressed general shock.

"You're married." Grandma Maple looked at her. "You can if you want to. He sounds like a nice man. Now, don't have one by a bum. Lord Jesus."

"He's very nice," said Jo primly.

Berry took out another cigarette. This was stressing her too much. She should've never replied. God, these people.

***

After the gifts were opened for the young nieces and nephews, Berry went outside and sat on the steps. The kids were playing ball in the front yard.

One of her little cousins rushed over and sat beside her.

"Can I smoke one?" he asked.

"Absolutely not." She whipped it out of his reach.

"Why?" said Paulie. "You do it."

"I'm grown, that's why."

"It looks so cool. I wanna try it."

"Don't try to look cool. Cool doesn't matter." She scowled at him. "Are all you kids this annoying? I really am glad I don't have any now."

"That's not nice," Paulie said, pulling a face. He was twelve years old, his fingernails were caked with dirt, his knees were ashy, and he had a nasally preteen voice.

"Truth hurts," she said, blowing smoke in his face.

Shoulders slumped, Paulie went back to playing with the other kids. Berry went back to smoking. And worrying about Jo. Worrying about what they would do. If they could really love each other like this, if her mind could take even another day of her stressful job. What if one day she just couldn't take it anymore?

Hard to believe life had taken her all the way here. But here she was. Ivy League educated. A hotshot lawyer and the only Black person, second woman at the firm. Divorced. Childless. Her heels were sewn to her feet, and she moved in places that made her unrelatable to other women. No one could even begin to comprehend how hard she'd worked, the things she'd done, or the perspective she'd gained on the world. She was in an isolating class all alone.

Maybe one day, those things that she was would no longer make her so alien. She didn't want to have made it. Peter and Richard hadn't made it in the sense she had. People expected them to be where they were. Nobody said, Man, you did it, because for them it was normal. Their ambitions were normal. She wanted to be normal.

Why couldn't this world have been built for her?

She'd asked herself that every day of her life since she gained consciousness.

Jo, sitting in that house now and drinking herself to a calm stupor, was the only person who would ever truly relate to her. White women didn't count, and too many other Black women looked at her like she was crazy. Religion and their beloved men was what they worshiped. She didn't care too much for either. No hate like before, just resignation, now. And resignation was even more final.

Where else was she going to find another woman like herself? Someone who knew the pain of not fitting in, never being able to, and the resolution of finally giving up and going where she wanted and doing as she pleased?

Jo knew it all. They didn't even have to talk about those serious things when they were together. Instead they talked about college, clothes, music, and food. Other topics were understood. There wasn't going to be much of another experience available for them in the American regime. They had each other. They were made for each other.

Berry sighed, squashed the butt on the gravel under her foot, and lit a new cigarette.

Returning would be dreadful. There'd be the same people, same places, same routines. She'd go crazy. Jo would go back to Leonard. Maybe Glenn. Hopefully not him. And then Berry would worry all over again that they didn't love each other, that she'd never, ever again find someone who matched her in so many ways—physically, and in the ways that really mattered, mentally, spiritually, emotionally.

And she worried and worried and worried, and wondered how they could be together and if that would ever be possible, and how much it hurt that they couldn't tell anyone, how sometimes she didn't even really know if she wanted this herself, and she worried and worried and smoked and worried.

A creak made her think someone was coming outside, but it was no one after all. She turned, staring up at the house above her. Then she saw a door—not the one of this house, but one in her mind. Painted red. And she knew what she had to do, it had been waiting for her to do for years.

Chapter 88

Grandma Maple washed the dishes while Berry dried them. Christmas was over.

"Bernie," said Grandma Maple as they worked on the stack of pots and bowls. "I respect your choices. I know it's hard to find a good man. I know it is."

"It is," said Berry. "It really is." She put up some plates and braced herself.

"I know most of 'em ain't worth the ground they walking on," said Grandma Maple.

"Grandma, they're worth less than that. The land got value. Land appreciates."

Grandma Maple smiled. Not quite a laugh, but close enough.

"You couldn't find any man, baby? Not after Tommy?" Grandma Maple glanced at her.

"Nobody could match me." Berry randomly almost told her that if she were straight she would've married David, but every single line of that sentence would be far too much to explain.

"I see, I see."

"You didn't get married again after my granddaddy."

"I didn't."

"Yeah, so why not?"

Grandma Maple shook her head and made a face like she tasted something nasty. "Heck no. I was happier. I like to breathe free."

If she understood all that, then why was she pushing Berry? There was no need for this conversation to go any further.

But Grandma Maple wasn't done. "So what do you do?" she asked. "You don't have a boyfriend? Nobody on the side you just see?"

"I just don't need one."

"Let me ask you something, Bernie. What's Josephine to you? I know she got a husband, but are you in love with her?"

"What, Grandma?"

"Are you in love with her? Are you one of those people, those women?"

"Hell no."

"Is she in love with you?"

"Hell no."

"You promise."

"Promise it."

"Alright then."

The two of them were facing each other at the cabinets, holding each other's gazes.

"I swear I'm not," said Berry. And every time she denied it, she believed it a little more.

Grandma Maple rested her hand on the sink. "She's married," she said. "I was hoping you weren't strange, because you've been single so long."

"You see how Tommy did me."

"I know. That's not what I'm saying when I say I wish you had somebody. I just want you to live normal. You're young, you're a beautiful girl, you got life in you. You can still have children. I'm old, no use in me starting now with some fool that's gon worry my head."

"Yeah," said Berry. "You're not old though. You're really not."

"Well, I still feel good."

"Hey, that's what counts."

"But Bernie..."

Berry folded the dishcloth and swallowed.

"I'm just glad you ain't say that. The other thing. I already know 'bout men. But I never wanted a woman. Ain't nothing no goddamn woman can do for me."

"Right," said Berry, with a dry laugh. Didn't want men, but couldn't stand women. "Right."

Chapter 89

Nobody could tell her what to do. They weren't paying her bills, they weren't living her life, they were just sitting on the sidelines running their mouths. Only she knew what was right for her. Berry waited until they were back home to talk to Jo, sitting at Jo's kitchen table.

"You could divorce him," she said. "I looked into it already and you'd only have to be away for six months to do a no-fault."

"We'd have to split everything," Jo said when Berry was done. She didn't say: I don't want to. She said they would have to split. "I was thinking of just separating."

"As long as you're married, you're tied to him."

Jo was hesitant. Divorce would take so much.

"Separation, you're still married," Berry insisted.

"Bernie, I don't—"

"You told me when we met again that you wanted us back."

"If I divorce him," Jo said, very evenly. More evenly than she'd ever spoken before. She sat up straight, her hands folded on the table. "I'm essentially outing myself."

Berry looked at her, surprised again. No more Jo who moved rashly without caring of what others thought. Life really did change people. But it had also changed Berry. And she simply listened, giving Jo space to talk now that she had said her piece.

"We have the lease in both our names," Jo continued. "I have my money and he has his, but we do get tax breaks. Divorce...I just don't want it to ruin all of..."

"It freed me," said Berry. "I wanted freedom."

Jo put her head in her hands and sighed.

***

"You know I only want you, love." Jo kissed Berry as they lay together in Berry's bed in the dusky evening.

"Then do it," Berry said. "You already proved yourself. I've already proved myself. We've done our time."

"I'd break his heart."

"So break mine, then."

"Baby, stop." Jo put two fingers to her mouth.

Jo and Leon's lives were put together expertly. The way only clever people could arrange their plans. Leonard had his position at the college, and Jo had her career as a lawyer. They saved their money. They looked the other way when one of them took a lover. Leon played Jo's man, and behind closed doors, Jo comforted Leon.

"My ex-husband cleared my safe," Berry said, turning to the side to stare at Jo. "And I never cared for him emotionally. You have nothing to lose."

"Leon will be pissed," Jo said softly.

"So let him be pissed," murmured Berry.

***

Berry refused to go to some Baptist community event with Jo, for a friend. Jo said it was inconsiderate. The friend had said to bring a plus one. Berry said she'd rather sit in a cold lake for two hours before she went to any religious proceedings.

Jo said Berry didn't care about her feelings.

Berry said she did. But she just didn't want to go.

"That's okay, that's okay," Jo kept saying. She flew from the bathroom to the bedroom, preparing herself while Berry sat on the floor, reading a magazine. "But when it comes to me, you want me to give everything to you."

"Where you getting that from? You can't possibly believe that an event is as important as anything I've asked from you."

"You don't get it," said Jo testily. And she grabbed her shiny black handbag and walked out of the room. She was out and in the car by the time Berry had gotten up off the floor. Jo probably hadn't even realized she left Berry in the house alone.

Everything was just too high tension. All of it. The feelings. The obsessive need that everything be loving and right. The utter pain Berry felt when Jo didn't understand and love her every action. Berry sat on the couch and scrubbed her forehead, and after a while, she got up and went back to her own place.

The vision she'd had, sitting on the steps of her grandmother's house in North Carolina, returned. A few hours later, she went back to the house and Jo let her in. Jo's hair was messed and she wore a pink robe. Berry sat next to her on the couch. She pulled the heavy gray blanket over them both. She apologized for earlier.

"I got crazy about my anti-religious stance," said Berry. "I could've gone for you."

"It wasn't you," Jo said quietly. "I overreacted. I don't believe in their faith. I went for them. You know I pray to myself."

"Well, I'm sorry," Berry told her. "How was the event?"

"It was good. And I'm sorry too. You have to forgive me if I talk like I have no manners sometimes. I'm working on being nicer, believe it or not."

"Jo, I love you so much. Everything you do is okay." Berry kissed her cheek.

"I love you more," Jo whispered defiantly. "You keep forgetting that."

Jo's robe was nearly open, so Berry leaned over and touched her. They were so deeply part of each other that it always felt no different from loving herself, and by the way Jo pulled her in, Jo felt the same. That they were inseparable, one. Berry kissed Jo's hair, her neck, her collarbone. She tongued the nipples, palming her own as she did. Jo exhaled sharply, chest rising. And Berry kept on kissing her. Jo kept her eyes closed, and Berry kept kissing.

She whispered again, "I love you so much."

Jo said, this time, with tears lighting on her lashes, simply, "I love you too."

Berry barely realized that she was crying, too. She was overwhelmed by the fight, by herself, by feeling that everytime she touched Jo that they were one, because their bodies and their minds were so similar and so familiar. And now Jo was sliding Berry's left top strap down, leaning in to kiss her skin. She kissed her deeply, softly.

They did what felt right. They came so fast, so hard. So easily. Berry felt the stress pulse out of her like a swirl of release. It was the kind of orgasm that left her bereft of everything but satisfaction. Satisfaction, she was complete with it, her heart slowly returning to normal as she came back down to earth.

They were wound together, limbs tangled. The heat from their bodies made them warmer, not the heater that ran on the high setting.

"It has to be like that," Berry whispered, not referencing what. "I know it."

"Yeah," Jo whispered. "I know. It's the only way."

Berry sat up, pausing with her top in her hand. "I used to think something was wrong with me. I don't think that anymore."

Jo, sat up, too and gazed back at her, hugging her knees. Her face looked young, but serious and thoughtful. And Berry had a realization, her eyes locked on hers.

"You know we've always needed each other," said Berry. "That was okay, too. But now, I think we want each other."

Chapter 90

Jo moved a few items into Berry's one bedroom apartment. It was crowded but this was a temporary situation. She returned less and less to her place, and eventually was all but moved. She withdrew large chunks of money out of her accounts and put it into black safes at Berry's place.

They worked up to it. In February, Leonard finally realized something wasn't right. Jo was occasionally around on weekdays, but never at night. She barely talked to him. What was going on with her and Berry?

"I'm not explaining it to him alone," said Jo at the table. "I just can't deal with it. When you see how dramatic he gets, you'll know why."

"Violent?" Berry asked, immediately feeling alarmed.

"No, no," said Jo. "It's not violence. He'll be upset, very upset."

The three of them finally sat down in Leon's living room one night. Berry's hands itched for a cigarette. Her neck was sweating.

Jo scooted close and put her arm around her. "Lenny," she said. "We need to talk."

"I know you love her." Leon put up placating hands, ever ready to please. "And that's not a problem with me." He looked at Berry. "I don't mind you being here, Bernie. At all! You're welcome like all our friends."

"I didn't think she was over too much," Jo began directly.

Leon swallowed hard, looking surprised at the redirection.

"She's not just my friend," said Jo. "Not in the same way as my other friends."

Leon looked queasy. He glanced back and forth at them. Berry didn't blink.

Still holding onto Berry, her chin on her shoulder, Jo said calmly, "I want a divorce."

"What?" Leon whispered.

"I'm getting a divorce," Jo clarified. "I'm getting one."

Leon slumped, his face, his posture. The women were silent.

"So that's how you want it," he muttered.

Jo didn't move an inch.

"Wow," Leon said, his voice cracking.

Jo pinched the bridge of her nose and sighed. "Babycakes," she said. "We don't have to be afraid we'll be alone if we don't live exactly like this. This was meant to be temporary—our agreement."

Leon put his head in his hands. He groaned, deep and pained.

"You could be happy, too," Jo said. "Because I'm not good for you, babycakes. I can't love you the way you ought to be loved. You know that."

Leon wept, his face buried in his palms.

Across from him, Jo stroked Berry's arm, and Berry made herself breathe evenly. She felt bad for Leon, but she wasn't sad overall, far from it.

Chapter 91

Leonard cried and begged Jo not to leave him. But on the last day of February, Jo filed for a divorce. Her divorce lawyer, a crooked looking white man named Duncan Carwell, got the business together on Jo's end and wrapped it up as fast as he could.

By the end of August, Jo Walker was a legally single woman.

Leonard cried and cried. Jo was never his lover, but she was a great friend.

Jo was distant and to the point with him. And she got out without losing her money.

Berry was just relieved Leon hadn't been spiteful. The man was too nice to think of all the ways he could've complicated the divorce proceedings for Jo.

Maybe it was because of the shared tiny, massive fact about themselves that they all wanted to keep secret.

Nonetheless, Jo was out. Their friends were shocked. But when they saw Jo sitting next to Berry at events, and found out that they were bunking in an apartment together, they knew right away. A sly look in their eyes, a sniff of disdain, suspicion, sometimes even curiosity. As for the two women themselves, all they ever did was deny, deny, deny, deny.

One room, one bed, too small.

Berry saw again the flash of the red door. The apartment was too small, and she'd never liked this place anyway. She'd always wanted one thing more than anything else in this world—somewhere to be herself.

They decided to buy a house.

Chapter 92

Berry and Jo wanted a mansion, not a shack, not a humble abode. They wanted a mansion.

They called realtors, answered newspaper ads, and they were told crisp no's. Jo went to the banks. Berry went to the banks. Over and over again their loan applications were denied. They had money. So they knew why. But they'd never give up, not now.

Finally one day, they went to this one bank for the second time. Jo remembered something about some guy her boss, Glenn, knew. As it turned out, the man knew quite a few members of both Jo and Berry's professional circles. It was a long story, but anyway, he approved their application.

It was all going to happen. Berry couldn't believe that it was going to happen. Even though it hadn't yet, all she had to do was keep hunting. They drove up and down Virginia. Jo looking for the perfect spot, Berry looking for that flash of a red door. God works in mysterious ways. Things were either too ugly, too much to fix up, or inconvenient. White realtors were snooty, downright rude. Always lying to them. Where would two Black sisters find the money for these kinds of fancy homes?

Jo and Berry were sisters when they toured homes.

And the trouble they faced. The last thing they deserved was a nice place to live! These darned Black women, always trying to have something good in the world! Why couldn't they be content with crumbs?

Berry and Jo kept looking.

In September 1976, they put their money together and baited it for the realtors. Money answered everything, even when empathy and decency stood at the door knocking with no response. They were Black women, and it didn't matter that they were sophisticated attorneys who were also human, and should have a nice place to stay. Why couldn't they keep to something simple like an apartment? Why should they launch out for a beautiful house?

But they found it nonetheless. They offered nearly half in a cash down payment. Irresistible bait.

They toured the place. A five bedroom, four bath home near Arlington. It was wide, tall, not only like a mansion, it was a mansion. Rich red brick with black shutters and shingles. They walked up the low steps to the front, hoping it could be theirs. They stepped inside the clear empty foyer, holding their breath. They walked through to the living room, to the kitchen, to the dining room, through the wide bedrooms, the spacious bathrooms, their words of muted gasps echoing as they tried not to get too excited. They didn't want to scare away their blessing by being too loud and desperate about it.

But Berry knew Jo was thinking the same thing when they looked at each other. Every square foot of this place was made for them. Every part of it. When she emerged in the sunlight and turned around again, Berry knew. She could see herself rising here, walking out of here, loving here, living here, being here. A safety in the middle of the regime, sometimes it's found. Her one true dream, standing tall brick by brick.

They signed the papers for the house in three weeks.

Chapter 93

Berry drove, Jo perched in the passenger seat, unbuckled, leaning forward and looking anxious. Berry was just as nervous, her heart was in her stomach. All this time, all her life, she'd waited and waited for this. Her key was in her purse. Jo had hers in her cardigan pocket. It was one thing to view a house when it wasn't yours, and it was another thing entirely to behold it when you owned it. They stopped in the cement drive and got out.

The door wasn't red, but that flash on the deep gray tone hit her just the way it had in her intuition. Every time she looked at it, surreality flooded her veins and vision. God had always spoken to her, God who was all things spirit and knowledge and not a man like most people believed. God had been with her even when she didn't understand. Dreams always came true, with different details but precise feelings.

Berry looked around. Everything was quiet and still. The closest neighbors were a thousand feet on either side. A small, thin wood shaded the right side of the house.

As they approached the walk, Jo let out a little gasp.

And it really hit Berry then, too.

"It's beautiful," said Jo.

"Ours," gasped Berry, and tears rolled down her face.

Jo broke ahead to reach the front and dropped to the ground, kissing the earth, not caring about her skirt or her heels, pressing her palms down for balance. She kissed the ground again and again, as if that were the sweetest ground to ever kneel on. "Ours, ours, ours," said Berry, half under her breath, a quiet chant. She stepped past Jo, and then she was crying harder, crying so hard, and laughing.

And then she let out a squeal. Still kneeling behind her, Jo laughed.

Berry kept laughing, and then she started clapping, and then she started jumping in a spin. "Thank you, Jesus, thank you, sweet baby Jesus!" she whispered, and spun in circles while Jo laughed.

"Baby! Baby!" called Berry, laughing. "We did it! Yes!"

She spun again. Jo collapsed on the steps in laughter. Berry fell down beside her, laid out across the ground and steps, not caring about the dirt on her nice clothes or the angle of her chest digging into the boards. And she just cried. Never had nice things. Stood by and wondered why she had to watch everybody else have luxury, happiness, freedom, and safety, while she wanted and wanted and wanted and wanted.

She did everything for this. She owned this. This was hers.

"Oh, thank you sweet, sexy Jesus!" she said finally, kissing the step.

Jo rubbed her back in circles. Their eyes met when Berry opened her own. Jo, grinning, dabbed at her own face with a white handkerchief in her other hand.

Chapter 94

No pastor should lie and tell his members to wait to get to Heaven to receive their joy. Joy could be found right here on earth, if one worked hard enough to buy it. Berry, who'd once made homes sparkling clean while returning to her own raggedy one, was living proof. Berry who couldn't walk through her front door because she watched a woman be gunned down in its entrance. Berry, who'd once spent a night in a homeless shelter after being kicked out of her church group. Berry who never really had anywhere in this world until she found her own place to exist in freedom and safety.

Their kingdom of heaven needed a thorough cleaning, a paint job in the den, placement of its new furniture, and a final flourishing touch of decorations. Berry didn't mind that one bit. She'd do anything for this house.

Jo was equally zealous about the house. It was as much Jo's house as it was Berry's. They were so happy with what they had that even at first they forgot to fight with each other. Or maybe they had truly matured and learned how to properly communicate. Jo and Berry had learned not just to long for each other, or to understand each other, but to respect each other.

They cleaned and placed items. Berry decorated: she put up curtains, organized closets and bathrooms. She styled furniture until it satisfied her. She matched the duvets to the curtains. She put out mirrors and set up lamps. She put up art of various intricate things.

Jo added other touches. In the kitchen, in the dining room, in the bedrooms. Jo loved all things Afrocentric. So there were structures of mysterious-looking feminine idols, portraits of shaded faces rocking Afros, more idols. Candles. There were so many candles. But all of Jo's trinkets were appropriately, delicately, exquisitely placed.

Berry and Jo were on the same page. That was the most delightful thing about it all. Neither had to beg the other—Could you do that? Because Jo had wanted nice things as much as Berry wanted them. Because Jo Walker was a little Black girl from Harlem whose mother did drugs and degraded her dark skin and left her to survive on her own and Jo had said no, she deserved better than the shit people always flung at her, and that was how Jo knew the meaning, the value, the magic, of beautiful things. Jo deserved this as much as Berry.

Berry was awash in love. In joy.

The house was like a new baby or some other such thing. Privacy, freedom, a yard! Marble counters, spacious bathrooms. And all of it was theirs. Like someone holding something new, Berry and Jo couldn't stop turning, twisting, looking at it.

***

"Hi Richard, guess what," said Berry, standing outside his office.

Richard turned and asked what, his blue eyes fixed on her.

"I got a little hut," she said. "Dirt cheap."

"Really?" said Richard, sounding surprised. "Where'd you live before?"

"An even cheaper apartment," said Berry.

He raised his brows. They both laughed.

"A little hut," he said. "Hah."

"Yep," she said. "Just a little hut."

She briefly debated having a housewarming for their circle of friends, but then she decided not to. No need to have people peering too closely at the secrets of her and Jo. She did tell a few like-minded friends. She was on the phone, smoking, describing everything to a vibrant and excited Amara, who was coming down next month.

Chapter 95

Berry and Jo spent their first official night in the new house a week later. Everything was done, perfect, and touched by them. Jo slumped on the living room couch, clutching a pillow to her chest as she slept. Berry curled up with her blanket on the opposite end, staring at the ceiling.

Five years here, she and Jo had agreed, regardless. Berry was searching for a new opportunity after her time at Schwartz and Hagan, and Jo was currently interviewing for a different position at her government job. Even though they had their house, they were still ambitious.

Maybe they'd start their own firm—with more than one legal focus, or maybe they'd leave America and travel Europe with their new money. Maybe after another ten years they'd find rich Swiss or French husbands and sleep with each other behind the accessory men's backs, and this soil would never see them again. Who knew what they would do, what they could do?

But for now, though, this was right. This was holy ground. This was the right place.

Jo slept softly. Berry threw off her blanket and got up.

She wanted to see it again as if it were the first time. She wanted to see it as if she were walking into this place and dreaming of owning it.

She tiptoed to the front and closed her eyes. She took a deep breath and opened them. The dark brown of the foyer enveloped her. She took in the entryway to the living room, its beige interior silently and warmly inviting her.

She walked slowly down the hall, every step deliberate. She stopped, turned left, and stared into the kitchen. Pale, sophisticated gray sparkled back at her. The marble, silver-swirled countertops gleamed. Even the curved dark brown legs of the chairs and the tables seemed to end in fancy cursive. And so much space.

She turned off the kitchen light. She stopped at the main bedroom. She'd always wanted a soft lavender to make her happy in the morning, and she loved the trim. Suddenly, she flew to the walk-in closet and slid back the door. Rows of color coordinated outfits greeted her.

Remember? Nora Anderson and her color coordinated closet.

Berry had it, now.

She smiled to herself as she pulled it shut. She came back to the living room and stood in the doorway. Jo was still curled up. She looked so comfortable. She looked just right in this environment. French windows, white blinds, cream and gold curtains. The sofa stretched around, the TV played low. Berry thought of going upstairs to the other rooms and lower to the den, but she was suddenly tired, and Jo looked so cozy.

Berry lay beside her. At length, she reached for the blanket. She pulled it over them both, and Jo shifted towards her before they snuggled together, wordlessly.

***

In an effort to quit smoking, Berry turned to cooking. She still smoked four cigarettes a day, but that was better than a whole pack. When she got nic fits, she ate a grape. Each time her hands reached for her addiction, she asked herself why, and the answer was always the same: stress.

She told herself she could do it. She could quit. She didn't need to walk down Lilah's road with her eyes wide open. She'd always made her own choices.

Jo was crazy about her cooking.

"You haven't been eating until you eat it like we make it," Berry always said.

"Oh you're not lying, girl!" Jo would tell her, scarfing down whatever it was Berry had created. Jo never ate much, but she would take a second serving of Berry's food.

One Saturday day while Jo was gone on errands, Berry decided to make them chicken and dumplings and a chocolate cake. A thanksgiving in October, if you will. She wanted everything to be beautiful and perfect for Jo. Jo deserved the world. Women who knew how to love deserved everything Because Jo gave it all back to Berry, over and over, and so Jo deserved it all.

She finished cooking, warmed up vegetables, and waited until Jo was home to dive in. A nice cigarette would do for now.

Just one. Her first one today, so that was progress.

She'd just lit up when there was the sound of the car. Jo must be back.

Jo wouldn't like Berry smoking, but she didn't have a leg to stand on because that girl was a drinker. She was trying to drink less, but that was Jo's own battle.

Jo came down the hall towards the dining room, calling out in a sing-song.

The door opened, and Berry looked up, blowing out the smoke.

"Oh," said Jo, face brightening. "Yay, chocolate cake, my favorite!" She carried a wrap of yellow flowers and a white box of confetti cupcakes, which she set on the table. "I got these for you while I was out, I didn't know you were making cake."

"Now the table has decoration," said Berry, grinning as she held the cigarette in one hand and reached for a flower in the other.

Aristotle and Plato and those other dead old white men had it wrong. Nothing was purer than a woman's love. How could Jo love Berry just as hard as Berry loved her?

And they thought the same. That was the best part.

Nothing was better and purer than the love between two women.

Maybe to the world they were wrong, but what could be wrong with this?

Later that day, Jo decided to change the niche altar setup in the living room. She wanted to change the rotation of the figurines. Berry decided to paint a small ottoman. The phone rang. Jo was taking down decorations. She looked over at Berry.

"Did you have someone calling?" Berry asked.

"Not that I know of," Jo said, shaking her head. She sat down cross-legged before her shrine.

Berry shrugged. Sitting on the floor on a spread newspaper, she opened the case of paint and stirred it with the stick. The brown swirled, rich and deep.

In the front of the house, the phone rang off the hook.

Author's Note

Berry's motivations, the domestic work situation at the beginning of the story, the lesbian poetry club, her relationship with Jo, and finally, the women's successes—all are drawn from real-life inspiration, historical bits, and personal sentiments. Black American women like Berry Smith and Jo Walker, living in a world not made for them, had to make their own way. They leaned on each other. They led the way for everyone else. They did it tenaciously, victoriously, and proudly.

Many of the "first" Black women to break barriers were women who chose to live private lives outside the norm. Those women have done a lot of our heavy lifting. They were extraordinary. That certainly requires the kind of cleverness, resolve, and self-assuredness I've tried to depict in Berry and Jo. This book is a celebration and understanding of the Black feminine in more ways than one. And of course, we cannot forget the idea of a house. When the world is antithetical to all things that represent you, down to your very being, where else would you seek but a place of refuge?

***

I would love to know your thoughts on *BEAUTIFUL HOUSE*. Please write a review, however short or long, on Amazon and Goodreads. You can write too, just email ray@rayecain.com. If it's nothing crazy, I'll definitely respond to you.